★★ A WAR OF 1812 NOVEL ★★

Backlash

EARLY PRAISE FOR

Backlash

"The story of the War of 1812, which had no clear victor, is a conflict that will continually be debated among historians. It has been described as the war that both sides won and the war that nobody won. A Canadian historian suggested that Americans think that they won the war, that Canadians know that they won the war, and that the British are blissfully unaware that the conflict took place. It is a complex story. Using the War of 1812 as the setting for *Backlash*, Mike Klaassen has done a superb job of weaving his story around the facts. This novel is extremely engaging and with Klaassen's attention to detail and accurate portrayal of the life and times of that era, his book is not only highly entertaining but also very educational. Readers will enjoy the drama and are sure to learn something new. *Backlash* is a very welcome addition to recent fiction and nonfiction based on the colourful events at a time when America and Canada were anything but friendly neighbours."
—*Ron Dale, author, historian, and former Superintendent of Niagara National Historic Sites of Canada.*

"In *Backlash*, Michael Klaassen skillfully weaves the raw realities of war with the experiences and emotions of diverse and disparate characters to bring us an adult novel, rooted in historical fact and the core of human nature: a great read"
—*Keith A. Herkalo, President, War of 1812 Museum*

"Klaassen sticks closely to the facts and skillfully weaves real history into an enjoyable and absorbing narrative. This is historical fiction that even a stickler for accuracy and documentation will find pleasurable reading."
—*Rick Conwell, Museum and History Store manager, Tippecanoe Battlefield Museum, Battle Ground, Indiana.*

"*Backlash* is a fitting close to the War of 1812 bicentennial. It is packed full of details that will captivate readers who know the war. It's careening narrative will grab anyone looking for a great yarn."
—*Douglas Kohler, Erie County Historian*

ALSO BY MIKE KLAASSEN

YOUNG-ADULT NOVELS

The Brute

Cracks

NONFICTION

Fiction-Writing Modes:
Eleven essential tools for bringing your story to life

Scenes and Sequels: How to write page-turning fiction

★★ A WAR OF 1812 NOVEL ★★

Backlash

Mike Klaassen

Backlash: A War of 1812 Novel

Cover design by Toelke Associates

© 2016 Michael John Klaassen

Published by Bookbaby, Pennsauken, NJ

ISBN: (PRINT) 978-1-68222-971-2 (Ebook) 978-168222-972-9

DEDICATION

To my loving father, Theodore Kurt Klaassen (1922-1998), and countless others who have served in the armed forces to defend our liberties.

ACKNOWLEDGEMENTS

I'm grateful for the technical and literary assistance of self-employed editor Laurie Rosin. Also, thanks go to Ron Toelke, of Toelke Associates, who designed the cover.

This book would not have been possible without the support of my loving wife of thirty-five years, Carol S. Klaassen (1951-2012), who not only inspired and encouraged me but was also the first reader of early drafts of the manuscript.

Preamble

In the early nineteenth century, the American government struggled to survive as conflicting regional factions and political philosophies threatened to tear the federal system apart.

In 1812, with questionable justification and inadequate preparation, the American government declared war on Great Britain, the mightiest military power in the world. By 1814 America had nearly lost the war, even though Britain had been locked in a life-or-death struggle to prevent Napoleon Bonaparte from conquering all of Europe. On December 24, 1814, the British and the American governments signed a peace treaty that effectively declared the war a tie and returned captured territory to prewar boundaries.

The united American States emerged from the War of 1812 as the United States of America. With renewed vigor, respect, and sense of destiny, the nation entered a period of robust economic and territorial expansion.

Postwar expansion could be described as the crack of a whip, or whiplash, that snapped the nation forward. If so, the war that nearly ripped the new nation apart and brought it to the brink of bankruptcy could be described as a backlash.

CHAPTER ONE

NOVEMBER 1811, INDIANA TERRITORY

Sixteen-year-old Lemuel Wyckliffe woke from fitful sleep. Throughout the night, moisture from the ground had soaked through his blanket and clothes. He had tried to convince himself that everything would be all right. After all, he was lying next to his pappy, among dozens of other seasoned frontiersmen. And they were surrounded by nearly a thousand well-armed men. But the camp lay deep in the wilderness, within sight of a huge Indian village.

The order to remain fully armed had been understandable, but it hadn't made for a restful night. Lemuel pulled his pappy's old musket a little closer under the woolen blanket, then rolled slightly so his hip didn't mash against the handle of the hunting knife sheathed to his belt.

He figured it must be nearly dawn, but the starless sky showed no sign of light. A gentle breeze whispered through leafless branches high over-head, and an owl hooted in the distance. The air hung heavy with smoke and was ripe with the smell of cattle and horses. Flickering campfires sent shadows dancing across canvas tents nestled among stately trees. Freezing drizzle settled on his cheeks as he peered into the darkness around him.

Nearby, an armed guard slogged through rustling leaves and mud that sucked at his boots. The sound of the guard assured Lemuel that all was well, for now at least.

He relaxed a little, then began to think about the coming day. If the rumors were accurate, they would be facing Indians recruited by the great Shawnee leader Tecumseh. He had been encouraging tribes from the Great Lakes all the way down to the Gulf of Mexico to unite and halt American acquisition of native lands. In recent months, thousands of Indians had gathered near the juncture of the Wabash and Tippecanoe rivers. The village, named Prophet's Town after Tecumseh's brother, was to be the capital of the new Indian confederation.

The gathering of such a large body of Indians had alarmed the settlers of Indiana. When rumors circulated that British soldiers from Canada were arming the natives, the pioneers pressured Territorial Governor General William Henry Harrison to do something about it. Harrison, an experienced Indian fighter and successful treaty negotiator, asked for militia volunteers to augment his small army of uniformed regular soldiers. With visions of his mutilated mother and sister flashing through his mind, Lemuel joined his pappy as part of a Kentucky militia company of mounted riflemen that responded to the general's request for help.

In late September, Harrison's army headed north from the territorial capital of Vincennes with horse-drawn supply wagons and a small herd of cattle. They chopped their way through a hundred miles of wild woodland and forded numerous streams.

Entirely on their own in Indian country, they were in constant danger of ambush. Along the way, Lemuel's father and some of the other militiamen coached Lemuel in the skills of Indian fighting. After crossing to the west bank of the Wabash, they followed the river northeast toward Prophet's Town.

As they had neared the Indian village in the late afternoon, a warrior carrying a white flag approached the army. A delegation of chiefs assured Harrison that they wanted peace and friendship with the States. In response, Harrison assured the Indians he would not attack them if they would comply with his demands to disperse and return to their traditional villages. Both sides agreed that there would be no hostilities, at least until after Harrison met with the chiefs on the following day.

Ignoring the campsite suggested by the chiefs, the Americans bivouacked on a timbered ridge overlooking a steep creek bank to the west and a mile-wide marsh to the east. Blue-uniformed infantrymen and rough-clad militiamen bedded down just inside a rectangular perimeter over a hundred yards long. With wagons forming a barricade to corral the horses and cattle, sentries were posted and outposts established. Lemuel, his pappy, and the other militiamen were camped along the southern edge.

Lemuel's eyelids grew heavy as he began to doze again in the quiet of the night. He flinched at the sound of a musket shot. An Indian war cry made Lemuel cringe. The first war cry was followed by dozens more. A flurry of shots erupted from the northwest corner of camp. War cries rose up in a wave just outside the perimeter. The cries spread first along the northern line. Then along the long eastern front facing the marsh. Finally, around the southern edge of camp to the creek bank.

Lemuel froze, his insides churning. If thousands of natives suddenly rushed into camp, the Americans would be overwhelmed, butchered, and scalped. Lemuel wanted to run for the creek bank where he could hide, but his legs wouldn't move.

A ball whizzed past his head and thunked into a tree behind him. All around, men scrambled to their feet and rushed toward the perimeter. Lemuel flung his blanket aside and staggered to his feet. Musket held ready, he vowed to kill as many natives as possible before they got him.

His pappy was already up. "Stay with me, Son!"

A uniformed soldier near a campfire yanked the cover off a flagstaff. The regiment's battle flag unfurled in the breeze. Just then three Indians appeared out of the darkness, two brandishing war clubs, the third carrying a musket. In a flurry of American gunfire, two of the Indians fell. The third one stooped next to a campfire and fiddled with his musket. A burly frontiersman called Stubby shot the Indian, then drew a hunting knife to take the scalp.

Lemuel ran after his pappy. At the southern perimeter, Indians howled like demons. Militiamen fired into the darkness. Lemuel scooted next to his father and knelt. Trembling, Lemuel raised the old musket to his shoulder and pulled the hammer back. A musket flash illuminated an Indian about twenty paces outside the perimeter. Lemuel noted the spot, aimed, and pulled the trigger. The hammer snapped down on the frizzen but didn't produce a flash. Cursing, Lemuel realized his powder was wet. He dumped the damp powder and reached for his powder horn, hoping his pappy and the other men hadn't noticed.

The din of war cries waned, and musket fire ebbed.

"Put out the fires!"

Lemuel recognized the voice. He turned and saw General Harrison astride a horse. The fires were backlighting the Americans, especially the mounted officers, making them easier targets for the Indians. Behind the general, bark splintered and scattered as a ball ripped into a tree trunk. Arrows streaked past Harrison and disappeared into the night. The general calmly wheeled his horse and trotted away.

A militiaman next to Lemuel's father stumbled forward, clutched the front of his buckskin jacket, then slumped to the ground.

"Help with the fires, Son," said Lemuel's father.

Lemuel hesitated, not wanting to leave his pappy's side.

Lemuel slung the musket over his shoulder as he rushed to the nearest campfire. He grabbed a stout stick and swept it across the flaming logs and embers, scattering them over the soggy ground. Flames flickered from individual coals, but Lemuel stomped them out. Satisfied, he raced to the next fire as arrows and musket balls flew past him.

A dozen cattle emerged from between the wagons and milled in confusion. Alarmed that the army's food supply might be lost, Lemuel tried to shoo them back behind the wagons. An arrow whizzed past his head. He ducked behind a tree just as the cattle stampeded past him into the darkness. He hurried back to the wagons, hoping to keep the horses from stampeding. Then he remembered that each horse had been hobbled with a short rope.

From the northwest corner of the perimeter, the highest ground in the camp, rose war cries and a deafening roar of musket fire. Scores of flashes lit the trees amid a growing cloud of gun smoke. Lemuel prayed that the Americans could hold the natives back. After a few minutes, the roar of gunfire and war cries ebbed. Lemuel hoped the attack was over.

As he scattered the embers of the next campfire, another wave of war cries and gunfire surged, more intensely than before. Downhill, at the northeast corner of the perimeter, the orange flash of musket fire glowed through a cloud of smoke that billowed high into the trees. A handful of dragoons mounted horses, drew sabers, and charged in that direction.

The din of battle dwindled as Lemuel and several others finished putting out the campfires. War cries from outside the perimeter continued but with less intensity than just a few minutes before. Here and there, firearms popped.

Lemuel ran back to the southeast corner of the campsite and found the men in his company. He knelt between his pappy and Stubby at the very edge of the perimeter. A musket flashed. Lemuel fired back. Without knowing if he had hit his mark, he reloaded, grateful that the musket loaded much faster than a rifle. And since the fighting was up close, the greater accuracy and range of the rifle was no advantage.

The noise from outside the camp subsided, and Lemuel began to think the Indians had retreated. Just then, a war cry echoed through the trees right in front of him. The first scream was joined by hundreds more in a hideous chorus that clawed at Lemuel's nerves.

Out of the darkness rushed an Indian, then dozens more. A volley of American gunfire illuminated hundreds of warriors. Into the camp flooded screaming natives, war clubs arcing overhead. Lemuel pointed his musket at the nearest warrior's chest and pulled the trigger. The Indian disappeared in a cloud of smoke. Before Lemuel could reload, more warriors rushed through the American line. Lemuel let his musket drop and drew his hunting knife.

Someone crowded behind him. A bayonet-tipped musket barrel appeared over his shoulder and discharged point-blank into the advancing Indians. The musket was replaced by another, which also fired.

Ears ringing, Lemuel ducked as the deafening volley of musket fire cut into the screaming horde. The air became so thick with gun smoke that Lemuel coughed and could barely breathe. A uniformed soldier thrust forward, skewering an Indian with his bayonet. Scores of soldiers charged forward, shoving bayonets into any native who didn't retreat fast enough.

Lemuel retrieved his musket from the mud, quickly reloaded, and hurried after the infantrymen. They drove the Indians beyond the cloud of gun smoke. Ahead, the eastern sky had brightened.

Pounding hooves rumbled as a dozen screaming dragoons galloped, sabers drawn, past the infantrymen. The Indians fled, but the horsemen bore down on them, sabers slashing right and left. Lemuel rushed after the dragoons and infantrymen as they pursued the warriors to the edge of the marsh. There they fired at any Indian who hadn't ducked into the tall marsh grass.

Scores of Indians lay sprawled across the ground. Some appeared to be even younger than Lemuel. One of the warriors jumped to his feet. With tomahawk in hand and a chilling scream, the young native charged Lemuel.

In a blur of motion, the warrior swung his tomahawk at Lemuel's head. He raised his musket, and the tomahawk blade hit the barrel with a clang. As the blade scraped down the barrel, Lemuel swung the musket stock up and around with all his strength. The wooden stock hammered the warrior across the ear. The Indian's head snapped to the side, and he toppled to the ground. Lemuel straddled the sprawled warrior, then rammed the butt of the musket down again and again until the Indian's skull split.

Lemuel spun around, musket held ready to propel another attack. But the only Indians in sight appeared to be dead. The dragoons were walking their mounts back toward camp.

Lemuel glanced at the dead warrior before him. Visions of his butchered mother and sister returned. He set his jaw and pulled his hunting knife from his belt, trying to remember Stubby's instruction. Lemuel clutched a clump of the native's hair, pressed the razor-sharp edge into the scalp until it hit the scull. As the blade etched bone, he sliced a half-circle around the clump of hair. With another deft move, he sliced a second half-circle around the other side. He placed the bloody knife blade between his teeth and pressed his knees into the Indian's back. With a wrenching sideways yank, he ripped the patch of scalp free, leaving a bloody circle of exposed bone.

Lemuel felt a burst of energy. He held the blood-dripping trophy high and let out a scream that matched any of the Indian war cries. He wiped the scalp clean on the grass, then tied it around his belt.

With a watchful eye for more natives, Lemuel headed toward camp. The site already swarmed with activity as soldiers and militiamen hurried to reorganize in case of another attack. The southeastern corner of camp was strewn with dead and wounded Americans.

Stubby approached, his face grim. Without a word, the burly old frontiersman grabbed Lemuel and pulled him close. Before Lemuel could respond, Stubby stepped back, holding Lemuel firmly by the shoulders.

The bearded, wrinkle-faced man seemed to hesitate before he spoke. "I'm sorry, boy. It's your pa. He's dead."

CHAPTER TWO

NOVEMBER 1811, YORK, UPPER CANADA

Lieutenant George Sherbourne sat at the foot of the table and squirmed in his chair. He glanced at the other officers and hoped his uniform was as spotlessly clean and crisply scarlet as theirs.

Around the table sat three of the most senior officers governing Upper Canada. With York as its capital, the province included vast territory stretching west along the Great Lakes and beyond.

George reached for the glass of red wine in front of him, took a sip, then eased the crystal back to the white linen. He glanced at Major Morrison, then felt his face grow warm. Just last week Major Morrison had refused George permission to marry Anne, the major's daughter. She came from a distinguished family with aristocratic blood, the major had explained. It would be unthinkable for her to marry the son of a shopkeeper.

The major might just as well have slapped George across the face, the words had stung so deeply. He still seethed and imagined himself running a sword through the major's gut.

Not wishing to betray his inner rage to senior officers, George tried to think of something else. A dreary, midday shower tapped at the windows of the eloquently furnished dining room of Government House, and George pitied the men and officers with duty outside.

"The damned Yanks have made a bloody mess of everything," said Colonel Sheaffe, a portly, bulbous-nosed gentlemen.

"Quite right. Quite right," mumbled the gaunt, pock-faced Major Morrison seated across from the colonel.

At the head of the table sat General Isaac Brock. Without a word, the tall, dark-haired officer sipped his wine. Behind him, high on a stone hearth, hung an immense rack of moose antlers.

George figured that the other officers were at least twice his age, and unlike him, they had been born and raised in the British Isles. George's father, a prosperous fur trader and member of the provincial parliament, had pulled bureaucratic strings to wrangle a commission for George in the British army.

After growing weary of his initial assignment to recruit and train local militia units, George had requested a transfer to England. Knowing that he must distinguish himself in battle to gain rapid advancement, he hoped to be assigned to General Arthur Wellesley, who was fighting Napoleon Bonaparte in Portugal and Spain.

One of the servants whisked away the remains of the meal while another offered cigars to each of the men. George waited for the senior officers before lighting his own.

After the wine glasses had been refilled, Brock cleared his throat. "Gentlemen," he said, raising his glass, "let us congratulate Lieutenant Sherbourne on his good fortune and wish him Godspeed."

George's insides tightened as the men around the table acknowledged him and tasted their wine. George nodded back and took a sip.

"Lieutenant," said Colonel Sheaffe, "I daresay any one of us would gladly trade places with you." He glanced toward the vaulted ceiling. "Ah, to be heading back to England at a time when men-at-arms are in such great need. Alas, the rest of us must be content to serve His Majesty in distant colonies."

George noticed the disparagement in the colonel's voice when he mentioned the colonies. The other officers resented being stationed in the semi-wilderness of the Canadas while the British army continued its seemingly endless war against Bonaparte.

"Well," said Major Morrison, with a hint of disgust in his voice, "someone has to keep an eye on those damnable Yankees."

Brock puffed his cigar.

Sheaffe clenched his jaw and nodded. "You are correct, of course, my dear fellow. The American fantasy of casting aside royal oversight is inevitably doomed. Their experiment with self-government will degenerate into rule by mob. It is surely only a matter of time."

Morrison snorted. "Unfortunately their cockeyed notions have already spread to France." He smirked. "Come to think of it, I'm not sure who I loathe more—the Americans or the French."

The officers spoke as if they imparted news. George knew that just a few years after the rebellion of the American colonies, the French masses revolted and put their king to the guillotine. Then they systematically executed just about everybody with privilege and rank. But the French Revolution quickly deteriorated into such chaos that the people cheered Bonaparte when he seized control and restored order.

"Surely," said the major, "Ole Boney's reign as emperor signals the beginning of the end of such notions."

"Nonsense." Sheaffe sneered as he spoke. "Bonaparte claims the title of emperor for himself, but wherever he goes he casts out the nobility and establishes republican institutions. Now the contagion threatens established order throughout Europe."

"I fear you are correct," said the major. "We must crush Bonaparte and reinstate the royal family of France. Our own necks are at risk. What if Nelson hadn't stopped the French and Spanish at Trafalgar? Bonaparte might have captured England. I shudder to think what the world would be like without the divine guidance of King George."

The officers nodded with solemn expressions as if they hadn't already discussed these thoughts dozens of times. George realized that the conversation was directed toward him. This was their last chance to share their wisdom with a junior officer headed back to England.

"But let's not forget," said Sheaffe, stabbing his cigar toward George, "we must also curtail the epidemic here in North America. The expansion of the rebellious colonies must be thwarted."

"Hear! Hear!" blurted the pock-faced major.

"Our forces contain them from the north," continued the colonel, "and Spanish sovereignty over Florida blocks them from the south. But the Americans' westward encroachment needs to be checked. They must not be allowed to consolidate their hold on the Mississippi Valley and farther west."

"With a little encouragement and assistance," added Morrison, "our aboriginal allies may help us confine the Americans to the Atlantic coast and the Appalachians."

Colonel Sheaffe scoffed. "You put much too much faith in the nitchies, I fear. Remember, they're savages. Totally undependable. But maybe we shouldn't worry so about the Americans. Since they formed their government, it has blundered from one folly to another."

"I was reading one of their newspapers recently," said the major, "and it appears that some of the northeastern states are so disenchanted with their new government that they might eagerly return to His Majesty's rule."

"I'm not so sure," said General Brock, who had been listening quietly. "I, too, read their papers. There seems to be growing animosity toward the Crown, especially in the southern and western-most states. Many of those elected to their lower house of Congress last year openly call for war against Great Britain."

George was startled. He hadn't heard this before. But with its professional army and its formidable navy, Great Britain was many times more powerful than the American forces. "Surely, sir, they would not dare."

Colonel Sheaffe chuckled. "The Crown would crush them like bugs."

"That would at least break the monotony around here," said Morrison.

"Gentlemen, let us be careful what we wish for," said Brock as he ground his cigar butt into an ashtray. "On paper, at least, the American militia totals over seven hundred thousand. If reasonably trained and adequately led, they would be difficult to stop."

CHAPTER THREE

NOVEMBER 1811, MISSISSIPPI TERRITORY

Fifteen-year-old Hadjo trotted along a game trail occasionally lit by afternoon sunlight beaming through the forest's canopy. Around his neck hung two gutted cottontail rabbits snared that morning. He had been fortunate to catch both only a few miles from the village, but he also took pride in his hunting skills.

His insides tingled with anticipation at the thought of presenting the rabbits to a leather-skinned, gap-toothed widow in the village. His gift almost guaranteed that he would be invited to share the evening meal with the widow and her daughter, Prancing Fawn.

Hadjo had met Prancing Fawn earlier in the week, and since then he had been able to think of little else. Each day he left at dawn to hunt and set traps to kill game, and each day he had brought home enough to provide a solid meal for the three of them. He was determined to prove himself a capable provider and someday qualify as an acceptable suitor for Prancing Fawn. Just the thought of her mischievous smile and eyes spurred him faster along the trail.

As Hadjo approached the village, he stopped short and clutched the tomahawk tucked under his belt. Warriors he did not recognize entered the village on horseback. For weeks rumors had circulated that Tecumseh, leader of the Shawnees, would visit the Muscogee tribe's annual gathering.

Thousands of Muscogee had flocked to their capital of Tuckabatchee along the Tallapoosa River to see and hear Tecumseh. Even some Cherokee and Choctaw had joined the gathering. Hadjo had heard that Tecumseh's long trek south to his mother's people was not a social call. His mission was to recruit allies for his plan to halt the white man's theft of native lands.

Although Hadjo had heard of Tecumseh's skill as a hunter and warrior, he wondered if anyone could stop the land-grabbing whites. Certainly, the council of Muscogee chiefs had failed—white squatters eager for land promptly broke each treaty signed.

But as the Shawnee leader and his twenty-four warriors dismounted, Hadjo had to admit they made an impression. Unlike Hadjo and the other Muscogees, who wore clothes made of material purchased in trade with white men, the Shawnee visitors wore traditional buckskin hunting shirts and leggings decorated with fringe and beads.

Each wore a red headband with eagle feathers, red war paint smeared under their eyes, temples shaven clean, and long hair braided back. Silver bands decorated arms and wrists. Each carried a rifle, tomahawk, and scalping knife.

Taller than the other warriors, Tecumseh led his Shawnees single file along a pathway lined by the Muscogees. At the central square of the village, they silently lined up in front of the open, thatch-roofed council pavilion.

Without a word, the Muscogee chief stepped forward and offered his pipe to Tecumseh. After a ceremonial puff of smoke to pledge peaceful intentions, the Shawnee leader passed the pipe to each of his warriors. The village chief directed his guests to a large log cabin where they could rest for the afternoon.

That night just outside the cabin, Hadjo and hundreds of other Muscogees watched spellbound as Tecumseh and his warriors performed a ritual called the Dance of the Lakes. In the firelight with their lean, hard bodies stripped to loincloths, the Shawnees stomped and leaped to the beat of drums.

Over the next several days, Hadjo sat with the other young warriors outside the council pavilion, listening as the chiefs consulted with the Indian agent assigned to the Muscogees. The hours passed slowly, and Hadjo grew more and more frustrated. As they had so many times before, the chiefs complained to the Indian agent that the decline in the deerskin trade had diminished the Muscogees' means of trading for food, clothing, and rifles. Many would starve during the coming winter unless the situation was addressed.

As he had on previous occasions, the federal agent advised Muscogee men to take up the plow and Muscogee women to take up the spinning wheel and loom. With the advent of a new invention, the cotton gin, agriculture was the means by which the Muscogees could prosper and adapt to white civilization.

Several chiefs expressed doubts, telling the Indian agent that tilling the soil was squaw work, not suitable for warriors and hunters. The agent reminded them that some Muscogee families had already learned to grow cotton and had purchased black slaves to expand their plantations.

Hadjo squirmed at the mention of Muscogee plantation owners. They seemed to adopt white greed as well as their agricultural methods. In tribal villages, those with more than they needed shared with those of their clan, so none suffered unnecessarily. But the Muscogees adopting the white ways had also begun to accumulate wealth rather than sharing with their neighbors. And the gap between the newly rich Muscogee plantation owners and the struggling hunter-warriors seemed to be growing.

The Indian agent addressed the Muscogees through an interpreter, but Hadjo had little trouble understanding English. Although he had been born to a village leader, Hadjo had been orphaned by a plague. For several years he had lived with white settlers who tried to teach him their ways. He recalled that the pull of native ways had been too strong for him, and he had run away to a nearby village.

The Indian agent then announced that the U.S. government intended to build a road from east to west across tribal land. When the chiefs protested, the agent explained that the whites needed the road to transport goods to market and for defense against attack from the British and the Spanish in Florida.

The chiefs said they would not approve such a road. The agent then told them the road would be built whether they agreed to it or not. He advised them to accept the payment offered, or they would get nothing.

Throughout the Indian agent's visit, Tecumseh sat quietly, his face expressionless. Hadjo began to suspect that Tecumseh was no better than the Muscogee chiefs who had no effective plan to halt the whites' encroachment on tribal lands.

For over a week, Hadjo had looked forward to the time when Tecumseh would address the tribal council. But day after day the Shawnee leader made excuses as to why the timing was not right. Only after the Indian agent left the village did Tecumseh finally agree to speak to the Muscogees.

At midday Hadjo watched as Tecumseh and his two dozen warriors emerged from their lodge. Naked except for their loincloths and smeared with black paint, the Shawnees carried war clubs. The gathered throng parted as Tecumseh and his men marched single file along the path to the village square.

Silently, with their faces contorted in anger, the Shawnees marched three times around the town's central square. In a traditional purification ritual, Tecumseh scattered tobacco and sumac at the posts marking each corner and finally into the town's sacred flame at the center. The Shawnees strode into the open-sided council pavilion, and then, as one, they shattered the afternoon calm with a ferocious war cry.

All took seats on the ground, and Tecumseh presented to the Muscogee chief an impressive belt of wampum with five strands of different colors. The Muscogee chiefs passed the wampum around for all to admire, and Tecumseh produced the Shawnee peace pipe. Longer and larger than the Muscogee pipe, it was decorated with shells, beads, and porcupine needles. Still without a word being spoken, the Muscogee chief puffed on the pipe, then passed it around to the other chiefs.

After the formalities, Tecumseh stood, and the crowd outside the pavilion sat quietly as all strained to hear.

"In the days of our ancestors, the world was in balance. Tradition guided our lives, and we lived in harmony with the bounty around us. Young men learned to be hunters and warriors, and young women learned to tend their gardens."

Hadjo was struck by the fire in Tecumseh's eyes and the emotion in his gestures. Even before the translator explained the Shawnee words, Hadjo could feel the passion and strength of Tecumseh's speech.

"But then the palefaces arrived from across great waters," continued Tecumseh. "At first they wanted only a little of our land in exchange for gifts. Then they offered us cloth, axes, and muskets in trade for deerskins. Our fathers cast aside traditions and, for a time, prospered with the trade."

Tecumseh paused before continuing. "Now the deer are nearly gone, so we have fewer skins to buy the white man's goods. Traditions have been ignored, and our women and children go hungry and cold. Meanwhile, the whites have multiplied, and so has their lust for our land. If the paleface encroachment is not stopped, the red man will be reduced to the status of the black slaves."

A murmur of concern and anger rumbled from the Muscogees.

"Only decisive action will hold the paleface back and restore great-ness to all red men. We must throw off the trappings of white civilization and return to the traditional way of life. As our ancestors did, we must seek spiritual guidance from our shamans. All tribes of red men must join forces for war and drive the paleface out of our land."

Murmurs of agreement rose from the young warriors around the outskirts of the gathering.

But one of the Muscogee chiefs asked, "If you are so eager to go to war with the whites, why are you not already leading our northern brothers into battle?"

All fell quiet to hear Tecumseh's reply. "The palefaces have great numbers and powerful weapons. No one tribe can defeat them. We have already seen this too many times. To drive back the white men, all red men must put aside differences and work together."

One of the chiefs scoffed at Tecumseh. "War with the States would be the ruin of the Muscogee nation."

Tecumseh's eyes blazed as he replied. "Together, we shall prevail. Now is the time. Soon the States and Great Britain will be at war. The British remember that we fought bravely at their side during the last war. They want to help us regain our ancestral lands. The British will give us guns, ammunition, and supplies to fight the Americans."

One of the chiefs laughed. "The British care no more for us than they do the Americans."

Tecumseh asked, "Who do the Muscogees prefer to trade with? The Americans cheat us and sell inferior goods made in the States. The British trade fairly for quality goods made across the great waters."

Still the chiefs argued that the Americans were too many and too strong.

One of the Shawnees was a shaman, and he now stood as Tecumseh sat. "The spirits of our ancestors have spoken. They are displeased with our neglect of ancient traditions and have shown their displeasure in the misfortunes we now face. But if we cast aside the ways of the white man and return to our time-honored way of life, the spirits will protect us from the paleface weapons. "

The shaman paused briefly. "You may trust Tecumseh's words. On the night of his birth, a bright light streaked across the sky, and he was named accordingly. The spirits will send you a sign. You will know it when you see Tecumseh's arm of fire stretch across the dark sky and the earth opens up to swallow the whites."

As the shaman sat, Tecumseh stood, his body trembling with anger. With arms raised he looked toward the heavens. "Oh, Muscogee! Brethren of my mother. Brush from your eyelids the sleep of slavery. Rise and strike for vengeance and your land. Drive the white man back into the sea!"

Hadjo leapt to his feet, as did hundreds of warriors around him. They brandished their tomahawks, and their voices combined in deafening war cries.

CHAPTER FOUR

NOVEMBER 1811, ATLANTIC OCEAN

Seventeen-year-old Silas Shackleton clutched a rough wooden rail as the merchant ship *Utica* rose with the crest of a wave. The blue-gray horizon stretched wide for a moment before the bow dipped and the vessel plunged over the backside of the swell. As the ship surged again, the deck seemed to slide and roll.

Dozens of experienced seamen moved about, apparently oblivious to the pitch and yaw of the deck. Only a day out of New York City on his first voyage, Silas wasn't accustomed to the constant motion of the vessel. At first he had been relieved to secure a position on a crew. Now he wondered if he would survive the day. The ship and the sea seemed to spin slowly around him.

He longed for solid ground, but staying ashore would have meant almost certain death. Not that the prospects of an untimely death were new to him—he had grown up in the streets of New York City as an abandoned son of a prostitute.

Over the last year, he had worked along the docks and had come to admire the disciplined and organized crews of the naval vessels he helped load. For months he had tried to secure a job on a ship, but few such positions were available for an inexperienced hand.

Just days before, he and his buddies had been sitting around a fire in an alley feasting on roasted pigeons. Several members of a local gang jumped the boys and tried to steal the meat. A knife fight resulted in the death of a gang leader's brother. With bloodthirsty gang members after him, Silas had signed on the *Utica* just hours before she set sail. He feared he wouldn't have lasted another night in New York City, but running left him feeling like a coward. The streets of New York were his home, and he already yearned to return.

A stiff breeze cooled his face, and the sea air felt fresh and clean, but then mixed with odors from the chicken coop and hog pen on deck. A salty taste seeped into his mouth, and his insides twisted tight. He leaned over the wooden rail, and the contents of his stomach spewed out. Vomit blew back in his face, splattering his clothes and the bulwark.

"Damn it, lad," said a mature crewman named Bosworth, "if you're going to puke your guts out, go to the head." He grabbed Silas by the collar and shoved him to the front of the ship.

At the bow, Bosworth bent Silas over the bulwark, then grabbed his legs and heaved him over. Silas screamed as he imagined plunging into the frothy deep. Instead, he landed in a net of coarse rope slung under the bowsprit. Several crew members laughed.

Silas grabbed the netting and struggled upright as another swell raced toward him. The bowsprit shot skyward, shoving Silas hard against the ropes. For a moment the ship seemed to stop midair, then the bow plunged again. Out surged more of the contents of Silas's stomach. The breeze swept his puke forward and away. He spat to clear the sour taste from his mouth. Over and over again, the ship rose and fell in the swells.

Silas cursed his weakness in front of the crew as he vomited until there was nothing left to heave.

Feeling a little better, he clutched the cargo net and began to climb back into the ship. He stopped and blinked when he realized he was gazing upward at pale buttocks resting on a crude bench set over the bulwark. A stream of urine caught in the breeze and sprayed forward from the bow.

Silas had always assumed a ship's toilet would be located at the rear, but now he understood. It had been set at the bow so the breeze blowing from aft of the ship and filling the sails would carry excrement away and not foul the deck and hull.

The man seated at the head let his wiping material fly with the breeze, then stood and pulled up his trousers. Silas was shocked to see that it was the ship's captain, a short, frail man with a long, drawn-out nose.

Captain Schroop stared at Silas for a moment. "Come along now, young man. It's time for you to learn your duties."

A junior officer not much older than Silas approached the captain. "Sir, the frigate is signaling us to heave to."

"Damn." The captain turned toward the British warship that had been sighted several hours before off the northern horizon and had steadily closed on them. Heavy with cargo bound for Lisbon, the *Utica* had no chance of outrunning the frigate.

Silas climbed over the bulwark, and Bosworth handed him a bucket. The older seaman shaded his eyes against the sun and studied the frigate. "Arrogant bastards."

Captain Schroop scowled from the raised platform at the rear of the ship, the *quarterdeck*. Silas had little doubt what peeved the ship's commander. Great Britain had signed the Treaty of Paris in 1783, recognizing its former colonies as a nation and establishing its boundaries as the Atlantic, the Great Lakes, and everything east of the Mississippi River except New Orleans and Florida. But in recent years the British had become irritated that the Americans traded freely with Britain's enemies, especially with France under Napoleon Bonaparte. Royal Navy vessels routinely stopped American merchant ships on the open sea. Instead of merely reviewing the vessel's bills of lading, the time-honored means of inspection, the British physically searched the ships, often damaging the cargo.

As the war in Europe dragged on, Silas recalled, the Royal Navy ran short of able-bodied seamen. Not restricting themselves to forcing their own citizens into the king's service, the navy began to impress American seamen into duty aboard His Majesty's ships. These blatant affronts to the sovereignty of the new nation had nearly resulted in a declaration of war against Britain.

"Steady, men," said the captain. "She probably just wants us to carry dispatches to Europe."

But as His Majesty's Ship *Guerriere* pulled alongside, her gun ports opened, and out rolled a menacing row of cannon.

Bosworth groaned. Several seamen swore.

The warship lowered a rowboat, and in climbed half a dozen redcoat marines and a British naval officer dressed in dark blue. Within minutes they pulled alongside the *Utica*. A horse-faced naval lieutenant asked permission to come aboard.

"'Permission to come aboard?'" Captain Schroop nearly spat the words out. "With a broadside aimed my direction, you ask permission?" After a moment, the captain said, "Very well, then. If you must . . ."

Once on board, the blue-uniformed lieutenant faced Captain Schroop. "Your bills of lading, sir, if you please."

The American captain grumbled something but led the naval officer belowdecks to inspect the documents. After a few minutes the two returned topside. The British officer turned to one of the marines. "Corporal, you have your orders." The marines headed belowdecks to inspect the cargo.

"This is outrageous," screamed Captain Schroop. "You will pay for any damages!"

The naval officer stood quietly as the marines searched the ship from top to bottom. After half an hour, the marines returned to their officer's side.

"Captain," said the lieutenant, "would you assemble your crew?"

The captain's face turned dark. "To what purpose, may I ask?"

"I have orders to apprehend deserters."

"This is an unforgivable breach of our rights to travel the seas unmolested!" But with a glance at the frigate, its cannon bristling from gun ports, he said, "Very well, but I personally guarantee that every crewman aboard is an American citizen. There shall be no forced conscription this day."

Shortly, the naval officer strode down the line of American seamen. He stopped and studied Bosworth. "I recognize this man as a seaman from His Majesty's navy."

Bosworth tried to run but was seized by the redcoats.

"Lieutenant!" screamed the captain. "I must protest. This man is a naturalized American citizen, and he has the papers to prove it."

The naval officer scoffed. "Papers are cheap. Besides, once an English citizen, always an English citizen."

"You may be sure I will protest this to the highest possible authority."

The young lieutenant smirked. "As you wish, sir."

A seaman who had been standing next to Bosworth rushed one of the marines and attempted to drag him away from Bosworth. Several seamen broke ranks and joined in.

Silas flinched at the thunderous boom of a cannon on the *Guerriere*. Something whizzed overhead with a sizzling hiss, then splashed into the sea a hundred yards beyond the *Utica*.

With a flurry of swinging clubs, the marines drove the American sailors back into line. The British officer strode past Silas, then stopped and turned. "Where are you from, lad?"

For a moment Silas couldn't speak. Then he blurted out, "New York, sir."

"Haw!" said the lieutenant. "That's an English accent if I ever heard one." He nodded to the stout, muscular marines.

Silas bolted for an open hatch, but two of the marines grabbed him.

He planted his feet squarely on the deck and pulled back as the marines tried to drag him toward the bulwark. When a marine's grip tightened about Silas's arm, he wrenched it back and shoved the redcoat away. Silas turned to scramble back into the line of American seamen, but before he could make any progress, a redcoat grabbed him by the shoulder and spun him around. Another marine stepped forward. A wooden club arced overhead. Silas's mind blazed with light, then everything turned dark.

The next morning red-coated marines hauled Silas and Bosworth, arms and feet shackled, up the steps of a wooden ladder to the deck of the *Guerriere*. Silas scanned the sea to the horizon in every direction. The *Utica* was nowhere in sight.

A grizzled old seaman faced them. He wore a boatswain's flat-topped straw hat and a crooked smile. "Welcome to His Majesty's navy, lads. The captain has asked me to apprise you of your options for employment." He studied Silas and Bosworth for a moment before continuing. "You may serve your time aboard as pressed men, or if you prefer, you may volunteer and receive the pay and benefits accorded regular seamen. Pressed men, as you no doubt understand, draw harsher duty and treatment. You may indicate your decision to volunteer as a seaman by making one step forward."

Silas was confused. He and Bosworth had been taken by force from an American vessel. Now they were being offered a chance to volunteer?

He tried to think of a choice curse by which to reply. But Bosworth stepped forward.

"Are you crazy?" Silas asked.

"Silence!" yelled the boatswain as he stepped in front of Silas. "Your mate here is showing wisdom. Life in His Majesty's navy can be harsh, but it's much better to serve as a seaman than a pressed man. Use your head, laddy."

Silas was appalled. There was no way he would volunteer to serve in the British navy. Bosworth was an idiot.

The old boatswain studied Silas silently, then turned to Bosworth. "You have one minute to talk some sense into your young friend."

As the boatswain strode away, Bosworth leaned toward Silas. "There's no use fighting them, boyo. They have us for as long as they want us. We might as well make the best of a bad situation."

Silas glared at Bosworth. "I'll not volunteer. And hell will freeze over before they'll get a lick of work out of me."

"Listen, you little turd." Bosworth clutched Silas by the shoulder. "The captain of a Royal vessel doesn't give a rat's arse about your scruples, your politics—or your life. What he does care about is maintaining discipline. In a battle of wills, you lose."

The boatswain returned. "What's it going to be, lad?"

CHAPTER FIVE

NOVEMBER 1811, WASHINGTON CITY

The carriage creaked and swayed as it slowed. Twenty-year-old Rachel Thurston grabbed the leather armrest and peeked out the window. Evening dew mixed with smoke from fireplaces already well stoked against the autumn chill. The lantern-lit, columned porch of the president's mansion came into view. The devil's lair, she figured. The enemy's inner sanctum.

She glanced at her father, seated across from her in his forest-green suit. Mordecai Thurston had a reputation for being an intelligent and powerful businessman in Gloucester, and he had been chosen by merchants and bankers throughout Massachusetts to lobby the federal government on their behalf. Rachel was confident that his capabilities were more than a match for President Madison and his bumpkin friends.

Rachel was sure that, as a woman, she would never wield such influence. Still, she shared her father's desires to defeat the Madisons' plans. She welcomed the chance to meet President and Mrs. Madison, figuring that it was wise to know one's enemies.

The carriage eased to a stop under the towering portico, and Rachel noted the brightness of the lanterns. A sense of pride flowed through her when she realized the lamps were most likely fueled by the best whale oil from Massachusetts, probably Nantucket or New Bedford. No doubt, the candles inside the mansion were made from another whaling product, spermaceti.

A smartly clad young black man opened the carriage door. Rachel's father stepped to the cobblestones, then offered his hand as she eased down the steps. Rachel hesitated, resenting the implication that as a female she was incapable of stepping out of a carriage without assistance. Her father glared at her, daring her to resist his help and risk tripping in her floor-length gown. She forced herself to smile and accepted his hand. The black man latched the door, and the carriage pulled away.

Since arriving in Washington City, Rachel had marveled at the presence of so many black people. Unlike her home state of Massachusetts, here they seemed to be everywhere. She glanced at the somber-faced black and pitied him. She wished she could do something about the plight of slaves but realized there was little a young woman could do to help.

She gazed at the huge columns on either side of the entrance to the mansion. Although it was nothing compared to the homes she had visited the year before in England, the building was impressive.

Movement in the driveway caught her attention. Around the curve flew a team of four white horses pulling a gleaming globe. Two brightly clad coachmen stood solemn as sentinels at the rear. Gold-painted sides shimmered in the lantern light as the carriage glided to a stop at the mansion entrance.

Diamonds sparkled from the surface of the carriage door as it swung wide. Out stepped a flamboyantly dressed gentleman and a woman in a flowing gown. Although Rachel had been in Washington City for only a few days, she had heard of the carriage belonging to the French ministry.

Without a word Rachel's father offered her his arm and led her up the mansion's steps. They both despised the French and their notions about self-government.

In the foyer, more black servants directed them past a broad staircase. A well-dressed black man stood in the wide hallway. As they approached, he bowed slightly and spoke with a French accent. "Good evening, Mr. and Miss Thurston."

Rachel wondered how the man knew their names. Then she realized his job was to know and greet each of the guests.

The black man extended an arm toward a noisy room across the hallway. "President and Mrs. Madison invite you to join them in the drawing room."

As Rachel and her father headed toward a large room bustling with the conversation of several dozen guests, the well-dressed black man in the hallway welcomed the French minister and his wife in their native language.

At first Rachel had been confused by the greeting because there was no receiving line. Then she recalled her mother complaining that Thomas Jefferson had been a backwoods hick, thumbing his nose at established etiquette and turning the president's residence into a ramshackle barn. Jefferson envisioned the new nation as egalitarian, where no man held higher status than another. Even prominent guests at Jefferson's dinner table found themselves seated with backwoodsmen. Rachel's mother had predicted that as Jefferson's handpicked successor and fellow Virginian, Madison would be little better.

Rachel's father guided her through the crowd, and soon her attention was drawn to a woman with hair piled high and wrapped in a turban of green silk. Around her neck hung a string of pearls, and the low-cut neckline of her dress revealed ample cleavage. Below a high-fitting bodice, the flimsy white fabric of her gown flowed as freely as that of a Grecian goddess. Given the large number of people clustered around the woman, Rachel had no doubt this was the she-devil herself, Mrs. Madison.

Around the room other women wore turbans, some decorated with bright feathers. Several also wore the high-bodice dresses championed in Europe by Emperor Napoleon's former wife, Josephine. Rachel recalled that Mrs. Madison, herself a renowned dressmaker, had adapted Josephine's style to her own tastes, moderating the plunge of the neckline and rejecting the nearly transparent fabric popular in Paris. Mrs. Madison's styles were emulated throughout the States.

Her father eased her forward again, and Rachel was reminded why the president's wife was widely regarded as a woman of beauty. Her features included everything men regarded with favor—a plump, well-endowed figure with a lovely, rounded face.

Mrs. Madison glanced at Rachel, then at her father. With a smile of recognition, she said, "Mr. Thurston, how nice to see you again."

"Thank you, madam. May I introduce my daughter, Rachel?"

"My dear," said Mrs. Madison, "it is my great pleasure to meet you."

"Thank you, ma'am."

"Please, call me Dolley." The president's wife smiled warmly. "I had the great pleasure of meeting your mother several years ago. My compliments. You've certainly inherited her beauty."

Before Rachel could say anything, Dolley continued.

"Let me also say how sorry I was to hear of the loss of your mother. I do look forward to visiting with you later. But let me assure you, if you need anything while you're in Washington City, just let me know."

From behind her, Rachel could hear the French ambassador. Dolley's attention switched to the approaching couple, but she patted Rachel's hand lightly as her father led her away.

Rachel's father guided her through the crowd again. They stopped in front of a short, frail man dressed in black. Her father stepped forward, and President Madison extended his hand. Although he was barely as tall as Rachel, Madison looked distinguished in his white-powdered wig and black suit.

Rachel thought the man's breeches, stockings, and silver-buckled shoes terribly old-fashioned. With skin as pale as parchment, the president appeared to be nearly fifty, although his wife seemed many years younger. Despite herself, Rachel felt goose bumps at the sight of the man often referred to as the Father of the Constitution.

Madison smiled warmly with a mischievous glint to his eyes. "How very nice of you to join us, Mr. Thurston. I do look forward to chatting with you later this evening."

Mordecai Thurston nodded slightly. "It is always a pleasure, Mr. President."

Rachel thought the title "Mr. President" a little odd but figured it was less presumptuous than "Your Excellency," as President Washington had been addressed.

"May I present my daughter, Rachel?"

"Certainly." The president turned to her and extended his hand. "Welcome to Washington City, young lady."

She curtsied slightly and offered her hand. He clutched it warmly, bent at the waist, and kissed her fingers lightly.

"Thank you—Mr. President. It's an honor to meet you."

Madison shifted position slightly, as if he were at a loss for further conversation. But then he said, "My dear, I understand that you have only recently arrived in Washington City. What do you think of our nation's capital so far?"

She recalled her disappointment upon arrival. Compared to London or even Boston, Washington City was a backwater village. Other than a handful of government buildings, the capital was little more than a town surrounded by dense forest and swamp. "I'm sure it will be beautiful," she said, "when it is complete."

Madison chuckled. His blue eyes sparkled in the lantern light. "I assure you that it is quite magnificent—at least on paper."

Her father led her back into the crowd. She hadn't expected to like either the president or his wife, but she had to admit they were both charming.

In Gloucester, her mother had railed against the mob that had rebelled against Great Britain, damning the rebels and their presumption to break with the nation that had given birth to the colonies and nurtured their growth.

Rachel acknowledged that Great Britain had treated her American colonies unfairly, and she accepted the need for the colonies to break away. But the direction the new government was taking seemed all wrong and would surely lead to disaster.

Rachel noticed the beautiful red-velvet drapery framing the ceiling-high windows. A life-size portrait of George Washington dominated one wall. The room sparkled with candles and lanterns and mirrors. A faint aroma of spices mixed with smoke from the fireplaces.

Her father struck up a conversation with several well-dressed gentlemen, and Rachel eased over to a group of women. She hoped for an opportunity to introduce herself, but the conversation stopped abruptly and all eyes turned to someone behind her.

"Miss Thurston."

Rachel recognized the voice and turned. President Madison had approached her.

He bowed slightly. "Would you do me the honor of accompanying me to dinner?" He extended his arm. The whole room fell silent as the crowd looked in her direction.

Madison smiled and slipped her arm into the crook of his elbow. "Come along, my dear. I do believe Dolley has prepared something special this evening."

With nerves tingling, Rachel clutched the president's arm as he led her into the hallway and then through a doublewide door to a huge room filled with tables. At the far end of the room hung portraits of presidents Adams and Jefferson. Along the opposite wall stood a huge sideboard cabinet that would surely have taken up the entire length of the dining room of their three-story home in Gloucester.

There was no progression to dinner, as there had been in England, where guests proceeded to the meal in descending order of their rank or station in life. Here, the seating seemed to be mixed, with no particular order. Her mother had been a stickler for etiquette. Traditionally, the host invited an honored guest to sit with him for dinner. Surely the president would select the French minister or a senior senator as his guest of honor.

Her mother would have been disgusted with such a break in custom. In Massachusetts, as part of a wealthy shipping family, her father and mother would have been among the first seated, and rightfully so. Of course, in London, or even here in Washington City, they would expect to be much farther down the order of progression. Such was the natural order of things.

Rachel looked for the head table, no doubt where the president was heading. But Madison led her to a table near the middle of the room. A black-clad servant pulled out a chair and offered it to Rachel.

She assumed President Madison would take the head of the table. Instead, he waited for her to sit, then stood behind the chair at the foot, to Rachel's right. In another break from custom, Mrs. Madison took the seat at the head of the table, the position normally occupied by the host, whose duties included engaging all around the table in conversation. As Rachel's father sat to Dolley's right, two other gentlemen joined them. After Mrs. Madison settled into her chair, the men each took a seat.

Madison leaned close to Rachel and smiled. "Dolley does me the great favor of taking 'the honor' of the table so I may relax and enjoy the meal."

On the white linen in front of Rachel stood a folded place card inscribed with her name. The seating arrangement had been planned in advance. She glanced toward Dolley and wondered what the woman was up to.

Across from Rachel and her father sat two men she didn't recognize.

Madison patted Rachel's hand. "May I introduce you to Henry Clay of Kentucky, recently elected Speaker of the House of Representatives."

The man seated at Madison's right had a narrow face and a warm smile. Rachel guessed that despite his thinning hair, he was about age thirty.

Next to Clay, and at Dolley's left, was a tall, well-dressed gentleman with intense eyes and thick, curly brown hair. Madison introduced him as Robert Fulton. Steamboats had been running between New York City and Albany ever since Fulton made the first voyage in 1807. Word had just reached Washington City that Fulton's recently launched *New Orleans* had successfully steamed from Pittsburgh down the Ohio River to Louisville, Kentucky, despite nearly sinking when devastating earthquakes rocked the Mississippi Valley.

A platter of roasted wild turkey was placed in front of Rachel. Black servants filled glasses with wine and brought dish after dish filled with steaming food.

"Miss Thurston," asked the president, "would you pass the salt?"

Rachel froze. Her mother had warned her that passing the salt by itself would also pass bad luck to the receiver. Was this an opportunity to hex the president? Almost instantly, she rejected the idea. She might be spying on the Madisons, but that was no excuse to be rude. She grabbed both the salt shaker and the pepper shaker, smiled, and passed them to President Madison.

Henry Clay glanced toward Rachel as he helped himself to a mixture of pickled beets and onions. "I understand, young lady, that you have only recently arrived in Washington City. I trust you are finding your accommodations satisfactory?"

Rachel and her father had rented a house on New York Avenue, and she had spent most of the week unpacking and getting settled. Although she missed her mother terribly, Rachel found the task of organizing a household made time pass quickly. "Our house here is quite different from our home in Gloucester, but I'm sure it will work out nicely, thank you."

Henry Clay smiled. "I envy you the comforts a house provides. Many of us in the legislature make do with boardinghouses. Although the company is pleasant, the rooms are a bit cramped." He glanced at President Madison. "Of course, we all covet the accommodations available here at the Executive Residence."

Madison smiled. "And for that I credit my Dolley, who has worked tirelessly to create an environment in which all may take pride."

Mordecai Thurston raised his glass toward Mrs. Madison. "Quite so. Well done, my lady. I daresay, if Mr. Madison were inclined to declare himself king, he would already have a suitable palace."

Rachel could feel the tension rise around the table.

"Oh, heavens," said Madison, "I think we've quite had our fill of tyrants. Dolley and I yearn for the time when my days of public service are ended and we may retire to the relative quiet of our home in Virginia."

Mordecai Thurston passed a bowl of baked apples to Rachel. "Does that mean, Mr. President, that you won't accept a second term in office?"

Madison smiled, obviously enjoying the banter. "I serve at the pleasure of the electorate. And the next term is still a long way off. But, please, let us not bore our ladies with tedious details of politics."

"Quite right, Mr. President," said Rachel's father. Then with a glance toward Dolley, "My apologies, madam."

"No apologies necessary, Mr. Thurston." Dolley handed him a bowl. "But please try these candied yams. I do so love to test new recipes."

Rachel sighed. Just when the conversation was getting interesting . . .

As the small talk drifted from food to cotton gins to hot-air balloons, Rachel realized the dinner had provided her with an opportunity. The people seated around the table were a microcosm of the volatile new nation. Her father represented the Congregationalists of New England. Madison represented the Episcopalian, plantation aristocrats of the southern Atlantic Coast states. Dolley had been raised as a Quaker in Pennsylvania. Clay and Fulton represented a rapidly growing group her father called the "damned Irish," many of whom were from states admitted to the nation after the original thirteen.

Even though most of the residents of the new states didn't consider themselves Irish, her father had complained that they had been infected by Irish ways. When she asked what he meant, he explained that early in the 1700s thousands of Presbyterian Scots-Irish had moved from northern Ireland to the western frontier of Pennsylvania.

As Rachel's father had described it, the fiercely independent Scots-Irish bred like rodents and soon outgrew the communities they settled. Before long, they were scurrying south along the Appalachians, and when a trail was established through the mountains, they scampered through to Kentucky and beyond. As new territories were settled, they received admission to the nation as states. Each new state had its share of representatives to congress, including two senators.

Each time a new state was admitted, Rachel fumed. At the time the northern colonies ratified the Constitution, they shared power with the southern Atlantic states more or less equally. But the addition of new states meant New England slipped further into minority position. She feared that New England, instead of rightfully leading the new nation, would become its rump end, with less and less influence, no doubt leading all into ruin.

In addition to their backgrounds, Rachel recalled, the men seated around the table held vastly different political views. Madison and many new members of Congress, including Clay, were Democratic-Republicans, who favored states' rights and a very limited role for the central government. "Lovers of the French," as her father called them. Rachel and her father were Federalists, the party founded by Alexander Hamilton. They believed effective government required a strong chief executive, a central bank, a standing army, and taxes to support it all.

Clay was also part of a group known as the War Hawks, for their support of war against Britain. So far, the new congressmen didn't have enough votes to pass a declaration of war, but they did have enough influence to elect Henry Clay as Speaker of the House on the first day he took office. As Clay chatted with Madison, Rachel realized that they would be formidable adversaries.

Rachel had the distinct feeling she was surrounded by predators biding their time as they waited to devour each other. She had witnessed her father in fierce political debates with those he opposed, and she understood that to be the nature of politics, where opponents often regarded each other as traitors and argued their views with religious zeal. Shouting and violence were not uncommon. She marveled at how these men sat around the table and made small talk of the most innocent nature.

Rachel's gaze shifted to Mrs. Madison, with her turban towering above all. "Presidentess," as one Federalist newspaper had described her. "Queen Dolley," another had labeled her. To Rachel, the woman seemed all sweetness and civility as she orchestrated polite conversation among bitter political rivals. Even though Rachel was drawn into the conversation from time to time, she felt as if somehow she were being manipulated like a pawn.

Her fork stopped midway to her mouth when she understood. Her role was to play the innocent female, around whom the lions were to be on their best behavior. Rachel glanced again at Dolley and saw her as a spider whose web extended into the capital and well beyond.

Rachel could feel her temper rising, but quickly calmed herself as she waited for a lull in the conversation. "Mr. President," she asked politely, "will you declare war against Great Britain?"

Conversation around the table died. Across from her, Henry Clay studied her with renewed interest.

Madison dabbed at his mouth with a linen napkin before answering. "The question of war, my dear, rests with Congress." He nodded toward Clay. "Unfortunately, sometimes war is necessary. But rest assured that I am well aware of the lessons of history. Once war is commenced, it often lasts much longer, costs much more, and leads to much different consequences than intended by those who initiate it."

Rachel was ready with another question, but a servant reached around her, removed her plate, and replaced it with a bowl of ice cream. Pain stabbed through her ankle as her father gave her a discreet kick.

"Ah," said Madison, "my favorite dessert. Dolley knows how to spoil me."

Silently, Rachel fumed at having been cut off. For the remainder of the meal, conversation returned to mundane matters.

As Rachel and her father prepared to leave, a sense of foreboding coursed through her. Clay, Fulton, and the Madisons would no doubt be formidable adversaries of Federalist plans. If the new nation didn't pay more attention to the concerns of the northeastern states, her father and his allies intended to break New England away, form a new nation, and realign with Great Britain.

CHAPTER SIX

JUNE 1812, UPPER CANADA

Hadjo sat quietly in a sycamore tree deep in the forest many miles northwest of the Detroit River. Beneath him ran a game trail over which he hoped a deer would soon pass. Dressed in buckskin, he held a bow in his left hand, an arrow in his right.

His back ached and his muscles had grown sore from sitting in one position for hours. Despite the discomfort, he took pride in the use of traditional weapons. Hunting with bow and arrow rather than a rifle or musket required more patience and skill since the hunter had to get much closer to his prey for a kill. Hadjo also took satisfaction in shunning the use of the white man's weapons.

As Tecumseh had explained, only by returning to their traditional ways and its balance between man and nature would the red man be able to drive the whites back into the sea. Tecumseh was right, Hadjo knew. The red men would never be able to succeed if they were dependent upon the palefaces for trade and gifts.

To help himself ignore the discomfort of sitting in one position for so long, Hadjo thought about all that had happened during the previous year. In the fall when Tecumseh headed north from the land of the Muscogees, Hadjo had been one of thirty Muscogee warriors to accompany the Shawnee leader.

He recalled the devastation they found when Tecumseh led them into what had been his village at Tippecanoe. Hadjo took some satisfaction in seeing that the bodies of the buried Americans had already been dug up and scalped, then left exposed to be ravaged and scattered by wild animals.

Despite the loss of face, Tecumseh renewed his efforts to unite the lake tribes against the whites. His credibility rose again as the shamans' predictions came true about a bright light stretching across the night sky and of the spirits tearing the earth open with rumbles that could be heard for many miles.

In the following months, Hadjo learned the Shawnee language, and since he was one of the few warriors also fluent in English, he was often asked to serve as messenger for Tecumseh.

Tecumseh had warned his Muscogee followers that his path required much sacrifice. Winters in his native lands were much more severe than in the land of the Muscogee. He traveled light and fast, which meant that all loved ones must be left behind. The Muscogee warriors were not likely to return home for at least two summers.

Hadjo recalled his tearful farewell with Prancing Fawn. Even now, he longed for the warmth of her embrace, the glow of her smile, and the laughter of her eyes. He yearned for the day he could return to her and make her his bride. But first he must help drive the Big Knives away so that he and Prancing Fawn could live the life meant for them.

He shifted his position slightly on the tree limb. Then he froze. Up the trail, something had moved. He slipped the nock of his arrow onto the bowstring and held his breath. Through a screen of trees, he could see a large animal approaching. But not a deer. His heart raced when he realized it was a bear.

The spirits were indeed being generous to him. A bear would provide delicious meat and a valuable pelt. And to wear a necklace of the claws and teeth from a bear that he had killed himself would be a great honor, a testament to his bravery and prowess as a hunter.

On the other hand, if he only wounded the animal, it might attack him or run away wounded. To leave a wounded animal was shameful. He would have to stalk the beast through the woods, and he had heard tales of hunters mauled to death by wounded bears.

The bear paused and raised its head, sniffing the air. Hadjo's mind raced. If the animal caught his scent, it would lope into the woods before he had a decent shot. Fortunately he was downwind. Once again the spirits was being kind to him.

The bear resumed its journey, padding along the deer trail. As the beast drew within range of his arrow, Hadjo pulled the bowstring back to his right ear. He waited for just the right moment, then let the arrow fly.

In a blur, the arrow streaked toward the bear and then, with a thump, drove deep into the bear's side. The beast howled and spun around to meet its attacker. Finding no assailant, it bounded off the trail and disappeared into the underbrush.

Tingling with excitement, Hadjo swung down from the tree. He fit another arrow to the bowstring. With his eyes and ears straining, he carefully set off through the underbrush.

He had gone only a few yards when he found the bear's trail in the dried leaves carpeting the forest floor. Fresh blood splotched some of the leaves. The trail led to the edge of a ravine. Hadjo studied the woods around him to make sure the animal hadn't circled back, then he edged toward the lip of the deep gully.

At the bottom lay the bear, the feathered shaft of the arrow protruding from its side. Hadjo studied the carcass for any sign of life. Containing his excitement, he slipped and slid down the side of the ravine. He approached the carcass cautiously.

First he would slit the bear's throat, so the carcass would drain of blood. He could skin and butcher the bear himself if he needed to, but that was normally squaw work. Besides, the bear carcass was much too heavy for him to lug back to camp by himself. After carefully noting his location, he would have to go back to camp and get others to help.

Maybe even Tecumseh himself would come along to share in the excitement of taking a bear with a bow and arrow. Hadjo's heart soared as he imagined the look of approval on Tecumseh's face when he heard the news.

With an arrow drawn back in the bow, Hadjo sidled closer to the bear and nudged its rump with the toe of his moccasin. In a blur of motion, the bear was on its feet. Its teeth exposed in a rasping growl, the bear staggered toward Hadjo.

Hadjo turned and raced back up the side of the ravine, hoping the beast didn't have the strength to follow him. At the top of the bank, with his heart racing, he turned and drew the arrow back. The bear was still at the bottom of the ravine, and Hadjo let the arrow fly. In quick succession, he fired two more arrows deep into the beast's chest. The bear grunted, its breathing labored. Its legs wobbled, then buckled as it collapsed to the ground.

For several minutes Hadjo knelt at the top of the ravine, studying the carcass for signs of life. Once he was satisfied that the bear was dead, he climbed back into the ravine and drew his knife. Kneeling behind the bear's head, he reached across its neck, feeling through the warm, greasy fur for the animal's throat. He slipped his left hand under the bear's jaw and pulled the head back. With a powerful stroke, he slit the blade deep across the bear's throat. Blood gushed onto the ground.

Hadjo raised his arms to the sky and screamed his fiercest war cry. Someday he, too, would be recognized as a great hunter and warrior.

CHAPTER SEVEN

JUNE 1812, BLACK SWAMP, INDIANA TERRITORY

Lemuel Wyckliffe swung his axe in a powerful arc over his shoulder. The blade bit into the trunk of an ash, sending chips of wood flying. He wrenched the blade from the foot-thick timber and brought the handle back for another swing. As his pappy had taught him, he established a pace he could maintain until he finished the job.

The axe wasn't cutting as deep and cleanly as it had just minutes before. It needed sharpening, Lemuel realized, but he was nearly through the trunk. Soon the tree groaned. He glanced around to make sure no one was in the tree's likely path, then chopped until he heard wood splintering. The tree crashed to the ground with a rattle and *whoosh* of leaves.

Lemuel couldn't help but feel that his pappy would be proud of him. He was one of hundreds of militiamen blazing a road through the wilderness. Up and down the trail, axes thumped as frontiersmen felled trees, built bridges, and laid causeways through forest and swamp.

In the spring Lemuel had answered a call-up of militia in response to news that Tecumseh, after the destruction of Prophet's Town, was gathering thousands of Indians at Fort Malden, on the British side of the Detroit River where it emptied into Lake Erie.

Lemuel had hiked with his militia company to Dayton. There, General William Hull, the military governor of Michigan Territory and the new commander of the army of the northwest, had mustered his forces for a march north to protect the village of Detroit. If war was declared, they would cross the river to the Canadian side, seize Fort Malden, and then head east to drive the British out of North America.

Lemuel had never seen a redcoat, but as far back as he could remember, he recalled his father's distrust of the British. From what Lemuel could piece together, his family had descended from clans who dwelled in the lowlands on the border between Scotland and England. Over the centuries, the lowland Scots defended their homes from one group of invaders after another, including Romans, Norsemen, and Englishmen.

Not only had their homes been under attack but so had their religious beliefs. Over the centuries they converted from paganism to Catholicism and then followed the teachings of John Knox, breaking away from the Roman church and shunning the Church of England.

When the British grew weary of unruly Irish Catholics, they enticed thousands of lowland Scots to Ireland, especially in the Ulster area. But once the Irish were subdued, the British began anew to harass the lowland Scots, who were then being referred to as Scots-Irish.

Fed up with the British, thousands of Scots-Irish immigrated to America in the early 1700s. Many of them were invited by the state governor to western Pennsylvania, in the area of Lancaster, where they would act as a buffer against hostile natives farther west. From there the Scots-Irish spread down the Appalachians and, with the help of explorers such as Daniel Boone, into Kentucky.

Lemuel's dad had been one of the woodsmen who helped Daniel Boone mark the two-hundred-mile Wilderness Trail through the Cumberland Gap of the Appalachian Mountains. Over the coming years hundreds of thousands of settlers streamed through the Gap to claim free land in the wilds of Kentucky. Initially they met fierce resistance from the natives who occupied the vast wilderness, but the overwhelming onslaught of settlers eventually drove the Indians farther and farther west. In the years that followed, much of the wilderness became settled, and in 1792 Kentucky was admitted as the fifteenth state.

Lemuel yearned for the day when he could take off on his own and head west. Daniel Boone had settled in Missouri, but Lemuel had heard that even farther to the west were vast plains, towering mountains, and then a great ocean. He hoped to see it all.

Lemuel wiped sweat from his brow. Though only midmorning, the day had already grown hot. A swarm of big, black flies buzzed around him in an annoying, cockeyed pattern. He didn't know which he hated worse, the flies during the heat of the day or the gallnippers that swarmed at dawn and dusk.

An eagle shrieked. Lemuel shaded his eyes against the sun and saw the wide wingspan of the bird. From such a distance, he couldn't tell whether it was one of the white-headed bald eagles that had been designated the new nation's symbol. His pappy told him that old Ben Franklin had tried to give the wild turkey that honor. Lemuel had to agree that the turkey was also a noble bird, but somehow the eagle seemed right.

He pulled the stopper from his canteen and took a swig of warm, stale water. The flies and the mosquitoes were just part of the challenge of taming a vast wilderness for the benefit of decent white folk. As far back as Lemuel could remember, every few years his parents and likeminded neighbors would sell their farmsteads to new arrivals, then pack their possessions and head farther west.

Once again deep in the wilderness, they felled trees to build a strong blockhouse. Then each of the families would select its own homestead within a few miles of the blockhouse. Each family ran the ongoing risk of being attacked by marauding bands of natives, but under threat of a large-scale attack, the settlers could flee to the blockhouse. There, with fire-arms bristling through horizontal slits in the thick walls, they could mount a formidable defense, even against a large number of natives.

Lemuel took another swig of water, then fished the whetstone out of his knapsack. With steady, efficient strokes he began to hone the blade of his axe to a keen edge.

As he had dozens of times throughout the morning, Lemuel glanced toward his rifle, which was propped against a stump nearby, ready to fire in an instant. With care he studied the trees and brush around him. No one had reported seeing any redskins so far, but that didn't mean the damned heathen wouldn't ambush them at any moment.

The thought of marauding natives reminded him of the day his mother and little sister were murdered. He and his father had been head-ing home in Kentucky with a deer carcass slung on a pole between them. Lemuel had noticed a grayish-white haze of smoke streaming up against the blue sky.

"Hey, Pappy. Look," said Lemuel, pointing in the direction of the haze. The source of the smoke was probably a couple of miles away, in the direction of their cabin.

The deer-laden pole pounded hard against Lemuel's shoulder as his father dropped his end and ran ahead. Lemuel tossed his end aside and hurried after his pappy. They raced through the woods and across a creek. As they sprinted uphill, Lemuel's lungs burned, and he could hear his father breathing hard.

They approached the column of smoke surging skyward. Lemuel's dad slowed his pace and brought the rifle up, holding it diagonally across his chest. Lemuel stepped next to his pappy, a pace behind, and brought the loaded musket up where he could use it in a hurry. As his father had taught him, he turned occasionally to check behind them.

They stepped into the clearing, and Lemuel could see that the cabin was nearly consumed by flames that still crackled and popped with intense heat. He prayed his mother and little sister were safely outside, but there was no sign of either of them. Outside the cabin, household items lay strewn across the ground.

Lemuel followed his father around the outside of the cabin, cautiously glancing at the woods, their little barn, and the field beyond. One of their hogs lay dead outside the barn. Lemuel's dad rounded the corner of the cabin and stopped. He fell to his knees, dropping the rifle. "No!" he wailed.

Lemuel followed, expecting the worst. But what he saw caused his own knees to buckle, and he slumped to the ground.

His pappy staggered to the naked body of Lemuel's mother lying in the dirt. His father sobbed as he scooped the blood-smeared corpse into his arms. Lemuel groaned, and tears streamed down his cheeks when he saw the jagged circular patch of exposed skull where his mother had been scalped. As his father cradled her, Lemuel could see that his mother's blood-smeared body had been savagely mutilated.

The contents of his stomach surged onto the ground before him. Trembling, he heaved and heaved until nothing more came up.

His thoughts went to his little sister. She was nowhere in sight. He forced himself to his feet and began searching. He wailed when he found her by his mother's vegetable garden. From her gashed and scalped skull, blood trickled down her lifeless face. Lemuel felt himself stagger to the ground when he realized her pale, naked little body had been impaled upon one of the stakes bordering the garden.

Overhead, the eagle shrieked again, and Lemuel's attention returned to his axe and the blade that needed sharpening. He studied the forest edging the trail of freshly cut stumps, half hoping to see a warrior sneaking up on the trailblazers. He figured the natives were a lot like trees. The ones that stood in the way of progress would be destroyed. He thought of the scalp dangling from his belt. At least a fallen tree provided timber, something useful.

CHAPTER EIGHT

JUNE 1812, WASHINGTON CITY

Rachel Thurston picked up a wooden spoon and stirred the mixture of beef and vegetables simmering over the embers of her kitchen hearth. Her hand stopped as she recalled her mother saying that you could always tell whether a woman was a good cook by how she stirs. When someone stirs from left to right, she is sure to be a good cook, but if she stirs right to left . . . . What nonsense, thought Rachel. But when she resume her stirring, she made sure she moved the spoon from left to right.

The room had filled with the aroma of stew. She scooped a spoonful and tasted it, then wondered what she could add to make it better.

On a shelf above the fireplace stood a pepper shaker, but Rachel hesitated. The price of imported spices always seemed so high. But her father had assured her that his shipping interests, operated by his partners back in Massachusetts, were banking fat profits. She grabbed the shaker and shook a generous amount into the pot. After a few swirls with her spoon, she tasted it again.

Satisfied, she glanced out the back window of the house they had rented. Estimating the time as late afternoon, she swung the kettle a little to the side. The stew could simmer until her father returned. As did many of their new neighbors, her father walked to the Capitol each day, and he could return anytime during the next few hours.

She envied her father. Each day he left the house on some mission, while she was stuck at home. She didn't mind being alone, in fact, her father had hired various housekeepers and companions over the years, but Rachel had always found a way to run them off.

She settled into a chair behind her father's desk and picked up a sheet of paper. She had been drafting a letter for her father to submit to newspaper editors in each of the states. Rachel had listened carefully as her father had discussed the Federalist argument for maintaining a standing army. The letter outlined the need for a professional corps of officers and men, well equipped to defend the new nation if the occasion arose. The letter criticized the Democratic-Republican reliance on the informal militia of local citizen-soldiers made famous by the so-called minutemen of the Revolutionary War. Rachel grabbed a goose quill pen, dipped it in an ink well and drafted an additional point to the argument. Even though her father would sign the letter, she took pride in the quality of the case it made.

Rachel jumped with a start. Something had boomed like thunder. The house shook, and dishes rattled. She glanced out the window and could see the sky was clear and blue.

In rapid succession the house rattled again and again. Cannon fire, she realized. Her heart sank. She suspected what that meant. She sighed and stirred the pot a few more times, then set the spoon on a plate beside the hearth.

She wiped her hands on her apron as she headed for the front door. Cannons had been fired just a couple of months before, when Congress voted to admit Louisiana as the eighteenth state in the union. But Rachel suspected the cannon fire this day was more ominous. Muskets popped in the distance. People shouted and screamed with joy. She stepped outside. From down New York Avenue she heard someone yell, "War! It's to be war!"

Her fears confirmed, Rachel headed back inside. How could people be so happy about war? And how could they declare war on Great Britain? It was like attacking your own mother.

A bell tolled from a church in the distance. Rachel imagined that as word spread up and down the coast and out to the frontier, more shots would be fired in celebration and more bells rung, some in celebration, and some to bemoan the destruction likely to follow.

She wondered what had tipped the scale. Over the months, she had been reading her father's newspapers and had pieced together an understanding of the situation. The States were clearly upset with the British for a variety of reasons. The Americans were proud of their new independence but frustrated that Great Britain continued to treat them like bastard cousins rather than a sovereign nation. The Royal Navy violated what the Americans viewed as their rights in the open sea. The Crown supported Indians on the western frontier, possibly even encouraging the natives to attack white settlers.

But as her father had explained, that was all nonsense. Much of the new nation's economy was at a standstill, and it was the new government's fault. When protests to London hadn't worked, the American government under President Jefferson decided to hit Great Britain where it hurt, in its pocketbook. The U.S. outlawed all shipping to and from its shores.

Rachel recalled her father's ranting that the policy was insane, economic suicide. At first the self-imposed embargo had little impact in England, but eventually it did take a painful toll on the British government already stretched thin waging war against Napoleon.

The most severe impact, though, was on America's own economy, which was heavily dependent upon the export of agricultural products and the import of finished goods from Europe. Americans became so disenchanted with their new government that the law was changed to allow shipping with any country other than Britain and France. Now business was booming for merchants sending goods to Portugal. Ironically, even though Lisbon merchants bought the material, most of it was then sold to the British army in Portugal.

Disgust with the government and the economic situation provided fuel for those led by Henry Clay and John C. Calhoun, who advocated war with Great Britain to solve the nation's problems. Still, the War Hawks had failed to muster enough votes to pass the declaration.

Something rattled, and Rachel peeked out the window. Her father had opened the gate to their white picket fence. She assumed he would also be crushed by the declaration of war, but his step seemed lively as he approached their porch.

The front door creaked slightly as he entered, and she heard him hang his hat atop their coat rack.

He entered the library and kissed her on the cheek. "Good afternoon, my dear." He headed to the back of the room, where he stored liquor and glasses. After pouring himself a whiskey, he sat in his favorite chair, leaned back, and took a sip.

From a rectangular wooden box on his desk, he pulled a large cigar. With a pair of scissors, he snipped the end, and soon the room filled with billows of smoke. He leaned back and puffed a hazy ring toward the ceiling.

Rachel felt her temper rising. "You seem to be rather cheery," she said, "considering the events of the day."

Mordecai Thurston shrugged. "Maybe it's for the best. The deadlock could have dragged on forever." He gazed at the glowing end of the cigar. "This way the Hawks will get their little war. And after the Crown crushes them, we can pick up the pieces."

CHAPTER NINE

JUNE 1812, H.M.S. PANTHER,
OFF THE COAST OF VIRGINIA

Lieutenant George Sherbourne clutched the rail atop a bulwark as the ship rose and fell in gentle swells. Although the green shorelines on the western horizon signaled the end of his long voyage back across the Atlantic, he felt that his rightful place was with General Wellesley fighting the French in Spain.

Instead, after months of boring duty in London, he had been assigned to the British minister in Washington City, a position he considered beneath his capabilities and a threat to his hopes for distinction in battle and the corresponding potential for advancement, fame, and fortune.

Without fame and fortune he had no chance of gaining Colonel Morrison's permission to marry Anne. George closed his eyes and pictured her fair hair, blue eyes, and cheeks with just a hint of freckles. He longed to reach out and touch her.

A seagull screamed, and George's attention returned to the Virginia shoreline and the duty that awaited him. Not that the post to the States was without challenges, he admitted. The upstart American nation seemed to be perpetually angry at Great Britain. They seemed particularly irked about impressments of American sailors into British naval crews.

The former colonies had been whining in vain for years. They failed to acknowledge that Great Britain had been locked in a life-or-death struggle against a French dictator bent on conquering all of Europe. The British government was deeply in debt and paid its seamen a pittance compared to wages paid on American merchant vessels.

British seamen jumped ship and then claimed they were American. False citizenship papers were easily available for a small price. And since it took years to train an able-bodied seaman, who could blame the Royal Navy for reclaiming deserters wherever they found them.

George glanced back to the Virginia shoreline and sighed. He resolved to make the best of his assignment.

That evening around the dinner table, Captain Meredith introduced a gentleman who had boarded the ship that afternoon. "Please welcome Augustus Foster, Minister Plenipotentiary to the States."

A slim, thirtyish man with dark hair and a boyish face stood and bowed. "*Former* minister would be more accurate, my dear captain," said Foster. "Gentlemen, I've closed our ministry in Washington City. The Americans have declared war on Great Britain."

"Surely, sir, you jest," said a lieutenant dressed in the red uniform of the marines.

Several naval officers grumbled.

"Outrageous!" said one. "While His Majesty's forces are stretched thin trying to rid Europe of a monstrous dictator, these ungrateful upstarts declare war?"

"Cheeky bastards, wouldn't you say?" said a second lieutenant.

George kept quiet. His future suddenly looked brighter. Although he hated the thought of another long voyage across the rough waters of the Atlantic, he hoped he could now return to Britain and be assigned to one of the units fighting Bonaparte on the Continent. He imagined himself leading a company of infantry against French regulars.

After dinner, George rose with the other officers as they bid their leave to Captain Meredith and Ambassador Foster.

"Lieutenant Sherbourne," said the captain, "please join us."

George felt a growing sense of apprehension as the cabin door closed.

Ambassador Foster leaned back in his chair and gazed toward the ceiling as if gathering his thoughts, then massaged the back of his neck. "Lieutenant," he said, "it would seem the post to which you were assigned no longer exists." He fingered an ivory snuffbox. "What *am* I to do with you?" He opened the tiny box and glanced inside. "You were born and raised in the colonies, were you not?"

George bristled. He was a British citizen and considered his loyalty to the Crown equal to any. But many officials in His Majesty's service seemed to consider those born on foreign soil to be second-class citizens. "That is correct, sir."

Foster leaned slightly toward George. "As a diplomat between posts, I have no authority over you, of course. But it would seem you are in a unique position to provide invaluable service to the Crown."

George smelled a rat. "How so, sir?"

"With the declaration of war, all of His Majesty's official representatives have been pulled out of the States. I don't doubt some of our former colonists will provide us with information for a price." He sniffed. "It does seem as if almost any of the Yanks can be bought. However, there remains the problem of separating fact from fabrication." The ambassador paused, letting George dwell on that thought for a moment.

George wished the man would just spit it out. "May I ask what you are getting at, sir?"

"We will need information, Lieutenant. Reliable information. What are the Americans up to and why? What are their intentions? What are their capabilities?" Foster pinched a bit of powdered tobacco from the snuffbox. "With your background in the colonies and your military training, you could be uniquely helpful in assessing the situation." The minister raised his fingertips to his nose and inhaled with a quick snort.

George began to feel that he was being pushed into a corner. "I'm not sure I understand what you are suggesting, sir."

Foster turned to the side and sneezed with such force that the wine glasses rattled. "Oh, come now, my boy," he said as he dabbed his nose with a handkerchief. "We need someone who can be our eyes and ears on shore. Someone whose loyalty is unquestioned and who can interpret events from a military perspective."

"But, sir," said George, "I don't think the Americans are going to welcome a British officer on their soil. In fact, I suspect any of His Majesty's men will be promptly rounded up and imprisoned."

"Quite so. Quite so," said the minister as he blinked watery eyes. "Any officer in uniform or otherwise identified as in His Majesty's service would no doubt be taken into custody." He paused. "Of course, if an officer weren't in uniform and could blend in with the local population, he would have a good chance of going undiscovered."

Before George could stop himself, he said, "Sir, are you suggesting that I become a *spy*?" He was well aware of the fate of foreigners caught spying during wartime. Execution.

The minister and the captain sat quietly.

"Sir, I have trained and studied as an infantry officer. I have no expertise in the dark arts of espionage. Surely I should return to England for reassignment to the Continent."

"You are probably right," said Foster, his fingers steepled over his belly. "But you *were* assigned to the post in Washington City. Presumably your superiors at Horse Guards felt they could manage the campaign against Bonaparte without your assistance."

George gripped hard on the arms of his chair. "My orders were to report to our ambassador in Washington City. Since the post no longer exists, I believe it is my duty to return to London for reassignment."

"Yes, yes," said Foster as he leaned back in his chair. "No doubt you know your duty." He paused. "However, the good captain and I *could* draft letters to your commanding officers in London recommending that you take on an assignment ashore in the former colonies. I have the utmost confidence they would view the decision with favor." Foster's glare met George's. "On the other hand, if your superiors learned that you avoided a unique opportunity to provide the Crown with invaluable information regarding the enemy, they might feel you lack the initiative and courage for higher rank in the future."

George fought to control a rising sense of panic. His mind whirled through possibilities as he tried to think of an argument against the minister's proposal. But deep down he knew they had him. "Sir, what specifically do you have in mind?"

CHAPTER TEN

JUNE 1812, H.M.S. GUERRIERE,
HALIFAX HARBOR

Silas Shackleton knelt as he scrubbed the hardwood deck with a bible-sized block of sandstone the sailors called a *holystone*. With disgust he shoved the rock forward, then dragged it back, again and again. When that patch of decking had been scraped smooth, he scooted to the side and began another.

The midday sun seared the crisscross pattern of scars etched across his bare back. Pinpricks of pain reminded him of being flogged shortly after his impressment the previous fall. Since then, he had been extra vigilant in minding his duties and keeping his mouth shut. Once again, he had been given the "opportunity" of joining the royal navy. His face burned with shame for having given in to his captors rather than being forced to serve as a "pressed man." Treatment of regular sailors was better than treatment of pressed men, but to Silas it was still little better than slavery.

Silas stood and stretched to ease a crick in his spine. All around the frigate stood the lofty masts of scores of ships moored at Halifax. He glanced past the vessels to the warehouses and houses around the harbor.

He longed to make an escape and somehow make it back to New York, but marines in scarlet uniforms stationed around the deck held loaded muskets ready to shoot anyone who tried to jump ship.

"Back to work, Shackleton!" ordered Granger, the scar-faced, old boatswain.

Silas clenched his jaw, hatred seething within him. He wondered if he would ever be released from service in the British navy. He dropped to his knees and grabbed the sandstone block.

Over the last year, the days had run together in a blur of routine. Mindless, backbreaking work filled most of his waking hours. The crew loaded supplies into the hold, then hauled them topside as needed. They cranked the capstan to weigh anchor and to hoist cargo. They climbed up and down the rigging to reset sails. Besides the tasks needed to maneuver the ship, they had regular drills to hone their fighting skills of firing cannon, boarding ships, and fending off boarders.

Despite his growing hatred of the British, Silas didn't mind the work. In fact, he admired the organization and discipline of the navy. Every man had his jobs and, through training and repetition, could do them well and without hesitation.

When off duty, the men were left largely to themselves. Silas had become friends with Bosworth, who was teaching him to read and write. Under better conditions, it wouldn't have been a bad life. But the living conditions were appalling.

As did many of the other seamen, Silas still wore the clothes he had on when he first came on board. And since he had grown, the garments had split and stretched tight. Although thin and tattered, they wouldn't be replaced until they fell from his body. He wore the only clothes he had, regardless of the weather, from the scorching summers of the Caribbean to the freezing winters of Halifax.

The food was lousy, with meat often rotten, bread filled with weevils, and drinking water foul. They slept belowdecks amid lice and rats in quarters teaming with the stench of putrid bilge water and men in cramped quarters.

In addition to the inherent dangers of life at sea, Silas quickly learned that as one of the youngest crewmen he was subject to other risks. Many of the crew had been on board for years and, without the benefits of female companionship, had looked to other crewmen for sexual satisfaction. Some of the men paired as consenting mates. Others took what they wanted, beating and intimidating their victims until their demands were met. Gang rapes were not uncommon. Belowdecks the officers left the men to fend for themselves unless their behavior interfered with the operation of the ship.

During the first month onboard, Silas and Bosworth repeatedly fended off sexual advances, fighting their way out of several situations.

"Some of these men can smell fear," said Bosworth, "and it excites them. Never let them catch you alone. Never let your guard down. But if trouble arrives, act quickly."

He gave Silas a sharpened shank of bone, but Silas dreaded ever having to use it. After a few weeks, they had joined a group of crewmen who had banded together for mutual protection.

Word had spread recently that the States were considering war with Great Britain. Initially Silas had hoped that would mean he would be set free. But a British warship was little better than a floating prison, its crew hardly more than slaves. When the ship anchored at port, the pressed men were locked up or put under guard on deck to prevent escape. The other sailors were treated little better and were hardly ever allowed ashore when in port lest they desert. If a ship was expected to be in port for an extended period, all or part of the crew was transferred to an outgoing vessel. The navy would keep him for as long as it needed him or until he was no longer physically able to perform the work of a seaman.

Silas jumped as something heavy pounded onto the deck in front of him. Wet, warm material splattered his face, arms, and bare chest. Unable to see, he cursed and sat back on the deck. With both hands he wiped warm slime from his eyes, then shrieked and leaped to his feet. His hands dripped with fresh blood and gray matter.

All around him crewmen shouted. Bosworth grabbed the bucket and dowsed Silas with seawater. Frantically, Silas scrubbed the mess away. After another drenching, he shuddered and for the first time saw what lay in front of him.

The mangled body of a seaman lay on the deck. The unfortunate soul had fallen from high in the rigging. The carcass lay in a bloody heap of shattered bones and pulverized flesh. With horror, Silas realized the man had hit the deck headfirst, his skull bursting in a shower of blood and brains. Silas shuddered as he wiped a smear of gore from his forearm.

One of the officers approached. "Who was it?"

Bosworth stood close to the body. "Young Adams, sir."

At first Silas was shocked. Then he understood. The boy's death was no accident—it was suicide. Adams had been impressed a few months after Silas. Unlike Silas, the boy had become the subject of frequent abuse by predatory crewmen.

Shame flooded through Silas when he realized that he hadn't even attempted to protect Adams—and that without Bosworth's guidance and protection, his own guts could have been splattered across the deck.

CHAPTER ELEVEN

JULY 1812, UPPER CANADA,
NEAR THE DETROIT RIVER

Lemuel Wyckliffe rushed through the woods a dozen yards, then stopped behind a stout tree. He studied the terrain ahead and on both sides. Hoping there were no natives hiding nearby, he signaled Stubby to advance. Lemuel raised his rifle, ready to shoot if an Indian showed himself.

Stubby hustled past Lemuel until he faced thick underbrush. Raising a hand, he signaled Lemuel to wait for the other pairs of militiamen who were repeating the same leapfrog advance through the forest. They, and scores of other militiamen, had been sent ahead of the regular troops to flush out any Canadians or Indians who might be lurking in ambush.

As Lemuel waited for the others to catch up, he felt renewed excitement that, after weeks of inactivity, they were finally advancing on the enemy. When General Hull's army reached Detroit a few weeks before, they found a dirty settlement of eight hundred villagers already short on supplies. The newly arrived troops pitched tents in the open fields outside the palisade. The fort was armed with forty cannon, but some of the guns weren't mounted, and part of the field of fire was blocked by the village at the river's edge.

General Hull crossed the Detroit River near Hog Island, occupied the village of Sandwich without opposition, and began improving its defensive earthworks. He then issued a proclamation inviting the Canadians of Upper Canada to join the Americans in throwing out the British.

Any Canadians wishing to remain neutral in the conflict should just stay home—their persons, property, and rights would be respected. Any Canadians caught fighting beside the Indians, however, would be put to death. Many local residents were recent immigrants from the States in search of cheap land, and several hundred joined the Americans as an irregular cavalry unit.

Lemuel heard the chirp of a bird and listened carefully. Indians sometimes used birdcalls to communicate. Even through the woods, he could hear the rumble and rattle of Colonel Lewis Cass's mounted militia and blue-uniformed regulars as they marched along the road.

Lemuel couldn't imagine himself serving in the regular army. He didn't like their uniforms, the strict discipline, or that they were armed with muskets rather than rifles. He figured most of the officers received their commissions through wealth or political connections rather than merit in the field or anywhere else. He recalled his pappy saying that the thought of taking orders from a dandy, untested officer left a sour taste in his mouth.

When the other militiamen had caught up, Lemuel ducked low and pressed through the brush until he could no longer walk forward. He dropped to the ground and crawled with his rifle cradled on his elbows, praying that he didn't encounter any natives. Eventually the brush opened to a clearing bordered by a split-rail fence. Downhill, across a hundred yards of pasture, lay a bridge guarded by soldiers in red uniforms.

Stubby emerged from the brush and rested his rifle across the top of a post. "That must be the Canard River."

As militiamen poured out of the woods on either side of Lemuel, the redcoats opened fire. Lemuel aimed at one of the dozen redcoats on the near side of the bridge, then hesitated. This was the first time he had set his sights on a white man. His momma had taught him the Ten Commandments, and "Thou Shalt Not Kill" was near the top of the list. Shooting natives didn't count, of course, since they were more like wild animals than real people. But redcoats, that was different. And these soldiers were on the British side of the river. Lemuel, Stubby, and the other Americans were the invaders.

But then, Lemuel rationalized, the British had been supporting a gathering of natives around Fort Malden, just a few miles farther down the road. And from Fort Malden it was a short canoe trip across the Detroit River to the American side, where the redskins could kill and burn out settlers. The natives who had killed his mother and little sister might very well have started their murderous mission from right here where the British fed them and encouraged them.

Lemuel was sure that the only way to stop the British from stirring up the Indians was to drive the redcoats out of North America. He refocused on the redcoat leaning against the bridge but decided just to wing him.

Lemuel eased back the rooster-shaped hammer until it locked into position with a click. He aimed carefully at the redcoat a couple a hundred yards away, focusing on the man's left shoulder, then squeezed the trigger.

The firing mechanism of the rifle was similar to a musket, and Lemuel hardly thought about it as the spring-loaded hammer snapped forward to the steel flap, called a *frizzen*, that covered the powder-filled pan. The chip of flint clamped into the jaws of the hammer knocked the frizzen forward and showered sparks into the pan. The gunpowder ignited with a flash that seared through the narrow hole at the base of the barrel, igniting the powder inside the barrel. The tightly packed powder exploded, propelling the lead ball out the barrel.

The rifle butt kicked against Lemuel's shoulder, and he blinked at the flash and the sting of smoke in his eyes. Without moving, he stared down the length of the barrel and watched the redcoat spin to the side and fall.

As Lemuel reloaded, more of the militiamen opened fire. Smoke billowed from both sides of the road. The dozen redcoats on the near side of the river grabbed their wounded and retreated across the bridge. Colonel Cass's regulars marched into view a hundred yards from the bridge.

From bushes on the near side of the bridge, a redcoat staggered to his feet, then another. For a moment the two seemed confused, and Lemuel wondered if they were drunk. The redcoats pointed their muskets toward the advancing Americans. Lemuel aimed his rifle at the chest of one of the redcoats, but before he could pull the trigger, both men collapsed to the ground as the air crackled with rifle fire.

Lemuel and Stubby rushed to the bridge. Men shouted, tossed their hats in the air, and shot their firearms skyward. They had met the enemy and had driven them away in a quick and easy victory. Never mind, thought Lemuel, that the Americans had significantly outnumbered the British forces at the bridge.

Lemuel could see that on the far side of the bridge were more redcoats—maybe fifty, and who knew how many Indians hid in nearby forests. He wondered if Colonel Cass would order his men to charge across the bridge. Lemuel figured it could be taken, but the troops would face point-blank fire, and the casualties would be heavy. There was always the chance the men might refuse to obey orders that posed such an obvious risk to their lives.

Lemuel settled in behind a fallen tree on the riverbank. He laid his rifle across a dead branch and aimed toward a redcoat on the far side of the bridge.

Stubby approached and tapped Lemuel on the shoulder. "Come on lad. The colonel is leaving forty men to guard the bridge. The rest of us is headed north to ford the river."

The regulars marched along the road that paralleled the Canard River. Ahead of the uniformed regulars, riflemen on foot scoured the woods for skulking natives. They topped a rise in the road along the river, and Lemuel could see mounted militia race ahead north across a patchwork of cleared fields and pastures, where cavalry could be of most use.

Lemuel recalled having the jitters prior to the skirmish at the bridge, wondering if he would survive the day. Now, with the afternoon sun shining and a victory under their belt, he felt they could march right into Fort Malden and kick the redcoats out.

"Keep a sharp eye," said Stubby, "the natives could be hiding anywhere."

As Lemuel plodded along, he relished the moccasins that Stubby had recently showed him how to craft. Lemuel was accustomed to walking on callused bare feet, but he appreciated the soft-leather comfort and protection of the moccasins.

About five miles north of the Detroit River, the mounted militia turned east along a road that led down to the river. Their horses splashed through shallow, muddy water. Lemuel, Stubby, and the other frontiersmen crossed on foot, holding their rifles high to keep them dry.

Once across the river the mounted militia fell in behind the regular troops. The frontiersmen took the lead, spreading out on either side of the tree-lined road, rifles ready to pick off any Indians who attempted an ambush.

Several hours later as the sun set, they approached the bridge where they had driven away the redcoats earlier in the day. Lemuel's insides tingled with the prospect of facing a line of British regulars. But as he and Stubby approached the bridge, the redcoats marched away from the bridge, the last defensible position before Fort Malden, and disappeared down the road.

Amid renewed celebration, Lemuel imagined that General Hull would quickly reinforce them and promptly attack Fort Malden, just a few miles away. With control of the fort, they could seize Amhearstburg and its shipyards. That meant they would effectively control the lake and all the territory upstream to the north and west. Eventually they would march east toward Montreal, Quebec, and Halifax, driving the British out of North America.

As evening approached, Lemuel, Stubby, and other militiamen lounged in a shady clearing prior to settling in for the night.

An officer approached on a horse. "On your feet! We're moving out."

"Attack at night?"

"No," said the officer, "we're pulling back to Sandwich."

"But why?"

"We just got here!"

"Turn us loose, sir, and we'll capture the fort ourselves."

The officer swallowed hard. "Orders is orders. Do as you're told. General Hull wants to wait for cannon before attacking the fort."

Stubby cursed and leaned close to Lemuel. "I've a bad feelin' about this."

CHAPTER TWELVE

JULY 1812, BALTIMORE, MARYLAND

Lieutenant George Sherbourne pulled a copy of the *Federal Republican* from his pocket. He studied the address on the masthead then headed south on Charles Street.

He tried to ignore the stench of the port city as he carefully gauged his pace along the cobblestones. Walking too fast might seem like he was running from someone. Too slow might appear as if he was reconnoitering the neighborhood.

He felt relieved that his clothes resembled those worn by the merchants and craftsmen along the street. After the ambassador on board the *Panther* had persuaded him to accept this assignment, the captain ordered the steward to open the ship's clothing bin, or *slop*, as the sailors called it. The tattered civilian clothes weren't exactly what George had in mind, but they provided an alternative to wearing his uniform ashore.

With a sense of dread, he had carefully folded his uniform and packed it in his trunk. He reread the latest letter from Anne, savoring the scent of her perfume, then tucked the letter into the trunk.

Once on land, he selected material at a dry-goods store, then had a tailor make him pantaloons and ruffled shirts. He also purchased a pair of Hessians, tasseled leather boots that rose almost to his knees. As he walked along the street, he began to feel confident that his appearance wouldn't betray him as a spy.

His mind reeled from the news of recent days. He fumed at the arrogance and stupidity of the Americans. Word had arrived recently that the British government had repealed the Orders in Council. With a halt to the impressments of American sailors and the seizure of American vessels, much of the justification for the newly declared war with Great Britain had been removed. Surely, George had figured, President Madison would call off hostilities.

Instead the president, with the support of congress, vowed to fight on. Apparently President Madison and his supporters would lose face if they called off the war at this stage. Obviously some of the Americans were in the mood for a brawl—a fight not only to teach Great Britain a lesson but also to annex vast tracts of territory to the new nation.

Outrageous behavior, George figured, especially since Britain was already embroiled in a fight for its life against a French tyrant intent on controlling all of Europe, including the British Isles.

With no quick resolution to the conflict in sight, George resigned himself to fulfilling the duties to which he had been assigned. He had already learned that gathering intelligence about American war preparations was ridiculously easy. The local newspapers openly outlined American war plans.

What he had learned worried him. Assuming the reported accounts could be trusted, the strategy was relatively simple. First the Americans would send their navy—a mere dozen frigates—to sea. Simultaneously they would issue letters of marque to any ship-owner who applied, effectively turning hundreds of American pirates loose on the seas to attack British merchant vessels.

The land-based portion of the plans called for seizing British North America—Upper Canada, Lower Canada, New Brunswick, Nova Scotia, and Prince Edward Island. Vital to the plans were the waterways that provided communication and supply lines.

The war planners, George had read, viewed the northern colonies as a giant tree. Its taproots were the settlements along the Atlantic Ocean, especially Halifax. Its trunk was along the St. Lawrence River, including Quebec and Montreal. Its branches were the Great Lakes and surrounding territories.

By cutting the trunk of the tree as close to the roots as possible, everything to the west would fall into American hands, as the British would be denied access to the waterways.

The strategic plan called for three independent attacks. The first was to the west, where forces would seize Fort Malden at the western tip of Lake Erie. The second would overwhelm the British forts in the Niagara area, sealing off the links between lakes Erie and Ontario. The third would take Montreal, then Quebec, and eventually march on Halifax, effectively uprooting Great Britain from North America.

To George the basic plan had merit, and that did not bode well for British control of the Canadas. The colonies were lightly defended by a few thousand redcoats, and most of those not the best in His Majesty's service. Both sides would, of course, call up their militia forces, but that did not favor British success, either, since the civilian population of the Canadian colonies was in the thousands compared to the millions in the American states.

The prevailing American view was that the Canadians would welcome them with open arms, willingly shrugging off British rule. Admittedly, thought George, French-speaking Canadians openly expressed their disdain for anything British. Many of the Canadian frontiersmen were as independent minded as the Americans. But George's parents, like many others, were loyal to the Crown. Furthermore, even those, including the

Indians, who didn't particularly like British rule weren't likely to welcome American dominance as an alternative.

Britain controlled the oceans of the world with hundreds of warships, and George had no doubt the Royal Navy would make short work of both the tiny American navy and the greedy privateers. The situation on land was quite different. Even though Britain had one of the most powerful armies in the world, that army was fighting the French on the other side of the Atlantic.

George had read that former-president Thomas Jefferson had predicted that taking the Canadas would be a mere matter of marching. A local paper quoted Jefferson after the declaration, "Upon the whole, I have known no war entered into under more favorable auspices. Our present enemy will have the sea to herself, while we shall be equally predominant on land, and shall strip her of all her possessions on this continent."

George imagined thousands of armed Americans surrounding and storming the sparsely manned outposts on the frontier. The Americans, he feared, could not be stopped.

His boot caught on a cobblestone, and he nearly fell. Most of the buildings along the street were marked with signs that named the establishment and its business purpose. He stopped in front of a two-storied building surrounded by a brick wall. The gated entrance bore no identification other than its street number. George slipped the newspaper from his pocket again and checked the address—45 Charles Street.

Earlier, George had picked up a copy of the *Federal Republican* from a boy selling them on a street corner. The editorial damned the newly declared war as a risky venture for which the nation was ill prepared. Without the funds, forces, or fortifications to take on Great Britain, argued the editor, a confrontation could lead to destruction—followed by iron rule.

He recalled reading that just days after the declaration of war, Baltimore resident Alexander Contee Hanson, owner of the *Federal*

Republican, began publishing editorials damning the war as reckless and promised to use every legal means to undermine President Madison.

Baltimore citizens, largely entrepreneurs and artisans whose livelihoods had been threatened by British ships, were outraged. Other local editors blasted Hanson, further inciting local citizens. Ruffians stormed the publisher's place of business, tossing paper, print type, and presses into the street, then used grappling hooks to rip the building apart. Hanson himself had been fortunate to be out of town.

Now a month later, Hanson had apparently moved back to Baltimore and begun distributing his latest editorial, again damning the war declaration and those behind it. George hoped to develop Hanson as a potential source of useful information.

He eased through the gate, then knocked on the whitewashed door. A fist-sized peep-hole slid open. Before George could announce himself, a gruff voice demanded, "Identify yourself. State your business."

George held up the newspaper. "I've been reading Mr. Hanson's editorial and thought I would stop by to express my admiration for his views."

For a moment George thought he might be refused entry, but the door swung open. From the dim interior he heard the voice. "Well, hurry in, then, sir."

Inside, a man dressed in an ink-stained apron swung the door shut and dropped a wooden beam into its braces to bar the entrance. The printer peered out the peephole for a moment then slid its tiny door shut. He wiped his hands on an oily cloth. "Follow me, if you would, sir."

The publishing house smelled of ink, oil, and solvents. One side of the room had shelves stacked with paper. Printing presses and other machines dominated the center of the room. A man was setting type onto a wooden tray while others operated the presses and paper cutters.

The apron-clad printer escorted George to the back of the room and then up a flight of stairs. They emerged into a room filled with two dozen men chatting and laughing. The printer hurried to a well-dressed man with wispy dark hair, then nodded toward George.

The man smiled and offered George his hand. "Alexander Hanson, at your service."

"George Sherbourne. I've been reading your editorials and I couldn't agree more. If there is anything I can do to help, please let me know."

"I'm always delighted to visit with my readers." Hanson seemed to study George's face. "What are your specific areas of interest?"

George could feel his insides twist a little tighter. He hadn't expected to be interrogated. "Foremost on my mind is the question of what can be done to bring this war to an end before things get out of hand."

Hanson smiled. "Let me introduce you to likeminded men." He turned to a gentleman at his side. "This is General Henry Lee."

George was stunned. Even he had heard of "Light Horse Harry" and his raids on British supply lines during the American rebellion. In one engagement Lee, with only seven mounted troops behind him, reportedly caused the retreat of two hundred British cavalrymen. So highly regarded was General Lee, that it was he who delivered George Washington's funeral oration.

George delighted in his good fortune. To gain the acquaintance of such men might prove invaluable for obtaining useful insights and information. Maybe this spy business wouldn't be so difficult after all.

"Where are you from, young man?" asked General Lee.

George had anticipated this question. While a boy he had traveled into the States on business with his father. He recalled a town on the western shore of Lake Champlain. "New York. Up-state. Plattsburgh area."

Hanson and Lee introduced George to others in the room. As best as George could tell, some of the rest of the men were long-term friends and supporters of Hanson who had accompanied him from Georgetown. Many others were locals who showed up uninvited to support Hanson in case another mob tried to silence the *Federal Republican*. George was relieved that, among men who didn't all know each other, he wouldn't stand out as a stranger.

George met another revolutionary war veteran, General James Lingan. They talked for twenty minutes, exchanging views about President Madison and his chances for re-election in November. George congratulated himself on working his way into a group of influential men who could indeed provide him with valuable information.

An angry shout carried in from the street. General Lingan peeked through a shutter in one of the upstairs windows. "A crowd is gathering outside the wall. A score of boys and a handful of men."

George followed the others to the window.

Hanson cursed. "The bastards."

"There aren't that many," said Lingan.

"Ah, but I recognize these rabble-rousers," said Hanson. "And the evening is young." He pointed at a dark-bearded man dressed in a suit. "That's Dr. Gale. He won't easily be put off. And that one," he pointed to a broad-shouldered man with dark hair, "that's Mumma—a butcher with a particularly violent nature."

"We shan't let a mob silence us," said General Lee. "We have a stockpile of weapons nearby. I recommend that we send a few men out to retrieve them."

General Lingan agreed. "The touch of cold steel or hot lead will discourage these troublemakers rather quickly, I would think."

"Just to be safe," said General Lee, "we should ask General Stricker to muster the dragoons."

One by one, several men slipped out the front door.

"Mr. Sherbourne," said Hanson, "you may wish to take leave of us before you get caught up in whatever trouble might brew tonight."

George was tempted to accept the offer of a graceful exit. He didn't relish the idea of being trapped by an angry mob. But the situation presented him with an opportunity to ingratiate himself with these men. And who knew what doors that might open? "Wouldn't think of it, sir," he said. "I'd hate to miss any excitement."

General Lee slapped George on the back. "You look a fit and able young man," he said. "Would you stand watch?"

George agreed and took his place at one of the upstairs windows overlooking the wall. He noted that the crowd had grown to several hundred. He hoped he hadn't erred by deciding to stay.

An hour later, at about eight o'clock, a carriage drew up in front of the gate. Six armed men hurried out of the house to stand guard while others rushed to unload muskets and ammunition. The noise from the crowd swelled. Once empty, the carriage pulled away.

A ruffian from the crowd shouted, "Traitor!"

"Hanson's spewing lies again," shouted another.

"Come on, men," yelled a towering oaf with a wooden club, "let's teach the bastard a lesson."

General Lee opened the shutters of the window next to George and shouted out to the street, "This is General Harry Lee. I believe you know me by reputation as a veteran of the War of Independence. This is a nation of laws, and you are unlawfully threatening the safety of person and property."

The crowd jeered insults.

"When the law fails," someone in the crowd yelled, "the people will set things right. Tonight, the law sleeps. We will render justice!"

General Lee yelled back. "I must in fairness warn you that we are well armed and intend to defend ourselves and this establishment. Any attempt by you to enter this building will surely result in your bloodshed. I recommend that you desist at once and return peacefully to your homes."

In the fading twilight, George could see the mob crowding closer to the publishing house. Something dark streaked across the gray sky. A paving stone crashed through the window, sending shards across the room. A flurry of stones clattered against the building, shattering shutters and panes of glass.

George's shoulder lit up with pain as a stone pounded into it, then tumbled across the wooden floor. He cursed and rubbed his shoulder until the pain subsided.

He snatched up the rock and hurled it at the man Hanson had identified as Dr. Gale. George had intended to crack the man's head, but the stone fell short, only clipping a foot. George stifled a laugh as the doctor danced on one leg, howling in pain.

Dr. Gale renewed his screaming at the mob, egging them on. Following his lead, dozens of men poured through the gateway in the brick wall. With a stout beam, they rushed the front door and rammed it.

General Lee tapped George on the shoulder and handed him a musket. "We've set up a barricade in front of the stairs on the ground floor, but we need to send this rabble a warning." The general nodded toward the street. "Fire over their heads."

George and another man stepped to the window. George cocked the musket, aimed high, and hoped the ball would fall harmlessly into the harbor. Upon General Lee's order, they fired. The muskets roared and gun smoke filled the room.

The crowd fell silent, but when no more shots were fired they grew even louder.

"Why haven't the militia been called?" asked George.

Hanson laughed. "You are new in town, sir, so I can forgive your ignorance. General Stricker and Mayor Johnson are my political enemies. I would be surprised if they lift a finger in my defense."

Around eleven o'clock the mob grew even louder. Dr. Gale led more men as they swarmed through the gateway of the brick wall and bashed open the front door. George heard the mob rushing into the front room downstairs. Shouts echoed through the building.

A musket cracked from downstairs. Ten more thundered in quick succession. From his window, George could see smoke billowing from the front door. The crowd fell silent.

Someone screamed in pain. From the gateway several men rushed forward. They hurried back to the street carrying injured men. George recognized one of the wounded, his chest bright with blood.

"That's Dr. Gale," George said. "By the look of it, if he isn't already dead, he soon will be."

General Lee called the men together in the front room downstairs. "We have faced the rabble and stood our ground. Now might be a good time for us to depart. We've shown them that we mean what we say."

Several men agreed.

"Gentlemen," said Hanson, "I'm sure that the worst is over. If we leave now, the mob has won. But if we stay, we'll show that we will hold our ground, even in the face of intimidation."

General Lee expressed his doubts, but most of the men present were persuaded by Hanson's appeal to stay.

General Lingan addressed the crowd from the second floor and urged them to desist and leave. Over the next hour, the mob continued to grow in size and noise.

Midnight passed, then two or three more hours. In a chair beside the upstairs window, George fought to stay awake. He had almost nodded off when an outburst of cheers erupted from across the street.

The crowd parted as a half-dozen men rolled a cannon from the alley. With a heave on the carriage's trail, they pointed the barrel toward the publishing house.

George hopped out of his chair and ducked. The man standing watch at the other window raced for the stairs. "I'll report this to General Lee."

George cursed under his breath, wishing he had thought of that first. He peered though the torch-lit night to see if the cannoneers were preparing to fire their weapon.

Just yards from the gun, a man held a linstock high, its smoldering cord-tip glowing bright. If the hoodlum moved toward the cannon's touchhole, George would bolt for the stairs. He checked his escape route to the staircase. He didn't want to trip just in time to catch a cannonball up his backside. The ruffians argued amongst themselves, probably about the wisdom of firing the cannon and the likelihood of more bloodshed.

"The troop is coming!" shouted someone outside.

From down the street echoed the clatter of shod horses on cobblestone. Most of the crowd scattered from the street.

Out of the dim light rode a major uniformed in dark blue with white trim. Behind him trotted two dozen dragoons carrying flintlock pistols and sabers.

"It's Major Barney," said Hanson, who had slipped in behind George.

The major rode to the front of the walled building and wheeled his horse to face the crowd. His troops guided their mounts into position behind him, and an angry roar of protest rose from the crowd. The stern-faced major raised his hand to silence them, but the crowd yelled louder.

Across the street the ruffians still had their cannon aimed toward Hanson's building. One man held the smoldering linstock inches from the gun's touchhole.

Major Barney swung down from his mount and raced to the cannon. He grabbed the end of the barrel with both hands and stood with his chest against the muzzle.

An angry group of hooligans began to drag the major away. Others stopped them, shouting, "Hear him! Hear what he has to say!"

They released the major. He straightened his jacket and whisked his hand across the sleeves, then scrambled atop the gun carriage and studied the crowd. "Good citizens! I am your friend. I share many of your political views. My men and I are here to protect persons and property. You must disperse."

"By what authority are you here?" asked one of the leaders of the mob.

Major Barney removed a folded sheet of paper from his pocket and held it high. "My troops and I are under the orders of General Stricker. We will prevent those inside the building from escaping. In the morning they shall be taken to the jailhouse to face justice."

At eight o'clock in the morning, Major Barney's dragoons formed into a hollow square in the street outside the gate. George followed Hanson and General Lee as they led twenty men out of the house, through the gate, and into the protective cordon of mounted horsemen.

Almost immediately the crowd pressed close around the guards. "We must have blood for blood!" someone yelled. "We will not be satisfied til we put them to death!"

The crowd roared with approval. A paving stone arced over a mounted dragoon and into the cluster of prisoners. With a thud, it pounded onto cobblestone, then clattered across the street. A horse whinnied and skittered out of line until its rider reined it back into position. More stones sailed over the dragoons and onto the prisoners.

The crowd rushed into the printing house and began tossing furniture and printing supplies out the upstairs windows.

George huddled as close as he could behind Major Barney's mount and yelled, "For heaven's sake, Major, get us out of here!"

Barney coaxed his mount forward. When the crowd failed to yield, he drew his sword and jabbed at them. With plodding progress, the procession began its trek.

A steady barrage of stones flew over the horsemen as the crowd screamed insults. George covered his head with his arms as best as he could.

Next to George, General Lee grunted in pain and slumped to the ground. George and Hanson grabbed the general under his arms and pulled him to his feet.

George's mind lit up with fireworks as something smacked his forehead with the force of a hammer. He staggered and stumbled, then righted himself. Someone lifted him by his armpits. After a few seconds he regained his balance. With blood obscuring his vision, he covered his head and trudged onward.

George wished they were moving faster, but the pace was no more than a shuffle as the major wedged his troops through the mob. A cobblestone pounded into George's arm and he felt his hand go numb. Another stone cracked onto his right boot, smashing his shin so bad he could barely walk.

As they progressed north along Charles Street, the mob continued to barrage them with insults, threats, and rocks. The journey of a mile to the jail took over an hour. Finally, Major Barney stopped at the steps of the two-story jailhouse near a stream known as Jones Falls.

Some of the men from the publisher's house slipped between the horses, dashed up the steps, and disappeared into the jail. The crowd roared in anger. Ruffians stormed the railing along the steps as dismounted troopers fought to drive them away.

Alexander Hanson grabbed General Lee under one arm and George grabbed the other. Together they hobbled up the steps through a gauntlet of hooligans punching and kicking them. A club arced overhead and smacked George across the side of his head. He staggered, then toppled forward through the jailhouse doorway.

"It's only a short delay," someone yelled from the crowd. "We shall take them out of the jail and put them to death."

That evening the crowd returned and attempted to ram the door open. That failed, but someone let them in a side door. Light flashed down the hall from the jail cell. Voices from the jailhouse lobby shouted in alarm. Light flashed, and George feared an oil lamp had been overturned. He imagined an inferno quickly enveloping the whole building, and the horrible death of everyone inside. But the light quickly dimmed to darkness. Only a few candles flickered in the cell.

A hammer pounded on the lock of the cell door. With a roar of angry shouts, the mob rushed inside.

As the prisoners had planned earlier, the candles in the cell were quickly snuffed. George waited until the room was almost full, then he ducked and slipped into the crowd. The prisoners had agreed that if the ruffians broke in, every man would look out for himself. The hope was that they could escape in the darkness and confusion.

George kept low and wormed his way out the cell door, down the hallway, and into the lobby. Soon he could see the silhouette of the front door and pushed toward it.

As he approached the door, someone shouldered him aside and bolted outside. George couldn't identify the man but hoped it was one of the prisoners.

George squeezed between two men and hurried toward the door. Someone grabbed him by the collar and jerked him around. In the candle-light of the lobby, George recognized Mumma the butcher.

Without a word Mumma slugged George in the face, nearly knocking him out. Mumma shoved George to the door, where another man whacked him with a club and kicked him. He toppled forward, then tumbled head over heels down the stairs to the cobblestone street. Ruffians stomped and kicked him until their attention was diverted by another prisoner being pummeled down the stairs.

George lay stunned as, one at a time, a dozen prisoners were dragged or kicked to the street and tossed onto a pile. He tried to get up, but two of the prisoners lay draped across his body. He couldn't stand, much less run.

Once the jailhouse was empty, the crowd gathered around the pile of bodies. George couldn't tell if the men piled around him were unconscious, playing dead—or actually dead.

With no chance for escape at the moment, he decided that the best strategy was to play possum and hope for the best. Blood clouded his vision, but he could see the street in front of him.

Mumma the butcher approached the pile and lifted one of the men to his feet. "This one appears to have a little life left in him."

The prisoner struggled. "I am General James Lingan."

The crowd hooted with laughter.

"Surely you know me by reputation," said the general. "Does my service during the revolution count for naught?"

Someone yelled, "You're just an old Tory."

One of the ruffians stepped forward and punched the general in the gut.

"Please," said General Lingan, "I am old and infirm. My family depends on me for support. Spare me further harm."

One of the hoodlums slugged Lingan in the face, knocked him to the ground, then kicked him repeatedly. "Damn," the ruffian said, "This old rascal is the hardest dying of them all." While the old general lay helpless, the thug stomped on his chest.

Through his own bloodied eyes, George studied Lingan. With a shudder, he realized the old general was dead.

George watched as another body was selected from the pile and beaten. One after another the prisoners were clubbed, kicked, and stomped. Some of the ruffians carried penknives, with which they stabbed and sliced at their victims. Blood covered faces and hands, then splashed over capes, hats, and coats. The victims shrieked and cried out as the town's fire alarm tolled in the distance.

General Lee lay sprawled on the cobblestone. One of the ruffians rolled Lee to his back and straddled his chest. With one hand he forced the general's eye open. With the other he tipped a candle so molten grease dripped into the eye.

Another assailant grabbed hold of General Lee's nose and tried to cut it off with a penknife. Lee sprang to life and knocked the thugs aside. The penknife sliced across Lee's nose and cheek.

The mob swarmed over Lee. After another round of beatings, General Lee was knocked back to the ground and left for dead.

Several men dragged a cart close, and in it George could see a simmering pot of tar.

One of the prisoners, about thirty years old with thin, blond hair, was beaten nearly senseless, then dragged beside the cart and stripped naked. His screams filled the night as boiling tar was poured over his bleeding body. George watched in horror as the man was beaten with an iron bar and then sliced with a rusty sword. One of the thugs tried to gouge out tar-covered eyes.

The man lay motionless until someone set fire to his tar-covered flesh. He thrashed and rolled on the ground to douse the flames. "For God's sake," he screamed, "just kill me!"

"Who are the other men who sided with Hanson?" asked one of his tormentors.

When the blond-haired man didn't answer, he was beaten again.

"If you tell us, we will let you live. Will you give us their names?"

The man sobbed but nodded.

The ruffians tossed him onto the cart and hauled him away.

Another ruffian approached the pile. "Which one is Hanson?"

George realized that the prisoner's faces were so bloody that they were difficult to identify by torchlight. Someone grabbed George by an arm and dragged him out of the pile.

"Here he is!"

George nearly panicked, but he realized that if he resisted, he would surely end up as dead as General Lingan. Using all his willpower, he kept his body limp.

One of the ruffians propped George up straight and held him by the shoulders. With a grimace and a grunt, the man kneed George in the groin. In a wave of nausea, George slumped to the cobblestone and vomited.

"Hit him again, Mumma!"

"Pound'em! "

George woke to the sound of voices.

"Toss'm into the falls," someone yelled."

"Let's tar'n feather'm!"

"I say we slit their throats to make sure they're dead."

"We'll hang them in the morning."

"First, let's castrate them."

"What they deserve is dissection!"

George felt a new wave of nausea sweep over him. He had never seen it done, but he had heard of the ancient punishment of dissection. They hanged the prisoner until nearly unconscious. They cut off his genitals and dangled them before him. They sliced open his belly and drew out his entrails. They chopped off his limbs. They mounted his head on a pike and displayed it publicly until birds pecked the skull clean or it rotted to pieces.

As the ruffians continued to argue, George dreaded whatever horror might be in store for him.

A well-dressed man with a black bag approached the pile of bodies. He knelt beside a victim sprawled on the cobblestones and examined him.

After a quick check of the other prisoners, he turned to face the crowd. "You've had your sport," he said with obvious disgust. "Now in the name of God, leave these men in my care."

Many in the crowd objected. But Mumma the Butcher stepped forward and silenced them with a raised hand. "The doctor is right. They've been beaten enough to satisfy the devil himself."

As George watched the rabble disperse, he recalled a prediction that the American attempt at self-government would degenerate into rule by mob.

CHAPTER THIRTEEN

AUGUST 1812, NEAR THE DETROIT RIVER

Hadjo followed Tecumseh and several other warriors toward Fort Malden. Clutching his war club, Hadjo worried that the meeting involved more treachery by the white men. A council house stood just outside the palisade, and Tecumseh led his men inside.

Tecumseh had asked Hadjo to accompany him because he, too, understood English. Hadjo was told to remain silent, listen, and look fierce, and that Tecumseh would visit with him later about what they saw and heard.

Hadjo looked forward to the meeting with eager anticipation. An American army of several thousand had marched north that summer and occupied the fort at Detroit. Some of the Americans crossed the river and advanced toward Fort Malden, but then withdrew. Hadjo was certain that if they had marched in force to Fort Malden shortly after their arrival, they could have overwhelmed it, as only a few redcoats were stationed there.

Since then General Brock of the British army had arrived with a couple hundred reinforcements and had summoned the local militia. In his first meeting with Tecumseh, Brock seemed impressed that the natives had already fought the Americans twice and cut off Detroit's supply line through the vast Michigan wilderness. Afterwards the general listened as Tecumseh addressed hundreds of warriors.

Hadjo's attention turned to General Brock, a tall, thickset man with dark hair, as he entered the tent with an aide, sat at a table with chairs, and offered Tecumseh a seat. Hadjo stood to the side, his arms crossed.

After exchanging pleasantries, General Brock leaned toward Tecumseh. "I have great news, my friend. We captured a boat carrying General Hull's baggage, including his private letters. From those papers we have learned that the Americans are short of food." Brock smiled. "They are also terrified of your warriors."

Tecumseh seemed pleased.

"As soon as I learned that the Americans declared war," Brock told Tecumseh, "I sent messengers to our soldiers far to the north and west of Detroit, across the lake from the American Fort Mackinac." Brock paused and smiled. "Word just arrived that our soldiers, with their Canadian and native allies, surrounded the fort under cover of darkness. Outnumbered and caught by surprise, the Americans quickly surrendered."

"My spies," Brock continued, "tell me that General Hull is a nervous, overweight old man. The Americans far outnumber our forces, even including your hundreds of warriors, but American leadership might be their weakness."

Tecumseh seemed impressed, then said to Brock, "Warriors in increasing numbers are joining our confederacy to oppose the Americans. Together, I believe we may defeat them."

The Shawnee leader spread a piece of birch bark in front of Brock and drew a map of the area. Together, they planned an attack. First, Tecumseh and hundreds of warriors would cross the Detroit River and surround the fort and village. General Brock, with three hundred redcoats and a few hundred Canadian militiamen, would cross the river several miles below the fort.

A deepening sense of dread coursed through Lemuel Wyckliffe as he gazed over the wall of Fort Detroit. He frowned as he watched a rowboat flying a white flag cross the river to the Canadian side. Word had already spread among the American forces that two British officers had brought General William Hull a demand for surrender. After a three-hour meeting with the redcoats, General Hull had politely but firmly rejected their demand and assured them the Americans could handle any show of force the British might be tempted to display. As the little boat continued toward the far shore, Lemuel feared that the Americans were trapped in a situation with no favorable outcome.

Especially after their initial success in routing out the redcoats at the bridge over the Canard River, Lemuel had hoped General Hull would attack Fort Malden and its small garrison of redcoats. Instead, the general dithered for weeks, requesting supplies from Ohio and instructions from Washington.

Each passing week brought ominous news. The British captured the merchant boat to which Hull had entrusted his official documents and the army's medical supplies. Only then did word arrive by dispatch rider that Congress had declared war on Great Britain. Stubby had grumbled that if the politicians in Washington had seen fit to declare war, it would have been mighty helpful of them to inform the army facing the enemy on the frontier.

Friendly Indians informed them that Fort Mackinac, many miles to the northwest, had already fallen to the British in a surprise attack. That news was confirmed when the paroled garrison from Mackinac arrived by schooner.

The general ordered his troops back across the Detroit River to the fort and continued to dither. When the governor of Ohio sent supplies north along the two-hundred-mile supply line, Tecumseh's Indians blocked them from reaching Detroit. The American officers and troops nearly mutinied, calling Hull an old lady and accusing him of cowardice and incompetence. They demanded the general's replacement.

Meanwhile, reinforcements arrived for the British garrison at Fort Malden. As the summer progressed, the Americans began to dread a long winter in a village already short on food while natives, rumored to number in the thousands, blocked both incoming supplies and the harvest of local crops.

Lemuel and Stubby discussed the possibility of heading back to Kentucky. Several militiamen had already departed, and Lemuel was tempted to join them. The alternative seemed increasingly like freezing and starving all winter. Besides, he and Stubby figured they could return in the spring, when the real fighting might begin. They had agreed that unless offensive action began soon, they would head home for the winter.

Lemuel blinked in the afternoon sunlight. Downhill to the south lay the village of Detroit. Below the town, two long wharfs extended into the Detroit River, which flowed from Lake Sinclair southwest to Lake Erie.

In Lemuel's mind, Canada was always to the north of U.S. territory, but because of a bend in the wide river, the Canadian village of Sandwich lay across the river to the southeast. Eighteen miles farther south was Fort Malden and the British shipyard of Amherstburg.

Lemuel could see that the village of Detroit included over a hundred buildings, most one or two stories high, but a few had three. Although the fort had been built across Savoyard Creek from the village, a network of palisades surrounded most of the town and linked it to the fort. The fort itself had four sides, each a hundred feet long, with a bastion at the outermost points. Outside the fort's fourteen-foot-high, earth-and-timber walls was a dry moat bristling with rows of sharp stakes. Hundreds of regulars and militiamen manned the fort and the stockade surrounding the town.

Lemuel was jarred out of his thoughts as cannon flashed and thundered from the Canadian side of the river and from two British ships anchored on the far side. Something whistled overhead, and Lemuel ducked. A timber wall to his left exploded in a shower of splinters.

As cannon boomed again, Hadjo leaped from behind a tree and raced to a fallen warrior. He screamed a fierce war cry at the Pale Faces in the fort, then ducked as several puffs of smoke billowed from the stockade. Hadjo grabbed the arms of his fallen comrade and dragged him back into the woods as balls snapped through leaves overhead.

Hadjo was one of five hundred of Tecumseh's warriors who had crossed the river from Canada under the cover of darkness and had quietly surrounded the fort. He ducked back between the trees, ran a short distance, then leapt out in view of the fort and screamed again. As ordered by Tecumseh, the other warriors were doing the same to make the Americans think thousands of natives surrounded them rather than just hundreds.

British cannon on the Canadian side of the river had opened fire on the fort and village. Cannonballs ripped through the fort, tearing gaps through the earth and timber walls, but they appeared to do little real damage. The American cannon returned fire, but they didn't seem to hit anything.

Hadjo could barely contain his excitement as the beginning of the battle approached. This would be his first opportunity to kill whites, and he hoped to take many scalps. He clutched his bear-tooth necklace. His reputation as a hunter had soared after killing the bear, but taking scalps in battle would distinguish him as a warrior.

From out of the woods a mile away, across a wide clearing to the south, marched British redcoats in a long column. Hadjo watched as they paraded in plain view within cannon range of the American fort. Then, without having drawn any fire from the fort, they veered into a ravine and disappeared.

Figuring that the battle would begin shortly, Hadjo tightened his grip on his red battle club, the Muscogee symbol of war. He forced himself to remain calm, savoring the moment that had been a long time in coming.

That night, Brock sent a letter to the Americans demanding their immediate surrender and warning that the Indians would be beyond his control once fighting began. The American general refused to surrender.

Brock created a fake letter mentioning that the British forces were accompanied by five thousand Indians, then arranged for the letter to fall into American hands. To give the impression that he had more regulars with him than he really did, he issued red coats to the Canadian militiamen and had them march with his regulars.

A large group of Americans were many miles south of the fort trying to bring in supplies. Rather than wait for those Americans to come to the aid of the fort, Brock decided to attack immediately. Hadjo had been sent as a messenger to alert Tecumseh that the attack would begin shortly.

The thought of rushing toward the fort, protected by cannon and manned by American riflemen, caused Hadjo to tighten his grip on the red war club. Movement at the gate of the American stockade caught his attention. A large white cloth was being run up a flagpole on the bastion at the side of the fort closest to the river. When the cannon fire from across the river ceased, a horse and rider carrying a white flag emerged from the fort.

The blue-uniformed rider waved a white cloth over his head several times, then coaxed his horse forward. A few more riders in blue joined the first, and they rode slowly toward the redcoats across the clearing. Several British officers rode out to meet the Americans. They stopped as they approached each other, and Hadjo could see them talking. Soon, each side wheeled their horses and rode back to their respective positions.

An hour passed slowly. Some of the British troops emerged from the ravine and marched toward the fort. The gates of the stockade swung wide open and out walked some Americans. As more and more Americans streamed out of the fort, the redcoats marched inside.

When Hadjo realized what had happened, he hurled his war club to the ground. The cowardly white men had surrendered the fort without putting up a fight.

Lemuel stood outside the fort with hundreds of other militiamen. Shortly after noon, the redcoats lowered the American flag. Then they fired a salute with one of the fort's cannon. By the position of the gun, Lemuel realized it was the cannon that had been captured from the British during the Revolution. As a band played "God Save the King," the redcoats raised the Union Jack over Detroit for the first time in sixteen years.

Lemuel's lips trembled as he grit his teeth. He felt that his mind would explode with rage. The British had far fewer troops and Indians than they had been led to believe. General Hull had been tricked into surrendering Detroit without a fight.

As expected, the American regular-army troops had been ordered to stack their weapons and were then taken as prisoners of war. But the American militiamen were being allowed to keep their personal property, including their weapons in defense against the natives. Lemuel's face seared hot when he realized the British didn't consider the American militia much of a threat.

Lemuel's shoulders drooped. The American army had marched north for a quick and easy conquest of Canadian territory. Now, with the loss of the forts at Mackinac, Detroit, and possibly even Fort Dearborn on Lake Michigan, nothing prevented a flood of natives from sweeping down through the vast Northwest Territories. With horror, he imagined the coming burning, butchering, and killing.

CHAPTER FOURTEEN

AUGUST 1812, HMS GUERRIERE,
750 MILES EAST OF BOSTON

Silas Shackleton coiled a thick rope in neat loops on the quarter-deck. As he continued his work, he watched three men measure the ship's speed. One of them held an eighteen-inch wedge of wood that had been tied to a rope wound onto a spool. The wedge was tossed overboard, and a small hourglass was upended. As the ship moved forward, the woodchip bobbed in the water and dragged rope off the spool. The rope had been knotted every four feet, and one of the sailors counted aloud as each knot passed him. After half a minute, the midshipman holding the hourglass said, "Time." On a piece of paper, he recorded the number of knots that had unwound from the spool. The rope was rewound as the woodchip was retrieved, then the whole process was repeated. The midshipman headed belowdecks to record the speed in the ship's log.

Silas gathered his loops of rope together in the middle and wrapped the last of the line around them. He tucked most of the tail end under the last coil and pulled it tight to hold it all together. He hefted the bundle over his shoulder, lugged it to a hatchway, then tossed it down to another crewman who would stow it. Silas didn't mind the work. Hard labor reminded him of jobs along the wharves of New York City. He wondered if he would ever see his friends there again.

As Silas headed back to get another line, he glanced at the swells that stretched to the horizon. A brisk breeze cooled his skin. The *Guerriere* was headed north again. Although she had been one of the warships accompanying a convoy of merchantmen heading for the Caribbean, she had developed problems with her rudder that required a trip back to Halifax for repairs.

"Sail ho!" yelled the lookout from the top of the main mast. "Two points off the larboard bow!"

Silas shielded his eyes from the midafternoon sun and squinted toward the horizon. A speck of white flickered in and out of view as the *Guerriere* rose and fell in the swells. Not wanting to get caught malingering, he grabbed another stout line. As he worked, the sail on the horizon grew larger.

"Frigate!" yelled the lookout.

Over the last year Silas had picked up much of the lingo used by the sailors. The *Guerriere* was also a frigate, and as such had three masts and a single gun deck. Each mast was square rigged, with rectangular sails versus triangular, each set nearly perpendicular to the length of the ship, instead of nearly parallel.

The approaching ship sped through the afternoon swells, running before the wind with a full set of sails.

"A Yank!" screamed the lookout.

On the quarterdeck at the rear of the ship, the slim captain of the *Guerriere* lowered his telescope, then turned to the sailing master. Officers began shouting orders. Like so many ants on a hill, crew members scrambled on deck. Silas grabbed the lower rung of a web-shaped rope ladder and climbed. In short order he was high in the rigging at his preassigned position to trim sail. The captain was apparently going to let the American frigate catch up.

The *Guerriere* had not seen any action while Silas had been aboard over the last year. But he had learned, from more experienced seamen, that handling a sailing ship in battle was tricky. The objective was to maneuver the vessel so that the battery of guns on either side could be brought to bear on the enemy, without the enemy being able to do the same. The ideal situation was to rake the enemy ship, firing across her deck fore and aft from one end of the vessel to the other, tearing a path of destruction through men and equipment.

The wind played the key role in how the battle would be fought. No ship could sail directly into the wind, so the vessel most facing into the wind had a distinct disadvantage. The ship with the wind most at its back was said to have the "weather gauge" and could steer toward her opponent, while her enemy could not do the same.

"Clear for action!" came the command from the deck.

Silas hurried down the rope ladder. Anything not needed for battle was either stowed below or lashed against the deck, a bulwark, or a mast.

As the American warship approached, it clearly had the advantage of the wind. The British captain altered course to reduce the Yankees' advantage, and the two ships began a cat-and-mouse game to see who could maneuver into position to harm the other.

The British captain addressed his crew from the front of the quarterdeck. "Lads, we are about to teach these Yanks why they should think twice before taking on His Majesty's navy." The captain paused, his thin lips twisting into a crooked smirk. "Let's make some sport of it, shall we? Four month's pay to everyone on board if we destroy her within fifteen minutes of firing the first broadside."

Most of the sailors cheered.

"Mr. Smith," the captain shouted to a lieutenant, "see to the pressed men."

The pressed men were rounded up under gunpoint and warned that the consequences would be severe if they shirked their duties during the coming battle.

"Sir," said a red-haired sailor with a Scottish accent, "as a citizen of the States, I cannot assist in an attack against my own countrymen. I respectfully request to be treated as a prisoner of war."

Silas had the same concerns, but before he could speak, the British officer nodded to the sergeant in charge of the marines. In a blur of motion, a club arced overhead and cracked into the skull of the redhead. The sailor slumped to the deck.

As the unconscious man was dragged below, the naval officer turned back to the remainder of the pressed men. "Any more requests?"

Silas trembled, burning with shame at the reminder of his cowardice.

"All right, then," said the officer, "back to your stations."

As the distance between the two ships closed, the American frigate was identified as the *Constitution*. The *Guerriere*'s captain ordered the starboard battery to fire. It cut loose with a tremendous roar and gush of gray-white smoke, but the broadside splashed harmlessly short of the American frigate.

The British frigate *wore ship*, turning a tight half-circle, and fired the larboard battery. But that broadside went too high. Despite the captain's cockiness, thought Silas, the crew's marksmanship seemed a little rusty. So much for bonus pay.

Over the next few hours, the warships maneuvered for position, each trying to gain advantage. Both vessels used only their "fighting sails," the top sails and jib, to balance the conflicting needs for both speed and maneuverability.

By the time the sun dipped toward the horizon, Silas had concluded that the encounter would end in a draw. When night fell, the ships would probably lose each other in the dark. Then he noticed activity aboard the *Constitution* that made his heart sink. The American frigate had set her main-top gallant and foresail.

"Look, lads," yelled a sailor near Silas. "The Yank's decided to cut and run."

But instead of veering away, the *Constitution* turned sharply toward the *Guerriere*. A murmur of voices rose from the *Guerriere's* officers and crew. With the additional sails spread, the American ship rapidly closed the gap between the two frigates. The *Constitution* was suddenly within fifty yards of the *Guerriere*.

Silas felt like screaming encouragement to the Americans. Then he realized what would likely happen next. Before he could hit the deck, the cannon muzzles extending from the *Constitution's* gun ports flashed.

The air around Silas shrieked with projectiles. The deck buckled under him. Bulwarks to his left and right exploded in showers of splinters. Silas crawled for cover as rigging and masts shuddered, then tumbled to the deck.

The next few minutes became a blur of noise and motion as gun crews from both ships blasted away at each other. But the *Constitution's* first broadside had crippled some of the *Guerriere's* guns and had impaired her ability to maneuver. In rapid succession, the Americans poured one broadside after another into the British frigate. Then the *Constitution* wore ship and unleashed her other battery.

Through the confusion and destruction, the *Constitution* edged closer, its guns blazing. The *Guerriere's* mizzenmast fell with a thunderous crash over her starboard quarter. Her bowsprit lunged into the *Constitution's* mizzenmast.

"Prepare to repel boarders!"

For a few minutes the two frigates were locked together. An American lieutenant climbed to the top of a bulwark and urged his countrymen to follow him. Just before he jumped to the *Guerriere*'s deck, his head snapped to the side with a spray of blood.

British crewmen carrying pikes and axes rushed to repel the Americans. Marines stationed aloft fired muskets at the opposing officers and crew. Then with a sudden lurch, the *Guerriere* drifted away.

With his ears still ringing and his lungs parched with gun smoke, Silas grabbed hold of what remained of a bulwark and steadied himself. The *Guerriere* rolled and dipped in the heavy swells. With a shriek of splitting timber, both the fore and mainmast fell, dragging a tangle of rigging with them. What was left of the British frigate was now a floating, helpless wreck unable to maneuver or make forward progress. The *Guerriere* listed to larboard, and Silas imagined water gushing in through the hull below.

All around him lay broken timbers, snarled lines, and tattered sailcloth. Strewn among the ravaged equipment lay corpses and severed body parts. The deck, where still intact, ran red with blood. The roar of the guns had been replaced by the pitiful screams and moans of the wounded.

The scene stunned Silas. Someone had tied the British flag to one of the few remaining upright timbers. As the Union Jack fluttered defiantly in the breeze, the *Constitution* bore down on them again. Silas wondered if the British captain was so proud he would let his helpless wounded be fired upon. Would the American ship really cut loose with another devastating broadside against an obviously defenseless vessel? Above the cries of the wounded, the captain shouted the order to strike the colors.

CHAPTER FIFTEEN

AUGUST 1812, NEW YORK CITY

Lieutenant George Sherbourne stood in line outside the entrance of a theater lobby crowded with well-dressed ladies and gentlemen, including Robert Fulton. George handed his ticket to a bright-eyed attendant who tore off a stub and handed the rest back to him. He followed the slow-moving crowd through the massive doors of the auditorium.

George quickly found his seat, welcoming the opportunity to blend farther into the growing audience. He had been ordered to keep an eye on Robert Fulton, whose steamboats traveled inland waterways of the States. After George's contacts in the Royal Navy provided him with extra funds to purchase clothes and lodging suitable for men in a higher social circle, he took a stagecoach to New York, the base of Fulton's operations.

Fulton maintained a high social profile, and George had little difficulty finding him. George almost gasped aloud at his first sight of Fulton, whose left eye was nearly closed by a huge boil on the side of his nose.

George had been warned that there was more to Fulton and his inventions than steamboats. In 1799 Fulton built a submarine and torpedoes in

France, then tried to blow up British ships blockading French waters. Later in England, before a gathering of British naval officers and other dignitaries, Fulton demonstrated the potential of his torpedoes—by blowing the ship *Dorothea* to bits.

Upon arriving in New York, George purchased for a dollar a sixty-page pamphlet written by Fulton, "Torpedo War and Submarine Explosions." The most recent news validated the Royal Navy's concerns. Soon after the declaration of war, Fulton wrote the American Secretary of War that he had a dozen torpedoes ready for deployment.

George's attention was drawn to the stage of the auditorium, where a well-dressed, middle-aged man strode in front of the drawn curtains.

"Ladies and gentlemen, may I have your attention?"

The man waited until the audience fell silent.

"My name is Charles Redheffer. Thank you for granting me the honor of your presence. In return, I will demonstrate to you an invention which will astound you. An invention that I believe may ultimately be recognized as the invention of the century. An invention that provides a limitless source of energy, and thus the potential for untold wealth."

Murmurs of excitement passed through the crowd, and the speaker waited again until he had the crowd's attention. "Alas, I wish I could take full credit for this miraculous achievement, but in truth the concept was originally developed by none other than Leonardo da Vinci. Over the centuries other scientists and inventors have attempted to improve the machine to its full potential. Only recently, after many years of toil and failed attempts, did I develop the refinements for unlocking the machine's potential. I regret that the specifics of my improvements must remain a secret to protect them from theft."

Another wave of excited murmurs passed through the crowd.

"For a limited time only, a select group of fortunate investors will have the opportunity to provide the capital to bring the benefits of this invention to the world and thus share in the profits so generated."

Murmurs in the audience rose to a new level.

"Ladies and gentlemen, without further ado, I present to you Leonardo da Vinci's new and improved perpetual-motion machine."

The curtain receded from the stage, revealing an elaborate metal and wood contraption. The primary features of the machine included a four-legged stand supporting a large, vertical wheel with what looked like hammers loosely attached at regular intervals around the circumference.

Behind the machine stood three large mirrors positioned to show the audience the backside of the invention.

"As the name implies, once this amazing device is set in motion, it remains in motion indefinitely. To set the machine in motion, let me have the assistance of a volunteer from the audience. Who would like to make history by setting the machine in perpetual motion?"

Several hands went up, and the speaker gazed past them. He smiled and pointed to someone in the third row. "You, young lady. Would you be so kind as to give me a hand?"

The speaker stepped down from the stage and offered a hand to a blonde in a dark-green dress. George caught his breath. The woman reminded him of Anne. For a moment his mind wandered back to York, and he wondered how long it would be before he could see her again.

Redheffer escorted the young lady onto the stage. "That's the way. Step right up to the machine."

Redheffer turned back to the audience and cleared his throat. "The laws of physics still apply. As stated in Isaac Newton's first law of motion, an object at rest tends to stay at rest unless acted upon by an external force. So to set the wheel in motion, force must first be applied." He pointed to a crank at the center the wheel. "Young lady, would you do the honors of giving this handle a robust turn?"

The blonde gave the handle a solid crank, setting the wheel in motion.

"Excellent job! Thank you."

The wheel turned, and the hammers hanging from the bottom edge of the wheel swung freely. As a hammer rode over the top of the wheel it lay flat until the descent began on the other side. Then it flipped, yanking the wheel and providing another burst of energy to keep it turning.

The crowd watched silently, but the longer the wheel continued to spin, the more people began to chatter.

"By now," said Redheffer, "you would have expected the machine to slow and eventually to stop. Does anyone see any reduction in the rate of turn?"

George stared closely at the machine and could detect not the slightest diminishment in the rate of rotation. The mirrors behind the machine provided a view of the backside of the contraption, showing that the demonstration involved no trickery.

The crowd fell silent.

"Ladies and gentlemen, Newton's first law of motion also states that an object in motion tends to stay in motion unless acted upon by an outside force. You would normally expect this wheel to eventually stop as friction gradually slowed the wheel. As I have stated, only through years of effort have I developed refinements to the perpetual-motion machine. The secret is the structure and weight of each of the swinging hammers attached to the wheel. As each hammer tops the wheel it tips forward and plunges with gravity, another of Isaac Newton's discoveries. Gravity provides the external force that perpetually stimulates the wheel, providing an endless source of energy. Energy by which to power any machine—from a grist mill to a cotton gin. Just think of the potential applications."

The crowd buzzed with excitement. George noticed a number of open mouths.

Robert Fulton rose from his seat and climbed the steps to the stage.

Redheffer hurried to Fulton. "Sir, for your own safety I must ask that you return to your seat."

Fulton approached the machine and stooped to look closely. Then he began to walk behind the machine.

The speaker attempted to step in front of Fulton. "Sir, I must protest this disruption!"

Fulton eased past the speaker and lifted one of the large mirrors, then pushed aside the screen behind the mirror. Behind the screen sat a man turning a crank that in turn pulled a string attached to a pulley on the spinning wheel of the machine.

George heard gasps of dismay. And curses.

The man seated behind the machine stopped pulling the string, stood, then silently walked off the stage. The turning wheel began to slow visibly, then stopped.

Audience reaction turned to anger. "I want my money back!"

Someone threw a shoe at Redheffer, and he ducked.

"Charlatan!"

"Let's tar and feather him!"

The speaker bolted for the exit. Several men pursued him.

The remaining crowd cheered Fulton.

Despite the angry red boil on Fulton's nose, he smiled and bowed at the waist.

CHAPTER SIXTEEN

SEPTEMBER 1812, WASHINGTON CITY

Rachel Thurston glanced out the window of the drawing room of the president's mansion. A patch of clouds blocked the late-afternoon sun, casting a gray pall over the landscape. As the clouds drifted, a wedge of light beamed across the muddy tidal basin along the Potomac River. Then, as quickly as they appeared, the rays of sunlight vanished.

As usual for one of Dolley Madison's Wednesday gatherings, her guests filled the drawing room and the adjacent dining room, where the marine band played lively tunes. Rachel estimated over two hundred in attendance.

Many of the guests chatted about the war and its recent setbacks. Rachel could hardly believe the news that had arrived over the last several weeks. In rapid succession three forts in the territories far to the northwest had fallen. The War Hawks, who had predicted that capturing Canada would require little more than marching, were stunned.

Rachel and her father studied his maps to understand the situation. The American army, under General William Hull, had marched north and west to Detroit, but rather than striking swiftly with his greatly superior numbers to take Fort Malden, Hull had dithered. News spread quickly that Fort Mackinac, far northwest on Lake Huron, had fallen to a surprise British attack. Then, when British General Isaac Brock arrived in the Detroit area with reinforcements, he tricked Hull into surrendering. Some in Washington City were clamoring for Hull to be hung for cowardice—after a fair trial, of course.

Prior to surrendering Detroit, General Hull had ordered the garrison at Fort Dearborn, at the mouth of the Chicago River on Lake Michigan, to evacuate. The Americans obeyed his orders, but just a few miles outside the fort, Indians attacked and slaughtered them. Rachel shuddered—rumors claimed that an American officer's heart had been hacked from his chest and eaten raw by the natives.

With the fall of the frontier forts—Mackinac on Lake Huron, Detroit in Lake Erie, and Dearborn on Lake Michigan—the Indian tribes of the lakes would be free to swarm down on the settlers in Michigan, Indiana, and Ohio.

The more Rachel thought about the consequences of these events, the more upset she became. Of course, she took some satisfaction that the first phase of the American three-pronged strategy to seize Canada had not only failed, it had backfired. She did fear for the innocent lives at stake in the territories, but her real concern was the unintended consequences of General Brock's victory at Fort Dearborn. The loss of the Michigan Territory almost guaranteed that the Madison government would not accept a peaceful solution to the conflict with Great Britain. The loss of territory and credibility would be far too great. Rachel's heart ached to think that the war might continue indefinitely.

"Excuse me, miss." A young black servant held a lacquered tray filled with glasses. "Would you care for some refreshment?"

Rachel accepted a glass of red punch, and the man moved on to other guests. She sipped her drink and studied those around her—senators, congressmen, and department heads. Mixed among the dignitaries were clerks and laborers. She even recognized one of the coachmen helping himself to a pastry. In fine Democratic-Republican tradition, Dolley welcomed all. Rachel couldn't help think of how Dolley's drawing rooms, as they were called, resembled the public days of Britain, when the gentry allowed commoners into the palaces to be awed by their superiors and to ask for favors. Remarkably, thought Rachel, the Madisons managed to don the trappings of royalty so subtly. Rachel admired the way Dolley managed the charade, hypocritical though it might be.

Rachel studied the room for more clues to Dolley's handiwork. Rachel had always considered their home in Gloucester to be one of the nicest in that community and far more elegant than the houses of most Americans. But their residence in Massachusetts paled in comparison to the president's mansion. While many in the country had only hard-packed dirt or rough-cut timber for flooring, the president's drawing room had a polished hardwood floor partially covered by a fine oblong rug.

No doubt most American homes could be described as dull, dim, and rough. Here, the walls and high ceilings were brightly painted, and the ceiling-length windows sported red-velvet drapery. The curved southern wall gave the room an oval shape, and the windows provided a grand view of the terrace and the countryside beyond.

Even on a gloomy day, mirrors around the room reflected the sunlight and, together with the glow from candles and lanterns, caused the room to sparkle. Blending with the bright hues of the ladies' attire, the room swirled with movement and color.

Rachel wondered at the irony in Dolley's agenda. Despite the lavishness of the president's mansion, the Democratic-Republicans claimed to abhor anything that smacked of royalty. They championed the common man, embracing the concept that all men were created equal. Of course, that equality didn't extend to black people—or women.

Rachel wondered if she could be lucky enough to find a place to sit. All around the room were scattered Grecian-style, gilded cane chairs, each bearing a design resembling the Great Seal of the new government, an eagle clutching arrows in one set of talons and an olive branch in the other. But all the seats were occupied.

Even the large sofa facing the towering windows bore Greek designs, its back displaying a shield and laurel. Rachel had noticed the Greek and Roman symbols on previous visits and had mentioned to her father that Dolley must hold great admiration for old-world design. Mordecai Thurston had scoffed, then explained that it was all a subtle political statement. The Madisons wanted to depict themselves and the new government as modern-day bearers of ancient republican virtue. Hypocritical or not, thought Rachel, Dolley seemed to be able to portray herself and the president as entitled to leadership of the new nation.

Rachel felt a touch of envy. Of all the women in the new nation, Dolley was the most fortunate. As wife of the president, she could actually influence events and outcomes.

As usual at Dolley's Wednesdays, many young women were present as well as a large number of young men. Rachel had been told that Dolley had been conducting her gatherings since she and the president first moved to Washington City and that many young couples owed their meeting to Mrs. Madison.

To Rachel, the presence of so many eligible young men was exciting—especially since some were obviously interested in her—but she dreaded the prospect of marriage. She already had her hands full managing a home for her father. The thought of bearing and raising a houseful of children held little interest for her, especially since young mothers seemed so tired and so many died during childbirth. To her, domestic life seemed too much like slavery.

Near the crimson-clad windows, several young men engaged in earnest conversation. One glanced in Rachel's direction. She was in no mood for the mindless conversation of young men. She turned and hurried toward the east wall of the drawing room, where a table had been heaped with cookies, cakes, nuts, and fresh fruit. At the center of the table stood a large bowl of punch. To the side were containers of coffee, tea, and wine.

Rachel helped herself to a cookie, then slipped into a room much smaller than the drawing room. Dolley's parlor, obviously meant to be more intimate than the drawing room, had a distinct feminine quality, with its cushioned seats, yellow-painted walls, and, of course, its centerpiece—a portrait of Dolley.

Even here, the casual chatter among guests was about the war. In Rachel's mind, the military setbacks had diminished the prospects for the election of James Madison to a second term. Her father was busy behind the scenes drumming up support for DeWitt Clinton, lieutenant governor of New York, as the next president.

Of course, Madison wouldn't openly campaign for another term. That would be unseemly. Even his supporters wouldn't publicly endorse his candidacy. Madison would have to appear to be indifferent to re-election. But of course, he would be willing to provide ongoing service to the nation if a groundswell of support demanded it of him.

Rachel could see that a small crowd had gathered at the northern door of the parlor. As usual, Dolley was the center of attention. Her flowered, white-satin headdress towered above the men and women around her. She wore a dazzling, loose-fitting silk robe, which formed a cape at her neck as she worked the crowd.

So that's her game, Rachel realized. Dolley was subtly orchestrating Madison's re-election, using her weekly drawing rooms as campaign events. As Dolley moved from the parlor to the hallway, the mob followed her.

A servant entered the room carrying a tray with bowls of ice cream, and guests hurried to help themselves. As the servant walked by, Rachel snatched one of the last bowls and followed Dolley's group toward the dining room.

"Listen up, everybody," shouted someone. "Great news!

"On August 19, the frigate *Constitution* attacked and sank the British warship *Guerriere*."

The crowd cheered.

At first Rachel felt dismay that an American ship could defeat a Royal frigate. Then she realized the irony of the situation. The War Hawks had counted on a swift and decisive victory on land. Instead, the first prong in their attack had failed. They had put little faith in their own navy, yet one of their frigates had been victorious over a British warship.

Then again, Rachel realized, the effectiveness of the American navy shouldn't have surprised anyone. When Thomas Jefferson became president in 1801, he had inherited a small but potent navy that had served its country well by ending French privateering of American shipping in the West Indies. Although Jefferson had also used the navy to subdue the Barbary pirates of Northern Africa, he eventually sold off all but thirteen of the frigates and one popular schooner, the *Enterprise*.

Unlike in the American army, Rachel's father had explained, promotion in the navy was gained and held by merit instead of influence or favoritism. Though small, the American navy was well trained and efficient. And after the quasi-war with France and action against the Barbary pirates, the captains were experienced at naval warfare. The navy itself was good, according to her father, but the Navy Department was not. The secretary of the navy was a political appointee, seemed hardly competent, and by midday was seldom sober enough to conduct business.

Instead of a deep-water navy, President Jefferson had constructed a fleet of two hundred gunboats to protect American waters. To Rachel it seemed that President Madison showed even less interest in the navy, and largely ignored it.

Eventually, after declaring war, President Madison consulted his naval captains. They encouraged him to send them out, one by one or in small squadrons. Incredibly, thought Rachel, they didn't get their orders to proceed until September, nearly three months after war was declared. Three squadrons set out from New York to spread over the central Atlantic. With wide latitude, they were ordered to annoy the enemy and protect American commerce. The government also issued letters of marque to almost any vessel that wanted one, and hundreds had set sail to capture British merchant ships.

In contrast, the British navy had over six hundred warships at sea, including over a hundred of the huge ships of the line and over a hundred frigates. Rachel suspected the Royal Navy, with its size and prowess, would swat the pesky American pirates like so many flies. Then, thinking of the *Constitution*, she supposed the American frigates were more like hornets.

The crowd in the dining room fell silent as three men dressed in blue uniforms approached Dolley. The tallest spoke in a voice loud enough for all in the room to hear. "Madam, it is our distinct honor to present to you the colors of the captured frigate, the H.M.S. *Guerriere*." He handed Mrs. Madison a folded flag.

Dolley unfolded the Union Jack, letting the stained and tattered fabric spill to the floor.

Rachel gasped, and then quickly covered her mouth. To allow a flag to touch the ground was considered disrespectful. To drag a flag on the floor intentionally, even the enemy's colors, was insulting.

Dolley glanced toward the floor. "Whoops!" she said with a mischievous smile, then handed a corner of the flag to one of the naval officers. Together Dolley and the officer spread the flag and held it high for all to see.

The crowd went wild with applause and cheers. "Huzzah!" someone yelled.

Throughout the room men stood and shouted, "Huzzah!"

The room buzzed with excitement. Rachel caught bits of conversation around her.

"The *Constitution* was hit several times."

"A seaman reported seeing a cannonball bounce off the ship's hull."

"Her hull is so tough that cannonballs can't penetrate!"

"Now they're calling her Old Ironsides."

The man nearest Rachel turned to her. "That will show John Bull a thing or two, won't it?"

For a moment Rachel was dumbfounded. She stood quietly as the others cheered and slapped each other on the back. Then realizing that she might be bringing unwelcome attention to herself, she lifted her punch glass and smiled.

As the guests quieted and began to exit the mansion, Rachel could sense that the tone of the conversation had changed from just an hour before. Despite the staggering defeat on the northwest frontiers, the mood of the crowd had brightened. If the news of a single naval victory met with similar reaction across the States, Madison might escape blame for mismanagement of the war. And that too, Rachel realized with sadness, meant the end of the war was nowhere in sight.

CHAPTER SEVENTEEN

SEPTEMBER 1812, BOSTON

As the afternoon sun faded, Silas Shackleton and Bosworth wandered downhill along the cobblestone street just east of Boston Common. The trees on the spacious grounds showed the red, yellow, and brown of fall. A northerly breeze nipped at Silas's ears. He cupped his hands and blew warm breath between them, dreading another chilly night, as hunger gnawed at his insides. If he and Bosworth were to have anything to eat before dark, they would have to either beg or steal, as they had done several times since being put ashore nearly a month before.

After defeating the *Guerriere*, the U.S. Frigate *Constitution* scuttled the British ship and ferried the survivors to Boston harbor. Silas had been delighted to set foot on dry land again and to be free of the Royal Navy. But with his new freedom came harsh realities. Their days slipped into a routine of walking the streets seeking employment, and then cold, hungry nights huddled in alleys.

Silas wished he could return to New York City, but Bosworth had convinced him that meant a long walk with little food and shelter. Besides, Silas still had enemies in New York, and they weren't likely to forget him anytime soon. He knew Bosworth was right, but Silas still felt the shame of running away.

Bosworth chuckled. "Almost makes you yearn for the good ol' days aboard the *Guerriere*, doesn't it?"

Silas hated to admit it, but he missed the routine aboard ship. They had considered signing up with an outgoing merchantman, but few were taking on new crewmen.

His attention drifted to a small crowd outside a tavern on Avery Street. Soldiers in crisp, dark-blue uniforms stood at attention as a fife-and-drum team played "Yankee Doodle."

Silas and Bosworth joined the crowd. A soldier approached them and whispered, "Free liquor if you hear out the major."

Silas had grown accustomed to daily servings of grog on the *Guerriere*, but he hadn't had a drink in weeks.

On an upturned box, an officer addressed the gathered men. ". . . and serve your nation in its time of need. Meanwhile, you will be securing your own future. Besides a handsome bonus upon enlisting, you will be paid ten dollars per month, and a daily ration of liquor. Upon the completion of your enlistment term of five years, you will be granted three hundred twenty acres of your own land."

A tall, dark-haired youth snorted. "And where might this here land be situated, General?"

The officer glared at his questioner. "It's major, if you please, young man." He cleared his throat. "As you would expect, the land granted to soldiers completing their enlistments is located on the frontier. But just think, it will be your land to improve and, if you wish, to pass on to your heirs."

"So, what you're proposing, General, is that if we don't get shot to hell in the infantry, we get the privilege of breaking our back clearing wilderness timber—and the chance of losing our scalps?"

The major's jaw clenched tight. He studied his questioner a moment. "Lads," continued the major, "there are many rewards for enlisting in your nation's army. I've done my best to bring them to your attention in a fair manner. But the harsh reality is that our cold-weather friend Jack Frost is the army's most effective recruiter."

The major paused and studied the crowd. "Do you feel the bite in the air? It could be a chilly one again tonight, boys. And that's just the beginning of another long winter." He glanced in Silas's direction. "Each recruit will be issued new boots, socks, trousers, and a wool coat. If you enlist this evening, you'll be given a hot meal, assigned a bunk, and issued a wool blanket." The major paused. "You have my gratitude for listening."

He turned to a thickset soldier at his side. "Sergeant Martin, would you see to the distribution of the liquor tokens?"

The uniformed soldiers began handing out brass buttons as tokens. Most of the men grumbled, took a token, then hurried into the tavern, but a short line of applicants formed in front of the recruiting table.

Silas glanced at Bosworth. The older man returned his gaze and nodded. They each accepted a button, and then stepped to the end of the line at the table. Ahead of them were rough-looking white men and a few blacks. All wore tattered rags. When the blacks' turn came, Sergeant Martin shooed them away.

Silas had visited briefly with the recruit ahead of him and noticed that he had almost no front teeth. Just one on top and one on the bottom.

When the recruit stepped up to the table, Sergeant Martin stared at him for a moment, then dug into his pocket and pulled out a tube of paper, a musket cartridge. He handed the cartridge to the nearly toothless recruit. "Tear this open with your teeth."

The man nodded, half turned toward Silas, and tore into the paper tube. Suddenly his expression changed. With eyes wide, he spat black powder to the ground.

The sergeant nodded and pushed the roster in front of the nearly toothless man. "Make your mark."

When Silas's turn finally came, the sergeant eyed him suspiciously. "Let me guess. Scots-Irish. Right?"

Silas didn't know what to say.

"You're of Scots-Irish decent, are you not?"

Silas blushed. He had never met his father. "No, Sergeant. I'm a New Yorker."

Someone behind Silas chuckled. The sergeant frowned and glared, as if trying to decide whether Silas was smarting off at him.

The sergeant told Silas to open his mouth, then grunted. He asked Silas his name and wrote it on the paper in front of him, then told Silas to sign or make his mark.

As Silas leaned over the table to make his mark, he felt a sting from old wounds on his back. He hesitated, then asked, "Does the army flog soldiers?"

"Flogging?" Sergeant Martin glanced toward the major, then answered in a voice loud enough for the officer to hear. "No, young man. Flogging has been banned in the army." Then leaning across the table, he asked more softly, "Why? Are you planning to make trouble?"

Bosworth stepped forward. "I can vouch for him, Sergeant. He's no troublemaker—but sometimes trouble seems to find *him.*"

"Oh, yeah?" asked Martin. "And just who's going to vouch for *you*?"

"We just completed a year as guests aboard His Majesty's ship *Guerriere*, Sergeant. If we're going to serve, we'd just as soon do it for our own country."

The sergeant studied the two of them a moment, then nodded. "Name?" He scrawled something in his book again, then shoved the recruitment roster toward them. "Each of you, make your mark."

Silas could see that each of the recruits above his name had signed with a simple *X*. He dipped the goose quill into a tiny pot of black ink and signed his name.

Bosworth did the same.

The sergeant studied their signatures. "You can both read and write?"

Silas spoke first. "Bosworth's been teach'n me, Sergeant."

Martin stared at Bosworth. "I need an acting corporal. You interested?"

Bosworth came to attention. "Aye, aye, Sergeant."

Martin cringed. "Now, now, none of the navy gibberish. It's 'Yes, Sergeant. Or No, Sergeant.' You're in the army now."

CHAPTER EIGHTEEN

SEPTEMBER 1812, BLADENSBURG, MARYLAND

Lieutenant George Sherbourne had never witnessed a duel, so he eagerly followed a crowd of well-dressed gentlemen as they headed into the woods just outside town. Two men stood in a clearing, each loading flint-lock pistols as a third supervised. When the firearms were loaded, the men exchanged words, nodded, and turned away. The two with pistols strode in opposite directions, each to another man at the far end of the clearing.

Some of the trees were just beginning to show a little fall color. George glanced at the early morning sun, hoping he had enough time to watch the duel before locating the local tavern where he planned to rendezvous with an agent of the Crown. George had scouted the area and sketched maps of possible invasion routes into Baltimore, Annapolis, and Washington City.

Although he had never seen a duel, he recalled some of the rules. The concept had been handed down through generations. Gentlemen— and men who aspired to be gentlemen—were forbidden from striking each other. After all, they weren't riffraff who settled differences with unseemly brawls.

Even back to the time of knights, gentlemen were allowed by custom to challenge each other in combat. Initially the accepted means of confrontation was hand-to-hand combat with swords or by mounted jousts with lances. With the advent of firearms, a couple of Irishmen saw a need to refine and record the rules in what became known as the Irish Code Duello of 1777.

Offenses leading to a challenge included physical blows and accusations of lying, cheating, or even worse—impugning a lady's reputation. All of which were prohibited among gentlemen. The code emphasized the reconciliation of differences. Combat was the last resort, after all effort at peaceful resolution had failed.

As George recalled, to provide a cooling-off period, a challenge was prohibited before dawn of the next day, and the actual duel was not allowed until the day after that. George recalled his father's admonition to control his temper and liquor consumption, lest he commit an offense leading to a duel. A careless act or word over drinks on a Friday evening could lead to a challenge on Saturday, and then a potentially deadly duel on Sunday morning. The challenged party was allowed to choose the weapons, time, and place.

Code Duello prescribed strict rules of satisfaction. Each person was to name a friend to act as his representative, or *second*. The initial duty of the seconds was to resolve the differences in a peaceful manner, if possible, and avoid the possibility of bloodshed. As a further incentive to broker reconciliation, if the seconds themselves failed to agree, they were also obliged to duel, at the same time but at right angles to their principals.

Dueling, George had learned, was a common occurrence at this particular clearing. Bladensburg itself was a port village on the East Branch of the Potomac River. Located on a busy road serving as the nation's main postal route that stretched north to Maine and south to Georgia, it was a prosperous town surrounded by houses of wealthy merchants and plantation owners. At a crossroads joining Washington, Baltimore, Annapolis, and Georgetown, it was also a gathering place for those drawn to its taverns. Dueling was prohibited in the federal District of Columbia but was legal in the state of Maryland. And since Bladensburg was just a short carriage ride from Washington City, it had become a convenient site for dueling.

George's face warmed as he recalled his last conversation with Anne's father, Major Morrison. After the major bluntly refused George as a suitor for Anne, George's temper had flared, and he'd briefly considered challenging the major to a duel for the insult to his honor.

George watched the two duelists and their seconds walk to the center of the clearing. The duelists turned their backs to each other, and the seconds withdrew.

"One!" yelled the man who had been supervising the loading of the weapons.

The duelists each stepped forward a pace.

The proctor continued counting as the duelists paced away from each other.

"Eight. Nine. Ten!"

Each stopped and turned.

"Gentlemen," said the proctor, "you may fire when ready."

Each combatant faced his opponent over his right shoulder, then raised his pistol and took aim.

George held his breath. Each duelist was allowed only one shot. Misfires, which were common, counted as a shot.

The duelist on the left fired first. The pistol flashed. White smoke billowed as the discharge cracked and echoed through the woods.

The other man cursed and slumped to a knee. A patch of blood oozed through the trousers of his right leg.

The air filled with the smell of gun smoke. The wounded duelist staggered back to his feet and raised his pistol toward his opponent. The pistol barrel wavered as the wounded duelist fought to steady it. George counted silently. To aim for more than three seconds was considered unsportsmanlike.

The duelist on the left stood his ground, waiting for the shot that might end his life.

The second pistol fired. The man on the left spun in a circle, then bent double. A red stain flowed across the right shoulder of his white shirt.

For a moment, the clearing was deathly silent.

"Mister Bosley," asked the proctor, "are you satisfied?"

The man with the wounded shoulder replied. "I am."

The proctor turned to the other duelist. "Mister Sumpter, do you publicly acknowledge that this matter of honor is resolved?"

"I do, sir."

With that, doctors stepped forward to attend to the men's wounds. The crowd began to disperse.

As George followed a group of men back to the nearest tavern, he thought of the parallels between the duelists and the two nations at war. Each seemed as much about a sense of honor as anything of substance. Yet the cost had already become much more severe than two slightly wounded men. He feared many more men would be killed or maimed before it was over. And it was such a silly war, thought George, so unlike the war in Europe where Great Britain valiantly battled an evil dictator seemingly intent on ruling the world.

The end of the American war seemed to be nowhere in sight. Ironically, thought George, General Brock's capture of Detroit had probably killed any chance of a diplomatic breakthrough.

CHAPTER NINETEEN

OCTOBER 1812, NIAGARA RIVER, NEW YORK

Private Silas Shackleton stood in formation, his back hunched against the bitter predawn wind. Sleet pelted him. He slipped his fingers under the stiff collar around his neck and gently rubbed chaffed skin. As he had frequently done over the last several weeks, he cursed his decision to enlist in the army.

To Silas's right stood Bosworth, who had been promoted from acting corporal to corporal a week after their enlistment. To Silas's left stood the five main reasons Silas hated the army—his messmates, Privates McGuinness, Denison, Raines, Webb, and Hatfield. When the five weren't actually performing their duties for the army, they were either drinking, playing cards, or fighting. If they couldn't find others to fight, they fought among themselves. To make matters worse, Sergeant Martin had pegged the whole group as troublemakers—"Damned Irish," he called them—and assigned them one tedious job after another.

Other than his messmates, Silas's experience in the infantry had been close to what he had expected. His first night included a hot meal, a blanket, and a bunk in a warm barrack. The next day Silas, Bosworth, and the other recruits each received boots, a uniform, and a wool coat. Later they were issued muskets and practiced marching. They learned to load and fire their weapons, although without powder and musket ball, and instead of a flint, a chip of wood had been clamped to the musket's hammer.

After a week of such training, they were ordered west. For days they tromped past one farm after another, then over winding roads that rose into vast stretches of forested hills. After plodding through cold rain and mud, they finally arrived tired and drenched at Lewiston, New York, on the Niagara River.

As soon as they arrived, they were hurried to the river, where they set up camp. They had a meal and caught a few hours of sleep before being rousted to stand in formation. Silas, Bosworth, and hundreds of other soldiers and militiamen had been standing since midnight, waiting for orders to cross the Niagara River into British territory.

The soldier standing in formation next to Silas was fair-haired, freckle-faced Sean McGuinness. "I wish they would hurry up. I'm—"

"Quiet in the ranks!" warned Sergeant Martin.

Silas cringed at the sound of the sergeant's voice. One thing he had learned over his first weeks in the army was to stay out of the sergeant's book. Any infraction, from speaking in the ranks to a sloppy uniform, could get his name listed, and that meant being assigned to anything from kitchen work to digging latrines.

Silas tried to ignore the freezing raindrops that dribbled from his bucket-shaped shako hat and trickled down his face and neck. Even though he was miserable, he wasn't in any hurry for what might be next.

If the rumors were accurate, the Americans had six thousand men assembled on their side of the Niagara while the British supposedly had only a few hundred—and those were spread thinly along the other side of the river. The general assumption seemed to be that victory was assured— the Americans would swarm across the river and overwhelm the British with sheer numbers. Silas wasn't so confident. Surely, the British knew the Americans were gathering forces—and why.

Besides, the vast majority of the American troops were militia, and Sergeant Martin never said anything good about the militia. He had a particularly low opinion of that part of the militia comprised largely of farmers and shopkeepers who supplied their own weapons and wore their civilian clothes rather than uniforms. Other groups were more organized, with uniforms, equipment, and some training. Martin had warned the men not to count on the militia in the face of enemy fire. In his words, they were as useless as tits on a boar.

Silas also heard that the New York militia had been called up in a hurry, with little training and equipment. The farmers among them were anxious to return home to finish the fall harvest. To complicate things even further, under the state constitution, the militia couldn't be compelled to cross borders onto foreign soil.

Not to worry, the troops had been assured. Any real fighting would be conducted by the professional army regulars. Silas squirmed at that thought. He had heard that most of the troops hadn't been in uniform much longer than himself—just a few weeks. They had marched for hundreds of miles and were dog-tired. True, they had practiced loading and firing their muskets, but they had actually fired their muskets only a few times with real ammunition.

He figured the commanding officers knew what they were doing, but rumors had spread that the senior officers were still arguing about whom would be in command. From what Silas could gather, the regular-army officers refused to serve under state militia officers of any rank, and the high-ranking militia officers refused to take orders from lower-ranked regular-army officers. The stakes were high for the officers because whoever led the attack was almost sure to reap the honor and fame of a victory.

Rumors had circulated that the American regulars who had been surrendered at Fort Detroit by General Hull were being marched, coatless and shoeless, across the river along the road that would eventually lead them to Quebec. Silas had heard one of his messmates wonder aloud if they, too, would be "Hulled" by incompetent commanding officers.

An owl hooted in the distance. Silas wondered if it was really a bird. Rumors abounded that Indians had joined forces with the British. Silas felt his scalp tingle. Since childhood he had heard of the atrocities committed by natives.

He longed to return to New York City, but that wouldn't be wise for a while. At least he was back in the state of New York, unfortunately about as far north as the state extended—hundreds of miles from the city.

Someone approached, footsteps sloshing through mud and fallen leaves. Through the mist appeared the slender silhouette of their ensign. Silas and the others snapped to attention, shoulders back and chest out. When Silas had first seen the young officer, he had almost laughed. The baby-faced ensign was only sixteen years old and had apparently obtained his commission through political connections.

"This is it, men," whispered Ensign Hightower. "Sergeant, quietly now, to the boats."

Here we go, thought Silas. Part of him wanted to slip into the darkness and disappear, even though he had no idea where he would go or how he would make his way. Better to risk being caught as a deserter than face the risk of being killed and maybe scalped in battle. But on the sergeant's orders, they all turned to their right. Bosworth was now in front of him, and his messmates were right behind him. Any opportunity to slip away had just disappeared.

On the sergeant's orders they marched down a path. As they descended, the din of the river grew louder. All along the steep, rock-lined riverbank, soldiers trudged single file to wooden docks. A dozen huge, flat-bottomed rowboats, each with a pointed bow and stern, awaited them. Silas recognized them as the *bateaux* commonly used to carry freight along inland waterways.

He followed Bosworth into the nearest boat and sat cross-legged on the wooden deck. Seated at the bow were a cluster of officers, several in the blue-and-red uniform of the New York State Militia. One of the militia officers wore stars on his epaulet. Other than the senior officers in his boat, Silas noticed no militiamen.

Silas squirmed as he scanned the men around him until he located Sergeant Martin. He relaxed a little when he saw that the sergeant sat facing away from him. Martin always seemed extra touchy around officers, especially senior officers, and he was extra quick to write names into his book.

The bateaux eased away from the dock—and American soil. Oarsmen seated on benches began pulling hard in the deafening current. Freezing-cold water sprayed over the sides as the boat rocked and weaved in the swift current. Silas took a deep breath, then gasped for another. He imagined being swept downstream faster than the oarsmen could propel them across the river. He wondered if they would be captured by British boats downstream. Worse, what if a gun crew high on the far bank spotted them and opened fire. One cannonball could shatter the boat and spill them all into the current and certain death.

Silas took a deep breath and tried to think of something else. Since arriving on the Niagara Frontier, he had learned that there, at least, the river ran wide and deep. Twenty miles south, near Buffalo, the Niagara River flowed from Lake Erie. It ran north, past the village of Chippawa, and then it cascaded over huge falls into a gorge several hundred feet deep. From there it raced as powerful rapids eight miles north, then emerged between two mountainous plateaus that loomed high on Silas's left. From there the river flowed wider and deeper the last several miles north to Lake Ontario.

Through the mist Silas could see several of the other boats battling their way across the river as a log bobbed and spun in an eddy. During his service aboard the *Guerriere,* he had seen experienced seamen maneuver rowboats in all types of weather. He could tell by the awkward, inefficient use of their oars that these rowers weren't nearly as skilled. A couple of the boats seemed to be out of control and disappeared into the fog downstream. Silas felt his bowels rumble. He hoped he wouldn't lose control and disgrace himself.

Ahead on the left loomed the towering escarpment of Queenston Heights. To the right, along docks at water's edge, were tied empty boats and barges. Above the docks lay the loyalist village of Queenston.

As the ensign had explained, their mission was to take the escarpment overlooking the portage road connecting Lake Erie and Lake Ontario, effectively cutting off British supplies and communication. The Heights were also important because they provided a commanding view north to the lake along both sides of the river.

Silas glanced up at the silhouette of the towering Heights. He shivered. Taking the plateau seemed a daunting task, even if the enemy wasn't shooting at them.

The bateaux headed toward the rocky shore upstream from the village. Shortly, the hull scraped against rocks. British soil, thought Silas. Enemy territory. As quietly as he could, he climbed over the side, but the sound of hundreds of fully equipped men clambering out of wooden boats raised a considerable racket. Silas was amazed that no sentry raised an alarm as three hundred men, mostly blue-coated regulars, hurried to the steep riverbank and regrouped.

Silas nearly tripped on the rough, rock-strewn shore. With the officers leading the way, they climbed the brush-strewn riverbank and headed toward the village.

Ahead in the foggy half-light, someone yelled, "Fire!"

Muskets flashed and popped. All around Silas, men tumbled to the ground. With trembling hands, he raised his musket to his shoulder, pointed it toward the flashes, and pulled the trigger. With a shower of sparks, the hammer struck the frizzen, but the musket failed to fire. Silas cursed.

"Fall back!" someone screamed.

Silas stumbled over a body. Ensign Hightower lay sprawled across the ground, his face covered with blood, a dark hole in his forehead. Silas cringed and turned toward the river.

Someone grabbed him by the shoulder. "Give me a hand, lad," said Bosworth.

Silas wanted to bolt for the relative safety of the riverbank. Instead he slung his musket over his shoulder and slipped his hands under the young officer's armpits as Bosworth grabbed the feet. Musket balls whizzed past them as they lugged the ensign toward the river. At the bank, they rolled the body over the edge and slid down after it.

From Fort Gray, high on the cliffs above Lewiston on the American side of the river, cannon flashed through the mist. Each blast pounded Silas's ears, thumped the air around him, and rocked the ground under him. He was thankful that the guns were pointed at the British.

A gun roared from the south, the British position above him on Queenston Heights. Another cannon opened fire from the north, a mile downriver. Silas dreaded what might be next. To his side men were ripped apart as a cannonball tore through them.

Bosworth finished reloading his musket, propped the barrel over the edge of the riverbank, and fired.

"Come on, lad," said Bosworth. "Time to earn our pay."

Silas removed the metal prick tucked into one of the belts crossing his chest and cleaned the vent next to the frizzen of his musket. He tore open a new cartridge and reprimed the pan, then pointed the musket toward the enemy village. Dreading the kick and the blinding flash to come, he closed his eyes and pulled the trigger. As the musket boomed, the butt hammered his shoulder with bone-bruising force.

Unsure of what else to do, Silas pressed his back against the steep, earthen bank. Musket balls whizzed past him, and cannonballs sailed overhead. Most of his messmates had gathered near Bosworth.

"Fire at will!" someone commanded.

"Load and fire, you lazy bastards!" screamed the Sergeant Martin. "Load and fire!"

With trembling fingers, Silas pulled the hammer of his musket to half cock, then opened the cartridge box at his right hip. He plucked out a paper cartridge, bit off one end of the paper tube, and loaded his musket. He spat to clear away the charcoal taste of gunpowder, then fired a shot toward the village.

As dawn brightened, Silas and the other Americans along the riverbank exchanged musket fire with redcoats and Canadian militiamen in the village. American artillerymen from across the river pounded the village while British gun batteries on Queenston Heights and a mile downriver blasted away at the Americans with round shot.

Over and over again, boats arrived with reinforcements. Silas helped Bosworth heave Ensign Hightower's body into a boat. It seemed to Silas that wounded troops were being evacuated almost as fast as new troops arrived. Many of the dead and wounded were officers, including the militia general who had shared their boat. Nobody seemed to know what to do. Silas longed to climb into the boat and return to the American side of the river. But he knew that with Bosworth and his messmates nearby, he couldn't get away with it.

"Form a line!" someone ordered. "Form a line facing the captain!"

Sergeants and corporals up and down the riverbank began shoving and kicking the men away from the bank. An officer in his mid-twenties stood between the men and the river. Captain Wool, Silas recalled.

"Okay, men," yelled Wool, "let's clear those lobsterbacks out of here."

Sword in hand, the captain led them up a path along the bank. At the top they formed a line facing the village, fired a volley, then reloaded and marched ahead. The redcoats along the river began retreating. Finally, thought Silas, an officer who knows what he's doing.

A cannon roared from the battery a mile downriver. Silas stumbled to the ground as a tremendous explosion boomed overhead with blinding light. Bodies tumbled over him as scores of lead balls tore into the soldiers around him.

"Fall back!" someone screamed.

Silas grabbed a crippled soldier, Private Raines, and helped him back to the cover of the bank, then dragged him over rocks to a boat. As the boat cast off, Silas hurried back to the relative safety of the riverbank and plopped down. British balls whizzed overhead.

Captain Wool crawled into a space between Sergeant Martin and Silas. Several other officers joined him. Between cannon blasts, Silas heard Wool ask an ensign, "Are you sure it's there?"

The young officer squirmed. "Sure?" he stammered. "As a child, I watched the locals use the path to access the river for fishing."

Captain Wool grimaced and leaned to the side, the seat of his trousers soaked in blood. "How far?" he asked the ensign.

"About a mile upriver, sir."

"Very well, then," said Wool as he staggered to his feet. "We'll leave a hundred men here to entertain the redcoats. The rest of us shall go for a hike."

Silas and his messmates followed Bosworth as Captain Wool led several hundred men south along the rocky western bank of the narrow, thundering stretch of river. The nearly vertical walls of the gorge almost blocked out the early morning sky. After a mile of scrambling over the boulder-strewn riverbed, they reached a substantial gash in the rocks.

Wool climbed atop a boulder as the men gathered around him. He shouted above the roar of the river. "Our duty lies above us, men. There can be no faltering." He paused. "Officers, if any man attempts to turn back, shoot him."

Wool headed up the path. Silas and his messmates followed Bosworth, and soon they were edging up a slippery trail that cut back and forth along the wall.

By early morning light Silas could see the river racing through the gorge, three hundred feet below them. His musket seemed to grow heavier with each footstep. Finally he emerged from the path into woods atop the plateau, his legs aching and his lungs burning.

Across a carpet of slippery, wet leaves, they followed the captain north to a clearing. In whispered tones, the sergeants organized the men into formation. Captain Wool disappeared into the woods ahead. As ordered, Silas pulled his bayonet from its scabbard at his left thigh. Rattles echoed through the woods.

"Quietly, you fools," whispered Martin.

With shaking hands Silas slipped the socket of the bayonet over the muzzle of his musket and twisted it tight. Metal scraped on metal, again breaking the quiet of the woods.

Captain Wool hobbled back to them, his face grimaced in pain. In hushed tones, he gave his orders. They marched single file behind the captain as he led them to the north face of the Queenston Heights escarpment.

The view in the distance was obscured with haze and low clouds. But just below them, atop a ridge overlooking the river, lay a half-moon shaped gun battery. A *redan*, Silas recalled. Mounted on a gray-painted gun carriage surrounded by earthen berms stood a large cannon, an eighteen-pounder.

Silently Captain Wool deployed his men in a line along the edge of the clearing above the gun battery. A shockwave pounded earth and air, and smoke belched from the gun. Artillerymen inside the redan hurried to reload.

Captain Wool yelled, "Ready!"

Silas removed the musket from his shoulder and held it diagonally in front of himself, muzzle high on the left. At the same time, he thumbed the hammer back to the half-cocked position.

"Aim!"

As did the other men in line, Silas raised his weapon to his shoulder, pulled the hammer to full cock, and pointed the barrel toward the redcoats.

"Fire!"

Muskets roared, and smoke billowed toward the gun battery.

"Charge!"

As they had been trained, Silas and the others screamed their loudest when they rushed ahead, bayonet-tipped muskets pointed toward the enemy.

Ahead, the British artillery crew tossed their tools aside and raced downhill, abandoning their gun without spiking it.

Silas and the others swarmed over the gun battery.

"Huzzah!" someone shouted.

All around Silas, men shouted and tossed hats into the air. Many fired muskets skyward. On the pole above the redan, the British flag was hauled down. Silas cheered as the Stars and Stripes raced to the top of the pole.

Silas felt his chest swell as he watched the redcoats disappear between the buildings of the little village. A victory. It wouldn't erase the stripes scarring his back, he figured, but it ought to take some of the wind out of the British sails.

A couple hundred redcoats emerged from the village and headed uphill behind a low stone wall. A tall, stout British officer with gold epaulets and a colorful scarf drew his sword and sidestepped over the wall. As the officer yelled encouragement, his men formed a line.

"Well, looky here," said Private Denison. "We have a redcoat general coming to welcome us."

Uphill, from clusters of brush just fifty yards from the redcoats, American militiamen fired rifles. As the British returned fire, an American rifleman stepped from the brush, aimed at the general, and fired.

The redcoat general staggered to his knees, clutched his chest, then toppled to the ground. The men around him stopped. American muskets and rifles continued to blast away. A redcoat toppled over the downed officer. The redcoats gathered their wounded and retreated to the village.

Another British officer emerged from the village and led his men uphill. As the redcoats advanced uphill, the Americans fell back. The British approached the redan, and an American officer yanked a white handkerchief from his pocket and stuck it to the tip of his sword.

Captain Wool rushed to him, snatched the cloth away, and stuffed it inside his shirt. "There will be no surrender today," he yelled. "Now pour it to them, boys!"

In the renewed fire from the Americans, the British commanding officer fell, and the remaining redcoats hurried back to the village.

From across the river came more noise. Silas listened closely. Between the gusts of breeze and the sporadic gunfire, he could hear shouts of joy. He smiled as boats loaded with troops pushed off the far shoreline.

With much cursing, the sergeants and corporals began to restore order.

"Dig in!" yelled Sergeant Martin. "We might be here for a while. And those redcoats might try to knock us off this hill. They are surely going to send more balls our way."

"Dig in with what, Sergeant?" asked Private Denison. "Our trench'n tools are on the other side of the river."

"Well," the sergeant hesitated, "then use your bayonets or whatever you can find. Rip down those makeshift shelters along the ridge and use the timber to lay a barricade—anything to provide protection."

Silas glanced back at the boats hurrying across the river, hoping they were bringing supplies. He was already low on cartridges, water, and food. In the distance to the north, he could see a column of redcoats marching toward Queenston.

Silas's company was assigned to defend a grassy patch high on the face of the Heights. They piled logs and brush to form barricades, then used their bayonets to scratch shallow trenches into the rocky soil. Exhausted, thirsty, and hungry, they hunkered down to wait for reinforcements and supplies from across the Niagara. Despite their victory, Silas felt uneasy. The officers didn't seem to know what to do next. Supplies were nowhere in sight, and he could see redcoats pouring into the village from the north.

Musket fire continued as American infantry along the riverbank exchanged shots with redcoats in and around the village. Cannon boomed from a high point a mile north along the river as bateaux crossed and recrossed. American guns flashed from high on the escarpment across the river and down by the village of Lewiston as artillerymen continued to blast the village of Queenston. Several of the buildings had already been reduced to piles of rubble.

As Silas gazed over the scene, a cool breeze began to clear the clouds and smoke. The view from the towering escarpment opened far and wide. After a dogleg bend, the Niagara stretched a dozen miles north to Lake Ontario. To either side of the river lay a wide plain, mostly overgrown with forest. Between scattered clouds, arcs of sunshine beamed across the countryside, illuminating the fall splendor in brown, gold, and crimson. In the distance, farms and woods formed a quiltlike pattern, but nearer to the Heights, Silas could discern meadows, orchards, and tilled fields.

The portage road wound down the Heights to Queenston, where it served as the main street of the village, then snaked north along the left bank of the river. Silas noticed that the village itself was little more than a collection of homes and outbuildings plus a stone barrack for the redcoats. Between the village and the Heights lay gardens and meadows bordered by rail fences, low stone walls, and scattered clumps of trees and brush.

Boatloads of American regulars had reinforced the Heights and tossed up crude defensive works. Silas estimated six hundred troops had arrived on the Heights, but he wondered what they were supposed to do next. Captain Wool and the other officers had gathered uphill under the regimental colors. Silas hoped they had a plan.

Silas flinched at the boom of a cannon nearby. From the captured redan, smoke billowed from the eighteen-pounder. Silas grinned. Newly arrived American artillerymen must have turned the gun toward the British.

More troops crossed the river and assembled on the Heights. But British cannonball continued to rip through the Americans. Silas peeked from behind their crude barricade as a steady stream of dead and wounded were carried down the hill to be rowed back across the river.

One of the tallest men Silas had ever seen, a young colonel, strode onto the battlefield and called the officers together under their regimental flag. Under the colonel's supervision, Silas and the others were repositioned to build defenses facing west across the top of the Heights. A small cannon was set near the center of their line.

"Finally," said Bosworth, "we have an officer who seems to know what the hell he's doing."

Downhill, a cannonball hit the slope and kicked up a spray of dirt and rock. The shot bounced toward Silas, and he threw himself to the ground. The ball sailed over him. When he looked uphill, a trail of bodies marked the shot's passage. A man lay sprawled across the ground, his leg severed at the hip. Another had been cut in half at the waist, his entrails spilled across the grass.

At about one o'clock Silas felt his hair stand on end as scores of Indians whooped and screamed from the cover of the brush near the top of the escarpment. The natives didn't mount an attack, but they seemed to delight in harassing the Americans, firing at them from the timberline.

The day wore on, and Silas grew more tired, hungry, and thirsty. Some additional troops arrived from across the river, but Silas could see that they hadn't brought much food, water, or ammunition with them, either. Hour after hour the British artillery batteries downriver lobbed round shot at the boats crossing the river and their embarkation point on the American side. A couple of British six-pound field guns near the village fired round shot and grape at the American positions on the escarpment, killing and wounding dozens.

Silas thought of the thousands of militiamen gathered across the river and wondered why they hadn't joined the battle. He knew many of the militiamen had expressed enthusiasm for the attack even though their governor objected to the deployment of militia beyond the state's borders.

Silas figured the sight of wounded being evacuated across the river may have terrified some of the troops. And there were the deafening sounds of battle, including the howls of the natives. But surely, thought Silas, the militiamen, having come this far, wouldn't abandon their countrymen now that the fight had begun. Maybe Sergeant Martin was right, thought Silas. You couldn't count on the militia.

As more wounded were hauled off the field, the American ranks dwindled. Silas noticed that the men sent to help the wounded to the boats didn't return, and he saw scores sneak away into the woods. He swore under his breath in envy. He was out of water and food. And even after scavenging cartridges from the dead, he was running low on ammunition. Silas glanced at the sun and figured that it was almost three o'clock.

Bosworth cursed. Out of the woods a hundred yards to the west, marched British soldiers in brilliant-red uniforms crisscrossed with white belts. With parade-ground precision, hundreds of redcoats deployed in a wide line facing the Americans. The redcoats paused for a few seconds, and then, as one, the entire line fired a volley. A cloud of gray-white smoke gushed forward, obscuring the long red line.

Through the curtain of smoke redcoats emerged, marching steadily, their bayonets pointed toward the Americans. Silas's first impulse was to drop his musket and run.

"Steady, now!" yelled Sergeant Martin. "Aim! Fire!"

With trembling limbs Silas fired.

When the breeze cleared the smoke away, Silas could see that the redcoats were still marching onward, silently, with bayonet tips glistening in the sunlight.

Billy McGuinness dropped his musket and ran.

Sporadic gunfire popped from the trees to the south. Sergeant Martin groaned and slumped to the ground, blood spurting from a dark hole in his neck. The redcoats kept coming.

"Shite," said Silas. He dropped his musket, turned, and ran. His mind raced. The river was a couple hundred feet to the east, but cliffs towered above the riverbank. Only to the north, closer to the village of Queenston did the cliff approach the water. He galloped downhill, jumping bushes and fences that blocked his path.

Silas heard footsteps behind him. At the speed he was running, he didn't dare turn to look.

"I'm right behind you," yelled Bosworth.

With most of the steep escarpment above and behind him, Silas sped across a garden near the river. At the edge of the cliff, he stopped short. Breathing heavy, he bent forward, hands on his hips. Bosworth pulled up beside him with Denison, Webb, and Hatfield.

The cliff dropped nearly vertically to the rocky riverbank. Way too far to jump. Two boats were at the near shoreline. Men were helping the wounded aboard.

Silas searched the cliff to the right and the left. He spotted a trail leading down to the riverbed. "There!" Together they raced and slid down the trail.

By the time they reached the rock-strewn riverbank, all the boats were headed back toward the American side of the river, 250 yards away. No boats were headed back to the British side. They were marooned. Unless they could find another way across the river, they would have to surrender.

Silas noticed a log floating and bobbing in the current midstream. Up and down the riverbank lay driftwood of all shapes and sizes. He picked up a log nearly eight inches in diameter and over six feet long.

He glanced at Bosworth. "I have no desire to become a British prisoner again. Do you?"

Bosworth glanced downriver. "If we take our time and pace ourselves, we might be able to make it across."

Denison chuckled. "You're crazy! You'll freeze your balls off before you reach the other side."

Bosworth grabbed a stout log. "Every man make his own decision. Swim or surrender."

Denison, Webb, and Hatfield took a seat and watched as Silas and Bosworth slipped off their boots, tied them together, and draped them over their neck.

Silas glanced back up the escarpment of Queenston Heights, knowing there were still hundreds of Americans up there, either to be captured or killed. And he was abandoning them, deserting in the face of the enemy.

"I know what you're thinking, lad," said Bosworth. "But we won't do them any good dead or captured." He tossed his log into the river. "Besides, we're probably going to drown anyway." He jumped into the water and swam after the drifting wood.

Silas did the same, gasping at the freezing water as the current carried them away.

CHAPTER TWENTY

DECEMBER 1812, INDIANA TERRITORY

In predawn darkness Hadjo crept across frozen ground toward a crude fortification on the north bank of the Mississinewa River. With an outstretched hand he felt the coarse bark of a log laid flat at the northwest corner of the barricade built by American invaders the day before. The air reeked of horses and smoldering campfires.

Footsteps of a sentry inside the barricade approached. Hadjo held his breath, lest even that slight sound give his position away. He relaxed when the footsteps continued along the inside of the barricade.

Within the enclosure were hundreds of soldiers, frontier militiamen, and their horses. Also inside were native men, women, and children plus scores of ponies captured in the village that had occupied the site until the previous morning.

Hadjo tried to ignore the terrible cold. It seemed to radiate from the ground to his bones. He longed for the milder winters of his Muscogee homeland much farther south. Fortunately, as one of Tecumseh's warriors, he had been provided warm clothes that protected him from much of the cold.

He eased an arrow from his quiver and waited for the signal to attack. Shortly he and three hundred other warriors would storm the barricade and make the whites pay for their transgressions. He resisted the urge to climb the barricade, scream his fiercest war cry, and loose his arrows into the soldiers. The success of the attack depended upon surprise and on getting as many warriors as close to the barricade as possible. Confident that he would soon get a chance to kill, he forced himself to wait.

In early September after the fall of the forts at Detroit, Mackinac, and Dearborn, warriors had surrounded Fort Wayne, a key fort on the American route northwest. But General William Henry Harrison marched from Ohio with a large army and dispersed the natives. Then, after destroying the Indian villages nearest the fort, Harrison headed back to Ohio.

For several months the Americans had kept to themselves in their settlements to the east. Hadjo had been with a small party of Tecumseh's warriors recruiting warriors from tribes along the Mississinewa River when word arrived about the sneak attack on a peaceful village.

The local elders had been shocked by the unprovoked assault, especially during the dead of winter. As best as the elders could figure, within a few days the Americans had traveled nearly a hundred miles through bitter cold and deep snow. The elders were also perplexed about the reason for the invasion, since the villagers had just been trying to survive the winter and couldn't have been a threat to anyone.

After that initial assault, mounted soldiers pursued escaping Indians downriver, where they burned two more villages and shot the natives' cattle. By nightfall the horsemen returned to the site of the first attack, where infantrymen had built a barricade around their camp.

As best as the elders could tell from villagers who had escaped capture, nearly six hundred American soldiers and frontiersmen occupied the barricade. Apparently the Americans had traveled light, without bringing tents or large quantities of food.

After much discussion, the elders concluded that the intended target of the attack must have been the village of Mississineway, at the confluence of the Mississinewa and Wabash rivers, where hundreds of warriors had taken refuge after Harrison chased them from Fort Wayne. Very likely, once the Americans realized their mistake, they would march on Mississineway, only seventeen miles from the village first assaulted.

The local elders and Tecumseh's lieutenants decided to attack the invaders. If possible, they would wipe out the Americans and take their food, horses, and supplies. At the very least they hoped to inflict enough damage so the Americans would leave without first attacking Mississineway.

The barricade enclosed a large, square compound in the forest just north of the steep river bank. Redoubts, with higher walls of stacked logs, had been built at the corners. The attack plan was to overwhelm the redoubt at the northwest corner of the log fortification. Once inside the barricade, they hoped to slaughter the whites and free the women, children, and old men.

Hadjo's mind wandered to Prancing Fawn, and he wondered how she was fairing. Winter in the land of the Muscogees was not nearly as severe as farther north, but the challenges of food and shelter were real nonetheless. Here, winters were a life-and-death struggle under the best of conditions. Hadjo thought of the families displaced by the American attack, and realized many would freeze or starve unless taken in by other villages. The additional mouths to feed could jeopardize the survival of those who offered shelter.

Hadjo imagined that Prancing Fawn was one of those suffering at the hands of the Big Knives, and he could feel himself fill with rage. He was eager for the attack to begin, but he realized that some warriors would not survive. He vowed that if he was one of those unfortunates, he would go down fighting and take as many whites with him as possible.

In the twilight, a fierce war cry broke the quiet.

Hadjo screamed his loudest, but his war cry was drowned by the screams of hundreds of others. He scrambled to the top of the rough pile of logs. War cries from outside the barricade were answered by musket shots and the curses of what sounded like hundreds of soldiers inside the compound.

No campfires were burning inside the enclosure, and Hadjo could only discern the silhouettes of the soldiers and horses inside. He fit the nock of his arrow to the bowstring and felt the bow creak as he drew the string back to his ear. In the darkness he couldn't distinguish a target, so he just aimed at the milling mass and let the arrow fly, hoping his arrow wouldn't strike one of the villagers somewhere inside the compound.

Gunshots flashed and popped all around as warriors flooded over the barricade. One after another, as rapidly as he could fire, Hadjo loosed a dozen arrows into the compound. When his quiver was empty, he tossed the bow aside, drew his war club from his belt, and climbed into the compound.

All around him warriors and soldiers fought hand to hand. Out of the twilight a soldier swung the butt of a musket toward him. Hadjo ducked the blow and pounded the war club into the soldier's knee. When the soldier staggered to the side, Hadjo swung hard and landed a skull-cracking blow.

A new swell of war cries rose in celebration. The redoubt had been overwhelmed. Hadjo joined other warriors streaming into the main body of the compound. Light from sporadic flashes of gunfire helped to distinguish soldiers from natives as the battle moved south along the inside of the barricade. With each passing minute, the dawn grew brighter, and it became easier to distinguish friend from foe. Hadjo and the other warriors beat down one soldier after another.

By the flash of erratic gunfire, Hadjo caught a new sight through the haze of smoke. He could see the muzzles of scores of muskets pointed toward the barricade. Over the din of the battle, someone shouted, "Fire!" In unison, the whole row of muskets flashed orange and spewed smoke.

Musket balls whizzed past Hadjo, and warriors around him fell. Outraged, Hadjo screamed his loudest, raised his war club and joined others as they charged toward the line of muskets.

They barely made two steps when another row of muskets fired directly into them. A musket ball whizzed so close to Hadjo's cheek that he felt its heat. To Hadjo's left and right warriors fell. The survivors joined together and rushed the line of muskets again. But time after time, a new volley of musket fire cut the group to pieces.

All around Hadjo, warriors turned to climb back over the barricade. Fearing a musket ball through him at any moment, Hadjo raced over the barricade as fast as he could move.

Once back in the forest outside the compound, the warriors gathered for a new attack. But the morning had grown brighter, and gunfire from inside the barricade hit the warriors with greater accuracy. Hadjo joined the stampede to get out of sight of the barricade. Once they were beyond rifle range, they kept going lest they be caught by mounted soldiers, who could move fast and inflict terrible damage with their swords.

As Hadjo joined other warriors heading back to the village of Mississineway, he realized they had failed to wipe out the invaders. He hoped he and the other warriors had inflicted enough damage on the Americans to discourage further attacks along the river. Maybe the predawn attack had even crippled the Americans enough to persuade them to return east.

Five days later and many miles farther east, Hadjo lay flat in brush as he watched hundreds of mounted soldiers ride to the fleeing Americans. The whites had been joined by new arrivals, and that meant the end of his chances to kill them. He recalled with satisfaction that the Americans had suffered terribly, paying a heavy price for their unprovoked attack on villages along the Mississinewa.

After the attack on the barricade, Hadjo had been one of those sent back to keep an eye on the whites. Early that afternoon, the Americans left the compound and headed east. Apparently they had lost many of their horses during the attack, because dozens of the whites traveled on foot. But the soldiers were also taking their native captives with them, probably as hostages to discourage further attacks.

After the whites had gone, Hadjo and the others entered the compound and found a hundred dead horses. Some of the warriors wanted to find the American dead and scalp them, but the whites had disguised their graves well, probably under the ashes of one of the many huts still smoldering on the ground.

Hadjo and a handful of warriors followed the whites to make sure they didn't circle back to attack more villages. But Hadjo could tell that the invaders were in bad shape. They looked sick and weak. Many of the soldiers and captives were on foot, and progress was slow. On the first day, they camped just two miles from the battleground. They did better during the coming days but still only managed ten or twelve miles between sunrise and sunset.

Apparently they expected to be attacked at any time, because they went to the great trouble of chopping down trees to erect a barricade around their camp each night. Hadjo noticed that more and more of the soldiers limped each day. Others were being carried on crude stretchers made of blankets and poles slung between horses. As the weather turned worse with bitter cold, howling wind, and additional snow, Hadjo's heart went out to the native hostages deprived of their homes. At least some of the women and children were being allowed to ride the captive ponies.

One day, three men left the American group and headed east. Hadjo and a handful of other warriors pursued them, hoping to take their scalps. But the men were apparently experienced frontiersmen and moved very fast. They met with another large group of Americans, who headed west along the trail through the snow.

As Hadjo studied the soldiers who had attacked and burned defenseless villages, he realized that many were suffering from frostbite. Even if they survived it was unlikely that they would ever be capable of fighting again. Hadjo had heard that white doctors often cut off injured limbs, leaving the patients that survived terribly crippled. He shuddered at the thought.

He studied the scene carefully so he could describe what he saw when he returned to the Mississineway. He suspected that the news would inspire many more warriors to join Tecumseh in the coming months.

The leader had already decided that his Muscogee warriors should return to their homeland in the spring to teach others what Tecumseh had shown them. To Hadjo that meant he would also be reunited with Prancing Fawn.

CHAPTER TWENTY-ONE

DECEMBER 1812, WASHINGTON CITY

Cold wind blasted from the north, sending dry leaves tumbling across the heavily rutted road. Lieutenant George Sherbourne's black gelding skittered to the side. "Easy boy," said George as he reined the horse back to the frozen track.

Here and there on either side, the forest had been cleared for farms. Although each homestead differed somewhat, they shared common features that provided shelter and sustenance for the occupants. Most had a white, block-shaped house, a barn, a few outbuildings, gardens, and orchards. Around each farmstead, in pens of various sizes, were hogs, horses, a cow or two, some chickens, ducks, geese, and a small flock of sheep. Smoke trailed in the breeze from some of the chimneys, but many of the homes seemed empty, their inhabitants off to church on Sunday morning.

The scene reminded George of his home in York, where the ground was probably already covered with snow. No doubt Anne would be with her family in church, where they would join the entire congregation for a potluck meal after the services. He longed to return home—to Anne.

Ahead, the road dipped to a wide patch of broken ice. The geld-ing stepped into the first puddle and stopped short. Freezing wind stung George's cheeks, and he tugged his wool scarf over his chin. "Come on, boy, it can't be much farther." He tapped his heels against the horse's ribs. The gelding balked a little, then slogged ahead through the mud and shards of ice.

George had finished his task of scouting and mapping potential inva-sion routes into Baltimore. Next, he would do the same for Washington City. His present route was the road leading from Bladensburg. This would be his first visit to the capital city, his first chance to get close to the men who had declared war on Great Britain. He thought of recent developments in the war and seethed.

After capturing Detroit, General Isaac Brock had rushed most of his men back east to the Niagara area, between lakes Erie and Ontario. There he organized defenses against an American attack from across the river, the second strategic prong against British North America. Although the Americans crossed the Niagara, Crown forces defeated them, capturing nearly a thousand.

The price of the British victory had been steep. While leading an early counterattack, General Brock had been killed. George swore that the Americans would pay for the general's death.

More recently, word had arrived that the American frigate *United States* had captured the newly built British frigate *Macedonian* in a long-range gun battle off Madeira in the Atlantic. The U.S. frigate returned to Boston, where she showed off her new prize.

George had to admit that the American privateers had been more successful in disrupting British shipping than he had anticipated. Piracy seemed to come naturally to American sea captains, and they had taken scores of British merchant vessels. Although many of the captured ships never made it to American ports because they were recaptured by British warships, enough survived to fuel the enthusiasm of the ship-owners and their crews.

The success of the privateers and the resulting prize money was a boon to all those involved, but George had learned that the overall cost of the war had already pushed federal government debt to the staggering sum of fifteen million dollars.

To make matters worse for the Americans, thought George, the third prong in their strategy for capturing Canada hadn't progressed anywhere near as planned. American Major General Dearborn had gathered a substantial army for a bold strike to take control of the St. Lawrence River. He began his advance north from Lake Champlain, the route of advancing armies in both the French & Indian War and during the American rebellion against the Crown. Early on a November morning, under cover of darkness, his forward guard of six hundred regulars surrounded a blockhouse at Lacolle Mills. They didn't know that the Canadian garrison had pulled out the night before, and the blockhouse was undefended.

In early morning twilight the Americans opened fire on forces approaching the blockhouse. Eventually they realized that they were firing on a group of their own militiamen who had taken a different route to the blockhouse. Canadian militiamen and allied Indians arrived. After a short engagement, the Americans retreated to Champlain, shamefully leaving five dead and five wounded on the field. Then the Vermont and New York militia refused to cross the border into Canada. Major General Dearborn withdrew his force to Plattsburgh for the winter.

George felt proud of his fellow colonials and the British army for tweaking the American's noses. He had already concluded, however, that the British had considerable help from the Americans. By George's calculation, the average age of the American generals was over sixty. None had seen battle since the rebellion of the American colonies—the Revolutionary War as they called it. General Brock had utilized the few resources available to him to successfully defend British territory against a vastly superior number of invaders. The American generals, on the other hand, had been indecisive and unprepared to capitalize on their substantial advantages.

Also of help to the British, thought George, was the American issue of who controlled their state militia. Although the national government could call up the militia to defend *against* an invasion, some of the state governors refused to let their militias *conduct* an invasion across state lines.

After abuses by the armies of Europe, and more recently by the British army in the colonies, the Americans resisted the establishment of a standing army, preferring to rely on their local militia for defense. To George, they seemed to hold an almost mythical belief in the effectiveness of their minutemen, the legendary citizen-soldiers of the rebellious colonies. George was skeptical. Part-time amateurs were no substitute for a well-trained, well-equipped professional military. Conveniently, the Americans seemed to forget that to beat the British, George Washington had eventually built and commanded an army of trained regulars.

Ahead of George, a wagon approached, sloshing through the puddles. George reined his mount to the side of the road and stopped. The driver was a burly man with a floppy, wide-rimmed hat that had been tied down around his ears with a bandana.

George smiled and waved. "How far to Washington City?"

The driver chuckled. "You're in it!" When George didn't return the laugh, the man said, "Just over the hill, sir."

At the top of the rise, George passed an empty turnpike tollhouse, apparently closed for the Sabbath. He approached the edge of what appeared to be a village with neat rows of houses. Despite the biting wind, he laughed aloud. Beyond the leafless trees ahead, towered two box-shaped buildings. These, he realized, must be the seats of the two American houses of congress.

Inside the Hall of the House of Representatives, Rachel Thurston glanced at a large fireplace. Grateful for the heat radiating from its blazing logs, she slipped the shawl from her shoulders. The hall wasn't nearly as crowded as on most Sunday mornings. She figured the biting-cold wind had discouraged many from attending, especially those with a long carriage ride.

As was their weekly habit, Rachel and her father attended the Sunday-morning gathering at the Capitol. Some who lived in Washington City preferred one of several newly constructed churches. Others made the three-mile trip to Georgetown, but she and her father liked the mix of people at the Capitol. Compared to the stuffy atmosphere of most services, especially their church back home in Gloucester, the meeting at the Capitol was more like a social gathering. Besides, her father was always on the lookout for new intelligence and potential allies, and he found the gatherings useful. He usually stationed himself near the door and acted as an unofficial greeter.

Each Sunday she and her father made sure they arrived early enough to find seating on the floor of the hall. It offered an entirely different perspective than that of being high in the gallery, where late arrivals were often directed.

As usual, men and women dressed in their best had claimed whatever chairs were available. The floor of the House was a raised wooden platform with mahogany desks and chairs arranged to face the Speaker. The Speaker's seat was a canopied chair set on its own platform at the front of the room. Beside the Speaker's chair stood a marble statue of Liberty with a carved eagle held in one hand and a scroll representing the Constitution in the other, and one foot rested on a downtrodden crown. Above the Speaker's chair hung a clock, and above it loomed an immense eagle chiseled in marble, its wings spread wide.

Around the interior of the hall, enclosing the raised floor of the House, stood two-dozen Corinthian columns arranged in the shape of an oblong octagon. Red-velvet drapery formed a wall between the columns. Above the hall arched a domed ceiling with hundreds of small plate-glass windows, each adding to the glow already provided by scores of windows set high on the exterior walls.

Rachel's attention was directed back to the floor of the House as a gentleman in a black suit stepped to the podium and began a sermon. She recognized him as a congressman but didn't recall his name or the state he represented. His dark suit reminded her of President Madison's habit of dressing in black which, along with tri-cornered hats, had declined in popularity since the Revolutionary War.

As the congressman droned on, Rachel's mind wandered. Many of her adult acquaintances continued to go out of their way to introduce her to eligible young men. Initially, she found the attention thrilling, but most of the men, she discovered, were boring, and the whole thing had become a little annoying.

The black-clad congressman wrapped up his sermon and asked everyone to bow in prayer. The hall fell silent as he thanked the Almighty for blessings bestowed. He asked for divine guidance and wisdom. Then with a loud, clear voice he said, "And may the Lord bless King George, convert him, and take him to heaven, as we want no more of him." The preacher paused at the chuckles from around the room, then said, "Amen."

"Amen!" joined a chorus of voices.

Rachel bristled. She understood that many Americans held the king of England in low regard, especially with his diminished mental capacity in recent years. But to publicly pray for his death was outrageous, even sacrilegious.

All around the hall, conversation resumed. Several women near Rachel began to chat. One laughed, then asked, "Why would anyone name their town Pigeon Roost?"

Rachel had heard that name earlier in the week when disturb-ing news had arrived from the northwestern territories of Michigan and

Indiana. All across the frontier, Indians had attacked. Settlers took refuge in local blockhouses and forts. Fort Wayne in Indiana had been besieged until General William Henry Harrison marched an army in to drive the natives away.

One story from the frontier had been particularly heartbreaking. A dozen marauding Indians, possibly of the Shawnee tribe, had attacked settlers in Indiana at a settlement called Pigeon Roost. Apparently so many pigeons inhabited the area that when they flocked, they filled the sky.

Unfortunately the local settlers had neglected the frontier precaution of building a blockhouse as a last line of defense for the community. The Indians caught the settlers defenseless and killed over twenty men, women, and children, then burned their cabins. One woman, while hiding in the woods with two children and an infant, held a shawl over her baby's mouth to prevent it from crying out and revealing their location. When the Indians departed, the woman discovered that her infant had suffocated.

"Indians?" whispered a woman not far from Rachel. "I'm sick of hearing about Indians. Y'all will wish for a few Indians on the warpath if our niggers revolt. Remember 1791? When the slaves on the island of Saint Dominique rebelled? Murdering and raping, they killed all the whites."

The woman's attention focused on Rachel. "Honey, ya'll are from the North, aren't you? Be very careful. Remember, they're from Africa. Savages. My family has owned slaves for generations. Believe me, if the darkies rise up, we're all doomed."

Rachel didn't know how to respond. She didn't dare open her mouth, for fear of saying something stupid. Washington City seemed to be filled with black people, as was the surrounding countryside. She stood silently as other women joined the conversation, many agreeing that a slave revolt was a serious threat.

Rachel's discomfort turned to anger at herself for being incapable of carrying on the conversation in an awkward moment. She was sure that if

Dolley Madison had been in her shoes, she would have glided through the moment as lightly as a butterfly visiting a rose garden.

Rachel knew that her father considered Dolley Madison to be a manipulating bitch, pretending to be above politics, all the while she was in the thick of it. But Dolley had an uncanny memory for names and faces and a knack for making people feel good about her. Despite her father's dislike of Dolley, Rachel was sure the president's wife and her socializing had played a significant role in getting her husband re-elected. Madison's re-election was a significant blow for the Federalists, but Rachel had to admire Dolley's role in pulling it off.

Rachel focused on the woman concerned about a slave rebellion, trying to recall her name. Tayloe. That was it. The woman was related to one of the local plantation owners who maintained a residence in Washington City, the Octagon House.

Rachel waited for a lull in the conversation, then jumped in. "Mrs. Tayloe, I've heard that you serve a particularly good cherry pie. May I trouble you for the recipe?"

The woman's expression changed as she gazed at Rachel with renewed interest. "Why, most certainly. I'll have it sent over to you this week. Better yet, I'll call on you and deliver it myself, if that would be convenient. And I've heard your mother served an absolutely heavenly bread pudding. Would you, by chance, have her recipe?"

Rachel smiled. "I'll make sure I have a copy of it for when you drop by."

As George rode the gelding toward the two huge, stone buildings, he had the eerie feeling that the city of nearly ten thousand had been abandoned. The windswept streets were as bare as the trees. Other than an occasional tumbling leaf, little moved. A steel-gray sky provided a background for stark buildings.

To George's left, the southeast, stood a forest of bare masts, indicating the naval yard. The possibility of capturing ships and supplies would no doubt make a mouth-watering prize for His Majesty's navy.

George had heard that the location of the capital city had been selected by George Washington himself. To George the site seemed appalling. Nestled between the Potomac River and its east branch, much of the surrounding area was swampland and forests thick with undergrowth. Although the American capital included a handful of rather impressive government buildings, the city itself was little more than a large village crisscrossed with crude streets. A mile west on another hill, George could see the rooftops of a mansion and several official-looking buildings. He figured that must be the president's palace and buildings for the administration.

He hoped to find a boardinghouse, where he could rent a room and get a warm meal. While still mounted, though, he might as well get a feel for the American capital city.

As he approached the boxlike buildings, he could see a covered wooden walkway between them. The two buildings were actually the outer wings of one large project, no doubt the Capitol, which would be home to both of the houses of legislature. He tried to imagine the completed project with an impressive structure between the box-shaped bookends. Maybe a clock tower, or spire, or a towering, peaked rotunda between the two houses of Congress. Someday it might indeed present an impressive sight.

Smoke streamed from the southernmost of the two buildings, while outside stood scores of carriages and horses. He hadn't planned on taking a tour the first thing upon his arrival, but this might be an opportunity not easily repeated.

As George approached the Capitol, a black man emerged from a hut at the end of a long row of hitching rails. George felt a rising sense of panic. But he had already learned that the surest way to get by was to pretend that he knew what he was doing, that he belonged. He dismounted, and without a word the groom led the gelding away.

George glanced at the steps leading into the eastern side of the building. No guards were posted, but if he were caught inside and identified as a spy, his fate would be sealed.

He adjusted his scarf to block the wind, took a deep breath, then climbed the steps. At the top he grabbed hold of an iron handle and pulled. Half expecting to face guards, he swung the massive door open and stepped inside.

He paused to let his eyes adjust to the dim light. A pair of uniformed sentries stood silently in a foyer dominated by a massive staircase and towering marble columns. To give himself a little time to take in the scene, George loosened his scarf and stomped his feet.

His gaze was drawn to the top of the columns, and he nearly burst out laughing. The decorations crowning the columns weren't of classic Greek or Roman design, as he had seen in London. Here, each column was topped with uniquely American symbols—ears of corn.

He glanced at the nearest guard and hoped the man hadn't noticed his reaction. George sobered quickly when he realized he had a choice to make. Judging by the number of horses and carriages outside, somewhere in the building was a large gathering of people. Were they upstairs or downstairs? He could climb the stairs or head down the hallway to the right. If he chose incorrectly, the guards might decide to question him, and who knew where that might lead.

He stepped toward the right-hand banister of the stairs. But just before he began to climb, he heard people singing from down the hall. Without breaking his stride, he headed that way.

His boot steps echoed on the marble floor, and he cringed at the attention he might be drawing. The sound of singing grew louder. He recognized the song as a hymn. Ahead stood a huge double door, and from out of the shadows, stepped a black man in a dark suit. Without a word, the man nodded and opened one of the doors.

George stepped through the threshold and stopped as the song finished. There was a rustle of clothes and squeaks of furniture as the crowd found seats. George slipped his hands behind his back, wondering what he should do next. Maybe he could find an empty chair and just blend into the crowd.

He felt a rising sense of panic when he realized that he had made a mistake. He was dressed in riding clothes—Hessian boots, pantaloons, and a heavy coat that probably reeked of damp horse. The occupants of the chamber wore their Sunday best—fine shoes, knee-length breeches, ruffled shirts, and waist coats. George's anxiety rose as a distinguished man with a powdered wig approached.

"Young man, you've picked a nasty day to travel, but welcome." The gentleman smiled and offered his hand. "My name is Mordecai Thurston."

"George Sherbourne. It is a pleasure to meet you, sir."

George chatted with his new acquaintance and found the man to be quite interesting. After a few minutes, Thurston was joined by a pretty girl with hair piled high.

Mordecai Thurston glanced from George to Rachel, then cleared his throat. "Pardon my lack of manners." He slipped his arm around the girl's waist. "May I introduce you to my daughter, Rachel?"

CHAPTER TWENTY-TWO

JANUARY 1813, MICHIGAN TERRITORY

The last time Lemuel Wyckliffe had seen Lake Erie had been the previous summer, after General Hull's surrender of Detroit. Instead of the lush vegetation he remembered, bare trees and straw-colored foxtail reeds now lined the shore. Instead of blue water stretching east to the horizon, gray-white ice blanketed the lake and blended into an overcast sky in the distance. Instead of traveling along the rough-cut trail farther inland, now buried under deep snow, he and six hundred other militiamen hiked along the windswept, frozen shoreline. Instead of limping homeward in disgrace, they marched toward battle with high hopes of a victory.

Lemuel pulled his blanket tight around his chin as another blast of wind howled over the ice. Up and down the bleak shoreline, small groups of men stopped, spread bedrolls on the snow, and opened their knapsacks. Seth Murdoch, the burly redhead whom they had elected sergeant of their ten-man squad, ordered a halt for a quick midday break.

Lemuel wolfed down a mouthful of corn dodgers and took a swig of icy water from his canteen. Not much of a meal, he realized, but a little hard-baked cornbread was better than going without anything—as they had done so many times since the beginning of this campaign. He hoped they would be heading back to Kentucky soon.

As he sat hunched against the wind, he thought back to the ordeal of the last few months. His body began to shake, and his lips trembled. He felt tears well in his eyes. He turned away from the other men so they wouldn't see his weakness.

That last summer, as the remnants of General Hull's defeated command had trudged south toward home, they had been met by thousands of new volunteers. Lemuel had intended to continue his trek back to Kentucky—he'd had enough of war. But with regular meals his strength began to return, and the enthusiasm of the newly arrived Kentucky militiamen warmed him to the idea of joining them to kick the British out of North America.

Lemuel had wavered in his decision until he learned that the commander of the new army of the northwest would be none other than General William Henry Harrison, the hero of Tippecanoe. To Lemuel and the many thousands of Kentucky recruits, Harrison possessed all the leadership qualities that General Hull had lacked.

General Harrison had a big army at his disposal, ten thousand men. He organized them into four columns that would march north, then converge at the Maumee Rapids just southwest of Lake Erie. Lemuel was assigned to the western-most column, about 2,500 men under the command of General Winchester.

Harrison's plan was to sweep north from the Rapids and recapture Detroit, then cross the river to take Fort Malden from the Brits. With Malden and the nearby shipyard, the Americans would control much of Lake Erie and western Canada. A simple and bold plan, but it depended on dry weather. If it rained much that fall, the whole operation would have to wait until the ground and waterways froze hard.

Lemuel pulled the blanket tighter around his body and fought to control his shivering. The western column had begun its northward march filled with enthusiasm—and a long train of packhorses loaded with provisions. The wilderness of Indiana, however, soon began to take its toll. During hot weather the men had to drink water from wagon ruts, and sometimes they marched twenty-five miles a day without a drop. Thickets soon shredded clothing, then the deep muck of swamps wore down the horses. When their provisions declined and they butchered their last beef, the army had to rely on Indian corn as their primary source of food.

On the last day of September, they arrived at Fort Defiance, where the Maumee and Auglaize rivers joined. Even though they were deep in the wilderness and hadn't made contact with the British or hostile Indians, they built a strong breastwork around camp.

In mid-October the weather turned unseasonably cold and wet. Then it rained and rained and rained, well into November. Roads dissolved, streams overflowed, and swamps swelled.

Frustrated with their drafty tents, the men built makeshift huts to escape the bitter wet and cold. Rations were short, and they lacked winter clothing. The chance for additional supplies diminished as mud prevented cross-country passage of loaded wagons. Desperate to replace worn-out boots, the men cobbled moccasins out of green rawhide.

They churned one campsite after another into a muddy bog, and they picked surrounding forests clean of wood for fuel. General Winchester moved them frequently, but by early November, the camp faced another challenge—fever. Plagued by diarrhea, vomiting, and overexposure to the harsh winter weather, hardly a day went by without at least one burial. Their latest camp stank of sickness and death, and the men began calling it "Camp Starvation." Discipline suffered, and the men talked of mutiny. Only an unexpected visit by General Harrison restored some order and cheer to the men.

Hardship and disease had destroyed nearly half of Winchester's command. The Kentuckians' enlistment term had already been extended but would expire in February. They were eager to return home despite having taken terrible losses without even seeing the enemy.

At the end of December, Winchester ordered the remainder of the command, only about thirteen hundred men, farther downstream. Near the Maumee Rapids, just upstream from Lake Erie, the men found cattle and hogs running wild and hundreds of acres of Indian corn still hanging from dry stalks.

With corn and meat in their belly, the men gained renewed life. At the Rapids they built a blockhouse and equipment for pounding and sifting cornmeal. Miraculously, a wagonload of winter clothing arrived from the industrious ladies of Kentucky. The prospects of surviving the winter improved.

General Winchester ordered the men to build sleds, ostensibly for hauling supplies. But Lemuel and the other men suspected that the general intended to attack the British in February, his last chance before the Kentuckians' enlistment expired and they headed home. Not one horse in camp remained strong enough to haul a loaded sled. That meant horsepower would have to be replaced by manpower—six men to a sled.

Then, in mid-January, two Frenchmen entered camp with alarming news. A detachment of Canadian militia had occupied Frenchtown, a tiny village on the Raisin River where it flowed into southwestern Lake Erie. Lemuel vaguely recalled the settlement from his trek to Detroit the summer before. The friendly villagers, mostly of French descent, had helped develop the road to Detroit and had recruited local militiamen to defend it. Now the townspeople pleaded for help in kicking the Canadians and Indians out of the settlement before the natives destroyed it.

General Winchester called a council of officers that evening. Anticipating a quick little victory before they headed back to Kentucky— rather than going home without having fired a shot in battle—they eagerly agreed to march on Frenchtown.

Five hundred and fifty men set out for Frenchtown the next morning. When General Winchester learned that two more companies of Canadian militia and a growing horde of Indians had arrived at Frenchtown, he sent an additional hundred men.

Now, as Lemuel swallowed his last corndodger, he recalled that he and Stubby were the only members of their original ten-man squad to have survived the winter. Before Lemuel could dwell on that cheerful thought, a hundred armed frontiersmen, apparently French trappers, emerged from the wooded shoreline.

At once Lemuel envied their heavy winter clothing and felt a twinge of bitterness. As did the rest of the Kentuckians, he still wore the remnants of his tattered summer clothes overlain with a dirty blanket held in place by a broad leather belt. Few of the Kentuckians had coats or wool clothing. Under their slouched hats, the Kentuckians' hair had grown long, matted, and uncombed. Despite their rifles, and the butcher knives and axes tucked under their belts, he realized that the Kentuckians probably didn't look like much of an army to the men from the village.

After the lunch break, Seth had their squad reassemble. As usual Lemuel cringed when Seth gave orders. Since being designated sergeant a few months before, the tall redhead had become bossy and arrogant. Occasionally the man's mean streak bordered on cruelty, and several of the squad members had asked Stubby if he would serve as sergeant if they voted Seth out. Stubby had said he would think about it, but wouldn't consider a move until after their current mission.

Within minutes their squad and more than seven hundred militiamen hustled quietly northward along the stark shoreline. By midafternoon Lemuel could see fingers of smoke curling over the trees ahead and figured that must be the village.

They headed up the frozen River Raisin, leafless trees crowding the icy shoreline on each side. The crack of a musket shot broke the cold silence. More shots followed the first. They had been spotted.

Someone shouted an order to halt. Lemuel skidded to a stop, his crude moccasins of rawhide offering little traction on the ice. He flinched and ducked as a shot whizzed overhead. A cannon boomed from the village. Word spread that the Canadians had two cannon with them.

A French villager approached their squad. "Please, my friends," he said with a heavy accent. "Ignore their little popguns. They are hardly big enough to kill a mouse."

Glancing briefly to each side, Lemuel realized that even a small cannonball could rip a hole through the men standing in ragged rows as they waited for the officers to decide on the next move. Feet shuffled on the ice, and someone cleared his throat. Seth and another sergeant hurried over to their lieutenant to await instructions.

A second cannonball sailed overhead—closer. Lemuel wondered if the next one would tear through him.

Stubby cupped his weathered hands to his mouth and crowed like a rooster. "Come on," squeaked the old Indian fighter, "fire away with your mouse cannon!"

Lemuel laughed and joined the others on a cockamamie chorus of catcalls and animal sounds. Over the voices of the taunting men, drums beat. Lemuel recognized the long drum roll that signaled them all to charge.

Ahead, several men helped their injured captain onto his scrawny horse. "Let's go get'm, men!" yelled the officer. No sooner had the horse stepped forward when its front feet broke through the thin ice at the boggy edge of the river. The injured captain toppled into the water and shattered ice. Several men hustled forward, coaxed the nervous horse onto more solid ice, and hefted the captain back into his saddle.

Lemuel hurried as fast as he could across the ice-covered river, his grip tight on his rifle, his heart pounding. He imagined hundreds of Canadians and Indians firing at the mass of advancing Americans as they charged the village. The losses could be staggering. A cannon boomed, and a musket ball buzzed overhead as a staccato of gunfire erupted from the village on the far riverbank. Lemuel's foot slipped to the side, and he nearly fell.

Amid a billowing cloud of gun smoke, Indians and Canadians swarmed around the village. The mounted American captain approached the dense foxtail reeds lining the riverbank. He jerked, then slumped to the side in the saddle. The horse broke through the ice again, and the captain toppled off. A few soldiers hurried to help the injured captain remount, but the rest of the men rushed past, charging up the bank toward the village.

As soon as Lemuel reached solid ground, he broke into a run. Ahead, men stopped to aim and fire, some standing, some kneeling. As the ragged line of men in front reloaded, Lemuel and the others flooded past them toward the houses.

Through gun smoke Lemuel could see the village amounted to little more than a collection of rough-cut wood houses bordered on three sides by a thin, five-foot-high fence. From the village, muskets flashed and smoke billowed. The tin cup dangling to the side of Lemuel's pack suddenly flew up and away with a *ding*. Balls whizzed past him.

Before Lemuel could pick a target, the Americans reached the houses and stormed between them. Firearms blasted all around.

Inside the palisade, Lemuel jumped over scattered bodies and rushed house to house without seeing any live Indians or Canadian militia. Peering over the palisade on the backside of the village, he saw a few dozen Canadians and over a hundred Indians loping through the snow toward the woods to the north and west of the village.

He raised his rifle toward a fleeing Canadian wearing a dark-brown fur coat, then paused. He switched his aim to a native with a single feather in his hair, then pulled the trigger. The Indian cartwheeled into a snowdrift. Lemuel noted the location so he could go claim the scalp before someone else took it.

"Let'm go," rasped Stubby. "They're whipped."

Within seconds, the musket fire dwindled, then stopped. The village overflowed with cheering Kentuckians. A Canadian militiamen and three warriors lay dead. They had already been scalped by the frontiersman.

Lemuel could see no American bodies between the riverbank and the village and none on the ice-covered river. Apparently they had taken the village without losing a single man. The mounted captain seemed to be one of only a few injured as the Kentuckians charged up the enemy bank to the village. Several men carried the captain toward a house, his leg bleeding and clearly broken.

All around Lemuel the Kentuckians howled and danced, a few fired rifles in the air. A U.S. flag, faded and tattered from months in the wilderness, was hoisted up a pole, where it snapped in the freezing wind. Joining the men around him, Lemuel howled his loudest. He danced a little jig his father had taught him.

Gunfire crackled in the distance, and the celebration ceased.

A couple of officers stood next to the palisade. "That would be Colonel Allen's detachment engaging the retreating enemy," one said. The officer turned to the Kentuckians and yelled, "Let's give'm a hand, men!" The officer drew his sword and trotted off toward the gunfire. Hundreds of Kentuckians hurried after him.

"You heard the man!" yelled Seth. "Let's go!"

"Stay close to me, lad," said Stubby with a worried tone.

With a growing sense of apprehension, Lemuel hurried after the old frontiersman. A quick surprise attack on a lightly defended village was one thing. Fighting Indians and skilled frontiersmen in the woods might be quite another.

Several days later on the snow-covered ground just inside the Frenchtown palisade, Lemuel woke to the twilight of an overcast dawn. He hated the thought of leaving the relative comfort of his bedroll on a

freezing morning, but he could no longer ignore the pressure in his blad-
der. He rose and snatched up his loaded rifle. As Stubby had taught him,
he had carefully tied a leather patch cut from a cow's knee around the lock
and hammer to keep his powder dry.

Just outside the palisade a sentry sat slumped against a tree, sleeping
on duty. Lemuel strode over and nudged him roughly with a foot.

The sentry glanced around at the half-light of early morning, then
leaped to his feet. "I'm awake," he said, fumbling with his rifle. "Thought I
was napp'n, didn't ya?"

Lemuel grunted. He stepped to a stout tree, set his rifle against the
trunk, and dropped the front of his homespun pantaloons. As he relieved
himself onto the snow, he gazed at the silhouettes of the village houses. He
cursed silently when he recalled that many of the buildings were now filled
with wounded Americans.

That first day, after capturing Frenchtown with hardly a loss, the
Kentuckians had boldly pursued the retreating enemy into the woods.
Instead of running, the Canadians and Indians bushwhacked the advancing Americans, then faded into the woods, retreating tree to tree. The
Kentuckians chased them for miles, well into the night, before the enemy
slipped away in the darkness. Exhausted, the Americans straggled back to
camp with their wounded.

By morning news had spread that they had at least fifty wounded
and a dozen dead or missing. The hasty decision to pursue the enemy into
the woods had turned a quick-and-easy victory into a much more costly
endeavor.

Lemuel had been part of a hundred-man detail sent to find and
retrieve the missing. All but one of the bodies they recovered had been
scalped, stripped, then left naked in the snow. They carried frozen-stiff
corpses back to the village and buried them in a shallow common grave.

Doctors who had accompanied the ragtag army attended the
wounded. Lemuel's heart grew cold as he thought of Stubby and Seth, both

lying in a nearby cabin. The doctors had dug a musket ball out of Seth's shoulder, and he was expected to recover. But Stubby had been gut shot. Lemuel remembered another militiaman who had been shot in the belly, and the poor soul had writhed in agony for several days before dying.

When General Winchester arrived in Frenchtown the day after the fighting, Lemuel assumed that they would all either hurry back to the relative safety of the Maumee Rapids or rapidly improve the village defenses for an extended stay.

With no means of transporting so many wounded, General Winchester decided to stay. He moved into a comfortable house a half-mile away across the river. Many of the other officers billeted in the farmhouses scattered throughout the area. The village houses were already crowded with wounded, so the remaining men had to take shelter wherever they could. One company of regulars were ordered to camp in a snow-covered field just north and east of the village.

As Lemuel retied the drawstring of his pants, he glanced toward the palisade. Not much more than a picket fence of five-foot-high split poles, it had at least provided a little break from the biting-cold wind. He felt sorry for the soldiers camped in the windswept field with no protection.

Lemuel was still amazed that General Winchester had made no attempt to improve the palisade or to construct other defensive structures. Timber abounded, and most of the Kentuckians carried axes. Then again, a scouting party had been sent up the road toward Detroit, and they had found no sign of the British. Before dark that previous evening, Lemuel heard a couple of men grumbling that no pickets had been posted—even up the road to the north. He figured the officers must be pretty confident that the enemy wasn't going to make a move. Still, Fort Malden was just across frozen Lake Erie, a day's march away.

With his blanket pulled tightly around his shoulders, Lemuel stepped back inside the palisade and stomped his numb feet, trying to get some warmth flowing through them again. From outside the palisade, he heard the rattle of drums. Peeking over the tips of the weathered, split poles, he saw soldiers in dark blue beating reveille in the open field. Men around him rustled in their blankets. Someone muttered and cursed.

As Lemuel blew a long, warm breath between his cupped hands, he watched the drummers pack their drums and sticks. The sound of drums beating continued, however, but from farther away. Lemuel glanced to the northwest, where trees were barely visible in the murky twilight. What he saw almost caused him to drop his rifle. At the tree line, men wearing long gray coats dragged out a sled-mounted cannon and pointed it at the village. Out of the woods streamed a column of soldiers onto the snow-covered field.

Realizing that under the gray great coats, the soldiers wore the scarlet uniform of the British, Lemuel screamed, "Redcoats!"

A rifle shot ripped the crisp morning air, and a British soldier slumped to the ground.

Lemuel clawed the blanket off his shoulders as other men around him threw off their bedrolls. He untied the hide of a cow's-knee covering the mechanism of his rifle. He pulled the hammer back and locked it in position. Hoping his powder was still dry, he aimed toward the closely formed line of gray-coats across the field and fired. Without waiting to see if he had hit anyone, he stepped back from the palisade to reload.

On either side of Lemuel, shouting-and-cursing Kentuckians rushed to the picket fence. Shoulder-to-shoulder, they aimed and fired as hundreds of British soldiers deployed across the field. The sound of musket fire grew to a deafening roar as more Americans began shooting. Each rifleman fired, then stepped back from the wall to reload as the militiaman behind him stepped forward. Thunderous gunfire rolled, wave after wave, from the palisade.

Gun smoke quickly blurred the view of the redcoat line. Musket balls snapped into the wood of the palisade and whizzed overhead. Occasionally a militiaman cried out in pain or fell, but to Lemuel the Kentuckians seemed to be holding their own.

The British blasted away with their muskets and field cannon, but most of their fire appeared to be directed toward the blue-coated American regulars camped in the field.

"Aim toward the cannon!" someone yelled.

As Lemuel waited for the man in front of him to shoot, he studied the three small field guns, each positioned in front of one of the British formations. He wondered how the soldiers behind the cannon could fire at the Americans without hitting their own men loading the guns.

Lemuel aimed for one of the soldiers serving the cannon and saw a line of gray-coats behind his intended target. He pulled the trigger and turned away, confident that his shot hit either the man loading the cannon or one of the many soldiers lined up behind it. Good men on both sides of this war, he realized, were dying because of the stupidity of their generals.

As Lemuel reloaded, he could see the American regulars firing from neat lines in the snow. They shot volley after volley at the redcoats, but whenever a British cannon fired, a whole swath of the Americans fell flat. For a while, others filled in the gap. But after about twenty minutes, the regulars fell back to the river.

"The general is here," someone yelled.

Several of the frontiersmen cursed.

"Mighty nice of that bastard to join us."

"What'd he do? Stop for breakfast along the way?"

An officer hurried toward them. "Men, we're going to reinforce the regulars," he shouted. "Follow me!"

Winchester and a group of officers led about fifty men, including Lemuel, out of the palisade. Lemuel assumed the regulars had regrouped at the river, where the bank offered some protection from British fire and where the wide expanse of ice would make an attack from their rear difficult. But by the time Lemuel and the others reached the bank, the regulars were already across the river and out of sight down the snow-filled lane leading back to the Maumee Rapids. On horseback, General Winchester and some of his officers led Lemuel and the other militiamen across the ice to catch up to the retreating soldiers.

Gunshots and war cries from the woods ahead indicated that Indians were already across the river. In the village, the snow had been packed hard by foot traffic, but along the narrow, tree-lined lane, the snow had accumulated in drifts two to three feet deep. By the time General Winchester's group caught up to the regulars, many of them were already dead.

Lemuel slogged past a cluster of thirty soldiers, scalped and sprawled across blood-soaked snow. At first he assumed the men had made a valiant stand together and had gone down fighting, but he saw little sign of a fight. Lemuel looked closer. Each of the men had black powder burns around their wounds. They had been shot at close range, probably after surrendering.

Redskins howled and shrieked from the woods on both sides of the snow-filled lane and began to pour onto the path behind Lemuel. With no way back to the village and natives firing at them from the woods on each side, the Americans ahead of Lemuel started to run.

As he ran through the snow, Lemuel recalled that Stubby had warned him repeatedly that the worst thing you could do when fighting Indians was to break and run. "No matter what," he had said, "gather your people together and make a stand. Injuns don't like a fair fight."

Hurrying ahead, Lemuel hoped General Winchester would stop soon and fight. If not, Lemuel would join any of the men who would make a stand. As he hurried to catch up to the others, Indians closed in from behind. Time after time, Lemuel passed the bodies of dead regulars and militiamen, some in clusters and others alone here and there. Caught in a deadly, snow-filled gauntlet with no way out, Lemuel slogged through the snow as fast as he could while rifle fire from the woods cut down one man after another around him.

An officer ahead of Lemuel spun around as a ball hit him in the shoulder. Three Indians rushed him. The officer ran his sword through one of the natives, but the others quickly killed and scalped him. Lemuel shot one of the Indians through the chest, then ran on without reloading.

As the number of Americans declined, Lemuel realized his only chance was to outrun the natives. He tried to catch up to General Winchester's group, but they were riding their horses as fast as they could drive them through the powdery drifts. Lemuel decided that if he couldn't catch up to a group soon, he would slip into the woods alone and try to make his way back to the Maumee.

He angled over to a trail left by one of the horses and found the going a little easier. Most of the rifle fire from the woods had dwindled, but he could tell from the excited war cries that scores of natives were closing in on him.

He trudged ahead until he reached a wide field surrounded by a split-rail fence. A handful of militiamen on foot had waded through deep drifts lining the fence and now raced across the windswept field. General Winchester and the other mounted men rode to the left around the outside of the fence. With the howling Indians gaining on him, Lemuel plunged through the split rails and ran.

He reached the far side of the field as General Winchester and the officers had almost completed their detour around the fence. Lemuel's arms and legs ached with fatigue, and his lungs burned. The natives were right behind him.

As Lemuel dragged himself through the fence, something slammed into his leg. He toppled into the snow bank. An Indian snatched away Lemuel's rifle, yanked him upright, and shoved him forward.

Howling, the redskins surrounded General Winchester and his officers, then dragged them from their exhausted horses. One of the Indians

grabbed General Winchester's hat and put it on, then his coat and epaulets. With the general wearing little more than his underwear, the natives
prodded the Americans back toward Frenchtown. At first Lemuel feared
they would all be killed and scalped, but apparently they were being taken
prisoner, probably to be exchanged for ransom.

A wounded militiaman ahead of Lemuel stumbled into the snow. A
warrior rushed to his side, yelled, and kicked him. When the militiaman
wouldn't get up, the Indian hammered a tomahawk into the man's head. He
sliced a circle around the dead man's skull, grabbed a handful of hair, and
ripped off the scalp. With a scream, the native held his bloody trophy high.

Lemuel didn't dare stop to look at his wound or tend it, but he had
the impression he had just been nicked by a musket ball. Still, it hurt with
every step, and blood splattered his footprints in the snow. The long walk
back to Frenchtown seemed to take forever, and he lost track of the number
of American bodies he saw along the way. All had been scalped, stripped,
and left in the snow. By the time they got to the river, Lemuel feared he
wouldn't last much longer.

The Indians led them across the ice, and then through the woods
east of the village. They were driven toward the redcoats assembled well
north of the village palisade and presented to an officer someone identified
as General Proctor. As the British officer visited with General Winchester,
Lemuel could see scores of dead and wounded redcoats strewn across the
bloodstained battlefield, especially behind the cannon. Even the men not
wounded looked exhausted.

A British officer handed one of the American majors a white flag.
He stepped to the edge of the British line and waved the truce flag over his
head several times, then walked toward the Frenchtown palisade.

A murmur of voices rose from behind the palisade, and Lemuel
realized that many Kentucky militiamen still occupied it. The American
major disappeared into the palisade, and all fell quiet for a few minutes.

Suddenly angry voices rumbled from the village and spread to both ends of the palisade.

The blue-uniformed major with the white flag returned to the British general, consulted with him, then hurried back to the palisade. After a few more minutes, he returned with hundreds of Kentuckians following him. As the heavily armed militiamen lined up in the snow, Lemuel realized there were several hundred of them. Apparently only a few behind the palisade had been killed.

He glanced back to the redcoats tending their wounded. A sour taste filled his mouth, and he spit to the side. He glanced toward General Winchester standing in the snow wearing only his linen undergarments and wondered if the general realized that the Americans might have defeated the British if he hadn't ordered them to surrender.

By the time all the Kentuckians had assembled in the field, a large number of Indians had crowded in close. Several of the natives began taking things from the Americans. Shouts of protest could be heard up and down the American line.

One of the American officers stomped across the snow to General Proctor, and the crowd went silent. "General, you promised that we could keep our possessions and that we would be protected from the natives."

The British general sniffed. "The Indians are fierce and unmanageable. It cannot be done."

The American officer turned to the militiamen. "Kentuckians! Prepare to defend yourselves!"

With a clatter and rustle of gear, hundreds of rifles were pointed toward the British and Indians.

"Stop!" shouted the redcoat general.

A hush fell over the field. Proctor glanced toward the Indians, raised his hand, and waved them away.

A pair of redcoats escorted Lemuel to a group of militiamen deemed too wounded to make the march across the lake to Fort Malden. He considered protesting, but his leg had stiffened, and he could barely walk. Besides, he was reluctant to leave Stubby and Seth, still lying in one of the cabins. Word spread quickly that the British would leave guards behind to protect the wounded and their property. In the morning, sleds from Fort Malden were to be sent for them.

Lemuel was a little surprised how quickly the British prepared to leave, but it occurred to him that they might be worried that General Harrison was marching from the Maumee Rapids. Over the next hour, Lemuel watched as the last of the redcoats and over five hundred American prisoners disappeared up the road leading north. A handful of Canadian militiamen and Indian agents, who had been left behind to protect the wounded Americans, lounged around a barn at the northern edge of town.

Silence settled over the village—an eerie contrast to the roar of battle a few hours before. A buckskin-clad Indian wandered between the houses, apparently seeking plunder, but to Lemuel he didn't seem hostile. The rest of the Indians were nowhere in sight. Lemuel glanced toward the woods, searching the tree line. He hoped the natives had left the area.

He decided to check on Seth and Stubby, so he limped back to the cabin at the eastern end of the palisade. As Lemuel swung the rough-cut door inward and stepped through the threshold, the voices of men inside fell silent. Lemuel felt conspicuous as the wounded men nearest the door turned to face him. He stomped his feet against the wooden floor and rubbed his hands together briskly, as much to relieve the tension as to restore some warmth to his extremities. A couple of the men resumed their conversation.

The air reeked with the stench of festering wounds and the various potions administered by the doctors. After his eyes adjusted to the dim interior, Lemuel could see more than a dozen men packed into the room. Several shared a quilted bed, and some sat with their back against the walls, but most of the wounded lay on furs spread across the floor in irregular rows. A fire crackled in a stone hearth at the far end of the room. Some chairs, a table, and a dresser had been shoved against the back wall. One of the men chatting was Seth. Lemuel waved, and Seth nodded back.

Lemuel found Stubby on the floor in front of a dresser and eased down beside him. As he sat cross-legged next to the old Indian fighter, he was surprised at the heat radiating from the man. Lemuel lifted the edge of the blanket and was pleased to see a thick layer of furs under his old friend.

As he replaced the blanket, he heard a sound that made his skin crawl. Stubby's jaw move slightly, and Lemuel realized that he was grinding his teeth. Stubby shivered, but beads of perspiration glistened on his forehead.

Stubby's eyes flickered open, but Lemuel saw no sign that the old man recognized him. Shot through the gut and now bloated with foul vapors, Stubby was probably in terrible pain. Lemuel wondered if the doctors had given him anything to make him more comfortable. Usually a shot of whiskey was all they prescribed for pain. Not knowing what else to do for his friend, Lemuel just sat quietly as Seth talked to another wounded militiamen.

"I heard that the British general promised the Injuns a big frolic this evening at Stoney Creek."

Lemuel's insides tightened. The creek was only five or six miles from Frenchtown. He recalled the savagery of the Indians that morning. Few had seemed intoxicated. He wondered how they would behave after getting liquored up.

"The sooner those sleds from Malden arrives and gets us outta here, the better, as far as I'm concerned," said the militiaman next to Lemuel.

Lemuel thought of the handful of Canadian militiamen left behind. He doubted they would be able to hold back a determined bunch of hostiles, assuming they really wanted to.

The topic of Seth's conversation had shifted to the subject of taking scalps.

"Personally," said Seth, "I don't have much use for scalps. I reckon, if you're gonna take a trophy, make it something useful."

Lemuel considered that thought for a moment and realized Seth had finally said something worth considering.

The cabin door swung open, and Lemuel blinked at the sunlight. The buckskin-clad Indian Lemuel had seen earlier peeked into the room, then stepped inside. Lemuel was relieved to see that a villager he recognized accompanied the Indian. Pierre was short and stout, with broad shoulders.

The Indian began rifling through the wounded men's gear.

Several of the militiamen began to protest.

Pierre held up his hand. "Give him a souvenir to take home to his own village, and he'll probably leave."

The Indian flipped up the corner of Seth's blanket, revealing a long, wide strip of fresh rawhide in the shape of a razor strop. The hair on the back of Lemuel's neck tingled as he realized that the strip of hide was human, probably sliced from the thigh of an Indian.

The native shouted something at Seth. Pierre argued with the redskin, then shoved him out the door. Pierre stood quietly at the open door for a moment, apparently watching the Indian leave. When Pierre turned back to the men inside, Lemuel could see anger in his expression. The Frenchman seemed ready to chastise Seth, but just then one of the doctors entered the cabin. As the doctor began checking on his patients, Pierre stepped out and closed the door.

When the doctor approached Stubby, Lemuel said, "He seems to be in a lot of pain."

"They're all in pain, son. I've given each of them some whiskey, except those with gut wounds." The doctor glanced toward the ragged bandages Lemuel had wrapped around his leg. "Better let me take a look at that."

The doctor undid the bloody rags and studied the wound in the dim light. "Should be all right if you can avoid the putrefaction. Want me to put some ointment on it?"

Lemuel recalled that his father hadn't cared much for doctors, with all their eccentric brews and ointments. "I'd appreciate some new bandages."

The doctor shrugged. "We use what we have," he said as he recovered the wound with the filthy rags.

"Anything I can do to help, Doc?" asked Lemuel.

The doctor took a fresh look at Lemuel. "It would be comforting if you would plant yourself at the door and keep those heathen redskins out of here."

Lemuel spent a long night by the door, listening to howling wind and men groaning, and wondering what he could do if natives tried to force their way into the cabin.

He thought of the prisoners trekking to Malden and was grateful for the shelter and the warm fire. The British would probably lead them north along the lakeshore to Brownstown, then across the ice to Malden. He figured that even if men with sleds left immediately from the fort, it would be midmorning before they reached Frenchtown. Realistically, it could be much later.

At dawn, Lemuel stirred the ashes in the hearth, but the fire was out cold. Using material set nearby, he carefully built a little pile of thin twigs, leaving a small opening at the front. Then he placed larger pieces of kindling on top of the twigs. Near the hearth lay a bag of *tow*, the curly, straw-colored material left behind when linen fibers were extracted from flax. He grabbed a handful and arranged it in the shape of an open-topped bird's nest.

From his own pouch, he extracted a piece of flint, a short steel rod, and a tiny metal canister. He carefully removed a thin patch of charred rag from the tin container and placed it inside the bird's nest. With the flint in his left hand and the steel rod in his right hand, he struck the steel against the flint. Sparks chipped off the flint onto the cloth. He struck the steel against the flint three more times in rapid succession and saw one of the sparks glow red on the black cloth.

He fluffed some of the tow around the glowing spark, and eased the bird's nest inside the little pile of twigs. He gently blew on the spark, and the glow grew brighter. The cloth began to smoke, then suddenly burst into flames. The straw-colored bird's nest burned rapidly, with flames leaping into the twigs. The twigs smoked and began to crackle as their flames grew even hotter, igniting the larger kindling.

Lemuel tended his little fire until he was satisfied that it would stay lit, then added some firewood. He broke the ice in a wooden bucket and poured the water into an iron pot hanging by a hook in the hearth. To the side he found a pumpkin and sliced it into bite-sized pieces, then tossed them into the pot. They would have soup for breakfast. He warmed his hands in the glow of the fire for a few minutes, then grabbed an apple from a barrel in the corner and headed for the door.

Outside the air was crisp, but the wind had calmed. The rough-cut timber cabins presented a stark contrast to the snow. It was a lovely picture, but something seemed out of place. As Lemuel munched on the apple, he limped past one house after another. Then he realized it wasn't that anything was misplaced—it was what was missing that alarmed him—the Canadian guards were nowhere in sight.

Lemuel checked the barn where he last saw the Canadians, then hurried around the inside perimeter of the palisade, alternately searching between the houses and eyeing the fields and outbuildings around the village. At least there didn't seem to be any Indians around, but there weren't any guards in sight, either.

He stopped at one of the cabins that housed the wounded and limped inside. He found one of the doctors. "Doc, do you know where the guards are?"

The doctor seemed only partially awake but shook his head. Lemuel knocked on the door of the next house. A man answered in French. Lemuel couldn't understand him, and the Frenchman obviously couldn't understand English.

Lemuel hobbled to another house and knocked. He was relieved when he recognized the villager who opened the door. "Pierre," said Lemuel, "would you help me find the guards?"

The man blinked several times and muttered something in French.

"Where are the guards?" said Lemuel. "Do you know which house they're in?"

Lemuel accompanied Pierre from one house to another. They banged on each door until someone opened it, then Pierre spoke either French or English depending on the occupant. After they had visited each house and made a quick check of the outbuildings, it was obvious that the Canadians had abandoned them during the night.

Pierre wandered off, and Lemuel saw him visiting quietly with some of the other villagers. But the next time Lemuel looked in their direction, they were all gone.

Lemuel limped back to the cabins where the wounded were housed and told the doctors what had happened. About an hour later, a group of Indians appeared in town. Lemuel watched them from the cabin that housed Stubby and Seth. The redskins wandered around the village collecting various souvenirs. Lemuel was relieved that they didn't look intoxicated.

By midmorning the number of natives in town had grown to a couple of hundred, and several of the villagers, including Pierre, had returned. A small group of Indians headed for the houses where the wounded lay. Lemuel stepped in front of the door when they approached the cabin, but the warrior in the lead brandished a tomahawk and shoved Lemuel aside.

The natives crowded into the room of wounded and began searching through the militiamen's possessions. One forced the drawers of the bureau open and began stuffing its contents into a bag. Another pulled the feather mattress off the bed and sliced open the tick. He shook the feathers out, then slung the empty cloth over his shoulder.

An Indian tugged at Seth's overcoat and indicated that he should take it off. The burly frontiersman cursed but handed the coat over. The buckskin-clad Indian who had been scavenging in the cabin the previous afternoon flipped back Seth's bedroll, exposing the razor strop of raw Indian hide.

What happened next left Lemuel stunned. In a blur of motion, the redskin who had taken Seth's coat drew an axe from his belt, swung it high, then down into Seth's forehead. In rapid succession, the native whooped a victory cry, scalped Seth, and stripped him. Then the big militiaman's corpse was dragged feet first out of the cabin and dumped. Still seething with rage, the Indian chopped the axe down on Seth's neck again and again until his head rolled free on the blood-soaked snow.

The redskins grabbed a few more souvenirs, then wandered off to another cabin. After a few minutes, Lemuel asked Pierre, "What are the Indians going to do with us?"

"Kill you," said the Frenchman. "Some of the warriors want revenge for your attack of the villages on the Mississinewa."

"Plead for us. Help us reason with them. Or bribe them."

Pierre shrugged. "If I interpret for you, they will kill me."

Lemuel started to argue, but the villager raised a hand in protest. "Quiet. The chiefs are in council. Maybe only the seriously wounded are to be killed." As Pierre turned to leave, he glanced down at the dry bits of hair and hide hanging from Lemuel's belt. "If you value your life, get rid of those scalps."

Lemuel stripped the scalps off his belt, then tossed them into the fire. Not knowing what else to do, he sat next to Stubby. He was pleasantly surprised when the man blinked and said, "What's going on, lad?"

In a hushed tone, Lemuel explained the situation. He told his old friend that Seth was dead but left out the details and didn't mention Pierre's prediction about the wounded.

Stubby was quiet for a while, his breathing labored. Lemuel nearly jumped when Stubby reached out and placed his hand on Lemuel's arm. "Lad," said the old man with a hoarse voice, "sneak out now, while you still can."

Lemuel was shocked. There was no way he would desert Stubby and the rest of the wounded. Lemuel started to say something, but Stubby shook his head and tried to sit up. The effort was too much for the gut-shot Indian fighter, and he fell back on his bedroll.

Lemuel stayed with Stubby until he heard a growing number of excited voices outside the cabin. He went to the door and saw that the number of Indians in the village had grown, and most of them were now gathered outside the cabins housing the wounded Americans.

Pierre stepped close to Lemuel and whispered, "The chiefs have decided. In revenge for the American attacks on the Tippecanoe and Mississinewa rivers, all the wounded who can't walk are to be killed."

The Frenchman clutched Lemuel firmly by the arm and led him away from the cabin door. Pierre guided him through the crowd of Indians to a warrior with red and black war paint and a black panther skin over his head and shoulders. In his arms the Indian clutched an American soldier's uniform and boots.

Pierre spoke to the Indian briefly and pointed to Lemuel. The warrior shoved Lemuel away from the other Indians and pushed him toward a log at the edge of the frozen river. Near the riverbank the Indian tripped Lemuel to the ground and shoved the bloodstained uniform into his arms. The Indian drew his tomahawk and began shouting at Lemuel. He turned to Pierre and pointed at Lemuel.

"You have been taken hostage and are to be traded for ransom in Detroit. Guard these items," said Pierre, indicating the blue uniform, "while Kispoko goes to find more souvenirs. Do you understand?"

Lemuel nodded and glanced at the warrior.

Kispoko glared, then strode back to the cabins.

"If you want to live," said Pierre, "stay quiet and do what you're told."

An Indian screamed a war cry that made Lemuel's skin crawl. A wounded militiaman with heavily bandaged legs was being dragged by his arms from one of the cabins. He was shoved into the crowd of warriors, where he sprawled onto the snow-covered ground. Scores of Indians shrieked as tomahawks chopped into the American. When they finished with the first one, another wounded Kentuckian, stripped naked, was dragged out onto the snow and hacked to pieces.

Indians swarmed into the cabins, dragged out more of the wounded, stripped them, and slaughtered them. A militiaman bolted from a cabin and ran toward the woods. Three warriors raced after him, tackled him, and chopped off his head. Lemuel sat in the snow, numb with cold and fear, watching the massacre.

As the slaughter proceeded throughout the village, Kispoko returned to Lemuel several times and added to the pile of plunder.

Smoke began to stream out of one of the cabins, then another and another. Flames rose from the roofs. Lemuel heard a pitiful shriek of pain from the cabin nearest him. The warriors screamed with delight. One cabin after another became engulfed in roaring flames, and agonizing cries of men could be heard above the excited babble of the natives. Lemuel estimated the number of men he had seen butchered out in the snow and realized there were still dozens inside the cabins.

He thought of Stubby lying on the floor, hopefully unconscious. Maybe then he would escape the pain of being burned alive. Lemuel started to get up. He had to do something. Either he should rush to the aid of the wounded Americans, or he should use the distraction as an opportunity to flee across the river. Pierre's rough hand grabbed Lemuel by the shoulder and shoved him down.

Lemuel looked away from the burning cabins for a moment, then heard another outburst of war cries. A wounded Kentuckian, flames and smoke streaming from bandages across his arm and shoulder, staggered from a cabin. Before he could hobble more than a few yards, Indians hacked him down.

Another frontiersman staggered out the cabin door. Lemuel rose to his feet when he recognized Stubby. The man's nightshirt smoldered while his beard and curly white hair crackled in flames. The old Indian fighter paused for a moment as if taking in the scene around him. Then he lunged at the nearest redskin and clenched him around the neck. They toppled to the ground as the warriors nearby began chopping at Stubby with tomahawks.

Several Indians picked up Stubby's mangled body and held it high as they carried it to the cabin. They heaved the corpse through the door and into the raging fire. The natives cheered. Another group held Seth's headless corpse high and flung it into the inferno.

Lemuel's arms and legs began shaking uncontrollably. His insides contracted. He doubled over as the contents of his stomach surged onto the snow. Sweat streamed down his forehead as he wiped vomit from his lips and chin.

Knowing he could be scalped and killed at any moment, Lemuel sat quietly and watched as the Indians butchered and burned the wounded Americans in a blur of mayhem.

By midafternoon Pierre was gone, and Frenchtown had become a lifeless, smoldering ruin. Kispoko tossed a ragged wool blanket onto his three-foot-high pile of booty and signaled Lemuel to pick it up. As they headed up the road toward Detroit, they passed more corpses of men who had apparently been unable to keep up with the Indians.

Lemuel wasn't sure of the exact numbers, but he knew General Winchester had nearly a thousand men in Frenchtown before the British attacked. As he plodded ahead, Lemuel figured five hundred Americans had been captured and fewer than three dozen had escaped. That meant the number of men who had been killed in battle or massacred must have totaled well over four hundred.

He stopped and listened. Not even the chirp of a bird broke the silence. He and Kispoko were alone. He stared into the eyes of the native— then dropped the pile of booty to the ground.

The Indian's face flashed with anger as he screamed and charged Lemuel, war club raised. As Stubby had taught him, Lemuel grabbed the handle with both hands. The momentum of Kispoko's charge bowled Lemuel backward. Kispoko hit the ground face-first, and Lemuel wrenched the war club free.

He swung the club hard into Kispoko's forehead, splitting the skull. As blood and gray matter spewed from the Indian's head, Lemuel pounded it again and again long after the native was dead.

He used the Indian's knife to take the scalp. Then raised it high and screamed his loudest.

Realizing that he may have been heard by more natives, Lemuel snatched up Kispoko's hat and removed his moccasins, then headed warily back down the road toward the Maumee.

CHAPTER TWENTY-THREE

MARCH 1813, WASHINGTON CITY

Rachel Thurston clutched the collar of her coat against the wind gusting from the south. Gray clouds hung low, hiding the sun. She shivered but was grateful to be sandwiched between her father and George Sherbourne, where she was sheltered from the worst of the breeze. Earlier she had begged to come along, but now she just wanted to return to the warmth of home.

Her father had taken a liking to George, but Rachel couldn't help feeling confused. On his frequent visits to their house to discuss politics and the war with her father, he asked for her views about a wide range of topics. He listened intently, and they had lively discussions, some lasting hours into the evening. At times he seemed quite interested in her, but then he pulled back and avoided her. In recent weeks, all he seemed to care about was making money, especially in arranging supply contracts with the War Department.

Rachel's attention returned to the crowd of hundreds outside the southern section of the Capitol, the part that was home to the House of

Representatives. The building's mirror image, the northern half, housed the Senate, the Supreme Court, and the Library of Congress.

Down the slope to the west, gullies drained into the swamp along the Potomac River. In the distance to the southwest, Rachel could see the church steeples of Alexandria, Virginia.

Her father had a sketch of the plans for the capital. She recalled city blocks divided by wide avenues stretching from government centers like spokes in a wheel. Scattered throughout the design, at major intersections, were circles with space for fountains and statues. Grudgingly, she admitted that someday it might make quite an impression. Of course, if the new government failed, the whole area would fall into ruin.

To the side the marine band had set up its instruments. The conductor stepped to the front, and with a flourish of his baton, the musicians began a martial tune.

To the northwest, Pennsylvania Avenue ran the mile from the Capitol to the Executive Residence. Ruts and mud holes from a long, wet winter had recently been filled with stone chips from building projects around the city.

Between the leafless poplar trees lining both sides of Pennsylvania Avenue stood militiamen representing Washington City, Georgetown, and Alexandria, each unit with uniforms of distinctive color and style. A few of the officers rode white horses, and Rachel stifled a gasp. Her mother had told her that if a young woman counted ninety-nine white horses, she would marry the next man to tip his hat to her. Rachel's mind raced, trying to remember how many white horses she had seen. Had she been subconsciously counting them? George had the habit of tipping his hat to her and bowing slightly each time they met. Did that mean they were somehow destined for each other? She bit her lip as she pondered that possibility. After a moment, she decided the whole concept was silly. Just more of her mother's superstitious rubbish.

Coming down from the president's mansion to the west was the capital-city cavalry escorting President Madison's carriage.

The president's party approached the wooden bridge spanning the waterway between the two hills. Rachel recalled laughing the first time she had heard its name—Tiber Creek. What nonsense, she had thought. As if this backwater village could ever approach the grandeur of ancient Rome.

The presidential escort began the uphill climb toward the Capitol. Rachel had to admit that the inaugural progression, with its military display, the somber music, and the Capitol itself, made a dignified scene.

Her cheeks burned from the chilling breeze, and she was sure they had turned crimson. She stuffed her hands under her coat to keep them warm, and once again wished she was home. A wave of guilt washed over her as she realized her selfishness. Her own discomfort was nothing compared to that endured by others caught up in the ongoing war.

In January word had arrived from the northwest frontier that General Harrison had ordered a daring winter raid on Indians threatening his plans to recapture Detroit. Three hundred soldiers and militiamen marched eighty miles through the snow to attack a village on the Mississinewa River. Then after a bloody counterattack by the Indians the next morning, the troops marched back to Ohio. Many of the soldiers suffered from frostbite, but all of their Indian captives arrived safely. The raid had provided the American public with a dose of positive news after the setbacks of the previous year.

The week before, disturbing news had arrived from the same territories. Hundreds of Americans, mostly Kentucky militiamen, had been defeated and captured by British forces at the village of Frenchtown, on Lake Erie at the mouth of the Raisin River. Particularly upsetting were reports that wounded Americans had been abandoned by the British and then massacred by natives. The news had already generated calls for revenge.

Rachel hated the thought of innocent civilians suffering for the arrogance to their government leaders. What surprised her, though—and infuriated her father—was that the British, with all its military might, had not already crushed the wayward American government and disgraced them.

She had to remind herself that Great Britain was embroiled in a much larger war in Europe, against Napoleon. Of course, if the British hadn't already been engaged against a formidable enemy, she was sure that the Americans would never have dared declare war in the first place.

The nature of the war in America, she was confident, was about to change. Washington City buzzed with the news that British warships had been sighted in Lynnhaven Bay, at the mouth of the Chesapeake. Rumors abounded that London had sent an entire fleet under a tough commander with orders to bring the harsh realities of war home to American citizens. She hoped the British would quickly knock some sense into the Democrat-Republicans.

As Madison's carriage stopped at the steps of the Capitol, Rachel wondered whether the British would attack Washington City. Most people seemed to think that unlikely, as the capital had little strategic value and even less in terms of the spoils of war. Baltimore, on the other hand, with its crowded harbor and warehouses, would be a phenomenally attractive prize for the British navy.

Of course it seemed that every setback the Americans endured was accompanied by some little victory that gave them encouragement. The U.S. government had been virtually broke, with barely enough to pay its bills for a few weeks. While many New England banks were brimming with cash from profitable trade, legal or otherwise, they refused to fund what they called "Mr. Madison's war."

When the situation looked bleakest, one of America's richest men, John Jacob Astor, came to the government's rescue by raising millions through the sale of government bonds. Astor, a German-born immigrant, had built an empire trading furs. In recent years he had been adding to his fortune by trading with China. He even managed to turn the blockade of New York City to his advantage when his ships outran the British, then sold their cargo at wartime prices for incredible profits.

Rachel assumed that Astor was in the crowd somewhere. No doubt he, along with other men of power and influence, would get a choice seat for the president's inaugural address. The only women present, she was sure, would be the wives and daughters of such men.

Her attention was drawn back to the inaugural procession. As the marine band played and the militia stood at attention, President and Dolley Madison ascended the steps and entered the Capitol. George offered Rachel his arm as they headed inside. Rachel slipped her arm through the bend of his elbow and noticed the lean, hard muscle. She wondered if there was more to George than he let on.

CHAPTER TWENTY-FOUR

APRIL 1813, YORK, UPPER CANADA

Private Silas Shackleton leaned toward the bonfire and flexed his fingers. The heat helped relieve the aching stiffness in his hands after a long, cold night. He stomped his feet on the slushy snow, hoping to warm his toes. His messmates, including Bosworth, huddled around the fire in front of the battery near Government House, the provincial governor's residence and headquarters. The morning was crisp, and the sky was pristine blue except for a column of smoke across town.

Silas watched the plume, which he knew to be from the smoldering ruins of the parliament buildings of Upper Canada. Silently, he cursed. Victory had turned into disaster and then embarrassment. Still, he figured that was better than the humiliating defeat suffered at Queenston Heights, as the battle of the previous fall was being called.

The thought of Queenston reminded him of their narrow escape across the Niagara with the aid of driftwood for buoyancy. Instead of the current sweeping them downstream, back eddies carried them upriver. With frantic effort he and Bosworth reached the main current of the river and shot downriver for miles. Then as they got closer to the American side, back eddies pulled them back upriver. By the time they had reached the American side, they were nearly crippled from the cold water. Local residents hurried them into a warm house and wrapped them in blankets. As their uniforms dried, a patrol of militiamen arrived to escort them back to Lewiston.

Silas had assumed they would be called out as cowards and charged with desertion. Instead, no one said a thing about the whole embarrassing affair. Silas and Bosworth were assigned to a reorganized company and marched to Sackets Harbor, on the eastern half of Lake Ontario. There they spent a long winter alternating between guard duty and work details that seemed primarily designed to keep them out of trouble.

When the ice on the lake finally thawed, they boarded ships and sailed northwest for York. They served under Major General Dearborn, but the general had been feeling sickly, so direct command fell to Brigadier General Zebulon Pike. The whole army seemed to take pride in serving with the man who had explored the Louisiana Purchase, traversing vast desert plains and following the Arkansas River to its source high in mountains to the west. Clearly Pike was an officer destined for greatness.

Naval ships brought them to the shore west of York. Shortly after they landed, they were attacked by a combination of natives and British soldiers, some in red and some in dark green. But the British forces were quickly driven back, especially by the navy guns just offshore. Under General Pike's direction, over the next several hours the Americans pushed the British forces back toward their fort on the shore just outside the city.

British regular forces withdrew from the fort and the town of York, apparently leaving local militiamen to negotiate their own terms of surrender. As the Americans approached the fort, the magazine inside erupted in a tremendous explosion, tossing stone and debris skyward. When the dust settled, over a hundred Americans lay dead or dying, including General Pike, whose chest had been crushed by a falling rock.

Over the coming days, abandoned houses were ransacked and robbed. A few nights later someone torched the parliament building. No one would officially take credit, but rumor had it that a rowdy bunch of sailors had set it afire after finding what they claimed was an American scalp on display inside the building.

Silas rubbed his hands in the warm glow of the fire outside Government House. They had won the battle to take York, only to lose one of their youngest and best generals. Then rabble within the American troops shamed them all by stealing from private citizens and destroying public property.

Silas imagined how he would feel if enemy soldiers occupied his hometown of New York City, ransacked homes, and then set buildings on fire. Just the thought of it deepened resolve to win a war.

And the situation kept getting worse. Silas felt like screaming and running away because of what they had just been ordered to do.

"Everybody take one," yelled their sergeant.

A line formed. Silas was handed a crude torch. Bosworth was just ahead of him. They returned to the fire and held the end of their torches in the flames.

When everyone's torch was lit, the sergeant yelled, "Let's get on with it."

The men scattered amid the government buildings. Silas followed Bosworth to Government House. With torches smoldering and sputtering, they rushed into a large office suitable for a provincial governor.

Bosworth walked to a window, checked the view, then touched the torch to the drapery. Flames raced up the cloth to the ceiling. Smoke began to fill the room. Silas dabbed the torch onto a pile of official papers. He and Bosworth hurried from one room to another, setting combustibles ablaze.

By the time the men reassembled at the gun battery, flames were already roaring through the roof. Other buildings in the complex around the fort were also ablaze, each sending a column of smoke racing skyward.

Bosworth tossed his burned-out torch onto the bonfire. "We better win this war quickly, boys."

"Why's that?" asked Silas.

Bosworth spat tobacco juice to the ground. "This kind of action invites retribution."

CHAPTER TWENTY-FIVE

MAY 1813, MAUMEE RIVER, OHIO TERRITORY

As the sun set over the forest, Hadjo shivered. He sat cross-legged and wondered what, if anything, he and the other warriors accompanying Tecumseh would get for an evening meal. Tecumseh lay under a tree nearby, apparently oblivious to hunger. But Hadjo knew that Tecumseh hadn't had a meal all day, either. As was his custom, he set an example for his men, ignoring personal discomfort, as one would ignore annoying mosquitoes.

Hadjo relaxed his shoulders, closed his eyes, and tried to think of something other than his aching muscles and the emptiness gnawing at his insides.

Soon he and the other Muscogee warriors would begin their long journey home. He longed to see Prancing Fawn again and to hold her. With his improved hunting skills and his experience as a warrior, surely her mother would approve him as a suitor. They would be wed shortly after he returned, and then they would have their own hut and begin a family together.

Tecumseh had promised to send the Muscogee warriors on their way south as soon as they killed or drove away the American invaders along the Maumee River. Over the last two weeks he and hundreds of other warriors had accompanied Tecumseh as the British, led by General Proctor, hauled field cannon up the Maumee River to the American Fort Meigs. The fort was a formidable structure set on a sixty-foot plateau on the southeast bank of the river. It enclosed nearly ten acres behind a combination of earthen berms and twelve-foot-high log palisades and included seven blockhouses and five raised batteries with cannon. Within the compound a mixture of militiamen and blue-coated regulars totaled well over a thousand.

Upon arrival Tecumseh's warriors quickly and quietly surrounded the enclosure to prevent anyone from getting in or out. While hundreds of hungry warriors scoured the woods for stray livestock, Indian snipers shot at any Americans who showed themselves over the stockade.

The British set up their cannon on a plateau across the river from the American fort. Shortly, British guns began pounding away at the twenty-foot-high berm forming the closest wall of the American fort.

Hadjo assumed the first cannon shots would quickly tear the fort apart so the warriors could storm inside and destroy the Americans. But the walls of the fort were built of a combination of earthen embankments and heavy logs, and the cannonballs did little damage. Now the siege of Fort Meigs had already dragged on for nearly a week.

Hadjo rubbed his temples and again tried to think of something besides his raging hunger. The events of the day set his mind reeling. Morning had started routinely with a handful of corn mush and some dried venison. Then disaster struck.

Seemingly out of nowhere, hundreds of Americans had floated down the river in flatboats without being seen by either the British or Tecumseh's warriors. The frontiersmen screamed like demons, stormed into the British camp, and spiked the cannon.

Hadjo realized now that if the Americans had then simply taken shelter in the fort, they would have won the day. The British would probably have withdrawn back to Lake Erie. Instead, the newly arrived Americans—euphoric after their quick victory—pursued the British into the woods.

Tecumseh and Wyandot Chief Roundhead, who had been on the east side of the river, hurried across to aid the British and to attack the frontiersmen. Over the next several hours, dozens of Americans were killed. Eventually the British and Indians overwhelmed them. So complete was their victory that the British took five hundred prisoners.

Tecumseh and Proctor were delighted. They planned to use the prisoners as bargaining chips to negotiate a surrender of the American fort. Meanwhile, the prisoners were being herded into the remains of old Fort Miamis on the northwest bank of the river, the ruins of a four-acre British stockade a mile downriver from the British gun emplacements.

As Hadjo tried to block out the gnawing emptiness of his stomach, sporadic noise echoed through the dimly lit woods around him. Warriors still excited from a day of battle whooped and howled in celebration before settling down for the night.

Then, through the trees came a sound that caused Hadjo to open his eyes and listen intensely. Scores of warriors screamed war cries, then hundreds more. Tecumseh sprang to his feet and ran in the direction of the noise. Hadjo and the other warriors serving as his personal guard raced to catch up with their leader.

Tecumseh elbowed his way through hundreds of howling natives while Hadjo and the others muscled in behind him like a wedge. Tecumseh stepped to the edge of a fire-lit clearing at the center of the crowd. A pathway lay across a wooden bridge spanning a ditch outside the old British stockade. Strewn across the ground lay a dozen bloody bodies, Americans. General Proctor and several of his officers sat to the left at the far end of the clearing.

An American frontiersman with shaggy blond hair was shoved into an open space in front of the British. The woodsman sprawled face-first, then struggled to get up. A warrior rushed forward and swung his tomahawk down into the American's shoulder. The man reeled and staggered, but several more red men lunged, pummeling the frontiersman with blow after blow as he tried to run the gauntlet into the old fort. The American fell for the last time, and a warrior hurried to claim the scalp.

A murmur rumbled through the crowd as Tecumseh stepped into the clearing. The warrior kneeling next to the recently fallen American leapt to his feet and screamed, a bloody shock of curly blond hair held high. Hundreds of warriors howled in celebration.

Tecumseh strode to the center of the clearing and paused. He raised his hand, and a hush fell over the crowd. He waited a moment before speaking. "The killing of prisoners will stop."

All around, angry voices protested.

Tecumseh raised his hand high again, and the crowd fell silent. "Mighty warriors, there is no bravery in killing captives. There is no honor in taking the scalps of helpless victims."

A handful of warriors edged closer and protested. Revenge was due, they argued, for their comrades who had fallen that day. How else might injury be discouraged but for the time-honored tradition of revenge?

Hadjo eased his hand to the tomahawk tucked beneath his waistband. He had pledged to defend Tecumseh with his life, if need be.

Tecumseh's icy voice cut through the night air. "Anyone who intends to defy my orders, step forward now. And I will put you to death myself."

Hadjo's grip on his tomahawk tightened. Tecumseh didn't make idle threats. He dispensed justice swiftly and surely. But even Tecumseh wouldn't last long if scores of warriors attacked him at one time.

Silence hung heavy. Tecumseh glared at the British officers seated across the clearing, then turned to the edge of the clearing, where more

Americans were being held. "Take those prisoners into the old fort and bother them no more."

CHAPTER TWENTY-SIX

MAY 1813, LAKE ONTARIO

Silas Shackleton sat in a wide, flat-bottomed bateau crowded with dozens of fully armed soldiers. His butt ached, and his bayonet sheath jabbed into his thigh. He tried to shift his position, but he was jammed shoulder to shoulder between Bosworth and Samuel, one of his messmates. The only sound was the creak of wood as the boat rose and fell in the early morning swells. Fog lay low over the water, limiting visibility to fifty yards. The air hung heavy with the faint smell of fish.

Barely visible ahead was the stern of a large, single-mast boat, its sails furled tight. With no wind, the sloop was being towed by its own gig manned by sailors pulling oars through the gray water. Silas's boat was second in a line of six bateaux tied behind the sloop.

He had lost his sense of direction in the mist, but he figured the shoreline was to their left as they headed west. Ahead, the sailboat dropped its anchor.

They had been in the boats since midnight, and Silas wondered how much longer they would have to wait until the action began. He suspected the eerie quiet would end all too soon, and he dreaded what that might bring.

As the bateau wallowed, Silas stared at the white epaulet on each of Bosworth's shoulders and his new red sash. Since Silas had been the only other in their mess group who could read and write, one of Bosworth's first acts as sergeant was to recommend Silas for promotion to corporal, signified by the white epaulet on his right shoulder.

At first Silas hated the idea, and so did his messmates. But Bosworth had explained that they could either accept Silas's new rank or Bosworth would have to find someone from another mess group to oversee them. Rather than have a stranger brought in, they all agreed to support Silas, and so far it had worked out well.

In the boat just ahead, an enlisted man sat head-and-shoulders above the others. Silas was reminded of another tall soldier, Colonel Winfield Scott. After surrendering at Queenston Heights, Scott had been sent to Montreal then released in a prisoner exchange. In May, after being promoted to full colonel, he arrived in the Buffalo area as adjutant general to Major General Dearborn. The commanding officer was so old, fat, and sickly he couldn't mount a horse. Instead, he used a buggy to move around. Behind his back the troops called him "Granny."

Dearborn gave young and energetic Colonel Scott wide latitude in running the Army of the North. Scott had become an ardent student of Napoleon Bonaparte's methods and used them to reorganize the army's staff and to train his troops. Then he set about planning the next campaign.

Commanding officers didn't share their battle plans with enlisted men, but rumors flourished. As best as Silas could piece together, once again the target would be the portage road along the river linking Lake Erie and Lake Ontario. The first prong of the two-part plan called for the capture of Fort Erie, where Lake Erie flowed into the Niagara River. The second prong targeted Fort George to the north, where the Niagara flowed into Lake Ontario. Fort Erie was only lightly defended, but Fort George was garrisoned with over a thousand British regulars plus whatever Canadian militia happened to be around.

Colonel Scott had earned a reputation as a careful planner, and Silas noticed the difference in preparation compared to earlier campaigns. Two days prior to the attack, the American batteries across the Niagara began bombarding Fort George with hot shot.

On the morning of the attack, the assault force had embarked on pre-assigned rowboats, barges, and larger naval vessels. The naval sailboats towed the soldiers westward past the mouth of the Niagara and then to designated positions marked by buoys offshore and west of the British fort. Silas could see one of the buoys bobbing lazily a few yards off the bow of the sloop ahead.

Action would begin soon, he was sure. He vowed he would do his duty, no matter what. His hand trembled slightly, so he tightened his grip around the stock of his musket. His jaw clenched as he recalled the humiliating defeat at Queenston Heights that previous fall. Despite himself, he felt his face burn with the shame of it.

His stomach turned to think that the coming battle could mirror the chaos of Queenston Heights, only a dozen miles farther south, or lead to another disaster, like losing General Pike at York. He gazed out into the fog. Somewhere out there was the flagship *Madison*, with both General Dearborn and Colonel Scott aboard. Silas felt confident that Colonel Scott could lead them to a victory. But General Dearborn was Scott's commanding officer, and who knew what difference that might mean before the day was over.

Silas felt a cool breeze rush across the gently bobbing bateau. As the fog cleared, over a dozen larger vessels came into view. In a display that gave him goose bumps, over a hundred bateaux and Durham boats spanned a two-mile-wide crescent off the shore to the south.

To the southeast across the river mouth rose the French-built, stone structure of Fort Niagara, currently occupied by the Americans. On a point west of the river mouth stood a small, stone lighthouse, and behind it sat the village of Newark. A mile south of the town, overlooking the western bank of the Niagara, spread the earth-and-timber fortification of Fort George.

The thunder of cannon boomed across the water as Fort Niagara fired on Fort George. The Americans had been pounding it with heated shot for two days, and smoke drifted from its palisade and bastions.

Men cheered from the boat ahead of them. A bateau was being rowed briskly from the largest vessel of the flotilla, the *Madison*. A tall officer sat at the bow of the rowboat, and Silas recognized Colonel Scott. Something splashed ahead of Scott's boat, and water rose in a plume ten feet high.

Orange points of light flashed from the shoreline. Silas jumped as something splashed into the water to his right. Water cascaded over the side of the boat. Men cursed and squirmed as they were drenched. The boat rocked, and for a moment Silas feared they would capsize. A direct hit with a cannonball could shatter the bateau and send all of its heavily equipped passengers to the bottom of the lake.

With a deafening roar and billows of smoke, guns from the American vessels fired upon the batteries guarding the shoreline. The British returned a few shots, but the American naval gunners quickly pounded the shore batteries into silence.

Ensign Morgan, a fair-haired firebrand only a year older than Silas, was the only officer in their boat. During the night, Morgan had told them that they were in the advance guard of 800 who would lead the attack under the command of Colonel Scott.

Silas could see that the advance guard had been organized into three groups, and that their boat was in the middle. The boat carrying Colonel Scott rowed past.

"Here we go, men!" yelled Ensign Morgan. The towline on the bow of their boat was hauled in, and the rowers began pulling at the oars. They turned south, toward the shore west of the village and fort. The rowers leaned hard into the oars, and with a gentle breeze at their backs, the boat knifed through the calm water.

Silas flinched as a cannon boomed from the *Madison*. One after another the other vessels of the flotilla opened fire. Cannonballs whizzed overhead like a swarm of angry bees.

As they approached to within a hundred yards of the shoreline, Silas could see a brick farmhouse, and to its right the mouth of a creek. Small-arms fire crackled from atop the steep bank along the shoreline. Little spouts erupted in the water around the boats. Samuel slumped forward, blood gushing from the back of his head.

Silas ducked behind the men in front of him. Earlier, Ensign Morgan had announced that they were hand-picked men. Bosworth told Silas that they had probably been selected because of their combat experience. Silas wondered if desertion counted as combat experience or the arson they had committed at York. Or maybe somebody was out to get them killed.

The naval gunfire dwindled, then ceased. Colonel Scott's bateau was a boat-length ahead and reached the shore first. From the top of the steep bank came a roar of angry voices. Thirty men wearing dark-green uniforms with black trim and plumed shakos stood at the top of the bank and fired at the Americans.

Silas's boat scraped hard against sand and lurched to a stop. Ensign Morgan yelled, "Everybody out!"

Silas grabbed the gunwale to his side and climbed over. Water splashed to his knees, but he appreciated having solid ground underfoot again. The boat pulled away from the shore, hurrying back to bring troops from the sloop.

Ensign Morgan drew his sword and yelled, "Form a line on me!"

Naval guns opened fire on the green-clad men at the top of the bank, and they disappeared from view.

Morgan's men were quickly joined by dozens from other boats.

Colonel Scott approached Morgan. "Well done, ensign. Quickly now, get your men uphill."

Bosworth organized the men into a rough line. Ensign Morgan stepped to the front and faced the men, then brandished his sword high. "To the top!" He turned and ran up the bank.

Bosworth, Silas, and the rest of the men rushed after Morgan. A man next to Silas stumbled, and the tip of a bayonet flashed in front of Silas, narrowly missing his eye. Silas cursed and hurried to get ahead of the other men. At the crest stood an earthen bank several feet high. Silas shoved his musket in front of himself, then climbed with his elbows and knees.

On top of the ridge, Silas staggered to his feet. Before him to the south stretched a plain of fields. A quarter mile beyond rose a line of trees, probably growing from a ravine or creek. Out of the trees filed hundreds of soldiers, some in green and some in red. Three companies by Silas's estimation. With bayonets fixed, the British forces advanced toward the Americans.

Silas imagined getting stuck in the belly by one of the razor sharp bayonets. He aimed toward the British and pulled the trigger. Up and down the line, the Americans opened fire. As the green-clad British pressed forward, the Americans started falling back and hopping behind the ridge above the bank.

"Back! Back! Back!" yelled Ensign Morgan.

Silas turned and jumped back over the edge of the bank. All around him men were doing the same. Someone's bayonet sliced across Silas's sleeve, and he felt a sting as the tip etched across his upper arm.

Bosworth grabbed Silas by the arm and studied the wound. "It's just a scratch. No worries. Now, gather your messmates. Be ready to make another go of it." Bosworth grabbed the bill of Silas's shako and pulled his faced close. In an angry whisper, he said, "Next time, wait for orders before firing your weapon." He pushed Silas back, then gave him a wink.

The naval vessels had moved closer to shore, and now their gunfire resumed. Cannonballs whizzed overhead and pounded the British. Silas watched as scores of rowboats reached shore. Seven or eight hundred men piled out and hurried up the bank.

"Okay, men," yelled Ensign Morgan. "Over the top we go. Now! Now! Now!"

Silas and his messmates crawled over the ridge and fell into line facing the British, now just a hundred yards away. From the smoldering fort a mile to the east had flowed a stream of redcoats, now joining the green-uniformed troops, doubling their force. The British advanced silently, bayonets pointed forward.

Ensign Morgan stepped to the end of their line. "Ready," he screamed. "Aim!"

Silas felt his fingers tremble as he pointed the musket toward the British.

"Fire!"

Silas closed his eyes and squeezed the trigger. Sparks stung his cheeks. Muskets up and down the line discharged. He nearly choked at the acrid cloud of gray smoke.

Flaming bits of cartridge paper had scattered across the straw-colored grass in front of the line. Silas worried that the pasture might catch fire and engulf the battlefield, but each of the little fires smoldered for a moment and then died in the damp grass.

Before the Americans could reload, the British fired.

"Back! Back! Back!" yelled Ensign Morgan.

Silas ducked as something streaked overhead. A naval gun boomed from one of the vessels. Others quickly joined in hurling cannonballs at the British line.

A third wave of boats arrived. Silas figured the Americans now outnumbered the British by three to one and more men were still coming in.

Cannon had been unloaded from the boats. With no horses, the gun carriages were dragged up the bank by soldiers. The fieldpieces were quickly loaded and fired at the British.

"One more time, men," said Ensign Morgan. "This time we will defeat them!"

Colonel Scott stepped to front of the army, drew his sword, and pointed it to the sky. A hush fell over the men. Scott thrust the sword to the south and set off at a steady pace. Up and down the shoreline, columns hurried to keep up with their commander.

Silas estimated that the American and British troops were only thirty yards apart, then twenty, then ten. Both sides halted, straightened their lines, then fired.

Ensign Morgan tumbled to the ground, the side of his head torn away, blood spurting and gushing.

"Fire at will!" someone screamed.

Hands trembling, Silas loaded and fired. As he loaded again, someone stepped close behind him, laid a musket across his shoulder, and fired.

With his ears numb and ringing, Silas forced himself to finish loading. Men from behind him shouldered him aside and stepped to the front of the line. The American line swelled with reinforcements, adding firepower to a line already shrouded with smoke and rumbling with a continuous roll of thunder. Gaps appeared in the British formation as some units retreated in order, while some broke and ran for the trees.

Colonel Scott followed the British until they disappeared into a tree-lined ravine, then he turned left and signaled his troops to follow him. A mile to the east across the plain stood Fort George, still smoldering from days of bombardment with red-hot cannonballs.

Bosworth fell in behind Scott as Silas and his messmates hustled to keep up. From the gates of the fort marched British troops heading south along the portage road toward Queenston Heights.

Huffing and puffing under the weight of his gear and musket, Silas strained to keep up with the long-legged colonel as he passed the village of Newark on the left. They were still several hundred yards from the fort as Silas eyed the twelve-foot high palisade and hoped the gates were open and the fort abandoned.

Colonel Scott approached Fort George's charred gate, and someone brought him a horse.

Silas paused, ready to run for cover, images fresh in his mind of the explosion that killed General Zebulon Pike at York that summer. But Colonel Scott mounted his horse and headed toward the fort's gate.

A thunderous blast rocked the earth. Smoke and debris shot skyward from Fort George. The earth seemed to leap up at Silas as he stumbled to the ground. Stone, timber, and dirt rained all around.

As the dust cleared, Silas could see Colonel Scott's new mount floundering on the ground. When the horse staggered back to its feet, Silas snatched the reins and tried to calm the horse.

A few feet away, the colonel struggled to stand. He cursed and clutched his shoulder. The colonel's face contorted with pain as he climbed back into the saddle. Scott accepted the reins from Silas. "Thank you, Corporal."

Scott's shoulder drooped as he shouted to the soldiers gathered around him. "If we don't defeat them today, we'll have to fight them again another day. Let's catch those redcoats, men, and teach them a lesson. Follow me!" Without another word, he reeled the horse and headed south.

Bosworth hurried after the colonel. Silas cursed, having hoped the fighting was over for the day. He followed the colonel, as did hundreds of others, including riflemen and dragoons. Scott was in the mood for a fight, and his enthusiasm spread to the men.

Silas imagined chasing the Brits until they either stood and fought or surrendered. As he marched south after Colonel Scott, he savored the thought of capturing the British army fleeing Fort George. It would be appropriate revenge for the humiliation of Queenston Heights.

A company of British infantry blocked the road ahead. Scott stopped and ordered his dragoons forward. At the sight of the American horsemen, the British withdrew.

A mile farther down the road, Silas heard the hooves of a galloping horse approach from behind. Brigadier General Boyd reined in next to Colonel Scott. "General Lewis sends his compliments, colonel. He asks that you cease annoying the enemy and return to the fort."

From the sagging look of disappointment on Scott's face, Silas could tell that the colonel thought the order represented another lost opportunity to deal the British a crippling blow.

Bosworth leaned close to Silas and cursed. "How do they expect us to win this war if the generals hold us back?"

CHAPTER TWENTY-SEVEN

JUNE 1813, H.M.S. BARROSSA,
HAMPTON ROADS, VIRGINIA

Lieutenant George Sherbourne shifted his weight with the gentle pitch and roll of the deck as he studied the forested shoreline to the south. He was in a borrowed uniform while in the presence of Admiral Cockburn, who was onboard observing an attack on the Americans. George wiped sweat from his eyes as the early afternoon sun beat down on him.

News had just arrived that His Majesty's frigate *Shannon* had engaged the American frigate *Chesapeake* off Boston. In a mere fifteen minutes, the *Shannon* crippled the *Chesapeake* and captured her. That should cause the Americans to think twice before taking on the British navy, thought George. He hoped the news boded well for the operation about to begin. Unfortunately, not all the recent news had been so favorable to His Majesty's forces.

Fifty feet from the ship, a seagull plunged into the water, then emerged with something in its beak. George studied the water for a moment, trying to imagine a submerged boat sneaking its way toward the *Barrossa* to plant explosives that would blast the vessel to pieces, killing all on board.

He still found it amazing that Robert Fulton had managed to build such a boat, called the *Nautilus*, many years earlier in France. George had found no evidence that Fulton was constructing another such vessel in America. Instead, Fulton had focused on torpedoes.

Through the first months of the war, with the successes of the American navy and the privateers, Fulton's weapons had drawn little attention, and the inventor seemed to be content overseeing his steamboats. The extension of the British blockade of American ports had spurred new interest in Fulton's weapons as a means of breaking the stranglehold on the American economy. At Fulton's request, the American congress passed a law commonly known as the Torpedo Act. It authorized the use of Fulton's explosive devices against British warships and granted officers and crews deploying the devices the same immunity and prize money as privateers.

Apparently Fulton had wasted no time in training crews to use the torpedoes. Attacks had already been reported against the *Poicteirs* on the Delaware and against vessels off Baltimore. Most recently on a dark, rainy night on Lynnhaven Bay, the ship-of-the-line *Plantagenet* experienced a near miss.

According to the report George read in the *Niles Weekly Reporter*, the explosion caused a concussion resembling that of an earthquake and a sound louder than the heaviest thunder. A pyramid of water fifty feet in circumference was thrown up forty feet. It appeared vivid red, with tinges of purple on the sides. Upon ascending to its greatest height, it burst from the top in a tremendous explosion and fell in torrents on the deck of the ship, which rolled into the yawning chasm and nearly capsized.

A furious admiral Cockburn said, "The American government seems intent on thus disposing of us by a wholesale six hundred at a time."

Since then, the *Plantagenet* had taken new measures for protection, surrounding itself with a seventy-four-gun ship, two frigates, and three tenders. George had already noted the presence of extra watchmen on deck and in the rigging of the *Barrossa,* even though the torpedo attacks so far had been attempted only at night.

British naval officers damned the use of submersible vessels and submarine explosives as a barbaric, cowardly tactic unseemly in modern warfare. But, George noted, British use of their own advanced weapons, fragmenting spherical cannonballs designed by General Henry Shrapnel and the Congreve rockets, were perfectly acceptable forms of weaponry.

George's attention returned to the British troops and sailors working their way into position. Today their job would be to unnerve the enemy and provide a smokescreen as a force of over two thousand British soldiers forded the shallows to attack Craney Island from the south. Once again he felt irked to be missing the action, not only here but also in Europe and in the Canadas.

The war could be over at any time. Just recently, Admiral Warren had received a letter from Andre de Dashkoff, the Russian minister in Washington City, offering to act on behalf of the tsar to mediate peace negotiations. Apparently without waiting for a reply from the British, President Madison had sent a delegation to St. Petersburg to negotiate a peace.

The end of the war would likely also end any opportunity for George to distinguish himself in combat, but it might also mean he could return to York, where he hoped to persuade Major Morrison to let him marry Anne.

George accepted a telescope from one of the ship's junior officers, then trained the glass on Craney Island, a mile-wide, flat patch of mud at the mouth of the Elizabeth River. He could see partially completed fortifications and the Americans manning them.

Upriver to the southeast of the island, lay the towns of Norfolk and Portsmouth. Somewhere up the river was the American frigate *Constellation.* With a flotilla of His Majesty's ships guarding Hampton Roads, the frigate had little chance of escape, but to capture the *Constellation,* Crown forces would first have to overcome the Americans holding the fortified island.

"Now, Lieutenant," said a major standing next to George, "you shall see the result of superior planning and execution."

The major spoke as if only British forces were capable of executing military action. Of course, as they had all recently been made aware, American forces were also able to deliver a blow. George cursed under his breath at recent reports. In April, American forces had sailed across Lake Ontario and captured George's hometown of York. Having the Americans capture the provincial capital of Upper Canada was bad enough, but the scoundrels had actually torched the provincial parliament building and the governor's official residence.

The attack had been led by Brigadier General Zebulon Pike. George felt some conciliation when he heard that, shortly after the Americans had arrived, a gunpowder magazine in the fort at York had exploded, crushing the general under rocky debris. With Brock killed at Queenston Heights, each side had now lost its most promising young general. Still, George seethed at the attack on York, vowing revenge. He could only hope that his family and Anne were not harmed.

The month before, word arrived that the Americans had occupied the city of Mobile. The Yanks contended that Mobile had been part of the territory sold to the States by Napoleon Bonaparte as part of the Louisiana Purchase. The Spanish, however, considered Mobile part of western Florida and had no intention of giving it up. In April, American General Wilkinson marched a small army eastward from New Orleans. They thanked the Spanish for protecting the city and informed them that their garrison duty at Mobile was over. The Spanish troops, greatly outnumbered, had little choice but to turn the city over to the Americans. To George it was just another example of the audacity of the land-grabbing Yanks. Unfortunately the Americans would probably get away with it.

George moved the telescope slightly to his right and scanned the forest of the mainland. From the shoreline, a Congreve rocket shot skyward with a streak of smoke. It was immediately followed by scores more in a spectacular display of rocketry. Their sizzle and pop drifted across the waters of Hampton Roads.

The rockets usually did little real damage, but they were effective as a distraction. Cannon rumbled from the island as the Americans unleashed a barrage of artillery fire. A cloud of gray-white smoke quickly shrouded the island. George imagined lethal blasts of grape and canister ripping through the British troops across the water from the island.

Meanwhile a separate force of sailors and marines in fifty barges made its way toward the northeastern face of the island for an amphibious assault. Dozens of boats, oars pulling in unison, closed on the island. More cannon from the island fortifications boomed, sending billows of smoke toward the boats. Plumes of spray spouted skyward among the barges.

George cringed as one of the rowboats shattered in a shower of splinters, disgorging its crew and passengers into the water. Each boat held dozens of marines, each fully equipped for battle. In water over their heads, they had little chance to survive. As George gazed through the telescope, he was relieved to see the heads of men bobbing in the water. At least some of them could swim or had found a shallow bottom.

The barges scattered in disarray as the American guns sought them out with skilled marksmanship, picking off one boat after another. Several of the barges approached to within a hundred yards of the island. Marines began climbing over the side, where they spread out in the shallow water and waded toward shore. As one boat approached the island, Americans rushed out to capture it. The remaining barges, still laden with marines, began withdrawing from the island.

"By God," swore the officer next to George, "the Yanks are targeting our men in the water!"

George looked again but couldn't see any sign that was happening. It seemed unlikely, anyway. Why waste shots targeting men helplessly floundering when boatloads of men still posed a threat to the island?

George retrained the glass on the Virginia shoreline. Between wisps of smoke he could see the red uniforms of His Majesty's troops. His heart sank when he realized that they were trudging west—back to their boats. Apparently the American artillery or the depth of the water between the mainland and the island had thwarted them.

The American frigate *Constellation* was beyond British reach for the time being. George was still annoyed at being left onboard when there was action afoot, but part of him was also relieved not to be involved in an operation that had turned into a humiliating failure. The battle was probably insignificant in the overall strategy of the war, but George suspected the Americans would take their little victory to heart. They might even begin to think they could actually win the war—a false impression George was certain would only prolong the conflict until the inevitable outcome.

CHAPTER TWENTY-EIGHT

JULY 1813, MONTPELIER, ORANGE COUNTY, VIRGINIA

Rachel Thurston slipped out the front door of President Madison's brown-brick mansion and eased the door shut. Her head throbbed as she blinked in the bright afternoon sunlight. After a quick look to make sure she wasn't being watched, she hurried across the porch and down the steps. Gravel crunched under her shoes as she headed northeast along the driveway.

She left the drive and strode down a grass-covered slope to the temple, a dome-capped structure supported by white columns. Rachel raced up the steps to the wooden benches and wicker chairs set in the shade of the dome. She picked a seat facing northwest, toward the hazy vista of the Blue Ridge Mountains. As she leaned back in the chair, she massaged the sides of her head, kneading her fingers into her scalp.

For the last several weeks, she and her father had been on a summer tour through Virginia. He explained that if they were to beat their political foes, they must better understand them. They traveled from one plantation home to another throughout the state.

Rachel had been amazed at the hospitality they received. Upon arrival at each mansion, they were welcomed as if they were long-lost relatives and provided meals and lodging for as long as they cared to stay. Travelers of all sorts, even peddlers, stopped at the plantation homes and received food and accommodations. Dignitaries, family, and close friends were provided rooms within the mansion, while other travelers were offered a place to camp in the shade of sprawling trees.

The Madisons had extended an open invitation to them, so Montpelier, home of James and Dolley, was included in the tour. Rachel wondered if such a visit would be awkward. But her concerns about dropping in on the Madisons evaporated immediately when Dolley greeted them all at her front door. Although James Madison had been ill and Dolley spent much of her time with him, she made her guests feel welcome. Rachel and her father were each provided a room upstairs.

The coming and going of guests left Rachel's head spinning. She tried to imagine the expense the Madisons and the other plantation owners bore for providing such hospitality. But their hosts seemed to genuinely appreciate the company, and, of course, the guests brought a priceless commodity to rural homes—news from the outside world. Rachel's head throbbed when she thought about the most-recent developments.

During the midday meal the newest visitor, a peddler of buttons and sewing supplies, brought shocking word of the latest British raid on Chesapeake Bay. Three days after their humiliating failure to take Craney Island, Crown forces returned to the James River and attacked the village of Hampton. As expected, they confiscated or destroyed public property and requisitioned foodstuffs, but then the troops went berserk. They stole private property and torched houses. They murdered unarmed men. They raped and killed women—some by black troops, former slaves recruited into the British army.

Rachel prayed the stories weren't true. Even if the accounts were exaggerated, the implications were huge. If Crown forces committed atrocities against American civilians, there would be little chance for an agreement to end the war. And news of the raid might very well accomplish what James Madison and the War Hawks had been unable to do—rally American citizens to resist British forces more aggressively.

The raid on a tiny village would have had little strategic significance, but if the attacks rallied the citizens to higher levels of patriotic fervor, the Crown would have a harder time suppressing the States.

On the other hand, there could be a silver lining in the darkest of clouds. Maybe the Americans would be so terrified and demoralized that they would readily agree to cease hostilities. Maybe the war would end quickly. Maybe the Federalists would be in a stronger position to shape the nation's future or break away to form their own nation.

Rachel leaned back and rubbed the sides of her head. She needed to think about something else. She gazed at the mountains in the distance and sighed.

The war was dragging on and on. Her father worried that would not bode well for their cause. The month before, the British blockade of the coast had been extended. Now His Majesty's warships patrolled from Long Island all the way down to the Mississippi River. New England had been excluded, presumably with the hopes of encouraging the growing peace movement in that part of the country and, of course, to preserve the ongoing trade between New England and the British forces battling Napoleon in Portugal.

With the end of winter storms in the Atlantic, the British navy had begun raids on American communities along the coast, possibly as a diversion to draw American troops away from Canada.

News of the war in the rest of country had been spotty. British General Proctor and Indians under Tecumseh were reported to have General William Henry Harrison under siege at Fort Meigs in Ohio. The American army had captured Fort George at the mouth of the Niagara River.

In June, HMS *Shannon* engaged the American frigate *Chesapeake* off Boston. The American captain, James Lawrence, had been mortally wounded. Although his crew promptly surrendered the sinking ship, Lawrence's dying words had become a rallying cry for the navy—"Don't give up the ship!"

An American named Joshua Hailey living in Paris had purchased a vessel and renamed it the *True Blood Yankee*. Then operating as a privateer based out of France, he had cruised for over a month off Ireland and Scotland, taking more than a score of vessels as prizes. He raided a town in Scotland and burned the vessels in the harbor. He even captured an island off Ireland and held it for six days as he made repairs. Rachel worried that such brazen acts would lead to reprisals against innocent American civilians.

A crow glided over the temple and landed on the roof of the mansion. *Montpelier*. A French name for a house filled with French furniture, thought Rachel. The Madisons really were *Frenchified*, the label her father used as he would a curse word. According to him, the Democratic-Republicans worshipped all things French, as compatriots in the republican form of government.

She tried to think of something besides war and politics and began to wonder what George Sherbourne had been doing recently. She hadn't seen him since leaving Washington for the summer and found herself longing for his company.

Her attention had drifted across the wide lawn to one of the horse paddocks, where a stallion had climbed atop a mare. When Rachel realized what the horses were doing, she felt her face grow hot. She hoped no one had seen her staring.

A slave walked past the temple. The young man had a light complexion, "yellow-skinned," as some would say. Rachel wondered who had fathered the slave. She glanced back at the horses and tried to imagine James Madison coupling with a slave girl. That seemed so unlikely, but then again, as a younger, unattached man. . . . Rachel shuddered and tried not think about it.

Another slave, a gardener wearing a floppy hat, walked past the temple. The Madisons, Rachel realized, were such hypocrites. On one hand they professed to champion the equality of men, yet they could afford their mansion and their hospitality only through the wealth created by slave labor.

Rachel tried to imagine black people living peacefully in their native Africa. After being kidnapped by slavers, they had to endure a long, perilous voyage across the Atlantic. Then they would have been sold to plantation owners. Their children born into slavery. Family members separated from each other and sold as livestock, never to see each other again. Some, no doubt, had been worked to death. Rachel seethed. But what could she could do about it?

CHAPTER TWENTY-NINE

AUGUST 1813, FORT MIMS,
MISSISSIPPI TERRITORY

Hadjo peeked through reeds toward an acre-sized stockade a hundred yards to the west, and almost laughed. After seeing the much larger forts of Detroit and Meigs, with their sturdy log walls and earthen embankments, this one hardly deserved to be called a fort.

Perched atop a slight rise east of the Alabama River, the walls appeared to consist of poles dug into the ground every few feet with logs stacked horizontally between them. To the south, across a potato field, stood a row of dilapidated shacks for slaves. Around the fort in all directions lay a mixture of reeds, low-lying brush, and trees.

Hadjo peered down the road for any sign of the scouting patrols that had almost discovered his war party just six miles away the previous day. Seeing none, he edged back into the ravine where scores of other Red Stick warriors hid, waiting for the signal to rush the fort's gate.

As the sun approached its zenith, Hadjo wiped away the sweat that dribbled down his forehead. Although he was eager for the attack to begin, he appreciated the chance to rest. He had traveled many weeks to get back to his Muscogee homeland after spending two years far to the north. Not long after the siege of Fort Meigs ended, Tecumseh urged his remaining Red Stick followers to return home and encourage the Muscogees to rise up and destroy the whites.

When Hadjo finally reached the village of his birth, he had been crushed to learn that Prancing Fawn had married that spring. When Hadjo protested that he had promised to return, Prancing Fawn's mother scoffed at him and reminded him they had waited two summers and two winters for him. Without word otherwise, they had presumed him dead.

Prancing Fawn had married Antler, a man from another village. Although Hadjo had met him only once, Antler looked soft. Hadjo was sure that Antler was no real warrior or hunter. Only Hadjo's sense of honor had prevented him from bashing the man's head immediately. Besides, Hadjo figured the blame for losing Prancing Fawn lay with the white men, for causing him to be away so long. Today he would make many of them pay with their lives.

The devastating news about Prancing Fawn was not Hadjo's only frustration upon returning home. The Muscogee nation had erupted in civil war. Roughly half the Muscogee people favored helping the Americans against the British, or some form of neutrality between the rival nations. The other half opted to drive the white men out of their tribal lands and, calling themselves the Red Sticks, they also fought with any Muscogees who opposed them. Hadjo had been delighted to learn that many young warriors from his clan had already joined the Red Sticks. He promptly sided with them.

Red Sticks had been part of a group that had traveled south to Pensacola to obtain guns and ammunition from the Spanish. Although the Spanish had provided them with only a few kegs of gunpowder and miscellaneous supplies, local frontiersmen heard of the trip and set out to stop the Indians on their return from Pensacola. Several hundred whites ambushed the Red Sticks as they crossed Burnt Corn Creek.

The whites captured the gunpowder, but while the frontiersmen divided the spoils of their victory, the Red Sticks regrouped and counterattacked. They recovered some of the gunpowder and drove the whites back. Many of the frontiersmen fled, but eighty stood their ground and continued to fight from the cover of the woods. After several hours the whites slipped away, some even leaving their horses behind.

The fight at Burnt Corn Creek showed the Red Sticks that they could stand up to the whites and whip them. Spurred by rumors that the frontiersmen had mutilated dead Muscogees at Burnt Corn and the shamans' assurances that the Red Sticks would be invulnerable to the white's weapons, they decided to attack. An attractive target was a trading post called Fort Mims, where a number of the white and mixed-blood men who had participated in the Burnt Corn incident had taken refuge.

Hadjo wiped the sweat from his eyes again and glanced toward the sun glaring through the branches overhead. The attack would begin soon, he was sure. To avoid being discovered for as long as possible, they had been ordered to avoid any war cries until they were inside the fort. A birdcall signaled their handpicked band to make themselves ready. Hadjo and fifty other warriors crawled to the edge of the ravine.

Even though Hadjo was straining to hear it, he jumped at the sound of the soldiers' drums signaling the noontime meal inside the fort. Several minutes passed as the chief allowed time for those in the fort to busy themselves with the meal.

The chief gave the signal, and black-and-red-painted warriors, decorated with feathers and carrying red war clubs, bolted from the brush on Hadjo's left and right. He raced to keep up with them.

A lone sentry in a dark-blue uniform stood at the stockade's east gate with his back turned to the approaching warriors. Hadjo was relieved to see that the fort's main gate was still wide open. Under cover of darkness that previous night, he had been part of a small group led by Chief Red Eagle to reconnoiter the fort up close. They had made two important discoveries.

First, the gun portals in the stockade walls were only waist high. Second, the main gate had apparently been left open for a long time, and sand had drifted against it, making it impossible to close quickly. Before withdrawing for the night, Hadjo and the others had quietly shoved more sand against the bottom of the gate.

Four of the shamans had volunteered to lead the charge into the fort. They were only thirty paces from the gate when the sentry turned toward them.

"Indians!" the soldier screamed as he raised his musket and fired.

"Indians!" he shrieked as he stumbled back through the gate.

Hadjo could hear a chorus of panicked screams rise up from inside the fort, but the noise of the settlers was promptly smothered by the war cries of over seven hundred warriors bolting from the reeds and woods in all directions and racing toward the stockade.

The shamans rushed a couple of blue-coated soldiers who had hurried outside to swing the gate shut. The holy men clubbed the soldiers to the ground. Then with a show of fearlessness, the shamans strutted through the gate.

As Hadjo crowded in behind the holy men, he took in the scene before him. The fort had apparently been extended a hundred feet on the east side, but the original wall was still in place. To the right inside the eastern expansion of the fort dozens of tents had been pitched in neat rows. Closer to the gate were more sturdy structures, probably for the officers. Dozens of bluecoats rushed for their weapons.

Muskets blasted, and three of the four shamans in front of Hadjo crumpled to the ground. Hadjo froze, as did the warriors around him.

A soldier wearing an officer's uniform drew his sword and rushed toward the gate. Hadjo raised his rifle and fired into the soldier's belly. The officer doubled over at the waist, but hobbled toward the gate. He shouted encouragement to his soldiers, but the warriors around Hadjo sprang to life, clubbing the wounded officer until he tottered to the ground.

Without time to reload, Hadjo slung his rifle over his shoulder and joined the warriors flooding through the gate. He swung his war club left and right into the soldiers. Caught off-guard and outnumbered, all the soldiers inside the eastern stockade lay dead within minutes.

Hadjo and scores of warriors headed for the gateless opening to the main enclosure. Hundreds of screaming men, women, and children rushed for cover.

At the center of the fort was a house partially surrounded by a small palisade. Several small cabins were scattered inside the fort, and at the southwest corner of the stockade stood a blockhouse still under construction.

Along the south wall, dozens of uniformed soldiers battled warriors who had charged the outside of the palisade and were now firing point-blank through the waist-high gun ports. The roar of musket fire smothered all other sound, and billows of gun smoke filled the air. As the soldiers attempted to defend themselves, the Red Sticks who had stormed the gate swarmed over them. Within minutes the inside of the fort was strewn with dead soldiers.

As more screaming warriors poured in through the gate, a raccoon-capped frontiersman rushed toward Hadjo with a hunting knife. He swung his war club and caught the bearded man on the forehead with a skull-cracking blow. Hadjo screamed his loudest as the man slumped to the ground.

The initial roar of gunfire from within the stockade ebbed to a crackle as defenders, with no time to reload, used bayonets or other weapons. All around Hadjo, warriors shot, clubbed, and stabbed the white men and their mixed-race allies. Individual defenders and small groups caught in the open were quickly killed.

As scores of settlers inside the buildings fired upon them, Red Sticks knelt to claim scalps from the corpses littering the compound. Other warriors hurried to grab plunder of all sorts, including black slaves, and hustle their booty out the gate.

Defenders were routed out of one cabin after another and from behind improvised barricades. By midafternoon the gunfire had dwindled to a sporadic crackle, and most of the Red Sticks had grabbed their plunder and drifted out of the fort. As Hadjo left the stockade, he could see that the price of their victory had been steep—hundreds of Red Stick corpses lay intermingled with the whites and the mixed-bloods.

Hadjo joined the others as they gathered at a cabin beyond rifle range outside the fort. He watched and listened as the chiefs discussed the next move. Many wanted to take their plunder and go home, but Chief Red Eagle argued that they needed a decisive victory over the whites. He reminded them that only a few pockets of resistance remained. The house at the center of the enclosure. A barricade and cabin at the west gate. A sturdy building at the north wall. The partially completed blockhouse held by a lone soldier at the southwest corner.

After a short discussion, the chiefs decided that Red Eagle would lead another attack. In short order, the Red Sticks reorganized and stormed the stockade. Proud to be following a bold and decisive leader, Hadjo followed Chief Red Eagle to the outside of the west wall. There they chopped through the timbers of a small gate. Once inside, they slaughtered the defenders.

Hadjo strode into the main enclosure, then ducked when a warrior next to him slumped to the ground with a musket ball through his chest. Gun smoke billowed out of the blockhouse on the southwest corner of the stockade. The lone defender continued his stand, firing his musket from the gun loops high on the overhanging structure. Several warriors squatted low against the wall, waiting for an opportunity—or building the nerve— to take a shot through one of the gun ports. Hadjo crouched low and ran toward the stronghold.

He crowded close to the square-cut log wall, careful to stay away from the gun ports. The holes were above Hadjo's head, too high for him to peek inside. The soldier's musket fired round after round, and Hadjo grudgingly admired the speed with which the man could reload.

Hadjo spotted an empty keg against the stockade and rolled it next to the blockhouse wall. He tipped the keg on end and climbed on top. Peering through the loophole, he could see that the inside of the blockhouse was well lit by the sunlight streaming through the partially completed roof. He hadn't heard the soldier fire his musket for several minutes and wondered if the man had finally run out of ammunition.

Hadjo raised his rifle, ready to shoot if the soldier stepped into his view. Still seeing nothing, Hadjo shifted his position on the keg. There, low against the wall on the far side, crouched the soldier, his eyes wide. Before Hadjo could raise his rifle for a shot, another gun roared. The soldier's head burst like a ripe melon, blood and gray matter spraying the blockhouse wall. A warrior shrieked in triumph.

Hadjo hopped down from the keg and studied the smoky scene around him. Fires had been set on the eastern edge of the stockade and were spreading quickly. From the house at the center of the compound, gunshots fired from the windows on the ground floor and from openings in the rooftop. Flaming arrows streaked to the house, and it quickly caught fire.

Hadjo was suddenly knocked to his back. One of the burning cabins had exploded into a fireball with a thunderous roar. As he struggled to his feet, he could see that splinters and debris had cut down dozens of Red Sticks closer to the blast.

Stunned, with his ears ringing, Hadjo screamed in rage. The settlers must have hidden their gunpowder magazine in the cabin, and it had gone undetected until the fire caught it.

To the north, a stocky black man with an axe rushed out of a cabin. Screaming Red Sticks charged him from every direction. The black man cut down several warriors before being hacked down himself.

A white man rushed from the house on the north palisade. Hadjo dashed after him, then swung his war club down into the man's neck. The man pitched to the ground and screamed as blood spurted from his mouth. Hadjo grabbed a handful of the man's hair and held it tight. He drew his knife and sliced into the man's scalp. With a powerful yank, he ripped the man's scalp from the skull. Hadjo let the man fall to the ground, then with his most ferocious war cry, held high the bloody patch of hair and skin.

A woman screamed as she raced from the big house engulfed in flames. Women and children, some with smoldering clothes, fled in all directions from the building. Many were immediately hacked down by the Red Sticks.

Gunfire popped from the windows of the ground floor and from holes torn in the roof. Hadjo raised his rifle to take a shot, but just then the roof collapsed, plunging through the house with a *whoosh* and roar of flames. Men, women, and children shrieked as they burned alive.

Chief Red Eagle strode among the warriors, praising them for their victory and encouraging them to take their captives and plunder and leave the fort. But women and children were still being dragged out of their hideouts and slaughtered.

"Hold your fire!" yelled Red Eagle. "You have won a decisive victory. Now is the time to show mercy. Take the women and children as slaves or as captives to be ransomed if you must."

Red Eagle's pleas reminded Hadjo of Tecumseh's admonition that there was no honor in killing helpless captives.

A dozen warriors screamed at Red Eagle and raised their war clubs. Fearing for Red Eagle's safety, Hadjo and several other warriors crowded around Red Eagle and escorted him outside the stockade.

The savagery that followed stunned Hadjo. One by one the whites and their Muscogee and mixed-blood allies were dragged out of the log building at the north wall and killed. Children were picked up by their feet, and their heads bashed against the stockade until blood and brains painted the walls. Women were stripped, mutilated, and scalped. Hadjo saw a screaming woman's swollen belly sliced open, and her child ripped from her womb, then hacked to pieces before her eyes.

One of the fiercest fighters of the day, a young warrior Hadjo recognized as Cowihta, herded a woman and seven girls to the side and threatened any Red Sticks who tried to take them from him. As Hadjo approached the young Red Stick, Cowihta eyed him warily.

"This woman took me in and cared for me when I was a child," said Cowihta. "She and her daughters are now my captives and under my protection."

Recalling the kind white woman of his own youth, Hadjo helped the young warrior fend off Red Sticks bent on killing all the whites. Together they escorted the woman and her brood through the smoke and out the stockade gate.

As they left the clearing around the fort, Hadjo glanced back. The entire fort now blazed, and the destruction would soon be complete. He estimated that nearly three hundred whites, mixed bloods, and Muscogees siding with the whites had taken refuge in the fort. He doubted that more than two or three dozen had escaped.

But the victory had not been cheap for the seven hundred and fifty warriors who had attacked the fort. Despite the shamans' promises of protection by the spirits, several hundred Red Sticks now lay dead.

CHAPTER THIRTY

SEPTEMBER 1813, LAKE ERIE

"Sail ho!"

Lemuel Wyckliffe woke with a start, tossed his blanket to the side, and grabbed his rifle. He searched the early morning light for a clue as to his location. The planks beneath him swayed gently. The crisp, fall air hung heavy with the smell of fish. He was on a ship—actually a brig, since it had only two masts. Even after a month on board, he still struggled with the nautical jargon. The *Lawrence* was moored in Put-in-Bay off South Bass Island.

The cry of "Sail ho!" had come from the masthead high overhead. Lemuel wondered how the lookout could see anything with barely a glow of light from the east.

"Where away?" yelled the young officer of the watch.

"Off Rattlesnake Island!"

The lieutenant hurried belowdecks. Lemuel squinted at the sail in the distance. It was probably the schooner stationed out in the lake to watch for the British.

All across the deck, men stirred from their sleep. Remembering his duty to guard the brig from a sneak attack by boarders, Lemuel turned to the bulwark behind him and eyed the waters aft of the vessel in the twilight.

Seeing nothing threatening, Lemuel relaxed his grip on the rifle. He snapped to attention as Commodore Oliver Hazard Perry appeared on the quarterdeck. Perry, his sideburns trimmed in the shape of mutton chops, finished buttoning his dark-blue uniform, then strode to the bulwark next to Lemuel and pointed a telescope toward the west. After a moment, the dark-haired, baby-faced commodore turned to the sailing master. "Signal all vessels to get under way."

Within seconds, signal flags were hoisted to the maintop, and crewmen scurried onto the deck and into the rigging. With a 150 men on board, many as inexperienced as Lemuel, it was organized chaos at best. Cutting through the commotion, the shrill whistle of the boatswain's mates signaled, "Up anchor."

As he had been trained, Lemuel stowed his rifle and helped turn the huge horizontal wheel called the *capstan*. He and dozens of others pushed hard at the spokes temporarily inserted into the capstan to winch up one of the anchor cables. Lemuel hoped the Americans would finally engage the British and get it over with, one way or the other. The outcome of the battle would likely determine which side controlled Lake Erie. And with the lake went the vast Canadian territory around it and to the west.

Lemuel couldn't help but think back a year before when General Hull had had an opportunity to seize Fort Malden and take undisputed control of Lake Erie. Now the States could lose the lake and much of the territory around it.

If anyone could do it, thought Lemuel, it would be Commodore Perry. He had already overcome incredible odds just to assemble his flotilla and sail it out into the lake. One of the experienced seamen had told Lemuel that as the son of a Rhode Island captain, Perry first went to sea at age eleven. He had served during the war against the Barbary pirates of North Africa.

Newly promoted and eager for glory but unable to obtain a captaincy at sea, the twenty-seven-year-old Perry had volunteered to serve on the Lakes. He was promptly given command of Lake Erie's naval operations and ordered to build a fleet capable of wresting control of the lake from the British as soon as possible.

Several merchant vessels had been converted into warships, and a few had been captured from the British. The rest had to be constructed from scratch. The challenges had been enormous. Except for a few scattered villages, Lake Erie was surrounded by wilderness, much of it swampland. The only resource available for shipbuilding was timber. Everything else—rope, metal works, sailcloth, and experienced shipbuilders—had to be brought in from farther east.

Only a handful of experienced seamen and marines had been provided by the War Department, and Perry hadn't had nearly enough to man his new squadron. He pleaded for help from militia commanders and scoured the countryside for recruits. The result was a motley crew of sailors, marines, freed slaves, boys, and militiamen.

Still short of men, Perry persuaded General William Henry Harrison to lend him some troops. Lemuel had recently been accepted into a company of mounted Kentucky riflemen, but with the outfit temporarily short of horses, he was assigned to Perry.

Since British ships controlled the lake, Perry's newest and biggest vessels, the *Lawrence* and the *Niagara*, had to be built upriver at Presque Isle, where they could be protected. They had been ready to be floated down into the lake at late summer, but the river level had dropped. They wouldn't clear the sandbar at the mouth of the river, so special devices, called *camels* had to be improvised to float the ships over the bar. All this had to be carefully guarded and timed to avoid attack by the British patrolling offshore.

Once the American fleet was assembled and became a potential threat, however, the British squadron avoided contact. They simply holed up at the naval yard at Amherstburg under the protection of Fort Malden at the mouth of the Detroit River.

Impatient and knowing the eyes of the nation were upon him, Perry twice cruised to Malden to taunt the enemy into coming out for a fight. They wouldn't take the bait, but with winter approaching and their supplies running low, the British had to be getting desperate.

As Lemuel pushed at the capstan, he noticed that the wood planking of the deck was already warping and cracking. Rushed and without cured wood available, the shipbuilders had used green timber. When they complained to Commodore Perry about not being given the time to build the brigs properly, he replied, "Plain work is all that is required. They will only be wanted for one battle. If we win, that is all that is wanted of them. If the enemy is victorious, the work is good enough to be captured."

The morning brightened quickly over Put-in-Bay as the American squadron of nine vessels got under way. At 480 tons each, the *Lawrence* and her sister, the *Niagara*, were four or five times as big as the other vessels. As they cleared the bay to the north of South Bass Island, Lemuel looked northwest past Rattlesnake Island and could see the British squadron against blue sky on the horizon.

The wind blew from the southwest, and Lemuel realized that meant trouble. The *Lawrence* and the *Niagara* were square rigged—with sails mounted perpendicular to the keel of the ship. They sailed most efficiently with the wind at their back. Sailing to windward meant they would have to travel a considerable distance one way, then turn and sail back, hoping to claw out a little forward progress with each tack. Lemuel had come to admire Perry's skill and was confident that if there was a way, the commodore would find it.

"Man the braces!" ordered a petty officer.

Lemuel and the other crewmen hurried to their preassigned positions and hauled at the hemp lines that repositioned the sails. On the crowded closeness of the deck, sweaty men stumbled about, tripping and falling with each maneuver.

Before long, Lemuel's hands blistered from heaving at the rope. Blisters broke, and skin scraped away. As they worked the lines to keep the sails taut, sweat and hemp fibers ground into raw and bloody sores. Hour after hour they tacked back and forth between Rattlesnake Island and South Bass Island, trying to make headway toward the enemy sails in the distance.

Nearly exhausted and hands stinging, Lemuel could see that they weren't making much progress. Each leg of the tack cut a slice closer to the British, but the breeze blew them back almost as far as they had come.

The smaller vessels, the double-mast schooners and the single-mast sloops, with their triangular sails rigged nearly parallel to the keel of the ship, were faring much better. They could sail right to the edge of the wind and easily advanced, but then they had to wait for the square-rigged *Lawrence* and *Niagara*.

At midmorning, after three hours of tacking back and forth, Commodore Perry turned to the sailing master. Instead of the quiet but firm voice he normally used when addressing his officers, Perry shouted loud enough for all to hear. "Enough of this. Turn the ship into the wind."

"B-but, sir," said the sailing master, "the enemy has the wind advantage."

"I don't care!" shouted Perry. "To windward or to leeward, they shall fight today."

The sailing master hesitated, then barked out a string of orders that sent the crew scrambling to lower and man the ship's boats. Lemuel choked back a groan as he thought of pulling at one of the oars to tow the ship against the wind.

Before the sails could be furled, however, the wind died. For a moment everyone stood silent as sails hung limp overhead and the ship bobbed in the calm. From the southeast a fresh gust of wind rushed across the deck. Sails filled and snapped tight. The ship tipped slightly and shot forward. The crew cheered, and for a moment with the wind at its back, the brig advanced rapidly toward the enemy vessels still far ahead. Then the wind dwindled to a gentle breeze that barely pushed them forward. They would need the boats, after all, if they were to make speed.

"Sir," said a lieutenant with a telescope, "the Brits are wearing ship!"

Even though the British were still seven or eight miles away, Lemuel could see that the cluster of sails had turned to a westerly course. Perry pointed his own telescope toward the enemy. "They're going to wait for us, gentlemen." Perry turned back to his officers. "Let's not disappoint them. Man the boats. Clear for action!"

Lemuel grabbed his rifle and hurried to the left side, or *larboard*, bulwark of the quarterdeck as the rest of the crew hurried across the deck and into the rigging. The crews removed the wooden tampion from gun muzzles and stacked cannonballs, grapeshot, and canister onto racks. Boys, called *powder monkeys*, hurried below to the magazine and returned with cylindrical leather pouches filled with prepared cartridges. Buckets of water and racks of cutlasses, pikes, and boarding axes were stacked nearby. A slow match was lit and carefully laid in a tub of sand.

The marine lieutenant in charge of the riflemen strode past his men lined up on deck. He stopped to make sure Lemuel's flint was securely fixed on his rifle lock and that he had plenty of cartridges. Some marines and soldiers slung their firearms across their back and climbed into the rigging while others were stationed in short rows on deck.

Loose gear everywhere was either fastened down or stowed. In less than fifteen minutes the brig was ready for battle. The commotion subsided, and after an hour, they were less than a mile from the British.

Two of the American schooners were sailing at the head of the American line to prevent the British ships from cutting in front of the *Lawrence*. At first Lemuel was pleased to see that the British had only six vessels versus the American's nine. Then he realized all six of the enemy vessels were together, while several of Perry's still lagged a couple of miles behind.

With the shift in wind, the commodore now had the weather advantage, the *weather gage*, as the seamen called it, and he could dictate at which distance the battle would be fought. Unfortunately, the breeze was light. Time would drag on as the Americans closed with the British vessels. Lemuel knew that was a problem.

The *Lawrence* and the *Niagara* each sported eighteen thirty-two-pound carronades. Named after the Scottish town where they were originally cast, these stout guns were capable of inflicting incredible damage at ranges of under a quarter mile. British vessels, on the other hand, were equipped with twenty-four-pound long guns with a range of up to a mile. As Perry approached the British, he would be within range of the enemy's long guns but would be unable to fight back with his own carronades.

As the *Lawrence* crept toward the British, Perry climbed onto a carronade carriage midship on the larboard side. He unfolded a dark-blue banner. "Lads, this flag contains the last words of the brave Captain Lawrence." After a moment, Perry shouted, "Shall I hoist it?"

The response from the crew was immediate and enthusiastic. A tingle ran the length of Lemuel's spine as he recalled that those were the words of Captain James Lawrence for whom Perry had named his flagship.

The crew cheered as the banner streaked up a line to the top of the mast where it snapped in the breeze. On the banner, in rather crude white letters, was written, "Don't Give Up the Ship."

"My good fellows," yelled Perry, "it is not to be hauled down again!"

Lemuel's chest swelled with crisp morning air, and all across the deck, he heard chatter of excitement and approval. Then he recalled that the passionate words on Perry's banner were actually the dying declaration of a captain shortly before his sinking ship was surrendered to the British navy.

As they inched toward the enemy, Lemuel wondered how this battle would compare to the ones he had fought at Tippecanoe, Detroit, and Frenchtown. During their training over the last several weeks, the handful of experienced seamen in the crew had assured the new recruits that nothing was quite as horrible as a battle at sea.

The commodore ordered an early lunch and a ration of grog so the men wouldn't have to fight on an empty stomach. Then he strolled the deck inspecting each gun battery. "Well, boys, are you ready?"

"All ready, sir!"

As Lemuel nibbled at a bowl of peas and sipped on the watered-down whiskey, one of the seamen walked by with a bucket of sand, which he scattered across the deck. Lemuel wondered if the man would be punished for soiling the frequently scrubbed planks, then noticed that several other men were doing the same thing. When Lemuel realized the purpose of the grit, his insides twisted tight. The sand would help prevent the deck from becoming slippery when it ran with blood. He glanced at the peas still in his bowl, then dumped them into the pen housing the last of the ship's hogs.

As the hog smacked up the peas and squealed with pleasure, Lemuel downed his grog and tried to think of something else. He turned to the bulwark and studied the vessels behind the *Lawrence*. Two of the smallest were still a couple of miles behind. In the light breeze, on a windward course, the square-riggers sailed faster, while the schooners and sloops lagged. Even with rowboats clawing them forward, Lemuel couldn't see how they could possibly catch up before the *Lawrence* reached the British.

A militiaman scurried down from the rigging, stumbled to the bulwark, and puked over the side. Being up in the rigging was like perching atop a tall tree—a tree that bobbed and swayed on the lake. Lemuel had been seasick the first few times he had been stationed aloft. The marine corporal standing across the quarterdeck from Lemuel pointed at him, then up at the rigging.

Lemuel slung his rifle over his shoulder and began climbing a web-shaped rope ladder attached to the aft-most of the two towering masts. Near the top he tied one end of a line around his waist and the other to a stout timber the sailors called a *yard*.

As the mast swayed back and forth and side to side, Lemuel settled in for what could be a long wait. Except for the small, v-shaped wakes behind the vessels, the lake was calm and nearly as blue as the sky. From his perch he could see several tree-covered islands and the dark shoreline on the horizon. Other than the cry of a few gulls and occasional instructions shouted by the petty officers to adjust the sails, time passed silently.

The sun was high overhead when Lemuel heard something from across the water. A bugle, probably from the largest of the enemy vessels. That would be the newly constructed *Detroit*, named after the British capture of the American fort. She was square-rigged with three masts, classifying her as a *ship* in sailor's jargon. The *Detroit* seemed to be about the same size as the *Lawrence* and the *Niagara*, but she was twice as big as the second largest British vessel. The other four enemy vessels, including two brigs, were considerably smaller.

From across the water came the sound of a band playing. Lemuel strained to listen and recognized the tune as "Rule Britannia."

An orange flash from the deck of the *Detroit* was followed by a billow of gray-white smoke and the rumble of cannon. The calm surface of the lake near the *Lawrence* suddenly erupted into a ten-foot waterspout.

Lemuel shifted his position and propped his rifle across a sturdy yard. Even though he was still well out of range, he aimed toward the *Detroit*. As did the *Lawrence*, the British ship flew numerous flags used to communicate with the other ships in the squadron.

Another blast of smoke billowed from the British ship. Before Lemuel could brace himself for what might come next, there was a heavy crash, and splinters flew in all directions. The mast and rigging below him shuddered. Lemuel tightened his grip on the rigging. A gaping hole had been ripped in the starboard bulwark and several seamen lay sprawled across the blood-splattered deck.

A deafening boom rumbled from the foredeck as the *Lawrence* fired her bow-mounted twelve-pounder toward the *Detroit*. Cannon thundered in the distance as the British ships unleashed more of their long guns. The two American schooners ahead of the *Lawrence* opened fire with their bow-mounted guns.

Perry had been approaching at a slight angle to the British as they sailed northwest, but now he turned the *Lawrence* straight toward the *Detroit*. Lemuel understood that Perry was trying to get his carronades within range as quickly as possible, but the head-on angle exposed the ship to *raking* fire—where a well-aimed cannonball could sweep the entire length of the deck, tearing a path of destruction through men and equipment. One unlucky shot could dismast the *Lawrence* and put her out of action.

The *Lawrence* suddenly turned, exposing the starboard side to the British guns. As limp sails fluttered, every gun on the starboard fired in unison. The crew cheered the broadside even though the shot fell well short of the British. The gun crews adjusted their aim and fired again, but once more the cannonballs fell short.

Sails snapped in the breeze and men manning long oars, called sweeps, clawed at the water until the brig bobbed around far enough to catch the wind again. As the Americans worked their way forward, the British long guns blasted away. Many of the shots made harmless waterspouts around the *Lawrence*, and Lemuel realized that the British crew must be as inexperienced as the Americans. Enough of the shots found the

Lawrence to batter her hull, sails, and rigging. The surgeon's helpers kept busy hauling men down to the infirmary.

Lemuel glanced back to the southeast. Several of the American vessels were still miles behind.

As the sun reached its zenith, the *Lawrence* drew to within a quarter mile of the British. Perry abandoned his head-on approach and set a course nearly parallel to the enemy's northwesterly heading. Now they would find out if Perry's long-range target practice had paid off.

"Take good aim, my boys!" he yelled to the starboard gun crews. "Don't waste your shot." He paused. "Stand by." The crew was silent. "Fire!"

A shockwave of air slammed into Lemuel. The brig shuddered and rolled to the larboard as the carronades roared in unison. Six-inch-in-diameter, thirty-two-pound shot ripped into the *Detroit*. Timber flew in all directions. The rear-most of her three masts shuttered, then tipped to the side, dragging sails and rigging with it.

Lemuel cheered with the rest of the crew as the carronade crews reloaded.

The *Detroit* fired back, and to Lemuel the two vessels seemed evenly matched. He assumed the American *Niagara*, with its twenty guns, was rapidly approaching to take on the other British ship, but when he glanced back he saw that she languished just out of carronade range. She fired a couple of her long guns but didn't come any closer. Four of the smaller American vessels were still over a mile behind.

The *Lawrence* drew closer to the British vessels. Near the rear of the *Detroit*, Lemuel could see a man in a dark uniform, an officer, maybe even the captain. Lemuel recalled rumors that the British commander had bragged that he lost one arm fighting Napoleon and that he would beat the Yankees on Lake Erie or sacrifice his other arm in the attempt.

Lemuel aimed his rifle toward the officer. On land it would have been an easy shot. Here, he had to contend with not only the pitch and roll of the ship under him but also the movement of the enemy ship. Lemuel aimed carefully and squeezed the trigger. The rifle bucked in his hands, but the sound was drowned by the roar of the cannon below him. A rising cloud of smoke billowed up around each vessel, and Lemuel couldn't see if he had hit his target.

As he reloaded, he felt the brig shudder through the mast and spar each time a British shot found its mark. He tried to ignore the chaos below him.

A gust of wind swept some of the smoke away, and Lemuel aimed at a man dressed in buckskin high in the rigging of the British ship. Lemuel fired and missed. He wondered how to allow for the simultaneous motion of the two vessels. He aimed again, feeling the movement beneath him, watching the *Detroit* rise and fall on the gentle swells of the lake. With more of a feeling than any calculation, he squeezed the trigger. This time the man in the rigging jerked, then fell and dangled from a line about his waist.

The second-largest British ship drew closer to the *Detroit* and began firing at the *Lawrence*. Lemuel could see that the *Niagara* still languished just out of carronade range, and he wondered why she didn't close with the enemy as had Perry.

The rigging beneath Lemuel jerked tight. The stout wooden spar under him cracked and broke nearly in half. Something fell from above and knocked the rifle from his hands. He grabbed hold of the nearest line as the mast shuddered and groaned, then tipped. Everything around him—sails, lines, and timber—fell. His stomach seemed to rise into his throat as he plunged downward in a blur. He had just enough time to wonder if the fall would kill him, when he crashed into a tangled heap of sails and rigging.

As the starboard carronades continued to roar, men hacked and cut at the lines and dragged the debris to the larboard, where it was tossed over the side. The planking was littered with rigging and body parts. Blood ran everywhere.

As Lemuel staggered to his feet, a seaman next to him scooped up a tangled mess of rigging and started dragging it away. Something whizzed past Lemuel with a *whoosh*, and the sailor's head vanished. The headless body wobbled for a moment, a fountain of blood gushing from the neck. Then the corpse collapsed to the deck.

From the corner of his eye, Lemuel saw something swinging toward him. His mind erupted in a flash of brightness. Darkness engulfed him.

With a throbbing headache, Lemuel woke to the sound of moans and screams. By the light of flickering lanterns, he could see that the brig's hold was crowded with wounded. The stench of gun smoke blended with a hellish mixture of blood, vomit, and urine. Bulkheads jarred with each blast of the cannon above. The compartment bobbed and weaved as the brig pitched and rolled in battle-churned waters. Unable to control himself, Lemuel bent at the waist and threw up on the wooden deck. His vomit splashed himself and others lying next to him.

He touched the throbbing, sticky welt on the side of his head, then quickly checked himself over. The knot on his head seemed to be his only injury.

The ship's surgeon had a table set in a shaft of light beaming from a skylight on the main deck. At the edge of the sunlight was a bench arrayed with blood-smeared forceps, probes, knives, and saws. A brazier, nestled in a tub of sand, sprouted red-hot irons. As the doctor chewed on a cigar, he finished bandaging a black seaman's arm, and then helped him off the table.

Three of the surgeon's helpers carried another patient down the ladder and into the room. Lemuel recognized the lieutenant in command of the marines. Two of the helpers carried the marine by his arms while the third lifted him by a leg. Even across the room, Lemuel could see that lieutenant's leg and half of his pelvis had been blown away. The doctor cut away some of the man's uniform and studied the wound, then said something softly to the lieutenant.

As the marine was being lifted off the table, he screamed, "For God's sakes, Doctor, if you can't do anything for me, at least put me out of my misery!"

The doctor turned away to examine another patient as the marine was set down next to Lemuel. The man gasped and choked back a scream as a puddle of blood spread across the deck around him. Not knowing what else to do, Lemuel picked up the man's hand and held it. With a grateful glance, the marine grit his teeth and moaned.

After half an hour of what must have been terrible pain, Lemuel felt the lieutenant's hand go limp, then turn cold. Lemuel placed both the lieutenant's hands across his lifeless chest. With a blank expression, the marine seemed to stare at the ceiling. Lemuel reached over and gently closed the man's eyes.

Despite the horror around him, Lemuel took comfort in the solid bulkheads providing a shelter from the battle above. He watched as the doctor tended one patient after another.

Suddenly the bulkhead to Lemuel's side burst into a shower of splinters. When the dust cleared, a jagged hole in the far bulkhead glowed with sunlight. All that remained of the doctor's current patient was a bloody mass on the floor. Lemuel realized for the first time that the surgeon's little hospital was above the waterline. Another cannonball could blast through at any moment.

The doctor's cigar wavered between his lips for a moment as his helpers dragged the remains of the patient away.

For the next hour, as the battle raged outside, Lemuel watched a steady stream of sailors being helped into the infirmary. The doctor stopped wounds from bleeding and applied bandages and splints. The room became so hopelessly crowded, Lemuel wondered how there could possibly be anyone left on the main deck.

The doctor's current patient was a blue-eyed boy of about sixteen with curly blond hair. His right leg was a shattered-and-torn mess below the knee all the way down to where the foot had been.

"Doctor Parson!"

At first the doctor didn't seem to hear.

"Doctor Parson!"

The doctor seemed annoyed, then looked up into the skylight.

With a surprised expression, the doctor plucked the cigar from his mouth and said, "Yes, Commodore?"

"Would you be so kind as to send one of your helpers up to serve the cannon?"

The weary doctor glanced around the dimly lit room then back to the open hatch before replying, "Certainly, sir." The doctor nodded toward one of his helpers who then headed topside.

Turning his attention back to his patient, the doctor studied the partially severed leg, then said to the young militiaman, "I'm sorry, lad, but the leg needs to come off."

The militiaman howled and tried to get off the table. The surgeon's helpers grabbed hold and held him back.

The doctor glanced around the room, apparently searching for something. His gaze fixed on Lemuel. "You. Get over here and lend a hand."

As Lemuel stood, his head throbbed with pain. Even though he felt dizzy, he stepped to the doctor's side.

Parsons handed the young seaman a shot glass of whiskey.

"Son, either I take the leg off now, or you'll be dead before the week's out." The doctor paused. "What's it going to be?"

With a look of desperation, the pale-faced boy nodded, took the glass, and downed its contents.

At the doctor's command, Lemuel and the other helpers grabbed the boy and held him flat on the table. The doctor placed a cloth tourniquet around the leg just above the knee and twisted it tight with a stick. Someone shoved a strap of leather between the seaman's teeth.

As the doctor's knife sliced through flesh just below the knee, the boy screamed and writhed, then passed out. Warm blood spurted across Lemuel's face as the doctor sawed through meat and bone until the damaged leg fell away.

Donning leather gloves, the doctor grabbed a red-hot poker and pressed it into one of the squirting streams of blood at the ragged stump. With a sizzle and a billow of smoke that reeked of burnt flesh, the stream stopped, and the doctor moved on to the next spurting vessel. When all the bleeders were seared shut, he moved on to the smaller vessels still oozing onto the table. After the entire end of the stump was cauterized, the doctor loosened the tourniquet and removed it.

Although Lemuel felt a little light-headed, he continued to help the doctor. From time to time, Commodore Perry called down and asked for another of the helpers until all six were gone.

"Doctor Parsons, if there are any sick or wounded who can still fight, would you send them up here?"

Lemuel wiped the blood from his face and headed topside.

He stepped onto the main deck and blinked at the brightness of the midafternoon sun, only partially blocked by the cloud of gun smoke shrouding the vessel. The scene before him caused his insides to turn cold. The *Lawrence*'s battered masts and spars stood stripped of nearly every strand of rigging and cloth. What sailcloth remained hung in limp, pock-marked tatters. Bulwarks were riddled with jagged holes. The deck was gouged with great furrows of shredded planks and strewn with shattered timber, tangled lines, and torn sail. Guns and their carriages lay broken and tossed askew. Dead, dying, and bleeding men lay scattered among the debris. Most of the 150-man crew had been either killed or wounded. The ship's lone hog squealed and grunted as it wolfed down a severed hand. When the hog hobbled forward on its front legs, its torso and entrails dragged behind where its hind legs had been blown off.

A cannon close to Lemuel roared and recoiled from its gun port. Only a few of the guns still worked, their crews hustled to reload as British ships fired at them.

The starboard bulwark next to one of the remaining cannon exploded in a burst of flying timber as an enemy shot tore through it. The six seamen serving the cannon were blown back in the deadly shower of splinters.

Commodore Perry rushed to the crewless cannon and began clearing the debris away. Lemuel hurried to the other side of the cannon, where the mangled body of a seaman lay crumpled next to the gun carriage. Lemuel grabbed hold of a leg and dragged the corpse to the side as blood trailed over the already red-soaked deck.

"Sponge!"

Lemuel didn't realize that the order was directed at him until he felt a tap on his shoulder and turned to see Perry hand him a tool. Lemuel took the stout wooden shaft with a wool sponge on end. At first he wasn't sure what he should do with it. Perry set a bucket of water next to the cannon, and Lemuel plunged the sponge tip into it.

Recalling what he had seen others do, he stepped to the smoking end of the barrel and inserted the sponge end of the rammer. He shoved the rammer into the bore and twisted the sponge 'round and 'round as he forced it deep into the barrel. When he felt it hit the end, he pulled hard to drag the rammer back out. As the sponge emerged from the end of the hot barrel, he heard a hollow *whomp*, and steam trailed out from the barrel.

"Load!"

Lemuel barely had time to set the steaming sponge aside before Perry handed him a flannel cartridge of powder. He inserted the pack into the end of the barrel and used the rammer to shove it to the bottom of the gun barrel. He hoped the metal had cooled enough to avoid a premature explosion that would surely blast him to pieces.

Lemuel reached down to a nearby rack for a six-inch, thirty-two-pound shot and hefted it up to the cannon muzzle. He edged the ball into the muzzle and stuffed a wadded mass of shredded sailcloth after it to keep the shot from rolling back out. He shoved the rammer into the bore until he was sure the shot was snug against the powder charge.

Perry jammed an ice-pick-shaped instrument down through the vent at the end of the cannon and inserted a primer, then leaned down to make sure the gun was properly aimed. He blew softly on the end of the slow match until the end glowed and a tendril of smoke curled up and away. Lemuel stepped back, turned away, opened his mouth, and covered his ear closest to the muzzle as Perry touched the tip of the match to the primer. In rapid succession, the powder in the primer flashed, burned down through the vent in the barrel and into the canvas powder cartridge. The cannon roared and recoiled in its slide.

As British shot continued to wreak havoc around them, Lemuel, Perry, and a handful of other crewmen loaded and fired the carronade again and again. On their fifth shot, the cast iron of the barrel burst apart, flying across the deck and killing another seaman.

Lemuel hadn't realized that they had been firing the last functioning cannon until he noticed the silence around him.

With the Stars and Stripes still fluttering high on the broken main-mast, the British continued to fire on them.

Lemuel assumed the commodore's next move would be to order the flag down. But Perry was at the larboard bulwark—or what remained of it. A hundred yards or so to windward and almost abeam was the undamaged *Niagara*.

Perry pointed aft and beckoned a couple of seamen to assist him. Lemuel rushed to Perry's side. Incredibly, after hours of battle, one of the little boats being towed behind the *Lawrence* had survived. Lemuel scrambled over the debris-strewn deck to help find the line to the boat. They heaved at the rope until the rowboat, a cutter, was alongside. Three of the sailors crawled down into the little boat. Lemuel hesitated, suspecting what Perry had in mind—and that the chances were slim that any of them would survive. He took a deep breath and hustled down into the cutter.

Lemuel steadied the little boat as Perry tucked his battle flag under his arm and climbed down. The commodore turned to one of his junior officers, the highest ranking officer on board still capable of standing. "As soon as I am away, you will be in command and may strike the colors. Tend to the wounded as best as you can."

They pushed away from the brig's side and began rowing for the *Niagara*. With bleeding hands Lemuel pulled hard at one of the oars as the tattered Stars and Stripes descended from the mainmast of the *Lawrence*. Cannon fire from the British dwindled, then ceased.

For a while, the drifting and bobbing *Lawrence* obscured the British vessels from sight. As the cutter pulled farther away, the enemy came into view. Something splashed near the boat, and water spouted a dozen feet into the air, close enough to drench Lemuel and the others. If one of the cannonballs hit their little boat, they would probably all drown.

Something snapped into the wooden plank next to Lemuel, and a splinter nicked his wrist. Water trickled into the boat through a ragged, rifle-ball-sized hole in the side of the thin hull. Lemuel imagined a British sharpshooter taking aim at him. He pulled harder at the oars.

Plume after plume rose around them as cannon boomed from the British line. Cascades of water crashed down into the boat, almost swamping it. By the time they reached the *Niagara*, their clothes were soaked, and Lemuel's arms were numb from exertion.

Cheers rose from the *Niagara* crew as Perry and his men climbed over her side. The commodore and the *Niagara*'s commander consulted briefly before the *Niagara* commander headed for the rowboat. With a

fresh crew of oarsmen rowing hard, they headed toward the lagging schooners and sloops.

As Perry's pennant and battle flag were being hoisted to the *Niagara's*
topmast, Lemuel joined a group of militiamen lined up on the deck.
Someone handed him a rifle as Perry gave his orders.

"Give me all the fighting sail you have. Set a course for the center of
the British line. Load all cannon with double shot."

Almost untouched by the battle so far, the *Niagara* swung gracefully
to the starboard, then steadied on a course toward the British line.

The British ships had all but destroyed the *Lawrence*, but Lemuel
could see that she had done her job well. The *Detroit* was nearly dead in the
water as its sailors raced to haul damaged yards around and to clear away
ragged and tangled rigging.

The *Detroit* was turning sluggishly, probably attempting to bring
its unused starboard guns to bear. Meanwhile, a second heavily damaged
British ship suddenly veered into the *Detroit*, its bowsprit goring through
Detroit's three masts, then tangling in the rigging, skewering its flagship.
The *Detroit's* already-crooked mizzen topmast crashed into the tangled rig-
ging of both British ships, locking them together, at least for the moment.

The *Niagara* raced toward the center of the British line, where three
vessels, including the *Detroit*, lay to starboard and three to larboard—all
caught in a line. Perry shouted his orders. "Gun crews, fire as you bear!"

As they approached the line, the foremost cannon on each side
roared and belched gray-white smoke. Each cannon now fired not just a
thirty-two-pound shot, but also grapeshot, chain, or whatever scrap iron
was available. With the British ships now only fifty to seventy-five yards
away, men and equipment fell in swathes as projectiles ripped across the
decks.

Perry shortened sail, and the ship slowed. The next gun on each side
fired, then the next. Thunderous cannon fire rippled down the *Niagara's*

gun ports. She shuddered and rocked with simultaneous recoils from opposite sides.

The British ships were badly damaged but not beaten. They concentrated on the *Niagara*, and within minutes, iron, lead, and splinters tore the brig's rigging to shreds and cut down twenty crewmen.

As the *Niagara*'s gunners fired into the British ships at point-blank range again and again, Lemuel and the other militiamen shot at the British sailors trying to untangle the *Detroit*'s rigging. At that range, despite the pitch and roll of the ships, Lemuel seldom missed.

During the chaos, the smaller American vessels arrived and joined the battle with their heavy long guns.

The crews of the two snarled British ships hacked with axes at the tangled rigging until the ships separated and began to drift apart. But with their sails and rigging shot away, their masts damaged, and their hulls shattered, the ships could barely maneuver.

Lemuel set his rifle sights on a British officer. He was about to pull the trigger when he noticed the Union Jack being lowered. Within a few minutes, all of the larger British vessels surrendered.

A couple of the lesser-damaged small vessels tried to escape, but two of the American schooners raced after them and brought them back to the debris-strewn waters where the battle-damaged squadrons had anchored.

Lemuel joined the other militiamen as they collapsed against a bulwark. He watched as Perry rummaged through his pockets and produced a wrinkled, yellow envelope and a pencil. Setting his hat on top if his knee as a makeshift table, Perry scribbled something on the back of the paper.

When he had finished writing, he climbed atop a gun carriage. "This is my message to General Harrison. 'Dear General: We have met the enemy and they are ours: two Ships, two Brigs, one Schooner, and one Sloop. Yours with great respect and esteem. O.H. Perry'"

The men cheered. As the commodore folded the envelope, he seemed to be searching for someone among the many faces on the crowded deck. Perry's gaze settled on Lemuel.

"You're one of the men General Harrison was kind enough to loan me, are you not?"

Lemuel came to attention and stammered, "Y-yes, sir."

"Do you feel up to taking a message back to the general?"

"Yes, sir. I'd be honored."

As he was being rowed to the schooner that would hurry him back to shore, Lemuel gazed out across the water. Lake Erie was now entirely under American control. The only remaining threat to the area was the British army and its Indian allies at Fort Malden.

CHAPTER THIRTY-ONE

SEPTEMBER 1813, WASHINGTON CITY

Rachel Thurston sighed as she waited in line to meet a promising young author from New York City. The craze for autographs had swept into Washington City, and a crowd of women had gathered at a house a few blocks from the president's mansion to obtain the signature of Washington Irving.

Rachel clutched her autograph book, somewhat embarrassed that it had only a few signatures in it. Her small collection of epigrams did include one from Mrs. Madison, in which she had written, "Habit and hope are the crutches which support us through the vicissitudes of life." Rachel had expected to get one from the president himself, but Dolley had been firm in stating that during war, the president had no time for such frivolity.

Rachel had mixed emotions about collecting autographs. She recognized that it presented an opportunity to meet interesting people and for visiting the homes of the famous in Washington City. On the other hand, collecting epigrams from people of accomplishment seemed a poor substitute for actually accomplishing something one's self.

Ahead of Rachel in line stood a young woman she recognized from earlier in the week. The two of them had attended a meeting where the speaker had railed against the evils of slavery and urged its abolition in the States, as it already was in Europe. Rachel's heart ached for the plight of the slaves but recognized that southern plantations, such as Montpelier, depended upon cheap labor to survive.

Rachel was still trying to sort out the issue in her mind. She had heard and read the arguments in defense of slavery. It was the "natural order" that some would dominate others, whether it be over blacks, Indians—or women. Some agreed that slavery was an abhorrent institution but that once it was established it was a bit like holding a wolf by its ears. How did one let go without getting hurt?

The States had banned the importation of new slaves in 1808. To Rachel, that seemed like a step in the right direction, but her father had another observation. Banning the importation of slaves had the immediate effect of making those slaves already in the States more valuable, substantially adding to the wealth of slave owners, and making the prospect of giving them up even less likely.

The issue of slavery was not likely to be addressed anytime soon, she feared. The war kept dragging out. An Indian massacre of settlers in the Mississippi Territory had shocked the nation and threatened a new front in the conflict. News had recently arrived that the Americans had won a naval battle on Lake Erie. The end of the war seemed nowhere in sight.

As the line in front of her shortened, Rachel studied the handsome young man at the table. He had dark hair, which was fortunate according to her mother, as people with light hair tended to have poor eyesight. The man's eyes were dark and they were prominent, a sign that he was a great talker. Rachel noted the man's high brow, his large, hooked nose, and strong chin, all features her mother would have judged with approval. Clearly, if a facial features were a reliable indicator of personality, this man was destined for greatness.

When Rachel's turn came, she stepped forward. As he had with each of the other ladies, the young man of about thirty stood and bowed. "Washington Irving."

Rachel introduced herself, and said, "I read your history of New York and thought it delightful. May I ask what you plan to write next?"

Irving chuckled. "It's quite kind of you to ask. But, frankly I haven't a clue. Once the war is over, I hope to travel in Europe. Maybe that will provide me with ideas and inspiration. How about you? Are you a writer?"

Rachel sighed. She couldn't very well admit that she had penned dozens of letters to the editor on behalf of her father. "Other than personal correspondence, that really isn't an option for women, is it?"

Irving carefully wrote something in her book. "That doesn't seem fair, does it?"

CHAPTER THIRTY-TWO

SEPTEMBER 1813, ANNAPOLIS, MARYLAND

Lieutenant George Sherbourne woke for no apparent reason. He heard bedclothes rustle in the darkness, and recalled that he was in a boardinghouse. Except for the mild snoring of his roommate, the house seemed eerily quiet.

A door creaked from downstairs at the boardinghouse entrance. Footsteps thundered on the stairs as men in boots hurried up the steps. Imagining soldiers coming to arrest him as a spy, George rolled out of bed and hurried to the window. As he groped to find the window latches, the footsteps stopped in the hallway. From across the hall, a door opened, then slammed. Through the walls he heard several men laughing and cursing.

"Bloody drunks," George whispered as he climbed back into bed.

He stared at the dark ceiling, trying to think of something else. His countrymen up north were doing their part to keep the Yanks from overrunning the British colonies. Stories had trickled down about a woman from the village of Queenston, on the Niagara, who had hurried miles cross-country to warn British troops of an eminent attack by the

Americans. George supposed the story was more dramatic than the actual events, but that really didn't matter—the tale had the makings of a new legend of heroism. No doubt his fellow colonials would be retelling the story of Laura Secord well into the future.

Another name that had emerged from the incident was Lieutenant James Fitzgibbon, who had been commissioned from the rank of sergeant-major when Brock was still in command. Reportedly, upon hearing Laura Secord's warning of imminent attack, Fitzgibbon led his men and a horde of local Indians in an attack that resulted in the capture of hundreds of Americans at a place called Beaver Dams.

George stared into the darkness around him. While others such as Fitzgibbon were achieving fame that could someday lead to fortune, he was relegated to the duty of espionage. Even if he survived he wouldn't dare admit his role during the war lest it bring dishonor to him and his family, making marriage to Anne even less likely.

The war seemed to drag on, way too long for him. News had recently arrived of a battle on Lake Erie. The Americans had defeated the British and now controlled that lake.

Much farther south and west in the Mississippi Territory, a rebel group of Muskogee Indians called the Red Sticks had massacred dozens of soldiers and pioneers at Fort Mims on the Alabama River. A state militia commander from Tennessee led a ragtag army south to avenge the massacre and crush the hostiles. No doubt, thought George, when the native rebels were destroyed the Americans would use the uprising as an excuse to claim vast new territories for the States.

George heard another noise and listened carefully. More revelers were finding their way home after a night of carousing. He wondered if he could fall back to sleep before dawn. During the coming day, he hoped to learn if any of Robert Fulton's torpedoes were in Annapolis.

George had already pieced together, from a variety of sources, the makeup and operation of the weapons. Each torpedo consisted of a waterproof wooden box filled with gunpowder and a firing mechanism, which was to be set off by either a timepiece or a string yanked from afar.

Deployment of the torpedo was usually carried out under the cover of darkness, preferably on an overcast night. With oars muffled and the crew camouflaged in dark clothing, a small boat would approach the target ship. The powder-filled box was slipped overboard with an attached line, then, with the aid of wind and current, the box was floated alongside the enemy vessel and detonated.

To George, the whole operation seemed rather preposterous, but the inventions had demonstrated their capability for destruction. Even a few successful torpedoes could change the direction of the war.

CHAPTER THIRTY-THREE

OCTOBER 1813, THAMES RIVER, CANADA

Lemuel Wyckliffe grimaced and shifted in the saddle. He hadn't been on horseback for many weeks, and his body was paying the price. Muscles ached all over, and the inside of his thighs felt raw.

He rode with a dozen other mounted scouts along a well-trodden muddy road. King's Road, as the British called it, stretched northeast from Detroit running parallel to the Thames River, and then north of Lake Erie to the Niagara area. A snarled mass of trees and undergrowth in full fall color lined each side of the path. Somewhere ahead of them fled the British from Fort Malden and their Indian allies. The rider at the front of the group raised his right hand and reined his horse to a stop. Lemuel strained to see or hear any sign of an ambush. The back of Lemuel's neck tingled.

The rider in the lead was an old scout called Gramps because he had thirty grandchildren. Gramps silently signaled the others to follow. Lemuel tapped the heel of his moccasins against the ribs of his mount and trotted forward. He eyed the brush around him. The scouts were just a few miles ahead of General Harrison's army and were constantly at risk of attack.

To the left lay a vast swamp. To the right, beyond fifty yards of trees and underbrush, ran the Thames River with its steep earthen banks. From there the Thames flowed southwest to Lake St. Clair, which emptied into the Detroit River, and then Lake Erie. The thought of Lake Erie made Lemuel think back several weeks with mixed emotions.

After the battle on Lake Erie, he had been rushed to shore, where he quickly found General Harrison. News of the naval victory spread swiftly, and as Lemuel headed back to his regiment of mounted Kentucky riflemen, he saw celebration everywhere along the way.

General Harrison and Commodore Perry wasted no time in repairing damaged ships and moving men into position to attack Fort Malden. The mounted riflemen, distinctive in their red-fringed, black hunting shirts, were ordered northwest toward Detroit. En route they stopped at Frenchtown on the Raisin River and found the remains of the massacre victims still strewn where they had fallen in January. After gathering the sun-bleached bones of their fellow Kentuckians and burying them, the riflemen continued toward Detroit with renewed resolve to drive the Indians and British from the northwest territories.

The American army quickly reclaimed Detroit, and Commodore Perry ferried General Harrison's men across Lake Erie to Fort Malden. They found both the fort and the shipyard burnt to the ground. The British had fled, taking as much of their supplies and equipment as they could haul.

Harrison summoned the mounted riflemen. There seemed little chance of catching the British and their Indian allies, as they had a week's head start. Harrison was determined to drive them well out of the Detroit area and to capture as much of their valuable supplies and equipment as possible.

A call went out for scouts, and Lemuel, eager to ease the boredom of the long march, volunteered. Within a couple days, the scouts determined that the British traveled slowly, probably to allow their supply boats to stay abreast as they struggled up the Thames.

Soon the riflemen overtook abandoned boats as the enemy picked up the pace of its flight. Progress up King's Road went quickly for the Americans as the fleeing British hadn't bothered to destroy the bridges behind them nor had they created other obstacles to impede Harrison's pursuit. Tecumseh and his Indians had been caught once destroying a bridge, and they were quickly disbursed with cannon fire.

Lemuel glanced at steaming horse manure on the road and the mud freshly churned by cart wheels and horse hooves. The British and Indians were not far ahead.

Gramps again signaled the scouts to stop. The muddy road curved to the right, and the forest opened wide to a clearing only lightly wooded with small trees. Ahead the road crossed the clearing and disappeared around a tangled, swampy area. As Gramps advanced cautiously up the road, a rifle cracked from the brush to the right. Gramps slumped over the neck of his horse.

A volley of rifle fire erupted from the brush. Gramps' horse bucked and spun, nearly toppling its rider off. The other scouts turned and raced back down the dirt road.

Lemuel's first inclination was to follow them, but screaming Indians bolted from the thicket and raced toward Gramps. Lemuel dug his heels into the mare, and she shot forward.

He reached Gramps and snatched the frightened horse's reins. As rifle balls whizzed past him, he headed back down the road as fast as he could go.

Ahead, the other scouts had dismounted and were shooting at the Indians. To avoid their line of fire, Lemuel guided his horse to the right. By the time he dismounted, the Indians had retreated into the brush.

As the men helped Gramps from his horse, their lead scout, William Whitley, asked Lemuel if he had seen anything farther up the road. Lemuel admitted that in all the confusion, he hadn't even looked.

"We need to know if this is jest another war party left behind to slow us down or whether the British are gonna make a stand here. You three," he pointed to Lemuel and two others, "go check it out. Ride fast, get a look, then hightail it back."

The three headed up the road, slowly at first. Lemuel urged the mare to a trot, then a canter, hoping that the speed would make him a tough target for any Indians still lurking in the brush.

The road curved left, edging closer to the little swamp. Fearing more natives might be hiding there, Lemuel reined his horse to the right, keeping to the middle of the clearing.

Shots crackled from the brush to the right. Lemuel leaned forward over the mare's neck to present a smaller target. The other scouts turned and raced back down the road. A score of Indians poured out to the brush, firing rifles at the retreating scouts. Remembering his instructions to find out what was ahead, Lemuel reined his horse back toward the north and galloped ahead.

Screaming Indians chased after him as he sped across the meadow. Ahead, the road curved to the left around the little swamp, and then the clearing widened again.

Lemuel pulled back on his reins and forced his heels outward in the stirrups as the horse skidded in the mud and slid to a stop. Just a hundred yards ahead, a small cannon pointed directly at him. Guarding the cannon were a dozen mounted Canadian militiamen. Beyond the cannon and its crew, at the edge of the woods stood hundreds of redcoats. Lemuel looked closely, noting the details.

The howls of the Indians behind him grew closer. He was cut off from going back the way he had come. Gray-white smoke billowed from the redcoats in the woods. The sporadic pop of musket fire mixed with the eerie shriek of the natives behind him.

The clearing opened wide to the left, and Lemuel reined his horse that way. As he headed west at a gallop, the woods ahead came alive with natives, screaming and firing at him. Musket balls whizzed past him.

The clearing opened back to the south around the west side of the little swamp. Lemuel leaned forward and held the reins loosely, giving the mare her head. He grabbed his hat with his right hand and slapped it back against the horse's rump. She accelerated to a dead run straight through the brush and woods. Trees sped by in a blur as hundreds of Indians stepped out of the woods to the west. If the horse stumbled and fell, he would surely be caught and scalped.

He raced around the little swamp toward the other scouts as they fired at the natives in pursuit. When a few Indians dropped in the grass, the others grabbed the bodies and hurried back into the woods.

The other scouts listened as Lemuel told them about the redcoats ahead. Then Whitley said, "Ride back and tell General Harrison what you jest seen. If any o' those fancy-pants officers around the general try to stop you from see'n him, tell'm you have orders to see General Harrison hisself. And right quick."

As Lemuel rode hard and fast along the narrow, muddy road, he hoped the mare wouldn't slip and throw him. And that Indians wouldn't emerge from the woods in another ambush. Ahead he could see the advancing column of General Harrison's uniformed soldiers. He stopped at the first officer he saw. "Sir, I have an urgent report for the general."

"What is the nature of your report?"

"The redcoats have taken to ground just ahead. I have orders to tell the general what I saw."

The lieutenant squinted at Lemuel, then nodded. "Follow me." He led Lemuel back along the advancing column.

When they found Harrison, the general listened carefully as Lemuel described the situation ahead.

"Stick with me for now," said Harrison.

They continued their march until they reached the southern edge of the clearing. Harrison sent more scouts to reconnoiter the area and called his officers together. When Colonel Richard Johnson of the mounted riflemen arrived, Lemuel repeated his report.

"Cannon on the road?" asked Johnson. "How many? How big?"

"Just one, sir. A six-pounder. Guarded by twenty dragoons."

Lemuel grabbed a stick and etched a crude map in the thick mud. The officers gathered around him.

"The redcoats are scattered in the woods?" asked Johnson. "Are you sure they weren't lined up in close formation—shoulder to shoulder in straight lines?"

"They were scattered in the woods, sir."

The colonel scratched at his chin as he silently studied Lemuel's map. General Harrison's scouts returned and confirmed that the British and Indians were still deployed as Lemuel had described.

"General," said Johnson, "I believe the situation presents us with an opportunity." The colonel edged closer to the general and lowered his voice.

"That's not sanctioned by anything I've heard of," said the general cautiously, "but I'm convinced it might work. If it fails, we can always bring up the infantry and do it the hard way. Colonel Johnson, you may proceed."

Dreading the possibility that he might be kept at the rear with the officers during the coming action, Lemuel approached the general. "Sir, may I return to my company?"

"Yes, certainly. Well done, lad."

Lemuel had enjoyed scouting but was happy to be back with the riflemen now that the action was about to begin.

Because the clearing to the east of the little swamp wasn't wide enough to accommodate the entire regiment, Colonel Johnson divided his troops. One battalion, five hundred, men led by his brother Lieutenant Colonel James Johnson, would attack the redcoats. If the first attack was successful, Colonel Johnson would lead the charge against the more unpredictable, and potentially more dangerous, natives.

At midafternoon Lieutenant Colonel Johnson deployed his men in four double columns in the clearing to the east of the little swamp. He rode to the front of the formation, drew his sword, and extended it toward the overcast sky. "Remember the Raisin!" he shouted.

Lemuel thought of the mutilated corpses that had been left scattered in what remained of Frenchtown. He joined five hundred mounted riflemen as they screamed the battle cry.

With his sword resting on his right shoulder, Johnson turned his mount toward the British line. On his command, the troops walked their mounts forward, then increased their gait to a trot, then a gallop. As Johnson pointed his sword forward, he screamed "Charge!"

Bugles blared as the four columns thundered ahead at a dead run. Lemuel saw Canadian militiamen milling around the cannon at the center of the road directly in front of him. He recalled the devastation of the cannon on Lake Erie and dreaded what might be next. Again he screamed, "Remember the Raisin!" knowing they might be his last words.

Lemuel raced toward the cannon crew hastily attempting to load. He reined the mare directly at a militiaman holding a rammer to the right side of the cannon. The Canadian turned just in time to see Lemuel and scores of mounted troops barreling toward him. The militiaman barely had time to drop the rammer and dive under the gun carriage before the horses sped past him.

Ahead, scattered at the edge of the woods were hundreds of redcoats. Muskets popped, and smoke billowed out of the trees. As the mounted riflemen bore down on them, Lemuel saw a redcoat drop his musket and run.

Lemuel raced his horse between trees and scattered redcoats. Not until he was many yards past the British line did he rein in his mount, then wheel to face the enemy.

Five men handed Lemuel the reins to their mounts, then turned to fire at the British. As he tried to calm the horses, Lemuel saw a redcoat raise his musket and take aim. American rifles fired, and the redcoat crumpled to the ground. Most of the British threw down their muskets and raised their hands above their heads.

It was over. Lemuel figured the whole battle had taken only ten minutes.

Lieutenant Colonel Johnson rode nearby and shouted orders to round up the prisoners. Lemuel could see a big grin on Johnson's face. As the lieutenant colonel surveyed the battleground, his gaze fixed on Lemuel. He reined his horse closer. "You're the lad who brought General Harrison the report on the British position, aren't you?"

"Yes, sir."

"Well done, young man. Now ride back and tell Colonel Johnson what you saw here."

Lemuel raced the mare down the road and around the little swamp to the south end of the clearing where Colonel Johnson and his officers waited with the other battalion of mounted riflemen. As quickly and accurately as Lemuel could, he described Lieutenant Colonel Johnson's victory.

Colonel Johnson listened quietly, asked a few questions, then turned to one of his junior officers. "Lieutenant, in five minutes I will send in the Forlorn Hope. The rest of us will follow shortly thereafter."

At the mention of "Forlorn Hope," Lemuel felt his insides twist. A relatively small number of men would charge the enemy first to draw the initial round of fire. Then, before the enemy could reload, the main body of men would attack. Members of the Forlorn Hope were usually unmarried troops who volunteered for this task, since it was basically a suicide mission.

Nineteen riders advanced to the front of the assembled troops and formed a double column behind the lead scout, Charles Whitley. By the looks of them, most weren't much older than Lemuel. He wondered why anyone would volunteer. Then he remembered his mother and sister, his father, and the men slaughtered at Frenchtown, including Seth and Stubby. Some of the natives who had killed them might actually be in the woods ahead, maybe even that heathen-devil Tecumseh. This was his chance to take the fight directly to the natives, maybe even kill the murderers of his family and friends.

Lemuel mounted the mare and guided her to the end of the double column of young men. The rifleman nearest Lemuel turned to him. For a moment their eyes met, and the young man nodded. A lump formed in Lemuel's throat. He nodded back, then focused on the black-shirted riders ahead of him.

Colonel Johnson rode a white horse to the front of the column and wheeled to the side. "Remember the Raisin!" he shouted.

As one, the battalion repeated the cry. When the voices died down, Johnson nodded to the buglers, who promptly sounded the charge.

Lemuel and the others in the twenty-man column screamed their loudest as they galloped into the clearing west of the small swamp. Lemuel expected their advance to be greeted immediately by war cries and rifle fire from undisciplined natives. Instead the woods ahead seemed deserted. He wondered if the Indians had departed, or worse, waited in ambush somewhere else.

The Forlorn Hope was almost to the edge of the woods when a rifle fired—then scores more. In the hail of balls, most of the riders and horses ahead of Lemuel tumbled to the ground.

A handful of natives stepped out of the brush at the edge of the woods, aimed their weapons, and fired. They were quickly joined by hundreds more. Rifle balls buzzed like bees past Lemuel. The rifleman next to him slumped in his saddle and off his mount.

The woods ahead billowed with gray-white smoke and roared with gunfire. Some of the Indians, armed only with tomahawks and scalping knives, raced across the field. The mare was still barreling ahead when she suddenly pitched to the ground. In a blur, Lemuel tumbled over the horse's head, and then slid across the grass.

With the air knocked out of him, he lay stunned. The blood-tingling war cries of hundreds of natives spurred him to action. He rolled to his side. Dozens of Indians raced toward him.

His chest burning from having the wind knocked out of him, Lemuel staggered to his feet, his legs wobbling as he tried to decide what to do. The mare whinnied in pain. Her left front leg was broken at the knee and flopped out to the side as she attempted to walk. Blood trickled from mus-ket-ball holes across her chest, shoulder, and neck.

Lemuel's rifle was still slung in the sleeve below the saddle. He rushed for the horse. At his rapid approach, the horse flinched and tried to flee. With only three good legs, she stumbled to her side with a pitiful cry. Lemuel dodged her flailing hooves, reached for the butt of the rifle, and yanked it from the leather sleeve.

He knelt to one knee and cocked the rifle. With no time to aim, he pointed the barrel at the closest Indian and pulled the trigger. The rifle blasted, and the Indian dropped face-first at Lemuel's feet.

With two more Indians almost upon him, Lemuel dropped the rifle and drew the tomahawk and butcher knife from his belt. As the closest warrior swung his tomahawk, Lemuel brought his own up to meet it. The two weapons met with a wrist-jarring crack. Lemuel shoved the Indian back and slashed the butcher knife at the native's neck. The Indian blocked Lemuel's blow, then stepped closer, tomahawk raised. Lemuel lunged for-ward, deflected the tomahawk blow with his left arm, then stabbed the butcher knife into the warrior's belly. Lemuel pulled the Indian close as he shoved the blade deep and yanked up through innards.

Lemuel barely had time to pull his knife free before another warrior was upon him. He ducked low just as the Indian reached him, and the native tumbled over Lemuel's back. He swung his tomahawk down into the Indian's forehead with skull-splitting force.

A scream of rage caused Lemuel to turn just in time to see another Indian rushing him, tomahawk raised. Before Lemuel could react, a white horse flashed between them, knocking Lemuel to his back. The horse was gone as fast as it appeared, and standing across from Lemuel was his attacker, tomahawk still in hand.

Lemuel crouched ready to continue the fight but hesitated when he noticed the expression on the warrior's face. The native blinked once before blood flowed from his lips. The Indian's head tipped to the side and toppled off a cleanly sliced neck as a fountain of blood gushed into the air. The severed head bounced and wobbled across the ground. The tomahawk slipped from his hand and the headless body collapsed to the ground.

Dozens of horses thundered past Lemuel as they charged the Indians in the clearing. At the front of the mounted riflemen on his white horse was Colonel Johnson, sword slashing right and left as he drove through a cluster of Indians.

Lemuel's horse shrieked in pain as it lay on the ground, its eyes wide with terror. Carefully avoiding thrashing hooves, Lemuel knelt on the back of the horse's neck and forced its head back. He placed the blade of his razor-sharp knife against the horse's throat, then sliced hard and deep. Steaming blood spurted over Lemuel's hands and gushed to the ground.

Lemuel grabbed his rifle and hurried after Colonel Johnson. The undergrowth in the big swamp was dense, and the horses couldn't get through. Most of the riflemen dismounted and fought tree to tree as the Indians gave ground.

Colonel Johnson was still mounted, but Lemuel could see that the man was wounded in several places. The colonel's horse was peppered with red-stained holes.

An older warrior, maybe age forty-five, tall and muscular, with a bandaged arm fired a rifle at Johnson, hitting him in the hand. The native tossed down the rifle, drew a tomahawk, and rushed toward the colonel. Lemuel aimed just as Johnson fired a pistol into the warrior's chest. The Indian dropped dead at the hooves of Johnson's mount.

As the colonel slumped in his saddle, quiet fell over the battlefield. Lemuel and several soldiers helped him down, then carried him back toward the clearing. Lemuel turned back to the big swamp, ready to rejoin the battle, but the gunfire dwindled as an eerie chorus of Indian war cries rose from the swamp.

Suddenly drained, Lemuel found a sturdy log and took a seat. As the gun smoke cleared, he could see that the remaining Indians had fled deeper into the swamp and that the battle was over.

"Tecumseh is dead!" someone yelled.

A cheer rose among the riflemen.

Lemuel thought of the Indian Colonel Johnson had shot in the chest and wondered if he had been Tecumseh. With their great leader dead, the Indians in the Great Lakes area might finally quit attacking the settlers. Now with the last of the British soldiers and their Indian allies from Fort Malden defeated, most of Upper Canada was finally under American control.

Lemuel hoped the victory would also encourage and inspire other Americans to defeat the British. He suspected that the war was far from over.

A fallen warrior lay half-naked in front of Lemuel. He considered taking the scalp but recalled Seth's preference for a souvenir with some practical use. After a moment to consider the possibilities, Lemuel knelt and grabbed the warrior's ear. With quick, forceful moves, he sliced an arc over the Indian's ear, then down the side of the neck. He sliced down the Indian's back and figured that a new set of reins would come in handy.

CHAPTER THIRTY-FOUR

NOVEMBER 1813,
ST. LAWRENCE RIVER, UPPER CANADA

Corporal Silas Shackleton silently damned the generals, and wished he could go back to New York City. He glanced at midmorning clouds that seemed likely to drench him again, then blew into cupped hands that had grown numb with cold. Shivering in his rain-soaked uniform, he stomped his feet in the mud. Moisture oozed into his boots through holes worn in the soles. As wind blew from the west, a mixture of drizzle and snow began to fall.

On a slight rise overlooking the river, Silas and hundreds of others stood in formation waiting for orders. Occasionally an infantryman stepped out of rank and hobbled into the woods nearby. Most of the men had diarrhea and no longer asked permission to take care of personal business with what little privacy was available. Silas was thankful that his own bout of dysentery seemed to have run its course, though he still felt weak and shaky.

His stomach churned as he thought about the events of the previous month. Their battalion had been part of a major troop movement from the

Niagara area, on the western end of Lake Ontario, to Sacket's Harbor, on the eastern end of the lake. Five thousand regulars had embarked on boats that set sail for what should have been a journey of less than two days. But storms struck them mid-voyage, sending many of the vessels to the shoreline for shelter.

The boat carrying Silas and seventy other infantrymen headed for the safety of a bay, only to find their way blocked by a mudbar. As the storm raged, he and the others used spades to scrape a channel through the mud. When they finally arrived at Sacket's Harbor, nearly two weeks late, they were greeted by another violent thunderstorm.

Silas's battalion was assigned to Major General James Wilkinson's command as it organized for a major campaign. The plan, as rumored among the enlisted men, was for Wilkinson to proceed down the St. Lawrence River to attack Montreal from the west. A second American army was to march north along Lake Champlain and attack Montreal from the south. Once Montreal fell, all of Canada upriver, including the Great Lakes, would be cut off and would soon fall into American hands.

General Wilkinson left Sacket's Harbor with over seven thousand men loaded in an armada of small craft. They had barely assembled on Grenadier Island, just above the St. Lawrence, when another storm struck, this one dumping ten inches of snow on them. Remarkably, to Silas, the morale of his messmates had remained reasonably positive.

As they did almost everywhere they traveled, on either side of the border, soldiers scoured the countryside for food and anything else they might need. Like a swarm of locusts they stripped farms of fruit, vegetables, grain, poultry, hogs, cattle, and sheep. Rail fences and loose planks were commandeered for firewood. When the army moved on, it left behind a path of ruin.

As they left Grenadier Island, British naval vessels began hounding them from the rear. And once the Americans entered the St. Lawrence, with its hundreds of tiny islands, Canadian sharpshooters began harassing them with potshots.

Several days later they stopped again to camp for the night, this time just above Long Sault Rapids. To make sure the enemy wasn't lying in wait below the rapids, Wilkinson sent a couple thousand men downstream along King's Highway, a rut-filled trail along the northern shore of the St. Lawrence River.

Silas's regiment camped in an open field, and it rained most of the night. Early the next morning they marched east along King's Highway. Then without explanation, after miles of trudging through the mud, they were ordered back to the same plot of farmland they had occupied the evening before.

Rumors circulated that General Wilkinson was drunk. Or that he was ill and had taken too much laudanum, leaving him tipsy, but that he hadn't transferred command to a subordinate capable of making clear decisions and issuing orders. Silas cleared his throat and hawked a crusty blob to the ground.

Somewhere beyond the trees to the west lurked the British forces Wilkinson's men had encountered briefly the day before. Occasionally sporadic small-arms fire popped in the distance, and Silas figured the sentries were exchanging shots with Canadian militia. He had little doubt that if given the chance, the three American brigades could annihilate the relatively small enemy force. Then again, General Wilkinson's expedition had seemed plagued from the beginning.

When the army had reorganized at Sacket's Harbor, they had no time to train together. Some of the units had been instructed with one drill manual, some with another, according to the preference of their commander. Now they couldn't maneuver in a coordinated manner.

Silas jumped. Cannon boomed in the distance. Upriver, just below a large island in the St. Lawrence, were several large boats. Smoke billowed from their decks. Something splashed in the water near the American boats anchored off the riverbank, and water spouted into the air. Another cannon boomed in the distance.

Over the next hour as Silas stood shivering in formation, cannon-balls plunged harmlessly into the river or skipped like stones across the surface before sinking. Then the British guns fell silent, and most of the enemy vessels disappeared upriver.

At midday the clouds darkened, and rain poured out of the skies. For an hour winds shrieked with gale force, hurling drops that stung Silas's face like pebbles as he shivered and shook.

Finally, around two o'clock, an officer gave orders for them to move. Silas hoped physical activity would warm his aching bones. His regiment led the way as two thousand Americans marched westward across a slippery, plowed field. With each step mud gathered in heavy clumps on Silas's boots. Ahead lay woods, probably concealing a waterway or low area too boggy for farming.

They slogged across the field in attack-column formation, twenty men wide. But as they approached the tree line, they deployed to a wide double line. They fixed bayonets, then marched forward. As Silas's company entered the pinewoods, muskets fired, and smoke billowed from between the trees. Indians howled like wild animals.

All around Silas, Americans fired as fast as they could load. He spotted a Canadian militiaman wearing a bearskin hat. Silas aimed and fired, but by the time the smoke cleared and he had reloaded, the militiamen and Indians had disappeared.

Silas's company advanced farther into the swampy woods, heading north and west. Natives and Canadian militiamen fired at them from the cover of the pines, then fell back. The woods echoed with gunshots and the howls of the natives. Silas and soldiers in line to his left and right picked their way through the woods, detouring around trees, sidestepping over deadfall, and sloshing across boggy puddles. He nearly choked on the thick smoke, and he spat to clear some of the gunpowder from his mouth.

For another half an hour, the Americans advanced through the pine-woods as fast as the British forces fell back. Silas estimated that the enemy numbered only a couple hundred, but the hideous screams of the natives made his insides twist tight. Musket and rifle fire mixed with clouds of smoke as one blue-coated soldier after another fell. Finally they emerged from the pines, and the view opened.

"Oh, no!" said the man next to Silas.

Through the smoke, Silas took in the scene. To the southeast across an open field, hundreds of American regulars marched westward, slogging through thick mud. Many of the soldiers were firing at British dragoons across the field, even though they were well beyond musket range. To the south across the fields were two tree-lined gullies, King's Highway, and then the St. Lawrence River. In the distance along the river to the south-west stood a yellow, two-story farmhouse. To the west lay wide fields criss-crossed with split-rail fences. But the sight that riveted Silas's attention lay just a hundred yards to the southwest.

Across the field stood wide lines of British infantry. Facing east, they stretched from the gullies on the south to the woods on the north. The northernmost line wore traditional red coats, while the soldiers in the line just to the south of the redcoats donned long, gray greatcoats. To the immediate south of the gray-coats stood two artillery pieces. In all, Silas estimated the British forces numbered well over a thousand men, but that was far fewer than the Americans advancing toward them. The soldiers around Silas cheered. Many opened fire.

Silas jumped as the earth and air thumped with the boom of a cannon. Smoke billowed from one of the British fieldpieces. On Silas's left, a dozen men toppled to the ground, and Silas realized the British were firing either grape or case shot, which spread as it left the cannon muzzle.

Officers and sergeants tried to organize the men, but most continued firing at will. Many of the soldiers took cover behind logs and fence posts.

Ignoring Bosworth's commands to form a line, Silas took cover behind a tree and fired as fast as he could reload.

With relief, he noted that even though the British infantry was within effective musket range, its lines faced east, across the field to Silas's left. That meant they would have trouble firing at him and the other Americans still emerging from the woods.

Bosworth grabbed Silas by the collar. "Corporal, help me get these men in line."

Before Silas could comply with Bosworth's orders, he saw something that he had seen only once before, and that had been on a parade ground. In the northernmost British line, half of the redcoats turned about-face and marched away as the other half marched forward. In doing so, the entire British line closest to Silas wheeled a quarter turn. Now the redcoats faced him and hundreds of other Americans who had just emerged from the woods.

To Silas's left, something smacked into a soldier. Men groaned and fell. The right half of the British line billowed with smoke.

Silas fired toward the redcoats, then ducked behind a stump. The left half of the British line fired. Balls whizzed past Silas. Men fell to his left and right, and the American line faltered. Men took cover, then began to fire independently over and over again.

"Where the hell is our artillery?" someone yelled.

"Sergeant," yelled a soldier, "I'm out of ammunition."

Damn it, thought Silas. Not only had the officers failed to resupply the troops with ammunition, they had neglected to protect them with artillery. Like Queenston Heights a year before, this battle was disintegrating into a disaster.

Bosworth knelt next to a fallen infantrymen and removed the man's cartridge box. Bosworth handed the box to the soldier who had cried out for ammunition, then yelled, "If you need more ammunition, strip the dead and—" The expression on Bosworth's face changed. He stumbled to his knees, then slumped to the ground.

Silas rushed to his friend and rolled him over. Blood pumped in throbbing spurts from the side of his head.

"Fall back to the river!" someone shouted. "Bring the wounded!"

Men all around Silas began to run for the cover of the woods. Not knowing what else to do, Silas grabbed Bosworth under the arms, propped him up, then drooped him over his shoulder. With tears in his eyes, he hurried after the ensign leading them back toward the pines. Damn the generals, thought Silas.

As he and hundreds of men fled the battlefield, newly arriving troops poured out of the woods. The two groups mixed, officers cursing and screaming orders. The ensign disappeared among the pines. Silas raced after him as fast as he could carry Bosworth's body.

A few minutes later, Silas and the others emerged from the timber, well east of the British line. They slogged back across the muddy field they had crossed less than an hour before.

They reached King's Highway just as several horse-drawn artillery limbers raced across the muddy field behind them. The horses bucked and kicked as if they weren't accustomed to their harnesses. Silas noticed saddle marks on their backs, indicating that they had been used recently as mounts, probably by the dragoons.

A mounted lieutenant with gold-colored piping on his uniform led the artillerymen. "Ensign," said the artillery officer, "you and your men attach yourselves to my unit. We have work for you."

"With respect, sir," said the ensign, "I've been ordered to take the wounded to the river and to return to the frontline with more cartridges."

From east along the road, a dragoon approached at a brisk trot. Across the pummel of his saddle was balanced a keg of cartridges. He paused, apparently to listen to the sounds of battle then headed in that direction, across the field.

The artillery officer glanced toward the ensign. "Apparently the ammunition supply is being addressed." His gaze drifted to the wounded. He checked Bosworth and turned to Silas. "This man is dead. Put him down here." To the ensign, he said, "Your men who are actually needed to assist the wounded may proceed. This corporal and the rest of your men shall follow me."

Silas groaned inwardly, but said nothing. He eased the body to the side of the road. Bosworth's eyes stared blankly toward the sky. Fighting back tears and a sudden constriction in his throat, Silas brushed his fingers across Bosworth's eyes to close them. Silas took a deep, wavering breath, then turned and left his old friend.

Silas and a handful of his messmates followed the artillerymen west along King's Highway, a corduroy road made with logs and saplings laid sideways across the muddy path. At a ravine without a bridge, the heavily rutted road plummeted to muddy water. The artillerymen unhitched the fieldpieces from their limbers. They pulled shoulder harnesses from the limber boxes and attached them to hooks on the axel hubs. Silas and the other men slipped the harnesses over their shoulders and across their chests.

Men with long ropes dragged the cannon to the edge of the ravine as other men pulled from the back to prevent the two-ton cannon from rolling out of control. The cannon started to veer left. Silas pulled hard to keep the gun and its carriage from turning sideways and tipping over. He slipped and slid down the slippery bank. Soon, mud caked him head-to-toe.

At the bottom of the ravine, he slipped and fell, nearly choking on gritty, icy-cold water that clouded his eyes. He staggered to his feet and helped roll the gun across the waterway.

They sloshed to the front of the fieldpiece, then dragged it up the muddy western bank. The officer led the way north through another field until they had a clear view of the British forces. Silas bent at the waist and grabbed his knees as he fought to regain his breath.

"Let's not dally, now, lads," said the sergeant. "Hurry back for the next one."

As Silas helped bring two more guns across the water-filled ravine, the boom of American artillery began to answer that of the British. Silas could see that the enemy had advanced toward the east. Directly to his west, on the other side of a gulley, the British had deployed in two lines with a fieldpiece set between them. Several hundred yards farther north, he could see the same two lines he had faced when they emerged from the boggy pinewoods, the gray-coated line and then the northernmost line in red coats.

The American lieutenant was firing canister. Like a huge shotgun, each round hurled scores of musket balls across the field, ripping a gap in the British line. The lieutenant appeared to be aiming for the center of the gray-coat line. With nearly each blast, the battalion colors would topple and fall.

The Brits were well beyond musket range, but each time a hole appeared in the gray line, new troops rushed to fill the gap. Silas was in awe that the British would march into devastating fire with such discipline.

Through the haze of smoke, he could see the gray line come to a halt. Finally, he thought, the British officers would order their men to fall back out of canister range before they were destroyed.

The gray line rippled again with movement. Silas felt his insides quiver. Even with an overcast sky, sharpened steel glistened as bayonets were drawn from their scabbards and fixed to their muskets. Silas cursed. The British weren't retreating—they were attacking.

The lieutenant ordered his men to double their rate of fire, and each blast of canister ripped wide holes in the British line. Without breaking stride, the gray-coats just kept coming, filling in the gaps as they marched. Silas estimated that the British were only two hundred yards away.

"Save the guns!" yelled the lieutenant. The sergeant reorganized a team of men to drag one of the fieldpieces away. Someone tossed Silas a harness.

An artilleryman near Silas toppled into the mud, a hole through his chest. The sergeant snatched the harness from Silas. "Corporal, grab another canister. Help Lieutenant Smith serve the guns."

The boxes of ammunition were stored twenty-five yards behind the fieldpieces as a precaution against accidental explosion. As Silas hurried back to the supply area, he realized that a stray ball or spark might set off the whole pile. With tingling nerves, he grabbed a canister, then raced back to the cannon.

As he handed the canister to one of the men loading the gun, several men cheered. American dragoons had emerged from behind the ravine. Silas estimated a hundred and fifty of them, each wearing a blue cavalry uniform, including a leather helmet topped with a white tress. They turned north off the road and formed a double line facing the British. In unison, each dragoon drew his sword and rested it over his right shoulder.

Silas's heart pounded as he realized that the dragoons might have caught the British off guard. The gray-coats were in line with no time to form a hollow square, the infantry formation most effective against a cavalry charge. The dragoons could hit the gray-coat line hard and fast, with horses bowling over men and churning them under pounding hooves. Meanwhile, the dragoons' sabers would slash left and right, causing terrible wounds, even decapitation. In the general panic, the British infantry would probably break and run, leaving the field to the Americans.

"Go get'em, boys!"

"Huzzah!"

In a neat line, the horses began walking toward the gray-coats across the field. After a few seconds, they accelerated to a trot, kicking up clumps of mud. The line began to fray with the varied gait of the horses.

With rising concern, Silas could see that to reach the oncoming gray-coat line near the center of the field, the dragoons would first have to pass in front of the two redcoat lines beyond the gulley to the west. And then to the north, the dragoons would have to jump a split-rail fence.

From across the gulley, the southernmost line of redcoats fired in unison. Several dragoons fell. Horses tumbled to the ground, legs flailing. The horsemen increased their pace to a gallop, hoofs drumming and white tresses streaming. The line grew more ragged.

Between gunshots, the dragoon commander's voice carried across the field. "*Charge!*"

Each rider thrust his saber forward over his mount's ears as they sped ahead at a dead run, hooves thundering as they kicked up a cloud of flying mud.

The British fieldpiece across the gulley belched smoke and roared. A dozen horses and riders toppled head over hooves into the mud. As the remaining dragoons raced farther north, musket smoke billowed from the next line of redcoats. More horses and riders fell. With little cohesion left in their formation, the remaining horsemen galloped ahead.

Silas cursed when he saw that the target of the charge, the gray-coated line in the center of the field, had wheeled to face their attackers. Just as the dragoons reached the split-rail fence, hundreds of muskets fired. Dozens of dragoons toppled from their mounts. Riderless horses bucked and galloped off the field, tails high.

One dragoon, the commander, continued to race toward the British. Only the fence separated him from the enemy. He and his mount sailed over the split rails.

Gray-coated infantrymen with bayonet-tipped muskets rushed toward the lone rider. Silas feared the American commander would be captured or killed, but the dragoon wheeled his horse, raced toward the fence, and jumped it again. Erect in the saddle, he followed his men back to King's Highway.

Silas glanced across the field, and his heart sank. Scores of men and horses lay dead or wounded in the mud. As horses and men screamed in pain, the gray-coated line resumed marching, advancing directly toward the American artillery.

"Let'r rip!" yelled Lieutenant Smith.

The cannon boomed and bucked as white smoke purled from its barrel. Across the muddy field, a swath of the gray-coated line fell flat. Silas handed a canister to the nearest of the artillerymen, then rushed back to the supply boxes.

Along King's Highway, the sergeant and his party were still working two of the cannon back across the muddy waterway. Between cannon shots, small-arms fire popped from the west as the British silenced the injured horses floundering in the field. Balls whizzed past Silas as he hobbled back to the cannon.

Lieutenant Smith's cannon roared again, quaking air and earth. Artillerymen tugged on ropes fixed to the hubs of the gun carriage, rolling the fieldpiece forward in the ruts packed hard by previous shots.

Another artilleryman had fallen to the side, blood gushing from his neck. As Silas lugged the canister toward the front of the cannon, an artilleryman nodded toward the muzzle. Silas hefted the metallic cylinder into the muzzle and glanced toward the artilleryman. He nodded, and Silas shoved the canister into the bore. The artilleryman stepped forward and poked a wooden rammer inside, driving the canister as deep into the barrel as it would go.

By the time Silas got back with another canister, two more artillerymen had fallen. Lieutenant Smith grabbed the canister from Silas and set it on the ground. Smith dipped a wool-covered rammer into a bucket of water, then handed the dripping swab to Silas. The lieutenant held up a leather-gloved hand, signaling Silas to wait. Smith hurried to the other end of the barrel, pressed a thumb down on the barrel's vent, and nodded.

Silas shoved the rammer into the barrel. It was a tight fit, and Silas had to get directly behind it and shove with all his might. He hoped the wet sponge would extinguish any sparks remaining from the last shot. The lieutenant's thumb over the vent would deprive any such sparks the air needed to ignite. If a spark did set off any unburned powder in the barrel, the rammer would be blasted out of the barrel, quite possibly ripping Silas's arms off or driving the wooden shaft through his chest.

Silas felt the sponge hit the bottom of the bore. He twisted the handle to swab out the inside, then heaved the rammer back out. As the wool-tipped swab emerged from the muzzle, it made a hollow *thump*. Without waiting for further instructions, Silas picked up the canister, shoved it into the muzzle, then used the wooden rammer to force it deep.

The lieutenant cursed and stumbled to his knees. He clutched his shoulder as blood drenched the front of his jacket. Silas rushed to Smith, intending to help him across the gulley. But the lieutenant staggered back to his feet and pointed to the cannon. "One more shot."

Spread on the blanket in a neat row lay hollow tubes of goose quill filled with fine black powder. Silas grabbed one, stuck it into the vent, and shoved it deep.

The lieutenant held what looked like a crooked stick—a linstock. When Silas had finished inserting the fuse, Smith handed the linstock to Silas. "Fire away, Corporal."

Silas took the linstock, its white cord smoldering. He gently blew on the tip of the cord, and it glowed. The gray line of British were just a hundred yards away, and the cannon was pointed directly at them. Recalling how the gun recoiled, Silas stepped behind the wheel ruts, then stretched forward. His hands trembled, shaking the linstock. He focused on steadying the linstock as he lowered its tip to the exposed end of fuse.

The fuse lit with a burst of smoke and sparks. The gun roared, and its carriage slammed backward. A swath of gray-coats were knocked flat. An officer and a dozen gray-clad infantrymen continued to advance, so close Silas could hear their footsteps as they trudged through the mud.

Lieutenant Smith lay next to the cannon. Silas rushed to his side and could see blood flowing from a hole in the young officer's chest.

The gray-coats were nearly upon them, bayonets fixed.

Silas hesitated. Should he stay with Smith? Or save himself and leave the lieutenant to the mercies of the British? Would that be cowardice?

He glanced at the approaching soldiers, a score of razor-sharp bayonets pointed toward him. Silas ran as fast as he could to the gulley. He slipped and slid down the muddy bank.

As he slogged across the muddy waterway, he began to feel a little safer. But he also realized that a force of fewer than a thousand British regulars had met General Wilkinson's force of over seven thousand and had whipped them.

Silas thought of the dozens of Americans left dead on the field, including Bosworth. With the British advancing rapidly, there wouldn't even be time to make sure his old friend received a decent burial. His lips quivered, and he cursed the generals for their incompetence.

CHAPTER THIRTY-FIVE

DECEMBER 1813, FRANKFORT, KENTUCKY

Lemuel Wyckliffe sat erect in the saddle as he and scores of other mounted riflemen paraded past the state capitol. Cheering crowds lined both sides of the street to welcome the war heroes, many from the surrounding county. Lemuel recalled that he, his pappy, and old Stubby had ridden through town on their way to join General William Henry Harrison on his mission to disperse the Indians gathering along the Tippecanoe River over two years before.

Colonel Johnson led his militiamen through the community that had elected him to the U.S. House of Representatives prior to the war. Since the battle along the Thames River, Johnson had become a local war hero. Rumors had spread among the militiamen that he might be considered for higher offices, maybe even president.

Lemuel's mount flinched when a cannon boomed from a nearby park. As he steadied the black gelding, church bells tolled throughout the city. A man stepped from the crowd and held an open whiskey jug up to Lemuel. He took a swig of bourbon and handed the jug back with a nod of thanks. Lemuel savored the taste and felt it burn its way down his throat, imagining that for the next week or so he and the other riflemen would enjoy lots of free drinks.

Lemuel noted that the town had more than doubled in size since he had last seen it. His skin crawled as he rode past a freshly painted bank building, recalling his pappy's admonition that neither a borrower nor a lender he should be. Bankers were akin to lawyers as the vilest of creatures, lending money to hardworking farmers then conniving to rob them of the land they had cleared from the wilderness.

On either side of the street new stores offered a variety of wares. Another sign of progress was the influx of storekeepers, or *ribbon clerks*, as his pappy used to call them. Kentucky had come a long way since the days when Daniel Boone and other hunter/Indian traders had crossed the Cumberland and hacked a living out of the wilderness.

From the edge of the crowd, a blond-haired girl smiled and waved. Lemuel smiled back. Then he noticed scores of young women in the crowd. No doubt some were welcoming their husbands back home, but he knew many of the men who had ridden with Johnson were unmarried. He suspected quite a few would become suitors during the coming months.

On the long ride back to Kentucky, Lemuel had plenty of time to think about his future. He had considered heading west to Missouri, where Daniel Boone had relocated. The prospect of meeting the old trailblazer enticed him. Maybe he would head even farther west into the plains or the mountain country beyond.

But word had reached them that Muscogee Indians in the Mississippi Territory were still causing trouble for white settlers. General Andrew Jackson of Nashville had issued a call for militiamen to aid him in crushing the uprising. Several of the riflemen in Lemuel's company had already decided to head south to show the Tennessee boys how to deal with natives. Deep inside, Lemuel knew he would join them.

CHAPTER THIRTY-SIX

DECEMBER 1813, MISSISSIPPI TERRITORY

Hadjo lay behind a log just outside the village of Holy Ground, high on the bank of the Alabama River. On either side of him, scores of Red Stick warriors hid in the woods. He stared into the twilight of early morning, trying to discern movement indicating the approach of American frontiersmen. For the moment, nothing except a few birds seemed to be moving, and only the chorus of their songs broke the silence. A chill ran down his spine. Although he looked forward to the opportunity of killing more whites and lifting their scalps, he had an uneasy feeling.

After the successful attack on Fort Mims, Chief Red Eagle regrouped the Red Sticks at Holy Ground to celebrate and to recommit to the religious teachings of Tecumseh's brother, The Prophet. The ranks of the Red Sticks swelled as new recruits joined their cause.

Within weeks of the massacre at Fort Mims, however, General Andrew Jackson led an army down from Tennessee to attack the Red Sticks. Jackson's men crossed the Tennessee River and built a stockade they called Fort Strother. Using Strother as their headquarters, the American frontiersmen attacked villages that had aligned with the Red Sticks. Although the Americans usually managed to kill some of the Red Sticks, most of the warriors escaped each time.

Hadjo tightened his grip on the rifle. The chiefs had considered the village at Holy Ground to be so remote that the Americans wouldn't be able to touch it. But scouts had sighted Choctaw Indians guiding the Americans toward the village. In preparation for fighting the Big Knives, the Red Sticks ferried their women and children to safety across the river.

Prancing Fawn had been among the women, and Hadjo's heart ached as he recalled seeing her with swollen belly and glowing with anticipation of childbirth. A child that could have been his, rather than Antler's. On many occasions Hadjo had considered killing Antler, but knew that would not win Prancing Fawn back to him. Instead, Hadjo directed his rage toward the Big Knives whose aggression had been the cause of his absence for two summers. With a little luck he would take scalps this day.

Hadjo held his breath and listened. The birds were no longer singing. The forest had fallen quiet. Something moved between the trees—just a silhouette. Then another. A man. Then several more. They crept from tree to tree as the dawn brightened. One of the men wore a floppy hat, as did many of the American frontiersmen.

From Hadjo's left a musket fired. He aimed his rifle and fired. Without waiting to reload, he retreated uphill into the village. Shots popped from all around him. The Americans seemed to be attacking from several directions.

Over the next three hours, Hadjo and the other Red Sticks fought as their attackers closed in on the village. The Americans pushed the Red Sticks closer and closer to the river, and warriors began to disappear into the swamp or to slip down the steep bank into the swift current and swim away.

Hadjo and a handful of warriors rallied around Chief Red Eagle as the Americans closed in for the kill. Red Eagle was leaning against a thick tree trunk as he reloaded his musket when an American stepped out of the woods and aimed his rifle at the chief. Hadjo lunged toward Red Eagle, knocking him to the ground. Chips of bark showered them as a ball nicked the tree.

Red Eagle rolled to his feet, ready to pounce. He glared at Hadjo, then nodded. The chief's attention returned to the Americans advancing in a broad line toward the camp. Red Eagle turned to his warriors and yelled, "Save yourselves!"

There had been only a few horses in camp before the battle began, and most of those had already run away or been shot. Just two remained. Red Eagle untied one, handed the reins to Hadjo, and pointed to the riverbank. "That is the only way out."

Hadjo slipped the reins over the horse's neck and held his rifle in his left hand while he leaped to the horse's back. Shifting the rifle to his right hand, he tapped his heels back into the horse's ribs. The animal shot forward, and the edge of the river bank came into view. When the horse saw the twelve-foot drop to the water, Hadjo could feel it hesitate. Hadjo held his rifle high over his head, screamed his fiercest war cry, and kicked his heels back into the horse's ribs. The beast sped forward, leaping as it cleared the bank.

Hadjo held the reins low in his left hand and the rifle high in his right as he gripped the horse with his legs. For a moment the horse sailed higher as if trying to clear whatever obstacle lay before it. At the zenith of the leap, Hadjo felt weightless, and time seemed to slow. But then the horse's head dipped, and Hadjo felt his insides rise within him. He yelled his loudest as he and the horse plummeted toward the muddy river.

In a flash of panic, Hadjo imagined a tree or rock hidden just below the surface. Bone-breaking impact would leave him and the horse helpless as they gasped their last breath in a powerful current.

The horse plunged into the water, and Hadjo pounded down on the animal's back. He lost hold of the reins as water surged over him.

As the horse shot deeper, Hadjo feared he might drop the rifle. He knew he couldn't swim while holding the weapon. He had to hang on to the horse. Gripping the rifle tight, he draped his right arm over the horse's shoulder, then grabbed its mane with his left.

The horse churned its legs as it fought to surface. For a moment, Hadjo feared that both he and the horse would drown.

His lungs burned for air, and he knew he couldn't last much longer. His mind reeled with dread of having to release both the horse and the rifle so he could claw his way to the surface. Just then he felt air on his cheek. He gasped for breath.

From behind him he heard a fierce war cry. Over the cliff sailed the other horse, with Red Eagle astride it. Soon both of them drifted downstream as their mounts struggled to reach the far shore.

Angry voices shouted from behind them. Something whizzed over Hadjo's head. A waterspout splashed to his side. Rifle fire cracked from high on the bank as more balls smacked into the current around Hadjo.

Grateful for the brisk current as it rushed him and Red Eagle farther from the Americans, Hadjo kicked his legs, helping the horse make progress.

Soon their horses staggered onto the far shore. Red Eagle turned to face the American frontiersmen across the river. He raised his rifle and screamed his war cry. More balls whizzed past them as they led their horses into the cover of the trees.

Safely out of sight, Hadjo followed Red Eagle's example and tied his horse to a tree. The chief plopped to the dry leaves covering the forest floor. He growled and then chuckled. "Well done, my young friend. Let us rest a moment, and I will begin to devise a plan to make those white dogs pay for their evil deeds."

CHAPTER THIRTY-SEVEN

DECEMBER 1813, WASHINGTON CITY

Rachel Thurston savored the scent that filled the store—a mixture of coffee, molasses, and pepper. Her head throbbed as she realized that many of the prices had jumped again. Imported goods were in short supply, and some prices had doubled, even tripled, since the beginning of the war.

Her father had provided her with coins for shopping and assured her they had plenty more when she needed them. Rachel couldn't help feeling guilty for spending so much on basic household items. As she worked with the store clerk to accumulate her purchases, she wondered how less fortunate citizens were getting by. Her heart ached for the untold hardship wartime prices must be causing so many Americans, especially the poor and their children.

Rachel passed a bin of onions tied together by their dry stalks. She selected a bunch and continued down the aisle. One should have plenty of onions around the house, her mother had advised. Their smell would slow the spread of disease, and onions placed strategically around the house would absorb disease from the air.

Once her purchases were gathered on the store counter and the clerk had tallied her bill, she reached into her pocketbook and pulled out a handful of coins. She had one U.S. silver dollar, but mostly she had an assortment of Spanish coins. Her father had coached her on the value of each, so she wouldn't be cheated by an unscrupulous merchant. She sorted through the coins and handed several to the clerk. For change, he handed her a tiny Portuguese coin.

One of the Federalist complaints about the Democratic-Republicans was that they hadn't standardized the nation's currency. To lubricate the wheels of commerce, they needed a national bank to print currency and mint specie. All foreign tender should be prohibited, the Federalists argued, in favor of domestic coin and currency. But the Democratic-Republicans preferred a less-formal system.

As it was, the situation was a mess. In the federal district, of course, prices were usually quoted in dollars and cents, but in New England prices were often listed in pounds and pence. And since Spanish coins were universally common, prices were frequently quoted in Spanish *reales*. On the frontier, according to newspapers, coins were in such short supply that business was conducted almost entirely by barter.

Rachel recalled that, before the war, she had written a letter arguing that the federal government should mint enough coin and print enough currency to fill the needs of the nation, and then ban the use of foreign money. There was little chance of that happening until after the war ended.

The war had brought the nation's economy to a standstill. Even privateering, which had been so lucrative during the first months of the war, had declined as most British merchant ships traveled in convoys protected by warships. Rachel had heard that 250 ships were idled in Boston harbor, even though the British blockade had not been extended north to New England—at least not yet. Making matters even worse, President Madison had signed into law an extension of the trade embargo, prohibiting food and contraband from being taken to sea. Her father had fumed that the restriction was aimed primarily at New England in retaliation for the region's failure to support the war. After a year and a half of war, no end seemed in sight.

As the clerk loaded her packages into her carriage, a disheveled boy of about ten approached Rachel and offered her a newspaper. She handed him a tiny coin and noticed a front-page story declaring that recent rumors of a slave revolt in Georgia were unfounded. In Washington City, Rachel had discovered, rumors about a slave revolt seemed to circulate constantly.

CHAPTER THIRTY-EIGHT

DECEMBER 1813, WASHINGTON CITY

George Sherbourne listened as Robert Fulton wrapped up a presentation about his plans for a formidable new warship—a steam frigate.

"Ladies and gentlemen," announced Fulton, "I do not exaggerate when I state that the steam frigate will make the States equal to any nation in naval power." With a dramatic sweep of his arm, he bowed.

"Bravo!" someone shouted.

"Huzzah!" yelled another.

George joined the other guests as they stood and applauded. A small crowd swarmed around Fulton, peppering him with questions.

George smiled and made small talk with the other guests, but his mind reeled. If Fulton were successful in building and deploying the steam frigate as he described it, Britain's blockade of New York harbor could be challenged. Additional steam frigates could break the entire blockade of American ports. A few more such ships under capable leadership could very well threaten Britain's domination of the seas and impair her quest to defeat Napoleon.

As George sipped punch, he wondered if he should eliminate Robert Fulton as a threat to Crown forces. Apparently the inventor didn't have any bodyguards, so assassination with either a pistol or a knife would be relatively simple if Fulton could be caught alone.

George took another sip of punch. Whom was he kidding? He was a soldier, not a murderer. Espionage was bad enough. He certainly didn't care to add assassination to his list of dubious accomplishments. And what would Anne think of him if she ever found out? Still, Fulton's latest invention could lead to the horrible death of hundreds of British sailors. Was it his duty to kill Fulton if he could?

The party seemed to be winding down, so he thanked the host and hostess, then headed for the door. Outside, his lungs filled with crisp night air as he began the walk to his boardinghouse, just a few blocks away.

Another year of war was nearing an end, with mixed results for both sides. Unfortunately, thought George, that didn't bode well for a British victory. And if Fulton was successful in building his steam frigate, the balance of power could very well shift to the Americans.

Recently the war had taken new direction. The Mississippi Territory had been a focus of attention since thousands of troops, mostly Tennessee militiamen, converged on the area to stabilize it and to exact revenge upon renegade Muscogee Red Sticks for the massacre at Fort Mims.

George suspected that the British and their Spanish allies in Florida were providing support to the Red Sticks, but he doubted that would be enough to counter a determined American effort if they had effective leadership.

Even the war at sea had taken an unexpected turn. One of the American frigates, the *Essex*, had sailed from the East Coast in the fall of 1812 with orders to join with two others in the south Atlantic. Unable to find the other frigates, the *Essex* rounded Cape Horn at the southern tip of South America and began cruising north to the Galapagos Islands in search of British whaling ships. For months, she had hunted like a wolf in a pasture of unguarded sheep, devastating British commerce in the Pacific.

George wondered of the fate of the trading post at Astoria, far to the west where the Columbia River flowed into the Pacific. Founded and owned by John Jacob Astor, it included territory larger than that of the original thirteen American colonies. When George had been on board a British naval vessel recently, one of the officers speculated that London had already sent a ship to take control of Astoria. News of such events took months to reach the American East Coast, as the overland route was incredibly long and ships carrying news had to sail around the southern tip of South America.

From the Great Lakes region, word had arrived that after Commodore Oliver Perry defeated the British squadron on Lake Erie, American forces under General Harrison recaptured Detroit and then occupied Fort Malden. Harrison then caught up to British forces fleeing from Fort Malden, captured many of the soldiers, and wiped out the allied Indians, including the legendary Tecumseh.

A few weeks later the Americans launched two powerful armies north toward Montreal in a pincerlike movement to seize the city and cut vital communication and supply lines to the rest of Canada. The smaller force moved north, up the Champlain Valley, while the larger headed east down the St. Lawrence from Lake Ontario. Both attacks failed.

George had gathered bits and pieces of the story and was pleased to hear that besides the Indians and the British regulars in the force, Canadian militia had worked together—both English-speaking and French-speaking—to drive back the invading Americans.

The Americans abandoned Fort George on the Niagara and burned the nearby village of Newark. Reports were trickling in that British and Canadian forces had crossed the Niagara and St. Lawrence Rivers to destroy American settlements, wiping out much of the U.S. gains for the year and taking "hard war" to American soil.

The crisp night air echoed with the clip-clop of horses trotting down the street behind George. He imagined that a detachment of cavalry had been sent to arrest him. He considered bolting between the houses and then dashing to the livery where he stabled his horse. His mind raced. If the horsemen hadn't been sent for him, he would bring unwanted attention to himself by running. Surely if he had been found out, his pursuers could have arrested him at the party or as he left the house.

He forced himself to walk normally as the horses approached him from behind. His heart pounded when they pulled alongside. One of the riders, a civilian, tipped a fur hat as he passed. George returned the courtesy, and the riders continued down the street.

George chastised himself for being overly paranoid, then forced his thoughts back to the war, which seemed to be dragging on with neither side gaining clear advantage.

Then again, all that could change with recent progress in Europe. General Arthur Wellesley had broken the French legions in Spain and chased them over the Pyrenees into France. If Napoleon could be subdued, thousands of redcoats and dozens of warships could be freed for action against the Americans. The thought warmed George as he approached his boardinghouse. American resistance would be crushed, and peace would be imposed under terms dictated by the Crown.

CHAPTER THIRTY-NINE

JANUARY 1814, MISSISSIPPI TERRITORY

With a wary eye, Lemuel Wyckliffe studied the tree-lined banks along Enitachopco Creek. Seeing no sign of Indians, he slipped his canteen strap off his shoulder and stooped to the rocky edge of the stream. He pulled the stopper and lowered the wooden container into the clear, cold water. Bubbles gurgled out as the canteen filled.

Downstream, on the left bank, a six-horse team stood hitched to a cart with a six-pound cannon in tow. The gun's crew packed equipment onto the two-wheeled limber as they prepared to ford the creek. Lemuel recognized the young lieutenant and his men as part of the Nashville artillery company that had stayed with General Andrew Jackson when most of his troops had abandoned him during the winter. Seeing the gun crew reminded Lemuel of the challenges Jackson must have faced over the last several months.

Lemuel had learned from the other scouts that the American strategy against the Red Sticks was a three-pronged plan. Separate columns of troops were to advance into the Muscogee nation from Georgia on the east, from Mobile to the south, and from Tennessee on the north.

By the time Lemuel had caught up with General Jackson, the Tennesseans had trekked south across wilderness hill country to the northern edge of Muscogee country. There, along the Coosa River, Jackson had built Fort Strother.

Jackson had wasted little time in launching his troops against the Red Sticks as soon as his scouts located them. Before dawn one early November day, they surrounded a Red Stick village of several hundred warriors and surprised them. As described by one of the other mounted riflemen, David Crockett, "We shot them like dogs." After suffering defeats, at Talladega and Holy Ground, the Red Sticks learned to elude or escape Jackson and his inexperienced, untrained troops.

When winter approached, Jackson's army ran out of food and supplies. Without winter clothes and with the end of their three-month terms of enlistment approaching, the men prepared to head home. Jackson pleaded with them to stay and be ready to attack the Red Sticks as soon as supplies and reinforcements arrived. Conditions continued to decline, and Jackson resorted to threats and force to keep his shrinking army in place. One day Jackson used a company of militiamen to prevent a group of volunteers from leaving. The next day he used the volunteers to prevent the militiamen from leaving. But the men were starving and freezing, and with no eminent plans to fight the Red Sticks, one unit after another packed up and headed home to Tennessee.

Months later the Americans began to hear rumors that a large force of Red Stick warriors were gathering at a tight loop in the Tallapoosa River called Horseshoe Bend. Fearing that the Red Sticks might threaten the American column advancing from Georgia, Jackson set out to find the native stronghold as soon as he had new troops and supplies.

Jackson's probe to the south came under repeated harassment. The Red Sticks launched sneak attacks against Jackson's column during the day and his hollow-square camps at night. His scouts discovered that Horseshoe Bend was heavily fortified. Without adequate forces to engage the Red Stick encampment, Jackson turned his column around and headed it back north toward Fort Strother.

Lemuel's hand had grown numb with cold by the time his canteen filled. He stood and took a long swig of the icy water, then dipped the wooden container back into the creek. The cannon crew's limber driver had coaxed his team into the creek, and the horses were in the water up to their belly hauling for the far bank. Lemuel shuddered at the thought of wading across another freezing stream. On the march, with no fires to be lit until the evening camp, he dreaded wearing damp clothes through another chilly day.

Still, Lemuel wished the cannoneers would hurry, so he and the other scouts guarding them could ford the creek as well. The scouts, the cannon crew, and several hundred green volunteers were Jackson's rear guard. The rest of the army was already across the creek and heading north. As was Jackson's habit, his army was divided into three columns led by an advance guard and trailed by a rear guard.

Fording the creek was potentially the most dangerous moment for the rear guard. If attacked, they would be cut off from the main body of the army until troops turned and recrossed the stream. The standard plan if attacked from the rear was for Jackson to wheel his right and left columns and hurry them back to attack the flanks of the enemy, maybe even surrounding it, while the center column backtracked to reinforce the rear guard. Lemuel figured it was a sound plan, in theory.

He almost dropped his canteen when the blast of a musket shot echoed through the woods. The first shot was followed by the crackle of more gunfire and blood-chilling Indian war cries. With a curse, Lemuel secured the canteen strap over his shoulder and brought his rifle up to his chest. Ready to aim and fire in an instant, he studied the tree line along the creek bank.

He was tempted to rush up the bank and join the scouts under attack, but his instructions had been clear—he was to protect the cannon crew's flank. With a glance over his shoulder, he saw most of the cannoneers, bayonets fixed to their muskets, rush up the creek bank to meet the threat.

The team of horses pulling the limber had almost reached the far bank. Now the cannoneers hurried to unhitch the fieldpiece. The lieutenant and a half-dozen of his men attached thick ropes to hooks on the ends of the axels and started dragging the cannon back across the creek.

Lemuel slung his rifle and raced for the cannon. With some of the men pulling at the ropes, a couple of artillerists cranking each wheel, and the rest of them shoving from behind, there hardly seemed to be any room for him to lend a hand. But one of the cannoneers slipped and tumbled into the water. Lemuel took the fallen man's place and shoved at the gun carriage's wheel with all of his strength.

As they worked the cannon up the bank, the din of battle intensified. By the sound of the war cries, Lemuel could tell they faced hundreds of Red Sticks. Movement upstream caught his attention. Hundreds of the new recruits assigned to the rear guard were fleeing across the stream, running away from the battle. Cursing the deserters silently, he looked downstream and saw the same thing.

A dark-blue uniformed officer on horseback galloped his horse into the stream and drew his sword. It was Jackson. By the man's frantic gestures, Lemuel could tell that the general was trying to turn the retreating rearguard volunteers around. But the panicked militiamen continued to flee across the creek, then disappear into the woods.

Hearing the fight ahead intensify, Lemuel pushed harder as he and the cannoneers manhandled the gun up the slippery bank. At the crest of the rise, twenty of his fellow scouts were firing from the cover of trees. A handful of the artillerymen had formed a ragged line and were firing at will. Across a small clearing, hundreds of screaming Red Sticks emerged from the woods.

The cannon crew hustled to ready the gun. Lemuel took cover behind a fallen tree and fired at the nearest native, dropping him with a shot to the chest. Lemuel jumped and turned when he heard noise behind him. Colonel Carroll and thirty troops were hurrying up the creek bank.

Lemuel dropped another Red Stick with a shot to the head. As he reloaded he estimated that all told, the scouts, the artillerists, and Colonel Carroll's men totaled fewer than a hundred men. Before them, in the meadow and the woods, the natives numbered in the hundreds. He glanced at the cannoneers, hoping they would bring the gun to bear soon, else they would all be overrun.

As balls whizzed by, Lemuel heard one of the cannoneers curse, then shout, "Who has the rammer and pick?

After a moment one of the other men shouted back. "We put them in the limber to ford the creek!"

"Damn it!"

"Well, hurry back and get them!"

The Red Sticks pressed their attack. A massacre was in the making. A scout to Lemuel's left screamed and fell to the ground, blood gushing from an eye.

As the cannoneers cursed, Lemuel fired his rifle again. An artillery private shoved a canister cartridge into the gun's muzzle, then grabbed his musket and removed the bayonet. He shoved the musket barrel into the cannon muzzle, ramming the charge home.

More and more Red Sticks rushed out the woods and attacked.

Another cannoneer poured powder into the vent. "Ready!"

"Match!" someone screamed in panic. "Where's the match?"

The lieutenant in charge drew his pistol, laid the flintlock next to the cannon vent, and pulled the trigger. The pan flashed, and the cannon roared with a belch of white smoke as the gun carriage bucked back several feet. Across the meadow a half-dozen natives were knocked flat on their backs in a hail of canister shot.

As the sound of the cannon blast echoed through the woods, the Red Sticks fell silent. Then with renewed furor, they screamed and charged again.

The gun crew hurried to reload, but the lieutenant yelled to his men, "Save the cannon!" As the gun was rolled back down the creek bank, the soldiers shot volley after volley of musket fire at the advancing horde.

Lemuel jumped and turned when he heard something behind him. American troops were rushing up the bank to reinforce them, and behind them were many more crossing the creek. As the new arrivals opened fire, the natives began to fall back.

Lemuel couldn't tell who gave the command, but with a roar the American troops rushed forward, bayonets lowered. Lemuel drew his hatchet and sprinted after them, screaming his loudest.

A few warriors stood their ground, but they were quickly slaughtered. The rest of the Red Sticks turned and ran for the woods, some tossing aside blankets and other items that might slow them.

As Lemuel raced after the Indians, he realized that even though the Americans had avoided getting massacred, most of the Red Sticks had once again escaped to fight another day.

CHAPTER FORTY

FEBRUARY 1814, BLACK ROCK, NEW YORK

Corporal Silas Shackleton stood at attention with his musket propped over his shoulder. An overcast sky hid the noontime sun. He wiggled his toes and fingers to warm them and wondered what the weather was like in New York City. Maybe a little warmer, he figured, wondering if he would ever be able to return home.

Five prisoners, each wearing white nightshirts, were marched at bayonet point in front of Silas and the other soldiers assembled as a firing squad. The prisoners were about to receive their punishment for desertion. One by one, with hands tied behind their back, they were spaced several yards apart and forced to kneel before a shallow trench. A sergeant draped a hood of black cloth over each prisoner's head.

The youngest of the prisoners, a boy of only fifteen, was placed directly in front of Silas. As Silas waited for the lieutenant in charge to give the orders, he glanced at the grave that had been chipped out of frozen, rocky soil. It reminded him of the many he had helped dig over the winter months.

The army had established winter quarters near the towns of Black Rock and Buffalo, along the Niagara River. The area's rocky soil provided a relatively dry location for a camp, but the winter proved harsh. Many of the men had only their lightweight summer uniforms. Some no longer even had boots.

In the cold and wet, disease spread rapidly. Dysentery and cholera rampaged through camp. Men reported a headache, and within a few hours, they died. Each day several bodies were laid to rest in shallow graves. Desertion was common, and mutiny became a threat.

Silas studied the five hooded men in front of him. A wave of shame flowed over him as he recalled leaving Lieutenant Smith on the ground at the battle along the St. Lawrence River. Another wave of shame hit him as he recalled that he had been a deserter at Queenston Heights the previous year. Even further back, he had run from his problems in New York City. Silas swallowed hard and clenched his teeth, realizing that he was the one who should be in front of a firing squad. He might be worse than a deserter. He might be a coward.

The lieutenant drew his sword, rested it upon his shoulder, and then nodded to the sergeant.

The sergeant yelled, "Present!"

Silas lifted his musket from his shoulder and thumbed the hammer to half cock. He held the musket across his chest, barrel high to the left.

"Aim!"

Silas thumbed the hammer to full cock, then pulled the butt tight against his right shoulder. He aimed carefully for the red patch of cloth sewn over the fifteen-year-old deserter's heart.

"Fire!"

Silas closed his eyes and squeezed the trigger. The butt hammered his shoulder, and sparks peppered his cheeks. Gray-white smoke billowed forward. A breeze whisked the smoke away, revealing the boy's body on the ground. Silas glanced at the other four prisoners. Each lay writhing in a growing puddle of blood.

When Silas glanced back to the boy's body, he saw it twitch slightly. It moved again, then the boy sat up. Unlike the other prisoners, he showed no sign of blood on his nightshirt. The sergeant walked over to the youth and yanked his hood off. The boy blinked at the sunlight, then glanced around.

Silas chuckled, as did several others in the line. The court-martial had found the boy guilty of desertion but, in deference to his youth, had ordered that he face a firing squad with one difference. Silas's musket and those of the other men in front of the fifteen-year-old had been loaded with powder and wadding but no ball. The sergeant untied the boy, handed him a shovel, and ordered him to help bury the deserters who had been executed.

CHAPTER FORTY-ONE

FEBRUARY 1814, WASHINGTON CITY

As the marine band struck up a waltz, Rachel Thurston smiled at the young man facing her. He placed his right hand at the waist of her gossamer gown and took her hand with the other. Together with scores of other couples, they glided in circles around the wooden dance floor. The "ballroom" was a warehouse at the Naval Yard, one of the few buildings in Washington City with a floor expansive enough to accommodate the dance.

The young man was a promising attorney with curly red hair and sweaty palms. Her mother had told her that people with red hair tended to be quick tempered, but Rachel saw no such indication in his behavior. He seemed to be concentrating on his dance steps, and Rachel had little trouble keeping up with him.

Each of the young men who had lined up for a space on her dance card had seemed pleasant. Rachel supposed that most of her dance partners would someday make very nice husbands—for someone. None of the young men particularly interested her, and her thoughts drifted to George Sherbourne.

She hadn't seen him in over a week. She supposed he was trying to line up speculation in land out west, or maybe in a steamship, or in a bank. No, not a bank. She had heard her father counsel George that banks were far too speculative to be considered sound investments, especially new banks outside the original thirteen states.

Rachel had asked her father about George's mysterious disappearances, and he had reminded her that Washington City was only the governmental center of the nation. The commercial centers, where real business took place, were Baltimore, Philadelphia, New York City, and Boston. It was perfectly natural for a young man seeking financial opportunities to make visits to any, or even all, of those cities in search of investment opportunities. Her father went on to remind her that during wartime speculative opportunities multiplied, but so did their risk. A man like George could become wealthy or go broke—maybe both more than once—during his career. If she was looking for stability in her life, he had warned her, she should stay clear of George Sherbourne.

Rachel wondered what George was up to. He and her father always seemed to have interesting and challenging opportunities to pursue. Meanwhile, she was stuck with housework and dancing with uninteresting twits.

News of the war had been discouraging. As American forces abandoned Fort George on the Niagara River, they burned the nearby Canadian village of Newark. British forces soon retaliated by capturing Fort Niagara and by burning American villages all along the Niagara River. Farther south, in the Mississippi Territory, General Andrew Jackson's forces seemed to be ineffective in subduing hostile Indians. With all the suffering by civilians, Rachel wondered why they put up with the Democratic-Republicans.

Her attention snapped back to her dance partner when she realized that he was staring at her. She smiled as nicely as she could and met his gaze.

The waltz ended with a flourish, and the dancers applauded the marine band, which was serving as the orchestra for the evening. A young man with dark hair and a long pointed nose approached her and claimed the dance. He smiled as they waited for the music to begin again. She was about to ask if they could skip the next dance in favor of a trip to the punch bowl when she heard a voice she recognized.

"Excuse me, may I cut in?"

Facing Rachel's young dance partner was George Sherbourne, his face weather-beaten but his smile warm. He was dressed in a waistcoat over a white ruffled shirt and breeches. Rachel felt her heart beat faster at the sight of him.

For a moment she thought her new dance partner might refuse, but George stood firm, his jaw set. To start an argument, especially in public, might very well lead to a duel. Rachel was quite sure the young man had never been in a duel and wasn't ever likely to be. On the other hand, she could easily imagine George facing off against another man, pistol in hand.

A shiver ran down her spine. She placed a hand on the young man's shoulder. "Maybe another time?"

CHAPTER FORTY-TWO

MARCH 1814, TALLAPOOSA RIVER,
MISSISSIPPI TERRITORY

At midmorning Hadjo peeked over one of the pine logs forming the barricade across the neck of the thumb-shaped peninsula called Horseshoe Bend. To the north, blue-uniformed soldiers marched across a clearing and began to line up and face the fortification. Another group of soldiers accompanied two horse-drawn carts, each towing a cannon to a small hilltop less than a hundred yards from the barricade. Meanwhile hundreds and hundreds of plainly clad militiamen poured out of the woods to the north and extended the line across the four-hundred-yard neck of the peninsula.

Even with the sturdy fortification, Hadjo felt jittery about the arrival of the army. Since the attack on Fort Mims in August and the arrival of General Jackson that fall, the Red Sticks had had only mixed success in fighting the whites. After their frequent withdrawals, the Big Knives kept coming back—each time better armed, better supplied, and in greater numbers.

The fortification at Horseshoe Bend was by far the Red Sticks' strongest. Improving upon the natural defenses afforded by a tight loop in the

Tallapoosa River, they had constructed the bow-shaped barricade suggested by the Spanish in Pensacola. A frontal assault would subject any attacker to murderous crossfire from a double row of gun ports placed in the sides of the zigzag fortification. And if the attackers breached the wall, its inward bow and jagged pattern would prevent them from subjecting the defenders to murderous fire in a straight line in either direction along the back side. The wooded and overgrown peninsula provided natural cover for the Red Sticks to withdraw into if necessary, to ambush the attackers.

Up and down the breastwork, Red Sticks adorned with feathers and black-painted faces climbed atop the logs to brandish their weapons and scream their war cries. Some waved cow tails, and some rang bells.

Hadjo climbed the eight-foot-high wall of timbers and balanced himself on the topmost log. Facing the whites, he raised his rifle and red-painted war club toward the heavens and howled like a wolf. Something whizzed past his ear, then another. From a formation of white militiamen across the meadow puffed clouds of gun smoke. As the crackle of rifle and musket fire reached his ears, Hadjo ducked and nearly fell. He leaped back behind the breastwork.

Lemuel Wyckliffe sat quietly in the brush along the south bank of the river across from the Horseshoe Bend peninsula. Cannon fire boomed in the distance from the north. He had been sitting in the cold for hours as hundreds of restless Cherokees and allied Muscogee warriors hid along the bank . . . just out of sight of the Red Stick village across the river. The village looked deserted, but empty canoes were tied in clusters along the shoreline, providing an escape route for the Red Sticks if they needed one.

Jackson's intentions had been made clear. The Red Sticks were to be exterminated. His orders for the allied Indians and militiamen across the river had been simple—stay out of sight, then kill any Red Sticks attempting to escape across the river. So far the biggest challenge for Lemuel had been battling boredom and staying warm in the brisk March breeze.

To Lemuel's right on his side of the river, he noticed movement at the water's edge. He shifted his position slightly and peeked between the pine trees. Several Cherokees had slipped into the river and were swimming across. Lemuel cursed under his breath. The redskins didn't follow orders worth a damn.

As the Cherokees worked their way across the river, Lemuel wondered if he should find General Coffee and report what was happening. But Lemuel could see that the swimmers were heading toward the canoes tied along the far shore. He decided to see what happened next. Maybe this would work out well after all.

When the Cherokees neared the canoes, gun smoke billowed from the cliffs beyond the village, and musket shots crackled in the crisp air. One of the Cherokees floundered in the water, obviously hit. The others reached the canoes, crawled in, then began paddling furiously back across the river with more canoes in tow. Gunfire popped from the cliffs across the river. Tiny spouts peppered the water around the fleeing canoes.

Even before the Cherokees returned to the riverbank safely, scores of Cherokee and allied Muscogee warriors wearing white feathers or deer tails in their hair rushed out of the woods to the river. Within minutes canoes laden with warriors were speeding back across the river to the deserted village. Lemuel studied the scene carefully, then turned and hurried uphill through the brush. He untied his horse and galloped to where he hoped he would find General Coffee.

Lemuel raced his horse up the riverbank through trees and brush as fast as he dared. General Coffee had ordered him to find Jackson as quickly as possible and report what was happening at the river and village. Still drenched from crossing the river, he and his mount bolted out of the woods.

What he saw before him caused him to rein his mount to a stop. A wide swath of ground across the neck of the Horseshoe Bend peninsula had been cleared of trees. Stout logs had been stacked in a jagged, concave curve from the river on one side of the peninsula to the other side. Behind the barricade to the south lay a hundred acres of thick woods within the loop of the bend in the river. Only a few taunting, black-faced warriors were visible at the breastwork, but Lemuel understood that as many as a thousand Red Stick warriors were holed up there.

Several hundred yards to the north of the barricade was Jackson's army, three thousand men lined shoulder to shoulder from one stretch of the river to the other. Closer to the breastwork on a hilltop, one of Jackson's two fieldpieces roared, firing a round at the barricade. Lemuel recognized the six-pounder he had helped manhandle up the bank at Enitachopco Creek. Along the long line of troops, he spotted a cluster of flags and pennants that marked Jackson's field headquarters. He spurred his horse in that direction.

He leaped from his horse before she even stopped, then dodged through a cluster of uniformed officers. He found Jackson conferring with a portly colonel. The tall, gaunt-faced general quieted the colonel with a raised hand as Lemuel approached. After listening intently to Lemuel's report, Jackson turned and studied the smoke billowing over the trees to the south. Gunfire crackled from the high ground behind the breastwork.

Jackson pounded his fist into the palm of his open hand, then faced his officers. "Gentlemen, this is our opportunity. Return to your units immediately. We attack shortly."

Men hustled in every direction, and for a moment Lemuel felt lost in the melee. He looked around for familiar faces, but everyone seemed to be part of the newly arrived troops. He did recognize several men in the 39th Infantry Company lined up under their new blue pennant. The flag sported a cluster of eighteen stars, one for each state in the Union. Under the stars, an American eagle seemed to beat its wings as the flag snapped in the breeze. Lemuel felt a chill run down his spine.

He stepped in at the end of the infantry formation, a line several ranks deep. The major in charge of the unit stood in front of his men, facing them. He glanced toward Lemuel and nodded, then turned to face the enemy fortification. In front of Lemuel, closer to the line of infantrymen, was a young officer he recognized as Ensign Sam Houston.

As Lemuel waited for the attack to begin, he wondered if the newly arrived volunteers would cut and run as those at Enitachopco Creek had earlier in the year. But General Jackson had made sure each unit was led by capable, experienced officers. He also issued an icy declaration, "Any officer or soldier who flees before the enemy without being compelled to do so by superior force and actual necessity—shall suffer death." Few doubted Jackson's resolve. Just weeks before he had ordered the execution of a private who failed to follow orders.

Drums began the long roll that signaled an attack. The 39th's major drew his sword, pointed it skyward, then forward. Up and down the line, officers and men began to march briskly toward the barricade. Lemuel clutched his rifle and hurried to keep up with the uniformed soldiers. Gun smoke billowed from the portals in the barricade, and balls whizzed past Lemuel. A soldier in front of him fell to the ground, and Lemuel leaped over him, hurrying to keep up with Ensign Houston.

The march across the field was several hundred yards. Although the morning air was chilly, Lemuel soon felt sweat trickling down his forehead. The uniformed soldiers next to him marched with evenly spaced paces, their chests thrust out with gleaming muskets at their shoulders. Lemuel hunched down as far as he could, making himself a smaller target, expecting a musket ball to catch him at any moment.

As the infantrymen drew closer to the barricade, the major shouted an order, and bayonet-tipped muskets were pointed forward at waist level. With a roar, amid a shower of Red Stick arrows and balls, the soldiers charged toward the fortification now shrouded with a cloud of gun smoke.

The major was the first of the Americans to reach the barricade. He shoved his pistol into a portal and fired. To Lemuel's left as far as he could see, thousands of men stormed toward the breastwork.

The major scrambled to the top of the barricade, waved his hat and yelled for his men to follow him. At that moment the major's head snapped to the side with a spray of blood and gray matter. He toppled off the barricade.

Half expecting his own death or injury at any moment, Lemuel reached the barricade just behind Ensign Houston. A musket barrel poked out from the gun port in front of Lemuel. He shoved his own rifle barrel into the porthole and pulled the trigger. Without waiting to reload, he slung his rifle over his shoulder and drew his hatchet. All across the barricade in both directions, Americans and Red Sticks fought bayonet to war club and hatchet to tomahawk.

Ensign Houston reached the top of the barricade and fired his pistol. An arrow caught the young officer in his thigh, and he lurched forward. Lemuel crawled over the top, ducked a thrown spear, and leaped at a black-faced native rushing toward the injured ensign.

Lemuel knocked the Red Stick to the ground, but they both sprang back to their feet. The warrior swung his war club toward Lemuel's head. He caught the club with his hatchet, and for a moment their weapons locked. Lemuel pulled the knife from his belt and shoved it into the Indian's belly, then yanked up hard, slicing deep until the blade caught on the Indian's ribs. He threw the warrior to the ground and swung his hatchet deep into the native's skull.

Soldiers poured over the barricade. Natives who stood their ground were quickly cut down. The rest retreated into the brush with soldiers and militiamen right behind them.

Lemuel knelt to take the scalp of the warrior he had just killed. Nearby, a private was attending to Ensign Houston, and Lemuel could hear the young officer telling the soldier to pull the arrow from his thigh. When the soldier refused, Houston drew his pistol and pointed it at the private's chest. "Pull it out!"

The soldier grabbed hold of the arrow shaft and yanked. Houston screamed, but the arrow didn't budge. Again the young officer ordered the private to remove the arrow. As the private hesitated, Lemuel stepped closer for a better look. The barbed arrow point was obviously deep in the flesh of Houston's thigh, maybe even embedded in bone. The private was arguing that the ensign should let a surgeon remove the barbed arrow tip. Houston pointed the pistol toward Lemuel. "You pull it out."

Lemuel flinched, then said, "Lower the pistol. Then I'll see what I can do."

Houston eased the pistol to the ground. Lemuel placed his foot on the ensign's thigh and grabbed hold of the arrow's shaft at the point where it entered the leg. He stepped down hard as he tightened his grip in the arrow and pulled. The arrowhead was in deep and tight, so Lemuel twisted and turned the shaft as he pulled even harder. Houston screamed and blacked out. Lemuel pulled and twisted with all his strength as he ground his foot down into the officer's thigh. He toppled backward as the arrow slipped free.

The wound in Houston's thigh bled heavily, but it wasn't gushing as it would if a major artery had been severed. The ensign regained consciousness as the private wrapped a dirty handkerchief around the thigh and tied it tight.

A shadow moved across the ground as someone on horseback rode behind them. Lemuel turned and saw General Jackson. The general glanced at Houston. "You've had enough fighting today, young man. Get some rest." Without another word, Jackson wheeled his horse and headed toward the sound of gunfire.

Through the brush, Hadjo could hear the approaching frontiersmen and soldiers as they systematically searched the woods, shooting the Red Sticks at short range like varmints. Out of ammunition, Hadjo had discarded his rifle and readied his bow. He hid under thick brush until a white man stepped into his view. He aimed at the soldier's chest and let the arrow fly, then slipped farther back in the brush to find another ambush site.

The fighting had continued hour after hour as the sun inched toward the west. Hadjo heard soldiers all around him as he crawled deeper into the brush. The undergrowth opened to a small clearing with a cabin. Into the cabin rushed a dozen warriors, including one Hadjo recognized as Antler. Figuring that this would be their last stand, Hadjo ran to the cabin and ducked through the door.

From the darkness inside, he watched and listened as soldiers and militiamen surrounded the cabin. Through the door and windows, Hadjo and the other warriors shot each time a white showed himself. But soon Hadjo was running low on arrows, and so were the others. After he fired his last arrow, he tossed the bow aside and drew his war club. For a few minutes all remained quiet. Hadjo wondered if the Big Knives had had enough fighting for the day.

Something thumped on the roof of the cabin. Hadjo peeked through a crack in the wall and saw a flaming torch tumble end over end toward them. Another thump on the roof. Smoke began to fill the cabin as the roof crackled and hissed. Flaming debris cascaded from the ceiling. Hadjo's eyes watered and stung. He coughed as the air grew hot. With horror he remembered the screams of the settlers at Fort Mims as they burned alive.

Someone coughed next to him, and Hadjo recognized Antler. For a moment Hadjo was tempted once again to kill the man who had taken Prancing Fawn from him. Then Hadjo realized that both he and Antler were about to die, and she would be left alone in a hostile world.

The heat intensified, and Hadjo felt his skin and hair singe. Several warriors elbowed past him as they rushed through the cabin door. With eyes stinging and the smoke tearing at his lungs, Hadjo clutched his war club and bolted out the door. If death couldn't be avoided, he preferred to die like a warrior and take a Big Knife with him.

Behind him, the cabin roof collapsed in a *whoosh* of flames and smoke. The warriors trapped inside screamed in agony.

Hadjo bumped into one of the other warriors who had exited the cabin before him. In the sunshine, with eyes watering, he could barely see. Assuming the whites were somewhere ahead, he raised his war club and screamed his fiercest war cry. The woods seemed to explode with gunfire. The impact of balls knocked him to the ground. His mind erupted in a flash of light before darkness engulfed him.

Lemuel crouched on a rock ledge high on a cliff facing the river to the west. He had seen scores of Red Sticks trying to swim the river. Each had been picked off by riflemen from the far shore until the river ran red and was littered with bobbing corpses.

He held his rifle ready in case another Red Stick emerged from the overgrown ravine. An unknown number of the redskins were holed up in a cave cut into the cliff. Jackson's cannon had been drawn close and had fired load after load of canister into the ravine with no apparent effect. An army officer called for volunteers to go down and flush out the renegades. For a moment no one said a thing.

"I'll do it," said a voice Lemuel recognized.

Ensign Sam Houston limped forward, a blood-soaked bandage around his thigh. No one else volunteered as the young officer borrowed a musket and hobbled down the path into the ravine. Lemuel had almost decided he would join Houston when muskets blasted from the brush below. The lieutenant crumpled to the ground.

As a score of Tennessee rifles fired into the brush-covered ravine, Lemuel sidled down the path. He grabbed Houston by the collar of his jacket and dragged him up the dusty path as fast as he could. Not until he was safely away from the ravine did Lemuel stop and ease the ensign to the ground. The right sleeve of Houston's uniform was bloodstained, and so was the shoulder.

Several of the Tennesseans were building torches, and Lemuel knew what they had in mind. He grabbed a stick and several fistfuls of dry grass and soon had his own torch. Someone had started a small fire on the ground, and the torches were lit. The flaming sticks were tossed end over end into the brush-filled ravine. As smoke began to rise, the brush began to crackle and hiss. One by one, natives bolted from the ravine and were gunned down.

Lemuel suddenly felt weak. He plopped to the ground and sat with his back against a tree trunk. His hands tingled and quivered. Each of his arms was smeared with blood, and so were his clothes. He checked himself quickly and found no injury. But tied to his belt were ten fresh scalps of coal-black hair, each red with blood.

As he tried to sit more comfortably against the tree trunk, he shifted his leather pouch to his lap. The pouch seemed unusually light, so he checked the contents. His bag of rifle balls was nearly empty. Usually it contained several dozen.

The past several hours had been a blur of loading and firing. He had lost track of the number of shots he had taken, but he was sure that he had missed only once. That had been when a native had jumped him from the brush. Lemuel had killed that one with the butt of his rifle.

He glanced across the river and watched scores of bodies float in the current. He had seen hundreds of Red Stick corpses scattered across the peninsula. A few of the natives were probably still holed up in caves along the cliffs, but they would be flushed out and eliminated before long. Of the thousand warriors holed up at Horseshoe Bend before the battle, he doubted that more than a couple dozen had escaped.

He hoped that this had been the last stand of the Red Stick rebellion. With the natives out of the way, Jackson would be free to deal with the other enemy—the British and their Spanish allies.

Hadjo woke, his eyes caked shut with sticky blood. His body throbbed with pain. Something heavy lay across him, and he could barely move or breathe. He listened carefully, trying to figure out where he was. His bare skin touched other skin. Not the warm flesh of the living—but the cold, clammy flesh of the dead. He was in a pile of corpses.

Fighting an urge to scream and bolt, he lay quietly for a moment. Hearing nothing but the wind rushing through tree limbs, he pushed at the bodies covering him. With a swipe of his hand across his face, he cleared the blood from his eyes. He wondered if he had gone blind, then realized that the sun had set. As his eyes grew accustomed to the dark, he saw that he was in a pile of dead warriors tossed on top of one another in the clearing around the smoldering cabin.

Hadjo listened carefully for any whites lingering nearby. Hearing nothing he began to focus on his wounds. His forehead ached from a throbbing lump. One by one he moved his limbs, and pain seared from wounds all over his body.

He shoved bodies aside, then struggled to his feet. He made a tentative, painful step forward. Dragging one leg in front of the other, he shuffled slowly and quietly downhill. Pausing frequently to rest and to study the surrounding woods, he trudged to the river's edge.

The water was freezing cold, and he feared he wouldn't be able to swim far with his wounds, so he worked his way along the bank until he reached the burned-out village. He located a canoe and slipped it into the water. He eased into the canoe and pushed it into the current. Somewhere downstream he would surely find other warriors gathering to renew the fight.

CHAPTER FORTY-THREE

APRIL 1814, FLINT HILL CAMP, NEW YORK

Silas Shackleton stood naked and shivering on the bank of the Niagara River. At the sergeant's command, he and scores of others stepped into the river, soap in hand. He gasped at the first touch of the freezing water.

From previous experience he knew the best way was to hurry and get it over with. The water was only a few feet deep, but he dunked himself until his body and head were submerged. He stood and growled. He ran his fingers through his hair and scrubbed his head and face vigorously, then dipped into the freezing water again. He scrubbed his neck and torso, then below his waist. All around him men howled as they scrubbed and splashed each other.

When the lieutenant who was supervising the wash was satisfied, a whistle blew. Silas and the other men raced for the riverbank. Once on shore, he grabbed a rag and rubbed himself dry. The afternoon sun was already warming his skin by the time he pulled his uniform on.

Silas viewed the twice-per-week bath in the river with mixed emotions. He dreaded the cold water, but he had to admit that the baths and other recent changes had made a huge difference.

Brigadier General Winfield Scott had arrived with orders to establish a camp of instruction that would turn a ragtag collection of regiments into a cohesive army. One of his first acts was to establish a new policy regarding camp sanitation. He ordered latrines to be moved far from sleeping and cooking areas. Water had to be boiled before drinking. Cooking utensils had to be washed in hot water. Detailed procedures for food preparation were enforced. Together with the supervised baths, the results were remarkable. Within weeks, diarrhea virtually disappeared from camp. The death toll from camp diseases declined to a few a month.

Silas buttoned the jacket of his new uniform. He warmed quickly under the wool cloth. The gray color reminded him that General Scott had worked tirelessly to provide better food and clothing for his men, and they loved him for it. A shortage of blue wool thwarted the general's attempt to attire his men in regulation uniforms. Exasperated, he procured uniforms in a color more readily available—the gray wool commonly used for horse blankets.

General Scott established a daily training routine based upon the French infantry manual. They drilled as individual units before breakfast, then again until lunch. Over and over, they practiced maneuvering in long, narrow marching columns, then redeploying into seven-man-wide attack columns. They shifted to wide, two-man-deep lines to maximize musket firepower. They practiced forming hollow squares for defense against cavalry. They rehearsed moving from one formation to another, then practiced changing direction. In the afternoon, General Scott watched as the regiments maneuvered together as an army.

One morning, from horseback, General Scott had addressed their company. "Some of you have seen battle and have tasted victory. Some of you may have already felt defeat. And some of you have yet to face the enemy. Many of you may wonder if we can match the might of the British army."

Scott's mount whinnied, and he patted her on the neck before continuing. "The British have bullied us. They fail to respect our government. In particular, and not without justification, they lack respect for our infantry. You will change that. With appropriate training, equipment, and leadership, you are capable of being the most effective fighting force the world has ever seen."

General Scott paused for a moment. "More than our own pride is on the line. More than our own lives. At stake is the honor, even the very survival, of these united States."

Silas lifted his musket to his shoulder and fell in line with his freshly washed messmates as they prepared to march away from the river. They were scheduled for more drills. He had thought of the redcoat armies that had defeated them at Queenston Heights and along the St. Lawrence, the battle some had labeled Crysler's Farm. He couldn't help wondering how the newly trained American army would stack up against the British.

"Drill and cuss," complained a man next to Silas. "Our routine is drill and cuss."

Silas laughed. "I don't know if we will be any more effective against the enemy," he said, "but at least we've learned enough to die with some style."

CHAPTER FORTY-FOUR

MAY 1814, WASHINGTON CITY

George Sherbourne handed Rachel Thurston a glass of cider, then sipped his own. For a moment, George wondered if back in York Anne was being attended to by another man.

He leaned against the rail fence of Tayloe's, an oval-shaped horse track set in a large, open field between Washington City and Georgetown. Around the track hundreds had gathered, representing all walks of life, from plantation owners and government officials to slaves. Men dressed in their finest leaned against the rail. Women in bright dresses and hats chatted in carriages and on boxes among booths and tents for refreshments and gambling. Wild-flowers bloomed all around.

Amid the uproar of neighing horses, glasses clinked, and bettors argued. Thunder rumbled from dark clouds looming in the southwest. Recent showers had soaked the ground, turning the early afternoon air steamy and reeking of fresh manure. The first two races of the day had left the track pocked with hoof prints and strewn with clods.

The first flies of the season buzzed all around, and George brushed one from his face. Five riders guided their mounts to the starting line. George had bet a small sum on a horse paying five to one. The dappled gray took the inside lane, its rider wearing a white shirt.

George studied the horses. A pretty scruffy lot, but that was understandable, considering that horses of any quality were difficult to acquire during a war.

A stout gentleman with bushy sideburns climbed the ladder of a short tower set behind a stage for judges at the outside of the track. Spectators edged closer to the rail in anticipation of the next race. As the starter pointed a pistol skyward, the crowd fell silent. Riders leaned forward over the neck of their mount, and for a moment, only the annoying flies broke the silence.

The pistol fired, and all five horses shot forward, thundering past George. He ducked as muddy clods pelted him. He whisked a blob from his shoulder, then leaned over the rail to watch the horses as they rounded the first turn. The gray was in the lead by a full length. "Go! Go! Go!" screamed George.

As the horses sped along the far length of the track, a black horse with a rider in a red shirt gained on the gray. All around George, spectators screamed, some with excitement, some in frustration. As the horses rounded the far end of the track, the red-shirted rider was only a half-length behind the gray.

After the last curve, the riders whipped and spurred their mounts to full speed. They thundered along the straightaway. The gray and the black crossed the finish line nose to nose.

All fell quiet as the man on the starting tower consulted with the race judges. After a moment, the mustached starter announced that the black had won. George cursed under his breath.

On the far side of the track, more horses began their warm-up walk to the starting line for the next race. The dark clouds in the distance had moved much closer, and thunder rumbled, reminding George of cannon fire and the war being fought elsewhere.

He worried that a new generation of commanders was emerging in the American army. In 1812 the average age of the generals had been in the sixties, but by 1813 the average age was just over thirty. The youngest was Brigadier General Winfield Scott, who that previous spring had organized and led the capture of Fort George at the mouth of the Niagara River. George wondered how Winfield Scott had managed to return to action, since prisoners to be exchanged usually had to give their *parole*, or promise that they would not take up arms in the war again.

To the delight of the American public, news of the frigate *Essex* had reached the States. Under the command of Captain David Porter, the *Essex* had wreaked havoc amongst British whaling ships in the Pacific. More recent news, George recalled with satisfaction, had arrived that the *Essex* had been blockaded into the neutral port of Valparaiso in Chile. After being holed up for a month, she nearly escaped, but a sudden squall snapped her topmast. Crippled, she anchored a quarter mile off the Chilean shore, where a British warship moved in and blasted the *Essex* to pieces.

By March, George recalled, His Majesty's Navy had control of both the Pacific and Atlantic Oceans. Despite their smattering of exploits, the American frigates had not been able to alter the course of the war. Now the blockade had them corked into a bottle like so many hornets. Besides ruining the American economy, the blockade had reduced its ocean-going navy to a minor role.

That could all change within a few months, George realized. In March the U.S. Congress had approved funds for Robert Fulton to build his steam-powered frigate. If it lived up to Fulton's grand dreams, it could single-handedly break the British blockade.

In the Mississippi Territory, General Andrew Jackson had managed to corner and destroy the rebellious Red Sticks at a place called Horseshoe Bend. The Americans now controlled all of the territory upriver from

Mobile and New Orleans. To thwart the American expansion, the Crown needed to take New Orleans and control the Mississippi River. To do that, George realized, they needed many more troops and ships, but that was now within the realm of possibilities because the latest reports indicated that the British army was doing well against Napoleon. If General Wellesley defeated Napoleon, dozens of warships and thousands of redcoats could be brought to bear against the Americans. George was sure that a few thousand battle-hardened redcoats could crush the Americans in short order.

Rachel was delighted to be at the track. It gave her an opportunity to think of something besides the war, which had not been going well for the Federalists. As she watched the horses race, she wondered if she should learn to ride. She was sure her father would not approve.

A gust of wind blew Rachel's bonnet to the side. As she tied its ribbon under her chin, something on the ground caught her attention. A horseshoe. What good fortune, she thought, and at a racetrack, too. She should place a bet immediately. If she could sneak the horseshoe home, she would hang it over the outside of their door with the open side of the shoe up so the luck wouldn't run out. Would her father object, she wondered? Of course, he would. Her face grew warm as she realized the absurdity of the whole idea. She wondered if anyone but her mother believed in such nonsense.

A black man with a tray of glasses approached the carriage and offered her a drink. Rachel could not tell, of course, whether the servant was a freedman or a slave. He reminded her, however, that the racetrack was yet another fruit of slavery, as no doubt, plantation profits had been used to construct the track.

Her awareness of the injustice of slavery had been heightened at a recent lecture. As usual the guest speaker—this time a man from Connecticut forming a society dedicated to ending slavery—had ranted against its evils.

This speaker had touched her consciousness in a different way. He praised the audience for attending the lecture and becoming informed about the subject. "Your presence here attests to your open mind and your concern," he observed. He noted the occasional article in newspapers and praised those who wrote and spoke out in favor of abolition. He praised those who contributed financially to the cause.

The young man also warned, as important as all of those activities were, they would not lead to victory. No, he argued, slavery would not be ended until people actually acted to do something about it. He argued that joining his fledgling organization helped swell its ranks so it could be a political force to reckon with. He pleaded with members of the audience to join the society and to contribute what they could, whether be it time, talent, or treasure.

Before leaving the room, Rachel made a point of introducing herself to the young man, registering as a member, and emptying her coin purse into the collection box. Part of her craved to do more, but she saw little opportunity for that.

A gust of wind whisked hats and bonnets into the air, then tumbled them across the ground. Thunder cracked and lightning flashed. Men and women hurried toward their carriages and mounts. Rachel searched the crowd, hoping to spot her father.

As he had on many occasions, George had been at their house the previous evening to play cards. Rachel had no particular interest in marriage, but she was puzzled that George didn't seem interested in courting her. It almost seemed as though he was using her and her father for some unstated purpose.

Even though she had known George for well over a year, she knew little about him. Whenever she had asked about his hometown or his childhood, he managed to answer in a manner that didn't reveal much.

Rachel looked at George more closely. Could it be that he was already married? Or maybe he was a sodomite? No. All of her instincts told her it must be something else.

CHAPTER FORTY-FIVE

JULY 1814, NIAGARA RIVER, UPPER CANADA

The afternoon sun beamed bright as Corporal Silas Shackleton trudged along the muddy ruts churned by the artillery limbers ahead of him. The day was warm and humid after the previous night's rain, and the smell of steaming horse manure overpowered the otherwise fresh air. General Winfield Scott's brigade marched north along the portage road paralleling the British side of the wide Niagara River. Ahead ran Street's Creek, its bridge newly restored with fresh planking.

The recently replaced timber reminded Silas of the challenges they had faced over the past forty-eight hours. After many months of hard training at the Flint Hill camp near Buffalo, the officers and men under Major General Jacob Brown had been eager to test their new skills against the British. Finally they received orders to cross the Niagara River and attack the enemy.

The campaign began in dense fog with an early morning row across the river. Once they landed, they chased away the Canadian sentries and set off for Fort Erie. The fort was defended by only a hundred and fifty men and a few cannon. After firing a couple shots as a matter of honor, the British forces surrendered the fort.

General Brown then sent Scott's brigade of a thousand men north to lead the way along the portage road as Brown himself followed with the rest of the army. The British and their Canadian and Indian irregulars fell back, tearing up bridges and then firing at the advancing Americans. Each time, General Scott's artillery blasted the defenders out of their positions. Then Scott's team of pioneers repaired the bridges, clearing the way to march forward, driving the Brits ahead of them.

On the day after Independence Day, they caught up to the British at the Chippawa River, one of the best defensive positions along the Niagara. As Scott's infantry approached, the Brits fired artillery. Then the redcoats torched the part of the village south of the river and removed the planks from the middle of the bridge. It had been late in the day, so General Scott ordered his men back across Street's Creek, a mile south of Chippawa, to camp for the night. The remainder of General Brown's army joined them before dusk. It rained heavily, and the men spent a miserable night in the mud.

In the morning Indians and Canadian militia began taking shots at the Americans from the adjoining forest. General Brown sent his own militia and Indians, wearing white headbands to distinguish them from their Canadian counterparts, to clear the woods.

General Scott fed his men a hearty meal, then ordered them north across the Street's Creek bridge for afternoon drills in the mile-wide clearing between the creek and the Chippawa River. Although the British forces defending Chippawa were reported to be few, General Scott ordered some of his artillery across the bridge as a precaution.

As Silas approached the bridge over Street's Creek, he felt pride in the gray-uniformed men. Still, he recalled the brutal efficiency of the redcoats at the battles of Queenston Heights and at Crysler's Farm.

As they crossed the bridge, newly laid wooden planks rumbled under foot. Trees and brush along the river had obscured the view, but now to Silas's right the stream opened to the wide, blue-gray Niagara River. From the corner of his eye, a blur of motion caught Silas's attention. At first he thought a fish had jumped or maybe a bird flew low across the river. When he looked closer, he nearly stopped in his tracks. Skipping like a stone across the water bounced a cannonball. The boom of cannon shattered the relative peace of the early afternoon. Three men in front of Silas suddenly burst in a spray of blood and flying body parts. Men all around Silas faltered and began to chatter. He fought to control his own rising panic.

"Silence in the ranks!" yelled Sergeant Holcomb. "Straighten those lines."

As trained, Silas and the men around him stepped over their fallen companions, filled in the gaps, and continued the march. They crossed the bridge and emerged from the trees lining the stream. Cannonballs bounced through their ranks, cutting down narrow swathes of men.

Ahead, a cannonball sailed over General Scott's head. He steadied his mount as he trained his field glass to the north. Scott turned to his officers and began shouting commands.

Finally, thought Silas, we have an officer we can follow with confidence.

Along the line a horse fell, spilling its rider to the ground. As the horse struggled to get up, it whinnied in pain. An officer stepped forward with pistol drawn, aimed point-blank at the horse's forehead, and pulled the trigger.

Another officer rode past Silas. A ball whizzed overhead, and the officer's cap flew from his head. Silas stepped forward and scooped up the hat. As he brushed away a smudge of mud, he noticed a musket-sized hole through the felt. He handed the hat back to the pale-faced, bareheaded officer. "Sir," said Silas, "an inch is as good as a mile."

With a slight smirk, the officer replaced the hat atop his head. "Quite right, Corporal. Carry on." He tapped his heels to his mount's ribs and rode farther down the line as British cannon roared.

Amid the chaos, Silas took in the scene before them with as much calm as he could muster. A few hundred yards to the north along the portage road stood white, wood-framed farmhouses and outbuildings. To the west, behind the buildings, lay a wide plain cleared for crops and pasture. Several hundred yards farther to the west stood more woods. To the north lay the village of Chippawa. But what shocked Silas and set his nerves tingling was what was happening a half-mile in front of him. Stretched across the cleared fields, from the portage road nearly to the forest in the west, were redcoats. Maybe a thousand of them. And they were deploying into a line.

An officer strode in front of the American line. "Steady, boys. This is what we've trained for."

Smoke blossomed from the far left of the British line as another field gun fired. A cannonball skipped and bounced across the muddy field, then disappeared into the trees to Silas's right. Guns roared again, and several men to Silas's left fell, one cut in half at the waist.

Silas stood behind his men. "Fill the gaps! You know the drill."

The artillerymen that had preceded General Scott across the bridge had unlimbered on the road just beyond the nearest farmhouse. They opened fire on the British cannon northwest across the field as the Brits shot at the American infantry still pouring onto the plain. At least this wouldn't be like Crysler's Farm, thought Silas, where the American artillery arrived too late to protect the infantry.

In a blur of motion, a cannonball ripped through the American artillery position. One of the guns seemed to leap off its carriage. It tumbled end over end, then toppled to the ground with a *thud*.

The lieutenant in charge of Silas's company ordered it forward to the nearest farm buildings, then west. With the same precision they had practiced hundreds of times, the men shifted from their marching column into a two-deep line facing the British several hundred yards north across the field. With a mixture of dread and excitement, Silas realized General Scott was throwing them forward to confront the redcoats.

Another cannonball bounced across the field and sliced through the American line. One man screamed and fell, his arm severed at the shoulder.

"Fill in the line!" Silas yelled. He watched as his men obeyed. Silas hoped they would continue to maintain their discipline under cannon fire. He was certain that after Queenston Heights and Crysler's Farm, the British held American troops in contempt. Today would be an opportunity to show the redcoats what the Americans could do.

From behind the British artillery position, where the ammunition limbers were stationed, a cloud of smoke and debris shot skyward, followed by a thunderous explosion. Cheers rose from the American line as soldiers waved their hats in the air. Under the direction of the officers, the men quickly settled back into their formation. Another cannonball tore a trail of mayhem through the line of men.

Silently, with precision that had earned it a reputation as the most disciplined army in the world, the British line marched closer. The redcoats paused a moment to dress up their lines, and then, with bayonets pointed forward, advanced again, this time to within a hundred yards.

Silas's lieutenant stood to the side of his unit. "Present!" he shouted.

"Aim!"

Muskets pointed toward the British line.

"Fire!"

The front row of muskets discharged in unison. Holes appeared in the British line but quickly filled. Smoke erupted from a section of the red line, and balls whizzed overhead. A man to the right of Silas cursed and fell.

One section after another of the enemy line opened fire. The American cannon blasted away, this time with canister, tearing big holes in the redcoat formation and peppering the British fieldpieces.

The next volley of American muskets crackled. Smoke clouded the line. The noise was deafening, and smoke obscured everything. A man in front of Silas fell.

"Fill the gap!" yelled Silas as he grabbed a man and shoved him into the space left by the fallen man. Another gap appeared, and Silas ordered it filled. When no one complied, he glanced right, then left. All of his men held in reserve were gone.

It was his turn to fill the gap, but he froze. His legs wouldn't take the step toward what seemed like certain death. He wanted to turn and run for the cover of the woods behind them.

Someone shoved him from behind.

"Fill the gap!" yelled Sergeant Holcomb.

Silas turned and saw his sergeant glaring at him.

"Fill the gap, Corporal, or I'll shoot you myself."

Silas felt his face burn with shame. He set his jaw, then strode between two soldiers and raised his musket. At the next command to fire, gunfire began crackling up and down the line in almost continuous roll. He doubted if he could hear his lieutenant. Silas aimed his musket toward the line of redcoats ahead of him in the growing cloud of smoke. He pulled the trigger and began to reload.

"Fire at will!" shouted the sergeant.

Silas fired and loaded as fast as he could, over and over again. Balls whined past him. To his right and left, men dropped.

Silas's ears rang hollow, as if stuffed with cotton. His mouth grew dry with the taste of gunpowder. His eyes stung from the thick smoke. After repeated firing, the barrel of his musket grew so hot, he could barely touch it when reloading. He prayed that the powder wouldn't discharge as he rammed in another ball.

The British returned volleys, but the Americans poured withering fire back into the red line. Like two boxers standing toe to toe, they slugged it out in a pure test of guts and strength.

At first tiny holes in the redcoat line were quickly filled. Then Silas noticed bigger gaps. Portions of the red line seemed to melt away.

"Present bayonets!" screamed their lieutenant.

Silas lowered his musket to his waist, bayonet pointed toward the enemy.

"Forward march!"

Silas had heard that a bayonet charge was largely a test of wills, seldom resulting in the actual use of bayonets against the enemy. Rather than face the carnage of hand-to-hand combat with bayonets, one side or the other usually lost its nerve and either retreated in good order or fled in panic.

The men would march to within a few yards of the enemy and would rush forward only at the last minute. Once the men broke out of marching discipline, they would be almost impossible to control until the battle was decided one way or the other.

To Silas's amazement, the red line ahead of them seemed to disintegrate. The British drummers sounded retreat, and the redcoats began to withdraw in good order, stepping backward with their bayonets pointed toward the Americans.

Silas hoped the redcoats would break and run, but more British cannon arrived and deployed on the left to protect the retreat across the river. Dozens of British dragoons rode forward to protect their cannon as they were limbered up and hauled back across the Chippawa River.

A cheer rose from the American forces. Hats sailed high into the air. Muskets fired. Silas was tempted to quiet his men and restore order, but he didn't have the heart. It had been a long time since they had had cause to celebrate.

He recalled how the Americans had been soundly beaten at Crysler's Farm that previous November when they had faced British regulars. The news had swept across the States with chilling effect. Now he glowed with confidence that news of this battle would spread like wildfire across the country, igniting new hope and confidence. American infantry had stood face to face against British regulars for half an hour and had whipped them.

Corporal Silas Shackleton woke to the sound of someone groaning. He tried to blink, but his eyelids squeezed tight at the glare of the early morning sun. Tears streamed down his cheeks. He tried to raise his left hand to shield his face, but pain stabbed through his arm. The sleeve of his gray-wool uniform was soaked with blood. The air reeked with a mixture of gun smoke and odors he couldn't identify.

As he lay sprawled across grass, he became more aware of his sur-roundings. Bodies lay all around him. He craned his neck and saw that he was on the knob of a hill overlooking a wide stretch of fields and meadows. All across the hill, and down to the tree line a half mile to the south, were strewn bodies. Bodies wearing gray. Bodies wearing red.

Just a mile to the east rose a towering cloud of mist, its billowy edges radiant with the early sunlight. At the sight of the cloud over the great falls of the Niagara River, Silas swallowed. His mouth felt parched and gritty with dust and gunpowder. His head throbbed, and pain coursed through his arm. He eased back to the ground and tried to remember how he got there.

He recalled the victory against the redcoats on the clearing south of Chippawa. But afterward, they had faced the tough prospect of attack-ing the entrenched British forces across the river. Rather than attack the British head-on, Major General Brown sent his pioneers upstream from the village. There they scavenged timber from local barns and improvised a pontoon bridge, enabling Brown's forces to ford the river.

Once it was apparent the Americans were about to outflank them, the British forces evacuated the village of Chippawa. General Brown hurried his men north along the portage road to Fort George at the mouth of the Niagara River. Even though the fort was only lightly defended, Brown was reluctant to attack it without naval support from the American fleet on Lake Ontario. That support did not arrive, so Brown withdrew his army south to Chippawa.

Brown didn't know the location of the British forces, so he sent General Scott back north from Chippawa to reconnoiter the area. As Scott's army approached the great falls of Niagara, his scouts reported seeing redcoat officers on horseback leaving a roadside tavern.

Scott and his officers questioned the proprietor of the tavern and were told there were eight hundred British regulars up the road a mile. After sending a messenger to General Brown asking that he bring his troops forward with all haste, General Scott continued north. Scott's forces sighted Indians in the woods, so he threw out a flank guard and pushed ahead cautiously.

Silas recalled hearing the boom of cannon ahead. He had looked forward to meeting the enemy again after marching all over the peninsula in search of them. The Americans marched along the narrow, tree-lined road, then turned west into an open field. They deployed in a line facing a rise to the northwest.

Silas recalled that his optimism disappeared once he got a full view of the situation. Across the wide ridge ahead stood a long line of redcoats. By Silas's estimation, they faced well over a thousand British regulars.

The more Silas had viewed the situation, the more concerned he became. He was sure that General Scott's first inclination in meeting the British would be to attack immediately. However, the redcoat army on the hill ahead was much larger than any rumored among the enlisted men.

To attack a superior force already positioned on the high ground would be foolhardy. And who knew how many other British forces were held in reserve out of sight, or en route to reinforce the troops within view.

The remainder of General Brown's army was still several miles behind General Scott's brigade. Brown's men would need hours to move forward along the narrow road to reinforce Scott.

Silas's mind had raced. Part of him hoped Scott would withdraw and retreat south until General Brown's forces could reinforce them. Silas also knew a retreat within sight of the enemy risked chaos, with a tremendous loss of personnel and precious artillery, to say nothing of the devastation to morale. Silas feared General Scott and his brigade were stuck, at least until General Brown's column reinforced them.

From previous marches along the portage road, Silas knew the terrain well. To the east of the road lay a quarter mile of dense woods, then the steep banks that dropped hundreds of feet to the Niagara. Across the top of the hill to the north, where the British forces stood, ran a secondary road called Lundy's Lane. Between the redcoats and General Scott's brigade lay a half-mile of open field crisscrossed with split-rail fences.

As shadows lengthened in the evening sun, General Scott's artillery had set up just west of the portage road. Skirmishers hurried forward to feel out enemy positions. They drove back some redcoats, but it was evident that the Americans were outnumbered and outgunned.

General Scott's men had been well out of musket range from the British, but they made easy targets for the enemy artillery positioned on the top of the hill. As the American infantry waited for General Brown, their artillery blasted away at the British guns but couldn't silence them. For an hour and a half, the troops General Scott had so carefully trained were shot to pieces by British artillery.

Silas blinked back tears as he recalled directing the men to close up ranks again and again after cannonballs ripped through them, severing limbs, heads, and bodies. Silas had been tempted to run for cover, but the officers and sergeants kept a close eye out for deserters. By dusk Scott's infantry and artillery forces had been decimated.

As night fell, General Brown arrived. Scott withdrew his men to the trees to rest and reorganize. Brown sent two groups to capture the enemy cannon on the hill. The first faked an attack from the south. The other unit crept up the hill under the cover of darkness and surprised the British cannoneers.

From then on, as best as Silas could tell, the fighting turned to chaos, with American and British forces firing at each other at close range in the dark. The Americans took the hill, the cannon, and the road, but the British kept coming, time after time.

General Scott pulled together the shattered pieces of his brigade and marched them up the hill in attack-column formation. He drove them forward between two U.S. regiments at the front of the line, then thrust them headlong into the British line until it broke.

In the darkness and confusion, Silas recalled, the Americans were fired upon by their own countrymen. Scott had two horses shot out from under him. General Brown and General Scott were both so severely wounded, they had to be carried from the field.

Finally, after numerous attempts to dislodge the Americans from the hill, the British withdrew, leaving the field of battle and several cannon to the Americans. The last thing Silas recalled from the previous night was that something had smacked his left arm and knocked him to the ground.

Now, with the sun rising beyond the towering cloud of mist to the east, he licked chapped lips and tasted gunpowder. He reached for his canteen, uncorked it, and tipped it to his mouth. Empty. He eyed the cloud of mist and heard the rumble of the falls in the distance. So much water, so close.

Around him, wounded men groaned and wept. The stench of gun smoke lingered, blending with the stink of death. Silas staggered to his feet.

The field was strewn with dead and wounded. He knelt next to a soldier but suddenly felt nauseated. He slumped back to the ground.

Movement to the north caught his attention. British artillerymen had arrived and begun removing fieldpieces from the hill. Silas had been surprised to see that the Americans hadn't taken the captured guns when they withdrew. The Americans surely wouldn't have left the valuable cannon behind, especially since they represented substantial bragging rights for the victor of the battle.

Silas recalled the pride of victory after the battle at the Chippawa River, then the devastation of the fight at Lundy's Lane. He hoped it was all worth it. He gazed around the battlefield. Damn the generals, he thought.

A group of militiamen loaded wounded onto wagons, then carted them north. Canadian militiamen piled fence rails, heaped bodies on top, then set the wood on fire.

Indians wandered, scavenging among the dead. When a wounded American refused to surrender his boots to an Indian, the native picked him up and tossed him onto the fire. Silas sat still, too numb to react. As the burning American soldier screamed, a Canadian militiaman raised his musket, shot the Indian, then tossed the Indian's body on the fire.

Silas fought to keep from passing out. As another wagonload of wounded headed north along the portage road toward Fort George, he imagined a British army surgeon sawing off his arm. He popped the stopper back in his empty canteen, then began crawling toward the woods. Once he was confident that he was out of sight of the local militiamen, he stood and headed for the sound of the river rushing over the falls.

CHAPTER FORTY-SIX

AUGUST 1814, MISSISSIPPI TERRITORY

As daylight waned, Lemuel studied the embers glowing bright red in his campfire. He had used dry sticks for fuel and kept the fire as tiny as he could to minimize the chances that hostiles would take notice. He gazed into the dark timber around him, trying to detect any sign that he was not alone.

Satisfied, he picked up the dead fox squirrel at his side. Its body was still warm and limp from when he had shot it out of a tall pine with a single ball. He strode into the woods until he was well away from his campsite.

He stretched the rust-colored body lengthwise along a fallen tree. With quick, confident slices he cut off the squirrel's head, then its feet. He rolled the carcass to its back and slit the skin from the neck to the tail. With skilled strokes he alternately cut and pulled until he freed the pelt. Another long slice opened the belly from the neck to the anus. He sliced and scooped until he cleared the body cavity of entrails. Leaving the discarded guts and body parts for scavengers, he strolled back to his campsite.

He skewered the squirrel's carcass with a long stick and laid it upon forked sticks set on opposite sides of the glowing embers. He took a long swig from his canteen and sat back to watch his supper cook. Weariness crept over him as he recalled the previous months.

After Jackson's victory at Horseshoe Bend that previous March, most of the villages that had sided with the Red Sticks surrendered. Troops hunted down and killed any Red Sticks who offered resistance, but many of the rebel leaders fled to Florida, apparently to regroup with the help of the Spanish and the British.

On the site of an old French stockade at the juncture of the Coosa and Tallapoosa rivers, Jackson constructed a new fortification for his head-quarters and named it Fort Jackson.

Lemuel had been waiting to deliver his scouting report one after-noon when a lone Indian rode into camp and stopped outside the general's tent. Lemuel expected the corporal of the guard to shoo the native out of camp, but the Indian identified himself as Chief Red Eagle. A flurry of excitement swept through the fort as the chief waited for his arrival to be announced. Lemuel recalled holding his rifle ready to put a ball through the chief's forehead if he caused any trouble.

Jackson invited the Red Stick chief into his tent as a growing crowd of angry frontiersmen and soldiers gathered outside. Later Lemuel learned that Red Eagle had explained that he would continue the fight if he could, but his warriors no longer listened to him. He admitted to Jackson that he had led the Red Sticks in the attack on Fort Mims but that he had urged his warriors to spare the women and children.

Red Eagle surrendered to Jackson, asking only that the Muscogee women and children hiding in the woods be fed. Jackson accepted the sur-render and pledged to feed the women and children. Jackson offered the chief a drink of brandy, then let him go free.

That summer Jackson ordered a gathering of Muscogee chiefs at Fort Jackson for his announcement of the terms of peace. What the general demanded had stunned Lemuel. The Muscogees, even those who had fought at Jackson's side, were to surrender over half of their territory, a vast tract stretching west from Georgia and south to the Gulf of Mexico. Furthermore, all the Muscogees, regardless of which side they had fought on, were to relocate their villages farther north where they would be beyond the influence of the British and Spanish agents along the gulf coast.

When the loyal Muscogee chiefs protested, Jackson told them that he wouldn't force anyone to sign the treaty, and any who decided not to sign would be free to go south to Florida. He also assured them that he and his troops would eventually follow them and destroy them. Reluctantly the chiefs signed.

Word spread rapidly that Jackson had imposed peace terms upon the Muscogees that forced them to cede over twenty million acres to the States.

The squirrel sizzled over embers, and Lemuel reached over to roll the carcass on the stick. The smell of charred meat made his mouth water.

Over the last year, he had come to respect General Jackson, but he didn't pretend to understand the man. On one occasion the general could be generous—as with Chief Red Eagle. On others, as with the peace treaty, he seemed heartless.

More recently Jackson had asked Lemuel to scout the Spanish town of Pensacola. Jackson worried that the Spanish were in cahoots with the British in arming the redskins. Lemuel's task was to scout out the surrounding area and, if possible, get into the town itself. He wasn't sure he wanted to just walk into town and look around without any apparent reason for his visit.

His hand brushed across the squirrel pelt, and he wondered how many furs he could accumulate before he reached Pensacola. With a collection of pelts, maybe even a fresh deer carcass, he would have goods to offer in trade and a reason for approaching the village.

The smell of charbroiled meat made his mouth water. Lemuel plucked the stick off its forked holders and studied the squirrel. He blew on the meat for a few seconds, then took a cautious bite. He savored the taste and took a bigger bite. Scouting for General Jackson wasn't half bad, he figured, if he didn't get killed while doing it.

CHAPTER FORTY-SEVEN

AUGUST 1814, WASHINGTON CITY

George Sherbourne dabbed a handkerchief at a drop of sweat as it ran down his forehead. He and Rachel sat with scores of other wedding guests at the French ministry, temporarily located at Octagon House. As they waited for the ceremony to begin, George squirmed. To accompany an unmarried woman to a wedding was bound to invite attention and speculation about their relationship. Neither of which did he welcome.

Mordecai Thurston was out of town for a month on business, and when Rachel asked George to accompany her to the wedding, he fought to conceal his sense of panic. He couldn't think of a viable excuse for not going, so he had accepted.

In the two years he had known her, Rachel had matured into a beautiful young woman, and when George accompanied her to various events around the city, he noticed the envious looks of other men, young and old. No doubt Rachel would make someone a lovely and dedicated wife.

In recent months, however, George had come to feel increasingly uneasy in his relationship with Rachel and her father. Without question his presence in their company, both at their home and in public, provided him with valuable cover as he spied on the American government. Quite possibly his association with the Thurstons had saved him from being discovered. He felt a tinge of guilt when he realized that their frequent ventures together in public and his companionship with her father may have discouraged other potential suitors.

For a moment, George's mind returned to York. He wondered if Anne had other suitors calling on her. No doubt she did, and he hated that thought. Even worse, he saw no way he could return to her anytime soon.

As had become his habit, George studied the faces in the crowd. Across the room a middle-aged man with a broad mustache glanced at George, then quickly looked away. George recognized him as the local head of law enforcement, and wondered if the man suspected George of espionage. Maybe he already knew. A squad of constables could be assembling outside the house, preparing to rush in and arrest him. That could be why the wedding was running late.

Trying to appear calm, George leaned close to Rachel and whispered, "Excuse me, I'm going to step out for a bit." Without waiting for her to reply, he began to rise. If he could slip out a back door, he might be able to evade arrest. If he could get to his horse, he might be able to escape entirely before they organized pursuit.

Just then a man dressed in black with a white collar strode to the front of the crowd. "Ladies and gentlemen, I apologize for the delay. My fault entirely. I should have repaired that wobbly carriage wheel weeks ago. But now," he said, and folded his hands, "let us proceed . . . ."

George eased back into the chair. Rachel placed her other hand on his and smiled.

Trying not to be too obvious, George let his gaze drift to the police chief across the room. The man sat next to a woman who could be his wife, and beyond the woman sat three young girls no older than ten years.

George breathed a sigh of relief, then glanced around the room to see if he had drawn extra attention to himself.

Even though the windows were open, the heat inside the house was nearly unbearable. As they waited for the bride to make her entrance, George studied the construction of the room. An interesting mixture of stone, brick, timber, and ironwork. The whole structure of Octagon House seemed to be an architectural experiment that included a circle, two rectangles, and a triangle as well as the shape for which the home was named. That Octagon House was remarkable, thought George, should be no surprise. After all, it had been designed by none other than Dr. William Thornton, the architect of the Capitol. Although the house was currently rented to the French, it was owned by Colonel John Tayloe, reputedly the wealthiest planter in Virginia.

With a great flourish of music, everyone in the room stood. The bride, a friend of Melanie Tayloe's, was escorted forth. George suspected that the unattached women in the room were each imagining themselves marching down the aisle before very long. He supposed Rachel shared those visions, although he had never noticed that she seemed to be in any particular hurry.

He hated the fact that he continued to deceive Rachel and her father, for he genuinely liked them. It wasn't that he didn't trust them, but even a casual slip of the tongue could result in his facing a firing squad. Besides, if they knew he was a spy, they would be in the terrible position of having to either report him to the authorities or risk being considered accomplices in his crimes.

He silently cursed the war, the idiot Americans for starting it, and the pigheaded British government that could have avoided it. The two governments were tangled in an unnecessary war, and he wasn't even in the fight.

When he had first joined the army, he had hoped that his service would one day lead to the kind of distinction that sometimes led to financial opportunities later in life. He had dreamed of the kind of wealth that would allow him to build a grand home such as the Octagon House. But his service as a spy would not earn him the fame and fortune he dreamed of. In fact, he was sure many would consider espionage unsavory behavior.

Fortunately, the war couldn't last much longer. With the recent defeat of Napoleon, Great Britain found itself with a surplus of ships and troops. George was thrilled to learn that battle-hardened redcoats had been pouring into the Canadian colonies all summer. He was sure it was just a matter of time before they flooded across the American border, crushing any resistance they encountered. Soon the Americans would be chastised for their arrogance. They would have to accept whatever terms the Crown allowed them.

At a minimum, George was sure, the Crown would annex the Penobscot River and the territory north of it to provide a reliable land route from the Atlantic to Quebec. They would take possession of the Great Lakes and surrounding territory. With a little luck, they might be able to break New England away from the States—maybe even New York.

As the preacher launched into a sermon about the sanctity of marriage, George's attention was drawn to a particularly nice piece of statuary in a far corner of the room. He wondered if it was made of the ceramic-like material called Coade stone, which was available only from England and must have been imported before the war and the inevitable trade restrictions.

The blockade currently extended along the entire American coast from northern Massachusetts to New Orleans and had brought domestic commerce to its knees. Surely the American people wouldn't tolerate the situation much longer. But, George thought, something always seemed to give them hope or inspiration. He fumed when he thought of the exploits of one of the few privateers still pestering His Majesty's forces.

The *Chausseur*, a twenty-gun schooner built in Baltimore, sailed the waters off England and Ireland. Skillfully evading vastly superior Royal

Navy forces, the *Chausseur* captured dozens of prizes, even taking on a British warship. In retaliation for the British blockade of American ports, the captain of the *Chausseur* sent a proclamation to be posted at Lloyd's coffeehouse in London announcing "the strict and rigorous" blockade of the British Isles. Cheeky bastard, thought George.

The bride and groom were exchanging vows, but George's mind drifted again to recent military action. News had just arrived from the Niagara area that newly trained American regulars took on British redcoats at Chippewa and at Lundy's Lane along the Niagara River. Both sides withdrew and claimed victory, but the Americans had shown that they could hold their own against British regulars.

That the Americans were getting better at the art of war concerned George. But with General Wellesley's seasoned troops arriving by the shipload in Halifax, no improvement in American skills and leadership would make a bit of difference in the final outcome.

George was sure the war would be over within months. He needed to find a way out of his assignment as a spy so he could get into the action before it was over.

Before leaving Washington City, however, he still hoped to determine the location of Robert Fulton's torpedoes. Most likely they were stored at the Naval Yard, but George had been unable to confirm it. If he could find the torpedoes, he hoped to destroy them before they were used against the Royal Navy.

The preacher finished the ceremony, then told the groom, "You may kiss the bride."

As the audience clapped, the front door of the house banged open. George spun around, half-expecting uniformed soldiers to rush in and arrest him. Instead a man shouted, "The British are sailing up the Patuxent River!"

Rachel Thurston hurried southwest along New York Avenue. Over the last couple of days, her neighbors had either left town or locked themselves inside their homes. That morning her father had gone in search of a wagon and horse. After waiting for him at home for several hours, she left a note saying that she was going for a walk but would return soon.

She tightened the ribbon securing her bonnet and tried to ignore the oppressive afternoon heat. The street was nearly deserted, a striking contrast to the scene of recent days. Word had arrived that British Admiral Cochrane's fleet was sailing up the Patuxent River in pursuit of Commodore Joshua Barney's flotilla of gunboats. If the boats were captured or destroyed, Chesapeake Bay would be left with no naval protection.

The streets of Washington City had turned to chaos. Wagons and carriages were loaded, and horses were commandeered as almost everyone tried to flee. Government documents were hauled away to safety. The secretary of War and his generals rushed about trying to organize defenses.

To support the few regular-army troops in the area, local militia were summoned, and help was requested from Maryland and Virginia. Within a few days nine thousand militiamen were assembled to assist in the defense of the capital.

Baltimore might still be the intended target of the British advance, but Rachel wished her father had made the decision to flee the city a little earlier. Now they might be too late.

With the approach of the British fleet, rumors circulated, renewing accounts of British atrocities, including arson, murder, and rape. Memories of British behavior in Copenhagen resurfaced, reminding everyone that in the 1807 attack on Copenhagen, the Royal Navy fired thousands of Congreve rockets into the city, killing over two thousand in the subsequent conflagration.

Local newspapers reported that in a recent raid of Leonardtown, Maryland, British marines ransacked a church, breaking tiles, robbing graves, and stabling their horses in the nave. Women were forced to strip for the entertainment of the officers. The *National Intelligencer* claimed that the behavior of Admiral Cockburn's men would have disgraced cannibals.

Rachel and her father had declined several invitations and pleas from neighbors to leave town with them. Although she didn't say so, she was confident that stories of British atrocities, whether at Copenhagen or on the Chesapeake, were grossly exaggerated. After all, British officers were gentlemen and wouldn't permit such evils.

She turned south onto 15th Street and stopped to gaze at the president's mansion.

"Miss Thurston?"

Rachel jumped at the voice behind her. She turned and saw a black man she recognized as French John, the Madison's chief usher.

"Miss Thurston, what are you doing out here all by yourself?"

Rachel hesitated, her mind racing. Then she stammered, "I, I thought I would drop by to see if Mrs. Madison was all right."

French John glanced toward the mansion, where two large cannon and a hundred uniformed troops guarded the gateway. "Mrs. Madison is very busy today, what with the British and all." Then he glanced at Rachel and smiled. "No doubt the best thing for Madam, right now, is a social call to help take her mind off this terrible war." He bowed slightly and extended his arm toward the columned entrance of the mansion.

They found Dolley at the west wall of the drawing room supervising two servants as they removed the red velvet drapes.

When French John announced Rachel's presence, Dolley looked surprised. "My dear, are you all right? I assumed you had fled long ago."

When Rachel explained that her father was looking for a wagon, Dolley gave her a big hug.

"Bless you, my dear. I so welcome your presence." Dolley sighed. "Unfortunately we might very well have unwelcome company before long, and we must prepare for the worst." Dolley took Rachel's hand and led her to the far side of the dining room and whispered, "Is there any word of a slave rebellion?"

For a moment Rachel was dumbfounded. "No, ma'am. I've not heard even a rumor of a rebellion in over a week."

"Oh, thank goodness." Dolley clutched her breast.

The servants finished folding the velvet drapes, and Dolley had them carried outside.

"Come along, my dear," she said to Rachel. "This won't take but a moment."

Dolley's carriage and wagon were already piled high with boxes of documents, silver plate, and various household items. Just then another heavily loaded wagon arrived with two gentlemen aboard.

"Clear out! Clear out!" one of the men yelled.

Dolley hurried to the new arrivals and greeted them as old friends. After a short conversation the men drove away.

Back inside the mansion, Dolley led Rachel into the sitting room, its wallpaper and drapery bright yellow. Dolley plopped into a chair. "What a relief! I need a little break to catch my breath." She handed Rachel a paper fan, and for a moment they sat quietly. "Tell me," asked Dolley with a worried voice, "do you have any news as to the whereabouts of the British?"

When Rachel said that she was sorry that she didn't, Dolley asked, "Have you by chance seen President Madison since midmorning today?"

When Rachel said no, Dolley pulled a tiny box from a drawer, pinched a tiny bit of snuff, held it to her nostrils, and inhaled. Rachel flinched as Dolley sneezed loudly.

Dolley produced a rag and, with a snort, blew her nose. The rag disappeared into a pocket and was quickly replaced with a dainty white handkerchief, with which the president's wife finished wiping her nose.

"I'm sorry, my dear. A nasty habit, I know. But it does seem to settle my nerves some." Her gaze drifted off into the distance for a moment, but then returned to Rachel. "How about your handsome Mr. Sherbourne? Have you seen him recently?"

Rachel blushed and shook her head. She hadn't seen George since he had ridden out of town with Secretary of State Monroe and a dozen dragoons to scout the British movements.

"Well," said Dolley, "let's go see if we can get a glimpse of them."

With speed and agility that challenged Rachel to keep up, Dolley raced down a hall, around a corner, then up one set of steps after another. Rachel lost count of the number of flights of stairs they climbed before reaching an open hatchway to the roof. From a cabinet set in the stairwell wall, Dolley snatched a telescope, then stepped outside.

Rachel struggled to regain her breath as she blinked at the brightness. The heat of the afternoon seemed to radiate off the dark, flat roof. As they approached the railed edge, Dolley raised the glass to her eyes.

Rachel tried to recognize the landmarks around her, but everything looked so different from this height, and she felt a little dizzy. She found the river, which would be to the west. She could see the twin buildings of the Capitol to the east. With the telescope, Dolley was studying the countryside to the northeast, and Rachel estimated that was in the direction of Baltimore, but closer lay the town of Bladensburg.

"My God," said Dolley. "I never believed it could happen." She dropped the field glass from her eyes and squinted. "Here," she said, handing the glass to Rachel. "You must see for yourself."

Rachel hadn't used a telescope in quite some time, and had trouble focusing it. "I see the tollgate for the Bladensburg turnpike."

"Look a little farther up the road."

Rachel followed the road north, and what she saw atop a hillcrest set her heart racing. Down the road in smart formation, marched a long column of redcoats. She nearly dropped the telescope, but then forced herself to study them for a few seconds, awed by the spectacle they created with their bright-red uniforms. Despite the cloud of dust the troops raised, she could see that several redcoats mounted on horses led the column, and she presumed they were officers.

Dolley and Rachel took turns searching the view in all directions. As Rachel put the telescope aside, she noticed that Dolley was staring down at the front gate of the mansion. Rachel's insides twisted tight. The American troops and their cannon were gone.

Dolley sighed. "I had so hoped I could wait until Mr. Madison returned. But I suppose it's not to be."

They rushed downstairs, and Dolley was ready to leave within minutes. She grabbed the cage of her pet parrot, and they headed out the door. When they reached the overfilled carriage and wagon, Dolley handed the cage to French John. "Would you take dear Polly to Octagon House and ask if the French minister will provide him sanctuary until I return?"

Dolley turned to Rachel. "My dear, maybe you should come with me. I'll make room for you."

Before Rachel could respond, she heard footsteps racing across the drive. Her father approached and bent double, his chest heaving.

After a moment her father bowed slightly to Dolley, "Mrs. Madison, I do hope my daughter has not been too much of a burden on this unsettling day."

"Nonsense, Mr. Thurston. I thrive on her presence. But I'm afraid I must leave. Won't you accompany me? I fear dreadfully for those staying behind."

"Madame, we are unarmed civilians," said Thurston. "I'm sure we will be fine."

Dolley took a deep breath and a long look at the president's mansion. Then returning her attention to Rachel and her father, she said, "Well, I must be off. If you see Mr. Madison please tell him that I am heading west across the river." She climbed into the wagon seat, and her coachman drove off.

Lieutenant George Sherbourne squinted in the glare of the setting sun. His horse reeked of sweat in the sweltering heat as they topped the last hill along the road from Bladensburg. The turnpike gate lay ahead, indicating they were just a mile and a half from the Capitol.

George wore a uniform and black chapeau bras as he rode behind General Ross, the no-nonsense, Irish-born veteran of the peninsular war, who was in command of the ground operation. Next to Ross rode Admiral Cockburn, in the dark-blue of the Royal Navy. On each flank marched redcoats, and ahead of them prowled skirmishers with rifles ready. To the rear were sailors in blue jackets—Cockburn's arsonists—and a rocket team.

Soon they approached the first houses at the northeastern edge of the capital, the first George had seen of Washington City in several days. He shifted his seat in the saddle to relieve his aching bones and muscles.

His horse skittered to the side of the road. An explosion rumbled in the distance. Over the houses and trees to the southeast, debris and smoke shot skyward. Planks tumbled end over end.

General Ross turned to George. "Any idea what that would be, Lieutenant?"

George checked his bearings before answering. "Sir, most likely that is the bridge over the East Branch."

The general studied the fading plume of smoke and debris, then shook his head. "They must have rigged it with a boatload of powder."

Smoke also rose in plumes to the south and west. At the general's request, George explained that those fires were probably at the naval shipyard and the long bridge across the Potomac.

George recalled his visits to the Naval Yard, with its storehouses of ordnance, cordage, sailcloth, and provisions. At the dock were tied the almost-finished frigate *Columbia*, its bottom ready for coppering, the sloop-of-war *Argus,* the new schooner *Lynx*, and the old frigates *Boston* and *General Greene*. George imagined that the fire would spread rapidly among scows and rowing galleys, creating monstrous fires, and when they encountered stores of gunpowder, deafening explosions.

George tingled with grim resolve at the thought of exacting revenge on the Americans for burning his hometown of York the previous year. At the same time, he glanced nervously at the houses lining the road. The capital city seemed deserted, but if the American forces appeared unexpectedly and attacked in force, the redcoats could be overwhelmed. He reminded himself that General Ross was a battle-hardened commander, having served with Wellesley against Napoleon.

They rode farther into Washington City, and the block-shaped buildings of the Capitol came into view. George flinched at the sound of gunshots. Smoke billowed from a three-story brick house to the right. Two redcoats fell and so did Ross's horse, toppling the general to the ground. Redcoats surrounded the house and searched it.

As General Ross brushed dust from his uniform, the wounded horse was put down with a pistol shot. Ross stared at the house for a moment, then turned to one of the other officers. "Burn it."

Another horse was found for Ross, and he led his men to the Capitol. As British drums signaled an invitation to parley, a couple of redcoat officers rode forward with white flags and waited for representatives of the city to come forward. No one ventured out.

General Ross cursed and turned to Admiral Cockburn. "I had rather hoped to ransom the city, but it seems there's no one left with whom to bargain."

George thought of the many officials, civilian and military, who so confidently dismissed the idea that Washington City would be attacked. Now those same officials and their families were no doubt fanning across Virginia seeking shelter. George couldn't bring himself to feel sorry for them, as some of those same officials had ordered American forces to invade the Canadas, where many British families were displaced, sometimes into the harshness of winter.

Night fell, and the sky glowed red from the fires around the capital. Ross led the men toward the twin buildings of the Capitol. There they deployed in a line and fired, shattering scores of windows. For a moment, all was quiet as they waited for return fire. The city seemed deserted.

After the buildings were searched, the general ordered a dozen rockets to be fired onto the roofs. When the rooftops failed to ignite, the general led a group inside the southernmost building. As they entered the hall of the House of Representatives, George was reminded of his first visit to the Capitol, and the first time he met Rachel Thurston.

At the front of the chamber stood the canopied chair of the Speaker, and above it hung a clock and a sculptured eagle with a wingspread of over twelve feet. Once inside the great chamber, Admiral Cockburn strode to the front of the House floor and climbed into the Speaker's chair. His eyes wild with mischief, he pounded on a table until he had everyone's attention. "What do you say, lads? Shall this harbor of Yankee democracy be put to the torch? All for it—say 'Aye'!"

"Aye!" yelled the men.

The admiral heaved the Speaker's chair to the center of the room. Redcoats began piling chairs, desks, and books on top of the raised wooden platform of the House floor. They stripped drapery from the windows and partitions. They ripped out doors and their frames. They tore shutters from windows and shattered the windows.

The general ordered nearly everyone out. As the room emptied, Cockburn's blue-coated crew of arsonists lit torches and raced out. Redcoats poured bucketfuls of powdery rocket fuel over the pile. The general turned to George. "Just retribution for York, I'd say. Would you do the honors?"

George thought of the government building burned in his hometown. He thought of his parents and of Anne. "Thank you, sir. I'd be delighted."

A corporal handed George a smoldering linstock. He touched the glowing tip to the fuse of a rocket. In a flash of sparks, smoke, and flames, the rocket streaked forward, igniting the heap.

Admiral Cockburn, a book under his arm as a souvenir, led his sailors out of the building. They tromped across the wooden walkway to the northern wing of the Capitol, which housed the Senate, the Supreme Court, and the Library of Congress. Soon it was ablaze, and everyone rushed outside to escape the smoke and rising heat.

Flames roared like thunder and lit the sky above Capitol Hill. Ross and Cockburn headed west along Pennsylvania Avenue to the president's house. An advance detail of redcoats had already surrounded the mansion.

George accompanied General Ross, Admiral Cockburn, and the other officers through the front door and into the dining room. There they found tables set for forty. With food from the pantry, they helped themselves to a meal.

They poured Madeira wine from cut-glass decanters, and General Ross proposed a toast. "To the health of the regent and success to His Majesty's arms by sea and land."

"Here! Here!"

"Peace with America and down with Madison!"

One of the officers asked if the general planned to keep Washington and use it to topple the American government and break the States apart.

Ross chuckled. "Lads, this is all just a diversion from the real action much farther north."

Admiral Cockburn took a cushion from a chair and held it high. To all present he announced, "I take this as a souvenir—to remind me of Dolley's seat."

The redcoats roared in laughter.

Cockburn raised President Madison's ceremonial chapeau bra on the tip of his sword. "Let's drink to Jemmy Madison's health. If we can't capture the little president, we'll parade his hat throughout England!"

At the admiral's orders, a midshipman and four sailors rushed upstairs to light beds and drapery. Ross rose, and at his direction, the table was upended, broken dishes scattering everywhere. Chairs, crimson sofas, writing and card tables, and window stools were piled against the table. Soon the whole mansion blazed.

The next morning Rachel Thurston clutched her father's arm as they hurried along Pennsylvania Avenue. Several ladies from their neighborhood led the way along the gravel road. Rachel coughed as a breeze brought her a whiff of smoke. Gray-white columns drifted skyward from the smoldering ruins of the Navy Yard, the Capitol, the Treasury, and the president's mansion. The building housing the War Department and the Department of State was now also ablaze.

The sight of such destruction saddened Rachael. Maybe now the American people would finally see the folly of Democratic-Republican policies and throw Madison out of office. There may yet be time for the Federalists to steer the new nation on a course toward peace with Britain and the prosperity that would surely follow.

On the street ahead stood the office of the *National Intelligencer*. A small crowd had gathered, part civilians but most were soldiers in red uniforms. At the sight of redcoats, Rachel felt a twinge of fear. She wondered if the neighborhood ladies were getting them all into a dangerous situation.

The sky had glowed orange all night as she and her father had stood in the street with their few remaining neighbors and watched for runaway fire or looters. They already knew that the Navy Yard had been set ablaze before the American military retreated. A couple of boys ran by after dusk and told them the Capitol and the president's mansion had been torched by the British.

The fires rumbled and roared like thunder all night. Occasionally, Rachel caught the sound of someone shouting or laughing in the distance. She figured the redcoats were having a real celebration.

At dawn, someone knocked on their front door. Thinking it might be looters, her father grabbed a loaded pistol and peeked around the curtains of an adjacent window. Instead of marauders, he found several ladies from nearby homes. They asked if Mordecai and Rachel would join them in imploring the British not to burn more buildings, as local residences might also catch fire. Surely, they said, they would all have safety in numbers, even in the presence of the invaders.

Rachel's toe caught in the gravel of Pennsylvania Avenue, and she nearly stumbled. As they approached the crowd outside the *National Intelligencer*, she could see that several of the redcoats were officers, including a rather stoic-looking general.

"Oh, my," said one of the neighbor ladies, "it looks like they plan to start another fire. I think I might faint."

Facing the civilians was an officer in the dark-blue uniform of the navy, a British admiral. Rachel felt her nerves tingle when she realized that the officer was probably the infamous Admiral Cockburn.

As the women approached, Cockburn smiled and bowed. "Good morning, ladies. To what do I owe the pleasure of your visit?"

The women who had so vocally railed against the arsonists fell silent.

Rachel had edged to the front of the crowd to get a better view. Her heart nearly leaped out of her chest when Admiral Cockburn's eyes seemed to lock on her.

"Come now, my ladies, how may I be of assistance?"

Even though Cockburn addressed the women, his eyes never left Rachel. Her face warmed as she realized the randy old salt had probably already undressed her with his eyes.

After an awkward moment, Rachel's father stepped forward. "Admiral, we have come to—"

Cockburn frowned and raised his hand, palm toward Mordecai Thurston. "Now, now," he said, "these lovely ladies have gallantly ventured out of their homes with some mission in mind. I would hate to disappoint them. Please, tell me what you desire."

As Cockburn continued to study Rachel, she waited for the women to answer him. When no one spoke up, she said, "Admiral Cockburn, we live nearby and are worried that the fires will spread to our homes. We implore you to refrain from setting more buildings ablaze. Even a brief change in wind direction could send the conflagration through our neighborhood, destroying all we have."

"Ah!" said Cockburn with a leering grin. "Not all you have, for sure."

A score of Cockburn's sailors hauled printing presses out of the office of the *National Intelligencer*. They dumped them onto the street and smashed them to pieces.

"That's the way, me hearties!" shouted Cockburn. "We'll teach Mister Joseph Gales, Junior to print lies about me."

A sailor carried a wide, wooden tray to the middle of the street and dumped its contents. With a clatter of metal, printing keys spread across the gravel.

Cockburn yelled to the sailor. "Make sure all the Cs are destroyed. I don't want those rascals abusing my name anymore."

When the sailors had all the printing presses, typeset, and other printing paraphernalia out of the building, a midshipman approached Cockburn with an unlit torch, and said, "Ready to light her up, sir."

The ladies shrieked.

"We implore you, kind sir," said Rachel, "A shift of wind, which is all too common in these parts, could send sparks onto our rooftops and destroy our homes."

Cockburn frowned, then seemed to consider the matter further. "Ah," he said, shaking his head as if in agony, "I can't bring myself to spare the property of a man who has libeled me with abandon all these many months."

Rachel's mind raced to find an argument that might change the admiral's mind. "But sir," she said, "Mr. Gales doesn't own the building. He only rents it. You would be injuring the wrong man. And you have promised you would spare private property."

Cockburn's gaze again settled on Rachel, and she endured his lecherous attention.

With a flourish of his arm that reminded Rachel of an actor on stage, Cockburn smiled. "Be assured, my dear ladies, I am a man of my word. I will provide you protection. The protection, I might add, not afforded you by your own president."

He turned to the sailors. "Put your torches out."

The ladies sighed as the sailors followed their orders.

"Now," shouted Cockburn, "tear the building down. Brick by brick!"

Within minutes, the sailors had grappling hooks onto the roof and ripped it apart. One by one, they grappled a wall and pulled until it toppled with a crash.

Rachel hated the destruction but was pleased that the British officers had conducted themselves as gentlemen.

Rachel noticed a young British lieutenant as he approached the stoic general who had been watching Admiral Cockburn entertain the ladies. She sensed something familiar about the way he walked. The lieutenant's back was toward her as he saluted the general.

Despite the noise of the sailors destroying the publishing office, she heard the lieutenant say, "Captain Willis sends his compliments, sir. I am to report a looter has been arrested. One of our men. A private."

The general frowned and cursed. After a moment, he said, "Very well, lieutenant. Escort these ladies safely back to their homes."

The lieutenant saluted and turned toward the ladies. He started to say something, then stopped short when his eyes met Rachel's.

Rachel was stunned. The British lieutenant standing before her in an immaculate scarlet uniform was George Sherbourne. At first she was confused, but she quickly realized that the man she had considered her friend was actually a British spy. And that he had been using her and her father over the last several years. Rachel felt her blood turn cold. She stepped close to George, and then with all of her strength she swung her hand. His head snapped to the side as her flattened palm cracked against the side of his face.

Late that night Lieutenant George Sherbourne topped the hill on the Bladensburg Turnpike and turned to look back at Washington City. He half expected to see a glow from the buildings set ablaze, but the sky was dark.

His cheek still burned from that morning when Rachel had slapped his face. He yearned to see her again—to explain himself, but the events of the day had precluded any such opportunity.

At midday the sky had darkened, and it began to pour, drenching all the fires. Wind roared as it ripped through the city, blowing drums like paper cups, uprooting trees, dismasting ships, and tearing the roofs off buildings. A three-pound cannon was overturned and hurled like a toy. British and Americans alike died in the storm that some called a hurricane, others a tornado.

In the aftermath around two o'clock, a terrible explosion rocked the earth. George had been part of a detachment sent to investigate. At Greenleaf's Point, where the East Branch flowed into the Potomac, they found dozens of dead and wounded redcoats around a deep crater. Two hundred men had been sent to destroy barrels of gunpowder in a magazine.

Apparently they had been dumping the powder down a water well when something set if off. Given the size of the crater, George was still amazed that casualties had only been thirty men killed and forty-four wounded.

Rumors quickly spread among officers and men that the whole invasion of the American capital had been jinxed, or that the storm and the explosion were unfavorable omens.

As nightfall approached, the redcoats spread the word to the locals that General Ross had ordered a strict dusk-till-dawn curfew. Anyone caught outside his or her home would be shot. Under the cover of darkness, General Ross marched his men out of the city.

From the rise along the Bladensburg turnpike, George took one more look in the direction of Washington City. In the space of twenty-four hours, the British had swept into the capital, burned government buildings, then vanished into the night on their way back to ships on the Patuxent River. George wished he could see Rachel again, but he suspected that their paths would never again cross.

CHAPTER FORTY-EIGHT

SEPTEMBER 1814, WASHINGTON CITY

As the stubble-faced liveryman held the bay gelding by the bit of its bridle, Rachel Thurston hiked her skirt and slipped her left foot into the stirrup. With the reins in her hands, she grabbed hold of the saddle's pommel and pulled herself up. She hooked her right knee around the leather horn jutting from the pommel. As she settled into the sidesaddle, she tugged at her skirt until it draped comfortably around her.

"Easy, Buck," she said, trying to sound reassuring. Rachel scooted slightly in the saddle to make sure she had her balance, then nodded to the liveryman.

He smiled and released the bridle. "Well done, Miss Thurston."

"Thank you, Mr. Newall," she said with pride. This was the first time she had mounted a horse without a leg up from the liveryman or first climbing a wooden riser.

She tapped her heel against Buck's ribs and said, "Giddyup."

Buck eased ahead, and she guided him onto the rut-filled street.

Despite her father's protests, she had been taking riding lessons from Hannah Gallitan, wife of Albert Gallitan, former secretary of the Treasury and now peace commissioner in Ghent, Belgium. They had met at one of Dolley's gatherings, and Rachel quickly discovered that Hannah didn't shy away from talking politics—or any other subject. They had quickly developed a friendship.

From the beginning of the lessons, Hannah had assured Rachel that despite his name, Buck was even-tempered and gentle. This was her first solo ride. She felt grateful that the saddle allowed her to ride while wearing a skirt, but she envied men their trousers and riding astride. She had asked Hannah if it would ever be acceptable for respectable women to wear trousers.

Hannah had puffed on her cigar and then chuckled. "Probably not in our lifetimes."

Rachel guided Buck across the meadow that covered much of Capitol Hill. As she gazed ahead, she wished she could urge Buck into a trot, and then a gallop. She imagined them flying at a dead run as her hair streamed back. Unfortunately, the sidesaddle didn't support her well enough to even consider a trot, much less a gallop. Maybe someday, she thought.

Ahead of her towered the ruins of the Capitol buildings. They stood roofless, windowless, and charred. With sadness she recalled the beautiful architecture and décor now reduced to ashes and cracked stone.

As Rachel stared at the ruins, she remembered the Sunday services she and her father had attended at the Capitol. Her face warmed as she also recalled that was where she first met George Sherbourne. If he ever showed up again, she would slam the door in his face. Of course, the chance that she would ever see him again was remote. Even if he survived whatever battles he might face, as an officer in the British army he would likely spend the rest of his career in the far reaches of the empire. The man was a louse. Good riddance.

She guided Buck northwest onto Pennsylvania Avenue and noted that the poplar trees lining the gravel road had yet to turn yellow for fall. She rode downhill across the wooden bridge over Tiber Creek.

As Buck plodded uphill she could see the rubble of the treasury, state, and war department buildings. The president's mansion had been reduced to an unroofed stand of blackened walls.

The state of the ruined buildings hadn't changed since James and Dolley returned to Washington City four days after the British left. Initially, the Madisons stayed at their old house on F Street, now the home of Dolley's daughter Anna and her husband, Richard Cutts.

Upon her return, Dolley had railed against Brits, and Rachel was sure that the president felt heartbroken and betrayed by his incompetent commanders. Of course, reasoned Rachel, that served him right for appointing them in the first place.

Washington City had been of no strategic value and hadn't offered the promise of rich plunder, so the Brits had obviously intended the raid to demoralize the Americans. Rachel fumed to think about it. She had hoped the invasion would leave the Madison administration discredited. Unwittingly, the attack on the capital city had backfired. Dolley's daring postponement of flight until the last minute had become a symbol of patriotism. As reported in the prestigious newsweekly *Niles Register*, "The spirit of the nation is roused."

More recently the Madisons had been lent Octagon House by their friend and fellow slave owner, Mr. Tayloe. At 8th Street and New York Avenue, Octagon House was now the largest entertaining place in the city. Once again, the Madisons were living in high style.

On September 21, two days after the return of congress, Dolley opened the social season with one of her drawing rooms. Local residents responded with record attendance. The *Washington City Gazette* expressed disappointment that the invasion of the capital hadn't also marked the end of Dolley's weekly gatherings.

President Madison set congress up at Blodgett's Hotel and encouraged them to begin the rebuilding effort. He met immediate resistance as others proposed moving the nation's capital back to Philadelphia, which had the distinct advantage of having buildings to house the government.

Rachel pulled back on the reins, and Buck stopped. She gazed back at the ruins stretching from the president's house to Capitol Hill and imagined it overgrown with trees and vines.

Despite the best efforts of the president and congress to reconvene the work of government, the ruins of the capital could very well become a metaphor for the future of the American states. Without even token naval resistance in Chesapeake Bay, the British could sail to Baltimore with impunity and pluck it like a Christmas goose. All summer tens of thousands of battle-hardened redcoats had been pouring into British North American, no doubt poised for an invasion that could shatter the States.

CHAPTER FORTY-NINE

SEPTEMBER 1814, CUMBERLAND BAY,
LAKE CHAMPLAIN, NEW YORK

Corporal Silas Shackleton dreaded the coming dawn as he steadied himself against the bulwark of the *Saratoga*. A rooster crowed from a coop at middeck as a rocket streaked across the predawn sky to the west. In the still of the morning, the sizzle of the rocket carried over the water. With a fiery burst, the rocket exploded above the American fortifications across the Saranac River south of Plattsburgh. Silas leaned against the ship's rail and spat in the direction of the British army occupying the town.

To the east across the water, the silhouette of the Vermont shores underscored a sky already glowing pink, orange, and purple. Silas had seen a map showing Lake Champlain as a dagger-shaped body separating upper New York on the west from Vermont on the east. To the north the lake emptied into a river that eventually flowed to the St. Lawrence near Montreal. The thought of Montreal made Silas's insides twist tight.

British troops, fresh from their victory over Napoleon Bonaparte, had been arriving in Canada all summer. By August their numbers had been rumored to be over fifteen thousand, and word had spread about a huge new ship the Royal Navy was building at the north end of the lake. Supposedly, it was a thirty-six-gun frigate capable of outgunning the entire American flotilla on the lake.

Silas was well aware that Lake Champlain had provided a north-south route for armies during the French and Indian War and then also in the Revolutionary War. The British might use it again. From near Montreal they could sail south a hundred miles, then march into the Hudson Valley and downriver to New York City.

With exactly that in mind, Plattsburgh on Lake Champlain had been selected for a major defensive buildup. Across the Saranac River on the southern edge of Plattsburgh rose a steep-sided peninsula that had the making of a natural fortress. On it Major General George Izard, who had trained as a military engineer in Europe, built three mutually supporting forts, two heavy blockhouses, and numerous interconnected batteries and trenches. He trained his six thousand regulars and stocked the fortifications with arms, ammunition, and supplies sufficient to withstand a three-week siege.

In August, the Secretary of War ordered Izard and his army to the Niagara area, leaving only a skeletal garrison at Plattsburgh. General Izard respectfully protested and asked that the orders be remanded. When no change of instructions arrived, Izard marched his army northwest, leaving Plattsburgh in the hands of Brigadier General Alexander Macomb with only fifteen hundred men, many of whom were sick or wounded, as had been Silas.

In early September, a small British force moved west along Lake Ontario as the War Department apparently anticipated, but a British army of many thousands thrust south along the western shore of Lake Champlain. Trying to buy precious time to prepare for battle, General Macomb ordered militiamen north to engage and slow the enemy. With little regard for the American forces, the redcoats advanced without even deploying from their marching formation. Most of the poorly trained, undisciplined American militia melted away, but the regulars fell back slowly, giving up ground grudgingly.

Silas had nearly recovered from the wound he had sustained at Lundy's Lane, and a sergeant put him in charge of a detail. They felled trees from both sides of the road to create a herringbone-shaped obstruction to impede the enemy's progress. They tore up bridges in the enemy's path and skirmished as they fell back. But the redcoats, many of them General Wellesley's battle-hardened "Invincibles," just kept coming.

With the British at their heels, Silas's company fell back to Plattsburgh. They tore the planks off the bridge spanning the Saranac River and stacked the timber to create a breastwork, then retreated to the fortified peninsula.

General Macomb called for more support. Militiamen and volunteers from New York and Vermont came to his aid. Within days the Plattsburgh defensive force swelled to four thousand men.

Meanwhile, the British built earthen ramparts for massive gun batteries in the village north of the river. Once the bombardment started, it continued day and night. Congreve rockets sizzled as they streaked across the sky, then exploded over the forts.

Silas had little doubt what the redcoats had in mind. They would take the Plattsburgh forts while the Royal Navy destroyed Commodore Thomas Macdonough's flotilla, now anchored in the bay.

With Plattsburgh and the lake under their control, the British could march south to the Hudson River, then all the way to New York City, cutting off and isolating New England from the rest of the States. And with mixed sentiments toward the new nation and its war, the British would demand that the occupied states renew their allegiance to Britain and break away from the republic. While Silas figured the people had the right to subject themselves to the Crown if they really wanted to, he had a hard time imagining the new American nation without the northeastern states.

British forces across the Saranac River had swelled to ten thousand troops. Silas had little doubt of the outcome of the battle. Sooner or later the battle-hardened British troops would crush American resistance.

He glanced at the ship's gig, a rowboat tied alongside the *Saratoga*. If he was quick he could be in the boat and rowing for shore before anyone missed him. Once on shore he would hide until the battle was over, then slip away in the following confusion.

He eased toward the boat, then stopped. Now he knew for sure that he was a coward. His face burned hot with shame and his insides seemed to melt.

His life seemed to flow through his mind. He recalled how he had fled the streets of New York rather than stand and fight. He had cowered to the Royal navy by volunteering for virtual slavery. He had enlisted in the army to avoid a cold and hungry winter. He had deserted at Queenston Heights. Yes, he had stood and fought at Chippewa and Lundy's Lane, but he knew he would have run if the sergeants hadn't stood ready to shoot anyone who stepped toward the rear.

And to think he had thought himself worthy of being a sergeant some-day. How could he have deceived himself into believing he could be their equal? A coward was lower than horse dung scraped off the boots of such men.

Silas stared into the dark water near the ship. If he grabbed a cannon-ball and jumped overboard, he would sink fast and deep. His shame would be over quickly. He edged over to a rack and lifted the nearest ball.

He jumped as a series of thunderous booms rocked the early morning calm. Cannon fire had come from beyond Cumberland Head. The British flotilla had arrived. Although the steep, heavily wooded peninsula blocked sight of the vessels, Silas imagined the ship masts and sails against the red glow of the eastern sky. In his mind's eye, he pictured one silhouette that stood much taller and wider than the others—the Royal Navy's new frigate *Confiance*.

At first he had assumed the cannon fire was the beginning of the battle, but the British ships were not yet in position even to see the American ships anchored in Cumberland Bay. Then he realized the British had probably fired their guns without cannonballs to scale the rust and dirt out of the bores and possibly to signal the British land forces to coordinate their attacks.

Silas glanced down at the cannonball cradled in his hands. He could still jump overboard and end his shame. But if he were to die this day, maybe he should make his life count for something. He eased the ball back onto the rack.

As the morning brightened, the shimmering water of Cumberland Bay came into view. To the southwest was the fortified peninsula held by General Macomb. On the western shore, beyond the docks lay the British-occupied village of Plattsburgh. The northern shoreline was formed by Cumberland Point, with Cumberland Head jutting into Lake Champlain.

Commodore Macdonough strode across the deck, gazing northeast toward Cumberland Head. He buttoned his jacket, then addressed his officers. "Clear for action."

As they had practiced numerous times over the previous days, essential gear was either stowed or lashed down. Everything else was tossed over the side. Soon the waters around the vessels were strewn with litter. Even chicken coops bobbed in the lake—the birds having been set free on the decks. A rooster in the rigging of the *Saratoga* flapped its wings and crowed.

Silas knew that he was one of only a few American crew members with any naval experience. Hundreds of soldiers had been loaned by General Macomb to Commodore Macdonough. Still desperately short of men, Macdonough persuaded the army commander to assign him the prisoners from the stockade to man the oars on the gunboats. When Macomb expressed concern that the malingers and drunks might cause more trouble than they were worth, Macdonough assured the general that after having rowed the gunboats across the lake, the men would have little energy for trouble. When more volunteers had been called for, several members of the band joined the crews.

Across the mouth of the bay, from Cumberland Head south to the shoals off Crab Island, Commodore Macdonough had anchored his vessels, now drifting tight on their anchor chains as the back current in the bay tugged at them. All sails had been furled against their yards.

Nearest Cumberland Head was the *Preble*, and just to its south was the second largest of the American vessels, the two-masted, square-rigged brig *Eagle*. Farther south was the biggest of the American vessels, Macdonough's flagship, the three-masted, sloop-of-war *Saratoga*. Next was the two-masted schooner *Ticonderoga*. In each of the gaps between the shoreline and the four largest vessels floated two seventy-five-foot-long, fifteen-foot-wide gunboats. Each sprouted a twenty-four-pound long gun at the bow and at the center a stout "smasher" columbiad cannon.

Southeast across the bay, a crowd of hospital patients gathered at a makeshift gun battery on the northern tip of Crab Island. Two naval cannon pointed toward the entrance of the bay. The unmanned battery provided an excellent vantage point for viewing the upcoming battle, and invalids had climbed atop the guns for a seat.

As townspeople began to assemble on the tree-lined north shore of the bay, a small vessel pulled around Cumberland Head and stopped in the choppy, wind-tossed waters. Silas figured the British commander from the *Confiance* was reconnoitering the American flotilla. Soon the British commodore's gig pulled back behind the peninsula.

The sun rose higher over the distant Vermont shores, and the day brightened. Through the white-capped waves off Cumberland Head sped the British flotilla, sails billowing.

Silas suspected what the British commodore had in mind—a quick, one-sided battle. With her longer-ranged guns, the *Confiance* could fire a broadside as she sailed just out of range of the American carronades. Once past the American anchorage, she could tack back in front of the

Americans, cutting loose with a salvo from her larboard side. She could repeat this over and over, in a figure-eight pattern, until the American fleet either sank or struck its colors.

As the British ships raced across the whitecaps whipped up by a brisk northeasterly breeze, Silas remembered the destruction aboard the *Guerriere* two years before. He recalled that ships at sea were constructed of oak, which, when cured, was nearly as tough as iron and, with sufficient thickness, could even absorb the impact of a cannonball. Vessels on the lake, however, were constructed of unseasoned local wood. When cannonballs hit unseasoned wood, it exploded in a shower of deadly splinters. With each exchange of broadsides, many brave men would be killed or maimed. Silas pitied the American crews, bobbing helplessly at anchor, for the slaughter they were about to suffer. He wondered how Commodore Macdonough could be so stupid as to let his flotilla be cornered so easily.

Then Silas recalled that he had heard that Commodore Macdonough was an ardent student of naval warfare and had served in the war against the Barbary pirates. Presumably Macdonough also knew the local waters and wind patterns better than the British commander. And maybe, thought Silas, the British crews were just as inexperienced as the Americans.

The first of the British vessels to round Cumberland Head was a little sloop, sails billowing in the breeze. Behind it was the frigate *Confiance*, then a brig, and then another sloop. A dozen gunboats followed. When Silas squinted he could barely see the oarsmen pulling hard to keep up with the sailboats. All the vessels sailed full speed into the bay, drums beating and crews cheering.

The remainder of the British vessels rounded Cumberland Head, and Silas braced for the coming blast. Reminding himself that he would see a flash and smoke before he heard the roar of cannon, he relaxed a bit and watched closely as the British ships entered the bay, their sails taut with the wind.

Silas felt his gut tighten as the *Confiance* headed straight for the *Saratoga*. The British plan, no doubt, would be to approach to a distance just beyond the range of the American carronades, then use their long guns to blast the *Saratoga*.

Just about the time Silas expected the *Confiance* to turn, exposing her starboard broadside to the Americans, the sails of the *Confiance* fluttered. He could hardly believe what he saw. The sails snapped as if gasping for air. Then, after quivering a couple of times, the sails fell limp.

Silas studied the scene before him, then cheered. The men around him turned toward him, and he laughed. "Don't you see? Cumberland Point is blocking the breeze in the bay."

The frigate had been sailing top speed straight at the American ships with the intention of turning to the south barely beyond American gun range. Now with her sails as limp as laundry on a still day and fighting an opposing current, the *Confiance* had lost her ability to maneuver.

As the bow of the frigate passed in front of the gun on his left, the Commodore Macdonough yelled, "As you bear. Fire!" The first cannon roared and bucked back in a cloud of smoke. Across the bay, shot ripped into the frigate's hull just above the waterline. Ignoring the cheers of the men around him, Silas rushed to help reload.

Guns from another American vessel roared, and Silas saw the anchor hanging from the bow of the *Confiance* plunge into the bay. She turned to her larboard, but her forward momentum carried her closer to the American line before she drifted to a stop, bobbing helplessly.

British yards and rigging toppled as the entire American flotilla opened fire on the ships opposite them.

Now Silas suspected Macdonough's battle plan. Familiar with the local winds and currents, he had carefully placed his flotilla to draw the British ships in where their long guns would be to no advantage. He had lured the British into a trap where they would have to fight as equals.

Macdonough's plan didn't assure a victory for the Americans against the *Confiance*, but it gave them an even chance.

Crippled but not beaten by the first American salvo, the *Confiance* dropped its remaining anchor, then fired back. Rigging aboard the *Saratoga* crumpled, and timber from the decks went flying.

The scene before Silas took on a surreal quality where action, sound, and time blended into the jumble of chaos. Cannon roared, masts toppled, sails shredded, and decks exploded. Gray-white smoke clouded everything.

Silas recalled the horror of the sea battle two years before between the *Guerriere* and the *Constitution*—just two ships maneuvering in and out of firing position. But that battle paled in comparison to the carnage occurring aboard anchored vessels at close range.

Over the next hour, officers and men scrambled through choking smoke to load, aim, and fire their guns in a deafening din of cannon fire. As timber and rigging fell on deck, masts and bulwarks were ripped apart. Severed arms, legs, and heads littered the deck now running with blood as the wounded groaned and screamed. Silas helped load a gun, and when a British shot knocked the gun off its carriage, he moved to another gun.

Between clouds of smoke, Silas could see that the northernmost of the British sloops had taken a terrible beating and seemed to be drifting helplessly toward the American gunboats. It struck its colors.

The southernmost of the British sloops seemed to be heavily damaged and had drifted toward Crab Island. Silas hoped the invalids had the gumption to take a shot or two at the damaged boat to prevent it from escaping.

The American brig *Eagle*, though heavily damaged, was trading broadsides with the British brig. The *Eagle* drifted for a while, then limped to a position slightly behind and to the side of the *Saratoga*. There, it turned its undamaged broadside on the British *Confiance*.

The battle raged for another hour, and by midmorning the damage to both the *Confiance* and the *Saratoga* was substantial. Silas wondered how either could continue fighting. The Saratoga fell silent, and Silas assumed Macdonough was letting the smoke clear so his crews could see their targets. But through the din, Silas heard MacDonough's command. "Wind ship!"

Silas's first reaction to the commodore's order was disbelief. To wind the ship now would require the remaining crew to leave their posts manning the guns, and crank the capstan. While they were turning the vessel, they would be defenseless and vulnerable to raking fire from the enemy.

But then he understood. The commodore had prepared for this from the start. Before the battle, Macdonough had each vessel set spring lines attached to anchors, and he had laid the heavy ropes low in the water to protect them from damage. Silas rushed to the capstan, grabbed a wooden stave, and shoved it into one of holes notched in the massive spindle. He and a dozen others heaved at it. Now as the *Saratoga*'s crew wound the capstan, and aided by the current, the sloop of war turned easily in place.

Silas glanced back at the *Confiance* and could see that she was also attempting to wind ship, racing to bring her own fresh broadside to bear.

The *Saratoga* completed its turn and now had an undamaged broadside of cannon facing the enemy. Across the bay, the *Confiance* was only halfway turned when the *Saratoga* cut loose. Cannonballs raked across the deck of the *Confiance* from one end of the frigate to the other. After a few more broadsides from the *Saratoga*, the *Confiance* was little more than a floating pile of junk. She struck her colors. In short order the remaining British vessels, including the sloop grounded off Crab Island, also struck their colors.

A handful of enemy gunboats pulled away from the bay and headed north. Silas hoped the commodore would send one of the vessels out to round them up. Then he realized that could not happen—not one of the

American vessels in the bay had a single mast standing on which a sail could be rigged.

At Commodore Macdonough's orders, the men began to look after their wounded. Silas could hear the roar of guns from the fortifications at Plattsburgh—not at the ships but back and forth between the American fortifications and the British across the river in Plattsburgh.

The smoke gradually cleared from the bay. The Stars and Stripes still flew over each of the forts, but Silas realized the flags would inevitably fall if the much-larger British force pressed its attack. The Americans could probably hold against a frontal assault across the river, but eventually the British would ford the river upstream and overwhelm the forts with superior numbers. The cost could be very high, but there seemed little doubt about the eventual outcome.

Silas glanced back at the defeated British flotilla and realized that the American fortifications at Plattsburgh were of no further value to the British. Without naval control of Lake Champlain, the British would have no way to supply their army through the coming winter. Without the possibility of winter supplies, the British would have little choice but to march their army back to Canada.

Silas did what he could to help the wounded around him, then found a seat on what remained of a splintered bulwark. He suspected that he had seen his last combat, but wondered how the rest of the nation was faring.

CHAPTER FIFTY

SEPTEMBER 1814, PATAPSCO RIVER, BALTIMORE, MARYLAND

George swung gently in a hammock and stared at the wooden deck above him. He had hoped to get a few hours of sleep, but every time he started to doze, another gun boomed, rattling the timbers of the boat. He muttered and rolled out of the hammock.

It had only been three days since George had disembarked with General Ross's forces onto the North Point peninsula fourteen miles south-east of Baltimore. George had been assigned to act as a guide for Ross's command, identifying the roads and surrounding terrain he had scouted over the last two years. After General Ross organized his seven-thou-sand-man force for a day, he sent his advance guard of riflemen northwest along the North Point Road toward Baltimore. All seemed to be going well until General Ross toppled from his horse with an American sniper's shot through his chest.

Colonel Brook promptly took charge and advanced his troops against American forces lined up across a narrow stretch of the peninsula. After a brief but spirited battle, the Americans withdrew to a heavily fortified hill on the eastern outskirts of Baltimore. Rather than gamble his troops in a high-risk assault on forces entrenched on high ground, Colonel Brook began a withdrawal. George had been sent back as a messenger to the ships on the Patapsco River.

George cursed his bad luck at, once again, being outside the action of the war, then climbed to the deck. He was aboard a sloop owned by Americans who had approached the fleet under the protection of a white flag. A couple of local lawyers were seeking the release of a popular physician taken as a prisoner of war after the burning of Washington City. The sloop and its passengers were being detained until the battle for Baltimore was decided.

Across the dark waters George could see the silhouette of the *Surprize*, Admiral Cochrane's flagship while in the shallow waters of Patapsco River. Beyond the *Surprize* lay over a dozen vessels firing upon Fort McHenry, the star-shaped structure guarding the entrance to Baltimore's harbor. As they had all night, cannon thundered and muzzles flashed. Mortar ships lobbed 200-pound shells that arced over the water and then plummeted toward the fort, either to burst overhead or to crash into the fort and then explode. Congreve rockets sizzled and rattled as they streaked from the *Erebus*, then descended and exploded over the fort.

Anchored just out of range of the American guns, the British ships were able to fire at will without the risk of return fire. The bombardment had continued almost constantly through the night with two purposes. The first was to cover the withdrawal of British troops from the peninsula east of Baltimore. The second was the destruction or capitulation of the fort. If the fort fell, the land forces guarding Baltimore would also likely crumble.

Admiral Cochrane, long frustrated with Baltimore and its "nest of pirates," had vowed to burn every house in the city. The harbor and its surrounding warehouses would make a huge prize for His Majesty's forces, and the proceeds from the sale of vessels and goods would make fortunes for each officer involved.

Another salvo of rockets soared from the *Erebus* and streaked toward Fort McHenry. Although the land attack against Baltimore had already failed, capitulation of the fort could still let Crown forces teach the rebellious Americans a lesson. George sensed that the approaching dawn would be the decisive moment after the disappointments of the previous days.

George studied the dark waters around the warships. He had been alarmed to hear that after the British left Washington City in flames, Robert Fulton had pulled several of his torpedoes out of hiding at Kolarama and entrusted them to a naval captain en route to Baltimore. George studied the silhouettes of the warships anchored in the wide river. He hoped the light from the gun flashes and the rockets was enough for the sentries to spot the Americans if they tried to deploy the devastating explosive devices. He glanced at the *Surprize* and imagined it bursting skyward in a pyramid of bright water, then crashing back to the surface as a thousand pieces of timber.

His attention drifted toward the northwest, to the fort, where the Royal Navy had laid a terrible barrage of hundreds, maybe thousands, of ten- to thirteen-inch shells. He also realized that with the long range between the ships and the fort, cutting fuses with sufficient accuracy to time a shell's explosion for maximum effect on the target was extremely difficult. Still, he imagined the horror the defenders must have endured throughout the night. He was sure that by now the Americans had either abandoned the fort or had run up a white flag that would be visible shortly.

As the morning brightened over Fort McHenry, George's heart sank. The Americans had hoisted an obnoxiously large flag over the fort, and it still fluttered in the breeze.

As the sun rose, signal flags aboard the *Surprize* were hauled down from the heights of the rigging, and new flags were run up. George didn't know the meaning of each pennant, but he suspected that Admiral Cochrane was ordering his ships to weigh anchor and leave Baltimore to the Americans.

CHAPTER FIFTY-ONE

SEPTEMBER 1814, MOBILE BAY

With the afternoon sun glaring in his eyes, Lemuel Wyckliffe galloped his mount along the shoreline toward the mouth of the bay. A tangle of overgrown brush lined the beach to his left, and the bay stretched wide and gray to his right. General Andrew Jackson had given him orders to scout between Mobile and Fort Bowyer, a semi-circular battery at the tip of a sandy isthmus that formed the eastern edge of the bay's entrance. Traveling along beaches and newly blazed trails through the woods, Lemuel had seen hardly anyone since leaving Mobile.

He felt his mount tiring from a long gallop, so he reined her to a stop and dismounted. He patted the black mare on her sweat-frothed neck and scratched her forehead. "Come on, girl, I'll stretch my legs while you take a breather." As he led her along the beach, seagulls screamed overhead and occasionally swooped to the water.

Despite the beautiful day, Lemuel couldn't help feeling uneasy. After the Treaty of Fort Jackson, Andrew Jackson had clearly emerged as the premier commander of the southwest sector of the war. A grateful president Monroe appointed him to the regular army with the rank of major general.

He was given command of the military district encompassing the states of Tennessee and Louisiana and the territory stretching from Alabama to the Mississippi River.

General Jackson feared a British invasion that could threaten the nation's future. As Lemuel walked his mount, he wondered if the war would ever end. The War Department warned Jackson of British preparations to attack New Orleans. Jackson believed the British would try to take Mobile first, then march west to Baton Rouge. Such action would isolate New Orleans and establish a foothold for British control of the Mississippi River Valley, north all the way to Canada. Jackson hurried his troops south to Mobile. There, he reinforced Fort Bowyer with 160 regular-army troops and ordered them to rebuild it.

As Lemuel led the black mare along the bay shore, he heard voices in the distance. From previous trips to Bowyer, he knew the fort was still several miles away along the narrow finger of sand dunes. He mounted the mare and headed through the brush and pines in the direction of the voices. As the voices grew louder, he dismounted and tied the horse to a tree, then crept forward through the brush. After a few minutes he peeked onto the gulf-coast beach.

What he saw made his nerves tingle. Along the beach marched sixty British marines in bright-red uniforms, a howitzer in tow. Following them were over a hundred Red Stick warriors. They were heading west toward Fort Bowyer.

Lemuel slipped back into the brush, found his mount, and led her back to the shore of the bay. Thankful that the mare was rested, he raced her full speed toward the fort.

As it came within view a mile ahead, Lemuel galloped up a sandy dune and screamed his loudest. He waved his floppy felt hat high over his head, screaming again and again as he pointed east along the gulf shore, hoping the soldiers in the fort could see the approaching British forces.

Seeing no response from the fort, he dug his heels into the mare's ribs. With sand kicking up behind them, the mare sped ahead.

As Lemuel approached the rampart, he heard a musket shot. He raced past the sentries guarding the entrance and sped inside. Everywhere blue-uniformed soldiers grabbed muskets and rushed to the fort's walls. Recognizing the fort's commander, Major Morgan, Lemuel leapt from his horse and quickly described what he had seen.

"That's not the worst of our problems," said Morgan, nodding out to sea.

Lemuel peeked over the rampart wall and cursed. To the south were four sets of sails, and he had little doubt that they each flew the Union Jack from their topmasts. Two of the ships approached rapidly and were soon working their way around the sandbars at the entrance of the bay.

Major Morgan told Lemuel to grab a fresh mount from the fort's stable and hurry back to Mobile to let Jackson know that they were under attack. As rapidly as he could, Lemuel switched his saddle from the mare to a light-brown gelding. Within minutes he was out of the fort, racing along the bayside shore of the sandy isthmus. He swung the long ends of his reins back and forth, snapping the sides of his mount. The beach seemed to flow by in a blur as the gelding sped at a dead run along the wet sand.

Out of the brush a hundred yards ahead of Lemuel poured dozens of Red Sticks. They stopped and pointed their muskets at him. Gun smoke billowed from the group of warriors, and musket balls whizzed past Lemuel. He pulled back on the reins so hard he nearly pitched forward over the gelding's neck as he slid to a stop.

The tip of the isthmus was so narrow that the Red Sticks and redcoats had already blocked his only path. He turned and sped back to the fort.

Lemuel made it back to the fort just as redcoats formed a line across the isthmus. On the highest ground in the middle of the narrow stretch of land, an artillery crew set up the howitzer and opened fire. A cannonball plunged into a log building inside the fort, sending splinters flying in all directions. Lemuel ducked behind the newly constructed timber and earthen rampart.

Most of the British line was just beyond range, but the American soldiers made halfhearted attempts with their muskets. Lemuel took careful aim with his rifle and dropped an Indian with his first shot. Before he could reload, the British and their Indian allies had retreated behind the sand dunes.

The American gun crews began firing back at the British. To Lemuel this wasn't going to be much more than a standoff until the Americans were either starved out of the fort or relieved by General Jackson's forces from Mobile. Lemuel didn't doubt Jackson would send reinforcements as soon as he learned the fort was under attack. And the sound of cannon fire was sure to alert Jackson of the British presence.

As the British ships drew close to the tip of the isthmus, they faced the semicircular battery of American guns. Great puffs of gray-white smoke streaked out from the ships, and cannonballs ripped through the ramparts of the fort. The ground under Lemuel shook as the American cannon fired back.

The two closest British ships dropped anchor off the point to hold their position against the ebbing tide as they blasted away at the fort.

As the evening wore on, the ships seemed to be getting the worst of the exchange. The British balls often reached the fort but did little damage to the earth-and-timber structure. On the other hand, the American cannoneers were shredding the ships' rigging and pounding their bulwarks.

The nearest ship began to drift closer to the fort, and Lemuel could no longer see its anchor chain. Maybe a lucky shot had cut her loose. Fort Bowyer's artillerymen concentrated their fire on the ship as it drifted south, right under the battery's guns.

The ship's rigging was a tattered mess by the time it floated south of the point and suddenly lurched to a stop on a sandbar. As the American guns continued to pound it, small boats loaded with marines and crew began to row for another ship. As the last boat pulled away from the British ship, flames leaped from its hold, spread across the deck and up the tattered rigging. The surviving ships weighed anchor and sailed eastward.

The sound of gunfire caused Lemuel to duck. The redcoats and Indians on shore were advancing toward the fort. He aimed and fired shot after shot as the American cannoneers blasted away at the attackers.

For a moment Lemuel wondered if the British were crazy enough to continue the attack, then he recalled how quickly some American forces had capitulated over the last couple of years. The British were testing the Americans' willpower as much as their firepower. And maybe the British just wanted to show off to the Indians. Whichever it was, the attack soon faltered. The redcoats retreated, regrouped, and marched east along the ocean shoreline toward Pensacola.

Lemuel reported to Major Morgan and was soon riding east along the shore of the bay toward Mobile. He pushed the gelding hard, but carefully preserved the horse's stamina by occasionally dismounting and walking briskly along the shoreline. On one such break well after dark, he glanced back toward the southwest. The sky suddenly flashed orange, and he heard a thunderous boom.

He assumed that the fire aboard the British ship had finally reached its powder magazine. He imagined timbers, masts, and cannon flying in all directions from the ship and then raining down on the surf. Within seconds the only evidence that the ship had been there would be the debris bobbing in the waves.

Lemuel suspected that the ship's explosion had been heard all the way to Mobile, and he looked forward to describing the action to General Jackson. Lemuel worried that the British would return to Fort Bowyer with more ships and men. He doubted that they would give up on their quest to take control of New Orleans and the Mississippi River.

CHAPTER FIFTY-TWO

NOVEMBER 1814, PENSACOLA, SPANISH WEST FLORIDA

Lemuel Wycliffe stood silently with hundreds of other militiamen and soldiers assembled in the crowded town square. A fife-and-drum team played a tune as the U.S. flag descended a pole in front of the governor's house. Lemuel swallowed hard as a color guard of blue-uniformed regulars folded the flag, then marched away.

The Spanish flag rose on the pole as another group of musicians played their national anthem. Major General Andrew Jackson turned to the Spanish governor of Pensacola and saluted him. Jackson then turned smartly and mounted his horse. Without further word, he headed down the road that eventually led to Mobile.

One by one, units of American regulars stepped out of formation and marched after Jackson. As Lemuel waited for his unit's turn, he glanced around with a mixture of frustration and pride. Jackson's Pensacola campaign had been both a victory and a disappointment.

After the British tried to take Fort Bowyer on Mobile Bay, Jackson became convinced that they would use Pensacola as a base from which to invade Louisiana. Although Pensacola was Spanish territory, four British sloops-of-war had anchored in the bay. A hundred redcoat marines moved into town and occupied the forts. They flew both Spanish and British flags over the forts, having effectively taken control of the village. Over the last several months, they had been actively recruiting Red Sticks and former slaves to join the ranks of the redcoats for an attack on Jackson's forces.

From Mobile, Jackson wrote letters to the Spanish governor demanding that the British troops be expelled and that several Red Stick chiefs seeking sanctuary in Pensacola be turned over to him. When the governor refused, Jackson promised "An eye for an eye, a tooth for a tooth, and a scalp for a scalp."

Jackson began the task of raising yet another army. This time, excited by recent victories and the probability that the war might soon be over, thousands of mounted Tennessee riflemen joined him. Lemuel hadn't been surprised when seven hundred Choctaws also answered the general's call. They always seemed ready for a fight. But he had been shocked when, even after being forced to give up half of their lands, a thousand Muscogees had also joined Jackson. Probably interested in plunder, thought Lemuel.

Jackson marched his four-thousand-man army east. When they approached Pensacola, they halted just out of cannon range of the forts that guarded the village and the British warships in the bay to the south. The village was little more than a few streets around a town square on the white sands at the edge of the bay. Two forts guarded the village, and two overlooked the entrance to the blue waters of the bay.

Under the protection of a white flag, Jackson tried to send a message demanding the surrender of the forts and the immediate evacuation of the redcoats. The British fired their cannon at the flag of truce, and the message had to be sent to the governor via a prisoner.

The Spanish governor rejected the demands despite Jackson's warning that he might not be able to control undisciplined militiamen and Indians after a battle began. The British slipped their troops out of the village and into Fort Barrancas, the western most and stronger of the two forts at the entrance of the bay, in effect, abandoning five-hundred Spanish troops to face the much larger American force.

Even though Jackson's army significantly outnumbered the Spanish garrison, Lemuel had been nervous about attacking forces defended by cannon in the forts and on the British ships. He had little doubt a frontal assault on Pensacola could result in staggering casualties. Lemuel recalled his delight when he learned what Jackson had planned.

As the sun set, the Americans settled in for the night and built numerous campfires. During the night Jackson left several hundred men in camp to tend the fires and make a ruckus. Then he led the bulk of his force into the woods, where they circled north and east around the village.

By the time cocks crowed to announce the coming morning, thousands of troops hid amid the brush-covered dunes northeast of the village. When the morning brightened enough to see the silhouettes of the buildings at the edge of the village, hundreds of uniformed soldiers advanced silently.

They were nearly to the town when the still of the morning was shattered by a musket shot from a fenced garden at the edge of town. Down one of the streets parallel to the shoreline, a battery of cannon had been placed behind a barricade. Hundreds of American soldiers had run, shouting and screaming, toward the gun emplacement.

Cannon roared and muskets popped from the houses and gardens on each side of the street. The officer leading the charge crumpled to the ground, his leg a bloody mess. As the Spanish cannon blasted again and more men fell, the regulars raced ahead. The soldiers in front of the charge reached the battery. They fired their bayonet-tipped muskets at the Spanish cannoneers and climbed over the barricade. Within seconds they captured the gun battery.

Gunfire crackled here and there around the village as hundreds of militiamen sped into town from the beach. Others had been assigned to attack from the north. Within a few minutes, Americans crowded the village streets.

A company of regulars hurried to the center of town to demand the governor's surrender. By the time they reached his house, a white sheet had already been hoisted up the flag-pole.

When Jackson arrived, the governor, an overweight old gentleman, emerged from the house. After the governor officially surrendered the town, Jackson instructed him to order the Spanish troops still holding the forts to lay down their weapons and evacuate immediately. The governor agreed, and messengers under the protection of white flags were sent to the forts.

But the Spanish soldiers delayed, possibly hoping the British in the warships would come to their rescue. Jackson fumed as the day dragged on. He needed to seize Fort Barrancas, with its guns overlooking the bay's entrance, if he was to maintain control of Pensacola. Without Barrancas, enemy warships could simply sail into the bay and blast apart any local defenses.

The British guns remained silent, but by the time the Spanish in the forts surrendered, the day was late. Jackson's attack on Fort Barrancas would have to wait until morning.

The next morning scouts told Jackson that the redcoats were departing Fort Barrancas and boarding ships anchored offshore. Before Jackson could give orders for securing the fort, a distant explosion shook the ground. Timber and sand sailed skyward over Barrancas, then cascaded back to earth.

Jackson had been furious. With Barrancas destroyed, he couldn't defend and keep his new conquest, a port that would certainly prove invaluable in settling the river valleys north of it. But the mission wasn't a complete loss. At least the British were out of Pensacola and wouldn't be using it as a base to stir up and arm the Indians. And the Red Sticks pinning their hopes for the future on support from Great Britain would certainly have been discouraged.

With the loss of Pensacola, the British might again try to take Mobile, this time with a greater force. Having no regular-army troops to spare in attempting to keep Pensacola, Jackson decided to march his men back west.

Lemuel heard the order for his company to march out of the town square. He took one last look at the village of Pensacola, mounted his horse, and began the long ride back to Mobile.

CHAPTER FIFTY-THREE

DECEMBER 1814, HARTFORD, CONNECTICUT

Rachel Thurston rocked her chair as she made tight, evenly spaced stitches in a seam of her new dress. The house her father had rented was not as grand as their home in Gloucester nor was it as new as the one they rented in Washington City, but she and her father agreed that it would suit them well until his business in Hartford was complete.

The wind howled outside, and the house shuddered. She paused and stared quietly through a second-story window overlooking the Connecticut River. The gray water matched the color of the leafless trees and overcast sky. Beyond warehouse roofs spiked a small forest of bare masts, their sails and lines long ago removed and stowed. Rachel wondered when the ships would be free to sail the seas again.

From the kitchen drifted the aroma of the cinnamon-apple pie she had baked that morning. Rachel paused, needle in hand, when she recalled that just a year before, in Washington City, she had served fresh pie to George Sherbourne. Rachel glanced back to the harbor, forcing George out of her mind, as she often did.

The idle ships in the harbor reminded her of embargoes and block-ades. The war seemed to have reached a precarious point. The British, with the defeat of Napoleon, had tremendous forces available to turn against the Americans. But most recently, Robert Fulton had offered the American government his steamships on the Mississippi as a means of transport-ing troops and supplies for the defense of New Orleans. And Fulton had launched the hull of his steam frigate *Demologos*, which when fully out-fitted was intended to smash the British blockade of New York Harbor. Already Baltimore and Philadelphia citizens were clamoring for Fulton to build them steam frigates as well.

The direction of the war would, of course, influence the success of her father's efforts. Mordecai Thurston was one of over two dozen dele-gates to a secret meeting of New England Federalists. Nearly half of those attending were from Massachusetts, but Connecticut, Rhode Island, New Hampshire, and Vermont had also sent representatives. Their agenda offered opportunity, but it was fraught with danger. Rachel shivered at a chilly draft and pulled her shawl tighter around her shoulders.

The location of the meeting had been kept secret. No records would be maintained, ostensibly so all could speak freely. Rachel suspected the lack of records meant a lack of evidence against the participants if they were arrested for treason.

All of the delegates were Federalists deeply dissatisfied with the direction the federal government had been heading. Her father expressed confidence that the delegates would see the wisdom of his plan for the New England states, and maybe even New York, to secede from the southern and western states and form a new republic with strong ties to Great Britain.

Her father would be a key figure in the new government, maybe even its leader. She wondered what the leader would be called. Governor? Prime minister? President? King? Surely not king. Rachel looked forward to working with her father as he charted New England's future, unshackled from reckless rule-by-mob experiments.

Rachel feared the more timid representatives lacked the zeal to carry the issues to their appropriate conclusion. Committees so often had to compromise to take any action whatsoever, and compromise often meant ineffective solutions. Privately to Rachel, her father had cursed when he learned that the group had selected a moderate as chairman of the meeting.

To free her mind, she pulled the two edges of embroidered muslin together again and continued to stitch. She stopped when she pricked a finger. A tiny spot of blood appeared, and Rachel wondered if that portended an omen.

As Rachel stared at her hands, she realized they were shaking. Deep down she knew if her father and the others failed, they might very well face criminal charges that could lead to disgrace, imprisonment, or even execution.

She heard the front door squeak as it opened. A blast of chilly air rushed into the room. She heard her father stomp his feet on the rug in the foyer.

Rachel put her sewing aside and found him at the cabinet behind his desk. He had already poured himself a glass of brandy. He plopped down in his chair with a look of defeat. "The fools!"

Rachel felt her heart sink. She put her arms around her father's shoulders and kissed him on the forehead. "No secession? No separate nation?"

He shook his head. "The moderates convinced the others to demand amendments to the constitution. Half-measures at best."

CHAPTER FIFTY-FOUR

DECEMBER 1814, NEW ORLEANS

Lemuel Wyckliffe leaned in his saddle and spat to the ground. As one of Jackson's scouts, he rode just behind the general's uniformed personal guards. Behind them rode and walked fifteen hundred volunteers, mostly from Tennessee and Kentucky. They were at the end of a leisurely eleven-day trek from Mobile, having stopped frequently while the general studied the terrain.

Palms and trees draped with Spanish moss gave way to shacks at the outskirts of the city. The dirt trail became a cobblestone avenue lined with two-story buildings, many of which had tiled roofs and open, second-floor balconies edged with wrought-iron grills. Cheering townspeople filled the street.

Jackson, his hair iron gray and his face sallow, rode erect in his saddle despite his unhealed wound and ongoing bout of dysentery. Half of Jackson's guard rode ahead of him to part the crowd. At first Lemuel was concerned that the people might be a threat to Jackson, but the townspeople cheered, obviously delighted to see the general who had pledged to save their city—or die trying. Lemuel relaxed a little as his horse plodded ahead.

The voices from the side of the street were mainly in French, but some were in Spanish, English, and at least one language Lemuel didn't recognize. Many in the crowd wore brightly colored clothes with outlandish styles. He saw white faces and black ones, but most ranged in shades between light and dark—probably the Creoles he had heard about.

On the long march Lemuel had learned that the city had been founded by France, then ceded to Spain as a concession for peace after the French & Indian War. But after Napoleon rose to power, he coerced the Spanish into returning New Orleans to France. Then when Napoleon ran low on money to finance his wars in Europe, he sold the city to the States as part of the Louisiana Purchase. With New Orleans as its capital, Louisiana was the newest state in the Union, the eighteenth white star on the nation's flag.

The street opened to a wide square bordered with Spanish-style buildings on the north, west, and south. The western edge was dominated by a cathedral and government buildings flying the Stars and Stripes. The square itself was packed with local citizens.

As Lemuel gazed east over the cheering crowd, he noticed that the square sloped to a wide body of water. He assumed it was a lake, but even from this distance he could see a rapidly moving current. Goose bumps prickled his skin when he realized that he was looking at the mile-wide Mississippi River.

Lemuel suddenly felt disoriented. He knew the Mississippi flowed south to the Gulf of Mexico, but here it was obviously running northward. Then he understood that the city was located on a crescent of high ground at a bow in the meandering river.

Gentlemen wearing hats, ties, and gloves escorted General Jackson into a government building. Lemuel and the other scouts dismounted to await the general's return.

No sooner had Lemuel's feet touched the ground when a local resident approached him, grabbed him by the shoulders, and kissed him on the cheek. Before Lemuel could react, the man kissed him on the other cheek. Lemuel stepped back, wiping a wet spot with the sleeve of his home-spun shirt. The frontiersmen around Lemuel snickered until the excited citizen said something in French and kissed another scout.

Over the next several weeks, Lemuel accompanied Jackson as he toured the military defenses throughout the area. Lemuel began to appre-ciate the challenges the general faced. New Orleans was nearly surrounded by water and was vulnerable to British attack from almost every direction.

The Mississippi River, with its mouth on the Gulf of Mexico, pro-vided a route from the south. Lake Borgne provided a route from the east. Lake Pontchartrain, separated from Lake Borgne by a narrow band of isles called the Rigolets, provided a route from the north. Barataria Bay and the surrounding waterways provided a route from the southwest.

Jackson toured the most likely approaches and improved the defenses where he could. Between New Orleans and the mouth of the Mississippi, he reinforced fortifications at several outposts. Jackson seemed most impressed with the fort that had been positioned at a sharp turn in the river. There, ships had to stop right under the fort's guns to wait for a change in the wind before sailing onward.

The wide Mississippi River, with its swift and unpredictable currents, would make attacking the city from the west and south difficult and risky, so Jackson focused his remaining defensive efforts to the north and east. He improved defenses along the creeks and bayous from Lake Pontchartrain and along the road from the Rigolets.

With relatively few men at his disposal and so many possible poten-tial attack points, Jackson dispersed his men carefully, with an eye to defending the most likely avenues of attack and the ability to reposition his troops quickly. He sent out pleas for men, arms, and ammunition from the upper states, knowing that help might not arrive in time. Hundreds of river boatmen and other volunteers floated down the Mississippi and offered their assistance.

Meanwhile, Jackson tried to enlist the citizens of New Orleans in the defense of their city. Lemuel could tell that this ,too, would be a major challenge. With a population of roughly twenty-five thousand, New Orleans was a fragmented mix of rival ethnic groups and social classes. In addition to the bitter resentment they held toward each other, many local citizens of French and Spanish ancestry considered the Americans greedy, ill-mannered upstarts.

Jackson established his headquarters in a three-story building with a balcony on the second floor. From there he addressed the people gathered in the street.

"Who are we?" he asked. "Are we the titled slaves of George the Third? The military conscripts of Napoleon the Great? Or the frozen peasants of the Russian Czar? I say no. We are the freeborn sons of America. The citizens of the only republic now existing in the world. And the only people on earth who possess rights, liberties, and property which they dare call their own."

Jackson appealed for help. "Good Citizens, you must all rally around me in this emergency. Cease all differences and unite with me in patriotic resolve to save this city from dishonor and disaster, which a presumptuous enemy threatens to inflict upon it."

Despite their differences, many of the citizens rallied to support Jackson. Militias were recruited and hospitals for the wounded were established. Local officials encouraged Jackson to accept help from the hundreds of pirates who operated out of Barataria Bay. For many years the pirates, led by Jean Lafitte, had been raiding English and Spanish cargo ships throughout the Caribbean. Despite their ruthless behavior in open water, they were quite popular locally because they smuggled their booty into New Orleans and sold it at discount prices.

At first Jackson would hear nothing of accepting Lafitte's help, calling the pirates "hellish banditti." But in a face-to-face meeting, Jackson listened to Lafitte's enthusiastic offer of ammunition, cannon, and men to fire them.

Jackson must have been impressed, because he immediately accepted the buccaneer's help.

The pirates were assigned the task of organizing the defense between the city and Barataria. Lafitte possessed extraordinary knowledge of local geography and provided invaluable maps. He organized three companies of artillery, and Jackson found him so helpful, he added Lafitte to his personal staff.

In mid-December, the British fleet was sighted near the entrance of Lake Borgne. They quickly captured the five American gunboats on the lake, depriving the general of further intelligence regarding British movements. Jackson ordered local militia and plantation owners to block the bayous and creeks around the city with felled trees and brush. He concentrated his troops around New Orleans and asked the state legislature to take bold action to defend their capital. When the legislators dithered, Jackson declared martial law and ordered virtually every able-bodied man in the area to serve in the defense of the city.

At Jackson's bidding, Lemuel scouted one possible invasion route after another as a flurry of rumors reported the British invasion was imminent.

Lieutenant George Sherbourne grabbed the gunwale as the large rowboat encountered a sizable swell on Lake Borgne, south and east of New Orleans. The rise and fall of the boat left George feeling queasy, and the air reeked of fish. Seagulls swarmed high over gray water that matched the color of the winter sky.

George gazed at the green shorelines ahead, looking forward to the security of solid ground once again. Somewhere beyond the shoreline lay the city of New Orleans, with its rich plunder and reputation for rowdy social life.

Sailors hauled at eighteen-foot oars as a fleet of boats lumbered ahead. Each was packed with redcoats sitting shoulder to shoulder wearing full gear, including extra ammunition. They had boarded the boats before dawn, and now the sun was past its zenith.

All around George were enlisted men, some chatting or cracking jokes. Some played cards. Others sat quietly with their eyes closed. To George it was almost unbearable boredom. Again, his mind returned to the letter he had received while the fleet was in Jamaica. He had been thrilled to see Anne's return address and had found himself an isolated section of bulwark before opening the letter in private. After reading the letter, he had let it drop and then watched it soak in brine and sink. Anne was engaged— and given the date of the letter, she was already married by the time he received it. Stunned by the news, he still hadn't fully accepted it.

As the boats rowed onward, he tucked his hands under his armpits and tried to think of something else. After being rebuffed by the Yanks at Baltimore, the fleet had sailed to Jamaica to prepare for an assault on New Orleans. Admiral Cochrane sent a squadron to capture Mobile, but the fortifications there were much stronger than they had been led to believe by their spies. The navy suffered another embarrassing setback when the Americans swept into Pensacola, effectively evicting the British from the port of its Spanish allies.

Initially, George had been thrilled to learn that he had been assigned to an infantry company with the invasion force. But after the letter from Anne, he felt less enthusiasm about everything, including the battle ahead.

The navy had already captured the entire flotilla of five American gunboats on Lake Borgne. George and his fellow officers had speculated about the route their commanders would select from the Gulf of Mexico to New Orleans. The Mississippi itself was already well fortified at two locations. George was confident that the navy could overcome the defenses, but the price would be high. The terrain around New Orleans offered numerous alternative routes. Best to pick one, get an invasion force on land, then strike rapidly for the city before defenses could be concentrated to meet the invasion.

One of the challenges they faced was that Jackson had ordered trees felled into all the bayous and creeks around New Orleans to deny their use to the invaders. But local fishermen of Spanish decent, acting as British spies, claimed that the bayou on one of the plantations between the lake and the Mississippi River had not been filled as ordered.

A detail had been sent to capture the plantation and secure it while the advance guard of the invasion force was brought forward. Unfortunately, the navy had neglected to bring shallow-draft vessels capable of negotiating the lake. Undeterred, the troops and their equipment were rowed the fifty miles from the anchorage to the plantation. Despite his personal discomfort during the long, slow journey, George had to admire the strength and stamina of the sailors manning the boats.

George noticed a particularly large swell ahead. Most of the boats met the wave head-on and rose with it. But one boat got caught sideways and was swamped. George gasped as the boat tipped with the next wave, then rolled upside down. One moment the boat had been filled with dozens of men. The next, the capsized hull bobbed listlessly, its fully clothed and armed redcoats nowhere to be seen.

George imagined his own boat capsizing and plunging him into the murky depths. As gulls screamed overhead, George fixed his gaze on the green shoreline. He feared the invasion was off to an ominous start.

Early in the afternoon Lemuel Wyckliffe strode into General Jackson's headquarters, at 106 Royal Street, to make his scouting report. He had been watching for the British invasion expected any day. Jackson was meeting with one of his officers, so Lemuel snatched a chair from the hallway and took a seat, grateful for a chance to rest.

Ignoring the blue-uniformed officers and men occasionally hustling by, Lemuel hoped he could grab a quick nap before seeing the general. But the chair was hard, and the bustle of men around him made it difficult to nod off.

From down the cobblestone street, he heard galloping horses. The clatter of hooves stopped just outside the door. Three men, plantation owners by their apparel, rushed into the building and were stopped by uniformed sentries. The captain of the guard hurried to Jackson's office, then escorted the new arrivals inside.

Lemuel listened as the excited men reported that the British had landed. The enemy was already at the Villeré plantation on the north bank of the Mississippi, just twenty miles east of the city. Lemuel had scouted the area and realized that someone must have failed to carry out Jackson's orders to obstruct the bayou between the plantation and Lake Borgne.

Jackson, who had been calmly sitting behind his desk, drew himself to his full height. Lemuel flinched. Jackson had pounded the table with a clenched fist, then swore, "By the eternal, they shall not sleep on our soil!"

Jackson summoned his officers, and they gathered in his office. "Gentlemen," said Jackson, "the British are below, and we must fight them tonight. I will smash them." The general issued a flurry of orders, and officers hurried out of his office. Jackson grabbed his hat and headed toward the street as the alarm gun boomed across the city.

Lemuel followed Jackson and his officers as they rode out of the city, then east atop the levee along the north bank of the Mississippi. Lemuel had scouted this same route and noted the plantations along the way. They passed the Macarty and Chalmette plantations eight or nine miles east of the city.

A vessel drifted down the river, and Lemuel recognized the schooner *Carolina*, now manned by Lafitte's men and one of only two real fighting vessels on the river. The gunboat continued downstream until she was across from the Villeré plantation, where she pulled up along the far river-bank and dropped anchor.

Most of the men with Jackson's formation were regulars. They fanned out in the brush and fields inland while a contingent of marines escorted Jackson and the artillerymen's two cannon along the levee road. Across the fields to the north, Lemuel could see General John Coffee's mounted militia advancing eastward along a cypress swamp.

Jackson halted his men well short of the Villeré plantation and waited for nightfall. Soon, British campfires were visible in the distance. Lemuel imagined the redcoats enjoying an evening meal and preparing for a good night's rest after what must have been a grueling boat ride.

George Sherbourne knelt in front of a cook pot hanging from a chain over glowing coals. He scooped a spoonful of watery stew into his mouth, grateful for a hot meal. Finally, they had reached the bayou and then the plantation buildings just off the Mississippi River. All afternoon, as boat-load after boatload arrived, he had helped organize the men. He looked forward to a rest but wondered how well he would sleep on the wet, spongy ground. The next day they would march on New Orleans. By nightfall they hoped to be sampling whatever pleasures the city offered its captors.

The letter from Anne crossed his mind again. On the long boat ride, he had begun to wonder if he had been unrealistic in his hopes to some-day marry Anne. Her father may never have approved the marriage, even if George had achieved fame and fortune. There was no guarantee in any battle that he could distinguish himself, or even survive. He wondered if he had been a fool.

The sky to the southwest flashed orange and white as if multiple bolts of lightning had struck in rapid succession. Something hissed over George's head. The cook pot clattered across the ground in a blizzard of sparks. One of the cooks had leaned over to stoke the fire, and his head burst in a spray of red. Several men were knocked flat. The air and ground shuddered at the crack of cannon less than a mile away. Men screamed and cursed. Officers yelled orders as more guns thundered from across the river and deadly projectiles streaked through the camp.

All around George, officers and men tried to take cover behind anything that might stop or slow the deadly rain of grapeshot. With a glare and a *whoosh*, a rocket streaked skyward out of camp, then across the river. Without any cannon of their own, they had nothing but rockets with which to respond to the American artillery attack.

Cannon flashed and roared again. The ground under Lemuel Wyckliffe and the air around him quaked. He pictured the *Carolina* across the river cutting loose with a broadside plus the swivel-mounted twelve-pounders fore and aft. No doubt they fired grapeshot to inflict the maximum possible damage on the redcoats.

In the darkness to the east, campfires in the British camp burst into a shower of embers. Bugles blared across the dark fields amid screams of pain and shouted commands.

"Hit 'em hard!" Jackson yelled. The regulars to the left and front of the general moved eastward, and the cannon crews hurried forward along the dark levee road.

A half-dozen streaks of fire snaked up from the British camp with a crackling sizzle, then exploded midair over the river. Congreve rockets. Lemuel had heard that they weren't particularly destructive, but he was thankful that they hadn't been aimed in his direction, at least so far. He crouched low, clutching his rifle, hoping he wouldn't trip in the dark as he hustled to keep up with the regulars. Once Jackson's cannon were within range, the gun crews fired round after round into the British camp.

A musket flashed and popped ahead of Lemuel, and he saw a red uniform. Men shouted. Muskets fired toward the Americans. Unable to see a target, Lemuel kept pace with the uniformed men around him. Musket balls whizzed overhead. As regulars next to him fired, Lemuel stepped ahead of them, then dropped to his knee and aimed his rifle. A musket flashed bright orange directly in front of him. Lemuel aimed for where the musket flash had been and pulled the trigger. Regulars rushed ahead of him. He reloaded and raced after the regulars.

The American regulars fired a volley, then advanced and fired again, driving the redcoat outposts back across the dark field. Lemuel hustled after them as they sidestepped over a wood fence, then sloshed through a water-filled ditch.

Between the boom of cannon and the sizzle of rockets, Lieutenant George Sherbourne heard a new sound. From the west crackled musket fire, not just one or two but a synchronized volley from regulars.

George rushed to find his infantry unit. He had no sooner reached it when a major strode out of the dark.

"Lieutenant, take your men west along the river levee and teach that rabble a lesson."

George led his men through the dark toward the pop and flash of musket fire. They encountered British sentries and outposts falling back in shameful disorder. He considered stopping to give the fleeing men a piece of his mind. Instead, he hurried his own men forward.

They approached the sound and flash of muskets, and George ordered his men to form a line. As the Americans drew closer, George yelled, "Fire!"

By the flash of muskets, Lemuel Wyckliffe saw scores of redcoats. They were lined three deep, the front row kneeling while the back row fired over the shoulders of those in the middle. Balls whizzed over Lemuel's head. A wave of British soldiers rushed the American regulars, driving them back. After a bit, Lemuel realized the Brits were after the cannon on the levee road.

Jackson's voice carried above the fray. "Save the guns, boys. At all costs!"

A flood of American regulars and marines poured forward, alternately firing and loading. They drove the redcoats back as the cannon were withdrawn along the levee.

Rifle fire crackled from the far left, toward the swamp. General Coffee's militia were also engaging the redcoats. Someone grabbed Lemuel by the shoulder. By moonlight, Lemuel recognized Jackson. "Go find General Coffee, lad, and tell him the advance along the river has been blocked."

Lemuel hurried north across the squishy field nestled between the river levee on the south and a cypress swamp on the north. He approached the swamp and found militiamen guarding hundreds of saddled horses.

He turned east toward the sound of gunfire and hustled to catch up to the dismounted riflemen. As he approached the fighting, Congreve rockets streaked and zigzagged above him.

He found hundreds of frontiersmen advancing toward the British camp. Lemuel passed militiamen as they stopped to reload. When he reached the front line, he aimed at the redcoats and fired. As dozens of militiamen surged forward, Lemuel paused to reload. The redcoats tossed their muskets to the ground and raised their arms in surrender.

Lemuel knew that the redcoats along the river were advancing against the Americans, so the group that had surrendered must have been an isolated detachment. He asked a militiaman kneeling nearby, "Where can I find General Coffee?"

The militiaman pointed to his left, and Lemuel ran in that direction as muskets and rifles flashed in the darkness. Unsure which shots were American and which were British, he held his fire.

He came across a large group of militiamen rushing forward, and hoping General Coffee was among them, he joined them. The shooters leapfrogged forward, each man in front firing, then stopping to reload as others stepped forward and fired. Redcoats seemed to be all around them. By the flash of gunfire and the light of smoldering fires, Lemuel could see that they were in the British camp.

A line of redcoats surged forward. Out of the dark, a soldier with a bayonet-tipped musket rushed toward Lemuel. He fired, and the redcoat dropped to the ground. Before Lemuel could reload, another redcoat tried to stab him. Lemuel swung his rifle just in time to deflect the blow, but the bayonet tip grazed his chest as the soldier's charge knocked Lemuel to his back.

The redcoat shoved hard on the bayonet, probably thinking he had skewered Lemuel. But the spire had only pierced Lemuel's shirt between his chest and left arm. As the redcoat thrust his bayonet into the soggy soil, Lemuel kicked hard and knocked his attacker down. Lemuel scrambled to his feet, then rammed his rifle butt into the man's head.

All around Lemuel, redcoats with bayonets closed in on the frontiersmen now fighting with hatchets and knives. Remembering Jackson's orders to find General Coffee, Lemuel ducked back into the darkness just as hundreds of redcoats swarmed about the militiamen and captured them.

All around Lemuel he could hear men screaming and cursing. Others shouted orders. The voices were all in English, and he couldn't tell which were British and which were American. A riderless horse suddenly appeared out of the dark. Lemuel tried to catch it, but the horse disappeared into the British camp.

After asking directions from several militiamen, Lemuel found General Coffee.

"Sir, General Jackson sends his complements, but wishes to advise you that the British are driving him back along the river. And, sir, may I speak freely?"

Coffee nodded.

"Between the river and here, sir, there is total confusion. We've captured some redcoats, but they've nabbed some of ours. In the dark you can't tell friend from foe. It's a mess, sir."

The general consulted with his officers, and then ordered his men to retreat.

By the time Lemuel found his way back to Jackson's command, the Americans had settled down for the night with orders not to light fires. Lemuel dreaded the long, cold night ahead, then heard the *Carolina*'s cannon rumble again. He imagined grapeshot ripping through the enemy camp. The Americans hadn't exactly pushed the Brits back into the sea, but true to Jackson's word, the redcoats wouldn't be getting any sleep on American soil that night.

A week later, Lieutenant George Sherbourne steadied the telescope and cussed. To the west, five hundred mounted American riflemen galloped around the open field in front of the British camp. As they had each morning since the landing, they stopped to take shots at the outposts. Then, after screaming in defiance, they wheeled and beat a hasty retreat. Meanwhile, natives supporting Jackson's troops filled the cypress swamp to the north, leaping from log to log, howling and shooting. George had to admit, at least to himself, that it was all a bit unnerving.

A captain stood next to George. "These Americans act more like assassins than soldiers."

"That they do, sir," said George. "Shocking behavior." The Americans seemed to delight in ignoring the conventions of 'civilized' warfare. After their initial attack on the first night, in an obvious tactic to buy time to improve their defensive position, the Americans cut the levee to let river water flood the sugarcane fields between the opposing armies.

The Americans didn't station a traditional chain of outposts and sentries, either by day or by night. Instead, at night, small bands of militiamen wandered around looking for British soldiers. They would sneak up on sentries and shoot them or hide in thickets to ambush redcoats passing by. The Americans stripped the dead of arms and valuable equipment, then disappeared into the night.

"Never you mind," said the captain. "These hooligans will get their due soon enough."

"No doubt, sir," said George. "But their tactics have been quite successful in delaying us. I've heard reports that Jackson's forces have been reinforcing their lines of defense."

The captain scoffed. "While you enjoyed soft duty on this side of the Atlantic, we stormed castles and fortresses in Europe. We met the best troops of Napoleon Bonaparte and crushed them. Jackson's mud wall will fall easily, and we will make sausage of his rabble army. Then you will see how battles are fought."

George felt his face burn at the rebuke. Not wanting to show his discomfort, he changed the subject. "I understand, sir, that many of these veterans are near the end of their enlistments. Will that complicate the situation?"

The captain lowered his telescope and smirked. "Well then, I guess we better get this mess over with. Once we have overrun Jackson's defenses and taken New Orleans, we will need only a fraction of these troops to hold the city. The rest may go home, stay here as civilians, or rot in hell."

Lemuel Wyckliffe sighed. He didn't know which was worse, the terror of battle or the seemingly endless boredom between engagements. After they had attacked the British on their first night ashore, Jackson ordered his forces to pull back two miles to the Macarty plantation, only eight miles east of New Orleans. A line of defense was established along an old millrace called Rodriguez Canal, a hundred yards east of the Macarty house. Although the canal was little more than a ten-foot-wide, four-foot-deep ditch, it spanned the narrowest approach to the city. With the river on the south, the canal ran only three-quarters of a mile north to a thick, almost impenetrable cypress swamp.

Jackson ordered Rodriquez Canal to be deepened and a rampart to be built on its western edge. Shovels, pick axes, saws, hoes, carts, and wagons were brought in from the city. Over the next several days, crews of soldiers, militiamen, local citizens, and slaves toiled to improve the defensive line. Units competed to build the highest mounds. A pattern of ramparts and artillery batteries emerged.

As the men dug deeper, water seeped in, and the dirt turned to slop. They scavenged wood from the fences in the area and cut cypress trees to shore up the rampart. Additional soil was hauled in, and cotton bales were laid in pits to provide a solid foundation for the cannon. Soon the rampart rose seven-feet from the bottom of the ditch. Second and third lines of defense, each a mile to the rear, were established as fallback positions in case the canal was overrun.

Lemuel's respect for Jackson had grown. The general worked tirelessly to prepare the defenses, going without sleep for five days and four nights. Instead of taking regular meals, he picked at food from horseback. When one of his officers begged him to rest, he replied, "No sir, there's no telling when or where these rascals will attack. They shall not catch me unprepared. When we have driven the damned redcoats into the swamp, there will be enough time to sleep."

As construction of the canal defenses progressed, the Americans continued to harass the British. The gunboat *Carolina* and the *Louisiana*, a sloop, regularly bombarded the enemy to demoralize them and to keep them from initiating an attack. As Lemuel gazed toward the east, he realized that life in the British camp must be downright miserable.

Lieutenant George Sherbourne stood to the side as a colonel and a major peered through telescopes. Nearly a half mile away the Stars and Stripes fluttered from a tall pole set just behind the fortified line established by Jackson.

That the Americans would attempt to defend the city was no surprise to George, but their success in doing so worried him. The Americans had been soundly routed during the invasion of Washington City, but they had achieved meaningful victories at Chippawa and Lake Champlain and had successfully defended Baltimore. The battle for New Orleans could go either way.

The number of Crown forces had swelled as boatloads of troops and supplies arrived almost continuously. On Christmas Day guns had been fired to welcome General Edward Pakenham, a veteran of the war against Napoleon. The general took command of the invasion forces. Day by day, the level of the river dropped, and the flooded fields between the Americans and the British began to clear.

George recalled with pleasure that Pakenham spurred his troops into action. On an early morning in late December, Pakenham's cannon fired hot shot and grape at the *Carolina*. Almost immediately the gunboat's rigging, spars, and bulwarks fell. The *Carolina* quickly caught on fire, forcing the crew to abandon ship. At midmorning the boat exploded.

British cannoneers then turned their guns on the *Louisiana*. The wind and the swift current made it impossible for the sloop to sail out of range, and she appeared to be doomed. George recalled his frustration as a hundred American crew members manned rowboats and towed her out of range.

That evening the British advanced out of their camp. They drove back the American advance guard, and within minutes they captured the Bienvenu and Chalmette plantations. The next morning British infantry, supported by cannon and Congreve rockets, advanced toward Rodriguez

Canal. George recalled with dismay that, after taking heavy losses, they had withdrawn.

Across the field, George could hear a band playing. He listened more closely and recognized "Yankee Doodle." He stifled a laugh and wondered if the Americans realized that the song they so proudly played had been first sung by British troops fighting against the French in North America. The *doodle* was a derivative of a German word for simpleton, and *macaroni* referred to a foppish wig. The tune implied that Americans were such fools that they thought sticking a feather in their cap would make it the height of fashion.

George's attention returned to the Americans, who were probably celebrating their little victory over the British. No doubt their festivities included the consumption of ample food and spirits. The thought of food reminded George that he and the other troops had been eating minimal rations.

"Lieutenant," said the major.

George came to attention. "Sir?"

The major handed George a folded piece of paper. "Take this to General Pakenham, at once."

George saluted and strode briskly back to the main camp. With the arrival of more-experienced infantry officers, he had been reassigned to the command staff, largely as a messenger. At first he had been angry at once again being denied opportunity on the battlefield. Lately, he began to feel relief. The buildup of American forces almost certainly meant that the battle for New Orleans would be a bloody affair, at best.

Lemuel Wyckliffe peered over the levee along the river and studied the British camp. After the British had destroyed the *Carolina* and occupied the Chalmette plantation, Jackson had ordered improvements in the line. The cotton bales were removed from the line, since many of them had caught fire during the British attack, blinding the cannoneers with smoke. The rampart was built even taller and wider, and the line was extended a quarter mile into the swamp. The rampart now included four gun batteries with wooden floors and a total of twenty-four fieldpieces.

Lemuel had been struck by the diversity of the assembled army. Besides the blue-uniformed regulars and the roughshod frontier militiamen, there were state militiamen in a variety of uniforms. Local citizens and men of color manned various units. The cypress swamp was filled with Choctaw Indians. Mississippi riverboat men and threadbare Tennessee volunteers had recently arrived to swell Jackson's ranks. The gun crews included a mixture of U.S. artillerymen, sailors, and Baratarian pirates.

Each morning as dawn approached, the rattle of drums woke Lemuel. Clusters of men gathered to eat a breakfast of cornbread, bacon, and coffee. Bands played lively music ranging from martial tunes to waltzes. A tent city sprang up behind the line, and the camp took on a carnival atmosphere. In contrast, from the British camp only an occasional bugle was heard.

After dark on New Year's Eve, sentinels reported hearing the British advance to within a few hundred yards of the ditch. Lemuel could hear digging and hammering and suspected the redcoats were building gun emplacements. When no attack came the next morning, the Americans gathered behind the fortified line to celebrate the beginning of the new year.

At midmorning the mist cleared, and a Congreve rocket shot up from the east. British cannon roared, belching tons of missiles at the Americans. Lemuel suspected that if the British had rushed the line at that moment, they may very well have succeeded before the Americans got themselves reorganized.

But soon the American gun crews fired back, and an artillery duel continued until noon. The British cannonballs tended to fly overhead or plop harmlessly into the muddy rampart, and Jackson's defenses remained largely intact. When the smoke cleared, the British batteries had been blasted to bits.

The *Louisiana* anchored across the river from Rodriguez Canal, where she could fire on any British troops advancing on the line. Jackson finally seemed satisfied that his defenses were as good as they were going to get. But redcoat deserters said the British troops were commanded by a general hardened by the war against Napoleon.

Through predawn darkness Lieutenant George Sherbourne hurried along a swampy path. He had just watched as the last of the barges shoved off from the riverbank. As had the dozens of boats before it, instead of rowing directly across the Mississippi as planned, the barge was quickly swept downstream by the current. George estimated the boats wouldn't reach the south shore until they were a couple miles downstream. The battle was off to an ominous start.

The plan called for over fourteen hundred men to cross the river, overwhelm the defenses across the Mississippi, then turn the American guns on Jackson's primary line of defense as Packenham's main force engaged in a frontal attack. Over the past several days, Admiral Cochrane had supervised the digging of a canal from the bayou to the river so barges could be used to row the men across the river. The project had turned into a nightmare. Soggy soil collapsed into the canal, clogging it for all except the smallest boats.

When the troops arrived to be transported across, they found no barges, so they had to drag the boats to the river themselves, delaying their departure by eight hours. Of the fourteen hundred men planned for the attack across the river, they had boats for only about four hundred. Prior to shoving off the riverbank, the colonel in charge of the operation had ordered George to find General Pakenham and report what he had observed. George dreaded giving the general bad news, but figured it was better than the nightmare the infantry commanders would face.

Lemuel Wyckliffe had just been roused to stand his turn at guard duty inside the Macarty plantation house, where General Jackson and his officers slept. An officer strode through the front door. Lemuel recognized him as an aide to General David Morgan, commander of the troops across the river. The captain of the guard led the aide to the door beside Lemuel and knocked lightly, then eased it open.

"Who's there?" demanded a voice Lemuel recognized as Jackson's.

The aide stepped forward. "General Morgan sends his compliments, sir. He believes an attack on the south side of the river is imminent, and he requests reinforcements."

Lemuel had been on the other side of the river several times during the past few days. An embankment had been built to prevent the British from using the south side of the river as a route to New Orleans, but the number of men stationed there was a small fraction of the men Jackson had gathered on the north side.

Lemuel heard Jackson rising from the couch. "Hurry back and tell the general that he is mistaken. The main attack will be on this side, and I have no men to spare. He must maintain his position at all hazards."

The aide left in a hurry.

All was quiet for a few minutes, then Jackson spoke again. "Gentlemen, we have slept enough. Rise. The enemy will be upon us in a few minutes."

Lemuel heard a bustle of activity as the general and his officers buckled their sword belts and gathered their pistols. General Jackson was the first out the door, and Lemuel hurried to keep up as the general and his staff headed north along a long rampart.

Even in the twilight Lemuel was struck by the immensity of the fortification that a few weeks before had been only a shallow ditch between sugarcane fields.

As Jackson and his officers continued to inspect one unit after another, the morning began to brighten. The Stars and Stripes hung limp atop the towering pole at the center of the line, but a thick, low-lying mist obscured the view beyond a few dozen yards.

Jackson finished his tour along the line and gazed into the fog. "I need to know what's going on out there, and we haven't had any recent reports from the outposts along the levee." He glanced at Lemuel. "Take a look and hurry back."

Lemuel hustled to the south end of the embankment. As he approached the river levee, he could see one of the improvements in their defenses since the artillery duel a week before. Jackson had ordered an earthen redoubt built on the site of an old brick kiln just outside the levee. Any redcoats reaching the canal would be subject to enfilade fire sweeping them from the side as they tried to storm the American line. The redoubt was surrounded by a ditch, with a single plank providing an escape route over the muddy canal if the position were overrun by redcoats.

Lemuel stepped off the embankment onto the plank. Carefully balancing himself as the beam bounced with each step, he made his way down to the redoubt. With a courteous wave to the blue-coated regulars manning the redoubt, he slid down the muddy berm to the field below and headed east along the levee. In the fog Lemuel passed one cluster of regulars after another until he reached the last outpost.

The corporal there recognized Lemuel as one of Jackson's scouts and reported that all had been quiet for hours. Lemuel jumped when the silence of the early dawn was shattered by a Congreve rocket screeching upward from the east. It ascended through the fog, snaking back and forth, hissing and wheezing, then fell silently out of sight.

The fog was lifting, but visibility was still only about thirty yards. Through the mist, Lemuel noticed movement. At first all he could see were a few red-coated soldiers, but soon there were scores more, advancing rapidly toward the American line. As they approached, a hundred more appeared.

Lemuel glanced toward the corporal. "This ain't no time to play hero. We're way outnumbered."

The corporal nodded and turned to his men. "Fall back!"

Lemuel ran as fast as he could through the mist-shrouded brush along the levee. The sound of footsteps told him the regulars were right behind him. As Lemuel passed one outpost after another, he warned the soldiers that they were about to be overrun.

Soon the redoubt came into view ahead in the fog. Lemuel raced up the steep, muddy slope and crawled inside. Some of the retreating soldiers followed him into the redoubt while others sloshed through the canal and scrambled over the slippery rampart.

Lemuel intended to hurry across the wooden beam and report to Jackson, but the mist to the east flashed orange and the air around him quaked with cannon fire. Cannonballs streaked overhead. The American guns returned fire. Above the low-lying fog, cannonballs crisscrossed mid-air. A cannonball hit the ground to the north of the redoubt, bounded over the canal, then plopped into the mud embankment.

From the fog along the river levee emerged hundreds of redcoats wielding bayonet-tipped muskets. Lemuel aimed his rifle at a soldier and fired. The redcoat slumped to one knee then toppled to the ground, but the fallen soldier's comrades never broke stride as they raced forward. Before Lemuel could reload, redcoats stormed over the top of the redoubt as American muskets blasted away at them.

A redcoat lunged toward Lemuel. He thrust his empty rifle up just in time to deflect the bayonet. More British soldiers poured into the redoubt. One ran his bayonet though the soldier next to Lemuel. He swung his rifle and caught the redcoat on the side of the head. Lemuel drew his hatchet, then joined several soldiers as they defended themselves. One after another, the Americans fell.

"It's no use, men!" shouted the sergeant next to Lemuel. "Save your-selves if you can!"

Lemuel and the regulars edged backward up the berm at the rear of the redoubt. The plank across the canal was still in place, and behind the rampart hundreds of Americans pointed their muskets at the redcoats still storming into the redoubt. An American soldier on the plank ahead of Lemuel took a shot in his back and pitched into the canal. Lemuel hustled across the bouncing plank, then plunged forward between the blue-uni-formed soldiers crowded behind the embankment.

A couple more Americans made it across the plank before a British officer emerged from the redoubt, brandished his sword, and screamed something to his men. The American infantrymen behind the rampart fired, and the British officer toppled into the ditch.

The gunboat *Louisiana*, anchored across the river, opened fire on the redoubt. The British soldiers still in the redoubt were cut down from two sides. The rest turned and ran, but they, too, fell in a hail of balls and grapeshot.

Lemuel found Jackson on a small rise behind the embankment. As the battle escalated and cannonballs sailed over him, the general had his telescope pointed toward the fog at the center of the field.

Between clouds of gun smoke, Lemuel could see the British lines beginning to crumble and melt away. The disciplined attach had disinte-grated into chaos.

Lemuel gazed in the direction Jackson was viewing. Out of the mist rushed a line of redcoats. On the swamp side, Lemuel could see frontiers-men retreating from their outposts, giving ground slowly at first, then turning and running to the canal where they slogged across the ditch and scrambled over the embankment.

With each passing moment, the fog thinned. High in the east, it glowed white with the rising sun while the mist across the field took on a scarlet hue. Lemuel looked closer and noticed that the redness before him seemed to be moving closer. A gust of wind swept much of the mist away. What Lemuel saw before him turned his insides cold.

A wall of scarlet-coated soldiers seemed to be marching directly toward him. To the right, next to the river, another wall of redcoats was advancing, and to the left, next to the cypress swamp, a third wall of red-coated men trudged forward. Lemuel felt his skin prickle. To the east stretched a broad river of red uniforms as far as Lemuel could see.

In front of the American line stood the massive might of the British Empire, Wellington's Heroes, the battle-hardened troops that had defeated Napoleon and helped Wellesley be made the Duke of Wellington. The scarlet uniforms glared bright with glistening accouterments. Flags and standards fluttered in the breeze. Thousands of men marched in precise formations stretching across two-thirds of the plain. The British were advancing rapidly, obviously intent on overrunning the American position in a matter of minutes.

For the first time, Lemuel understood what they were up against, and he realized that the ragtag army around him might not survive.

But all around Lemuel the Americans cheered. And from across the plain he could hear the cheers of the redcoats. Finally, the time for the showdown had arrived.

Through clouds of choking gun smoke, Lieutenant George Sherbourne found General Pakenham on a rise several hundred yards east of the American line. As the general studied the battle from atop a black horse, cannon from both sides thundered. Congreve rockets whooshed overhead, drums rattled in unison, and bugles blared.

The general listened carefully to George's report about the delays in the attack across the river, then muttered a curse and turned his attention back to the battle. After a minute the general said, "As I recall, Lieutenant, you have been clamoring for an infantry command. There seems to be some delay in bringing forward our ladders and fascines. Would you be so kind as to bring them forward and storm that wall?"

George came to attention and saluted, then rushed into the smoke, wondering how he could find anything in all the confusion.

From the rampart Lemuel Wyckliffe watched as a British column advanced along the edge of the swamp. They were still beyond the white-painted rocks set two hundred yards out to mark the most effective rifle range and out of reach of the *Louisiana*'s guns. As the redcoats came closer, an American artillery battery opened up with a roar. One after another, Jackson's artillery batteries fired level across the field directly into the faces of the redcoats.

Between billows of smoke Lemuel could see gaping holes ripped into the British formations, front to back, as men and body parts were hurled in every direction. Lemuel had expected the redcoats to advance in a wide line, just two or three men deep. But probably because of the narrow field of battle, or maybe for maximum strength in hitting Jackson's line, the Brits advanced in attack columns, dozens of men deep. When an American cannonball reached the redcoats, instead of merely hitting a few men, it tore through scores.

Some barrages mowed down entire sections of troops. Almost as quickly as the holes opened, they were filled by disciplined troops marching steadily ahead. A thunderous blast shook the rampart as the American cannoneers cut loose with their biggest gun, a thirty-two-pounder. Almost instantly, hundreds of redcoats fell flat in a single wave of destruction. Lemuel figured the gun must have been loaded to the brim with musket balls.

As the British approached the two-hundred-yard markers, the commander of the American riflemen shouted, "Steady boys, our turn will come."

Four lines of sharpshooters waited as the American artillery continued to pound the advancing British. Finally the redcoats reached the two-hundred-yard markers.

"Fire!" yelled the commander.

The entire front line of frontier riflemen opened fire. When the militiamen in front stepped back to reload, the next man in line stepped forward. The result was a continuous roll of rifle fire.

In turn, each rifleman laid his rifle over the top of the berm, exposing only part of his face to the enemy. The riflemen had been instructed to aim at the redcoats' most vulnerable spot—the neck, just above the red tunic. Lemuel had little doubt that most of the rifle balls found their mark.

The gun smoke grew so thick Lemuel could hardly breathe, and his eyes stung. He lost track of the number of times he loaded and fired. Between shots, he heard Jackson yell, "Stand to your guns! Don't waste your ammunition! See that every shot tells! Give it to them, my boys! Let's finish this business today!"

A new sound caught Lemuel's attention. From the British rear close to the river, Lemuel could hear a pitiful wail. Bagpipes. Diagonally across the field marched nearly a thousand troops, pipes blaring and bayonets glittering.

Lemuel watched the advancing Scotsmen as they came within range. The Americans opened fire on them with rifles and cannon. The Highlanders kept coming even as the Americans tore into their flanks. Lemuel searched the ranks looking for an officer. Finding none, he selected a man in the lead and dropped him.

At about a hundred yards distance from the American lines, the Highlanders stopped. Incredibly, apparently without orders to do otherwise, they stood their ground as American fire continued the slaughter. Finally, the few surviving Highlanders broke formation and fled.

On the north edge of the field, near the swamp, Lieutenant George Sherbourne found a company with the fascines and twelve-foot ladders. To the hatchet-faced captain in charge, he conveyed General Pakenham's orders to take the wall. George knew such orders were a virtual death sentence.

The captain's face turned ashen, but he drew his sword. "Very well, Lieutenant. Let's get about this murderous business."

They marched steadily into the clouds of gun smoke. George drew his own sword and pointed it toward the American line. The men behind him were experienced troops. Silently, George vowed not to falter or fail them. He felt his hands quivering and recalled a conversation he had had with another officer, a veteran of battles against Napoleon's armies. George had asked how the officer maintained his courage in the face of gunfire.

The officer told him to focus on the job at hand. "It also helps," he said, "to accept the likelihood that you are already doomed. The only question is the manner of your death. Will you perform your duty and die with honor? Or will you die in disgrace?"

As George marched toward his probable death, his mind raced. He realized now that he had been foolish to think he could ever marry Anne. His infatuation with Anne had clouded his judgment about Rachel, who he now realized he truly cared for. Even worse, his obsession about achieving battlefield distinction may have caused him to be less effective in performing his espionage duties as an officer of the Crown. Had his preoccupation prolonged the war or contributed to British defeats? Too late, now, to analyze such concerns. Now above all, regardless of the personal consequences, he must perform his duty. His long-term craving for honor on the battlefield seemed callous and silly. Whether he still wanted to or not, live or die, he was about to lead men into desperate battle.

The captain leading the company slumped to his knees then fell sideways into the mud. His face had been blown away, and with his eyes gone, blood dripped from the bone of his forehead.

Horrified at the sight, and the thought that he could be next, George stopped. His first inclination was to turn and run as far away as he could get. His legs wouldn't move.

A gust of wind cleared away some of the smoke. They were within a hundred yards of the American wall. Near George lay a man desperately trying to keep his bowels from spilling onto the blood-soaked ground. All around were strewn the bodies of dead and wounded, in places so numerous they formed drifts of corpses.

Ahead, George could see a company of redcoats with ladders and fascines being slaughtered as they tried to storm the American wall. All along the line American riflemen fired continuously. Even worse, the American artillery seemed to have an endless supply of ammunition to fire pointblank into the advancing troops.

George realized that this battle was lost, but he had his orders, and he had resolved to perform his duty, at all costs. But did duty require him to sacrifice the men now under his command once there was no hope for success? Should he order his men to retreat? Wouldn't they still be cut down by the merciless fire of the Americans? Should he order his men to lie down and take cover? Such an order would surely mark him as a coward, end his military career with a court martial, and brand him for life.

Another of his men pitched forward with a ball through his neck. George knew it was time for him to make a decision.

The smoke cleared in the breeze, and a salty taste crept into Lemuel's mouth. His stomach turned. A field of red stretched for several hundred yards to the east. In some places bodies lay in piles where entire platoons had been mowed down by a single cannon blast. From the levee on the south to the swamp on the north, the ground was littered with body parts—arms, legs, torsos, and heads.

Among the lifeless lay the writhing, twitching bodies of those in the final throes of death. Already, American scavengers were venturing out onto the field in search of souvenirs. The roar of cannon and rifle fire had ceased, and the men up and down the line fell silent. As Lemuel's ears adjusted to the lower volume of sound, the din was replaced by the pitiful groans and shrieks of the wounded and maimed.

He could see only a few Americans with even minor injuries. It looked as if the entire British force had been destroyed. Casualties must have run into the thousands, compared to a mere handful of Americans.

But soon, here and there across the field, he saw redcoats stand and step forward with their hands raised, apparently having played possum until the fighting was over.

Jackson called his officers together. Lemuel stood to the side, hoping he would be sent to scout out the remaining British positions.

Some of the commanders wanted to pursue the redcoats, but Jackson cut them short. "What more do you want? Your objective is gained. The city is saved. The British have retired." The general shook his head and took a deep breath. "I'm ordering a ceasefire."

CHAPTER FIFTY-FIVE

FEBRUARY 1815, SPANISH WEST FLORIDA

Hadjo sat cross-legged in front of a small fire set in the center of the largest hut in the new village. One by one, several dozen men entered the pavilion-style structure and took a seat facing the flames.

As smoke rose through a hole in the roof, the men sat quietly. Out of respect, they waited for the eldest to speak. A wrinkled man with gray-streaked hair selected a stick from a nearby pile and slipped it among the embers. He seemed to study the flames as if hoping they would reveal wisdom to guide his words.

After a few minutes, he struggled to his feet and spoke in the language of the Muskogee. "Our people have a long history and deep tradition, but this village is new, with men, women, and children from many villages far away. It is appropriate that we gather to discuss issues that must be addressed, especially given the trying times we face. No man should tell another what to do, but it is wise to listen to the concerns and ideas of others before making a decision. As is our tradition, all who wish to speak may do so, but only one may speak at a time as the rest listen respectfully." The old man eased back to the sandy, earthen floor.

For a moment, no one stirred. Then another of the older men stood. "The American frontiersmen have stolen our ancestral hunting grounds and have driven us away. We must find a new beginning."

The old man sat, and a young warrior jumped to his feet. "We must arm ourselves and strike the white man wherever we find him. When he sees that we are fierce and steadfast, he will leave us alone."

A man with a rattlesnake skin around his waist rose and spoke. "We have already tried the warpath as a means of dealing with the Big Knives. There are too many of them, and they have better weapons. We cannot defeat them or drive them away. We must find a different path."

"Some of our brethren have taken up the plow and are raising crops to trade with the white man," said another.

"Traitors!" someone yelled.

"I, for one," said another young man, "would rather die as a warrior fighting the Big Knives than stoop to doing the work of squaws."

One by one the other men spoke. Hadjo listened as young firebrands, little more than boys, ranted about the white man and demanded vengeance. Others joined in with war cries. Meanwhile, the old men sat with head bowed and shoulders slumped. Hadjo had seen and heard it all before in council meetings over the years, including the gathering many years before when he had first heard Tecumseh.

It all seemed so long ago when he had been a young man inspired by the words of the legendary Tecumseh, when they had all dreamed of pushing the whites back into the sea. Hadjo recalled his burning desire to be a great hunter and warrior, maybe even a chief.

Now talk of fighting the American frontiersmen saddened Hadjo. After the devastating defeat at Horseshoe Bend, and under cover of darkness, he had floated downriver until he was well beyond the American army. At dawn he dragged the canoe into bushes and slept until the sun rose high, then he continued downstream until he found a village.

Hadjo had assumed he would be welcomed as a visitor, even as a hero. Instead, he found the villagers angry with the Red Sticks for bringing down the wrath of the Big Knives. He left that village as soon as he could walk.

After traveling carefully and stopping frequently to rest, he reached his own village. He found Prancing Fawn outside her mother's hut nursing a baby girl. He informed her of the death of Antler. News of the Red Stick defeat had already reached the village, and Prancing Fawn seemed to accept the news of Antler's death as confirmation of what she already expected. She thanked him for bringing her the news.

Some of the villagers had decided to stay and make peace with the whites, however they could. Others were heading to Pensacola, where they hoped the Spanish would protect them and arm them. Even though his wounds were only partially healed, the elders encouraged Hadjo to join those heading to Florida. Hadjo expressed his love for Prancing Fawn, and she agreed to go with him as his wife.

In Florida, they hunted game and traded with the Spanish. But when General Jackson attacked Pensacola, Hadjo and the others fled farther east into the wilderness.

He had learned to appreciate having a woman to keep him warm at night. She had recently informed him that she was with child—his child.

He stared into the flames and worried about what might lay ahead for his new family. Tecumseh's plan to organize the tribes and drive out the whites had failed. The shamans' predictions of protection by the spirits had proven false. Hadjo feared there would be no stopping the Big Knives. They would continue to push the red men aside, taking their land and killing them if they resisted.

Canada might stay under British control, and Florida might remain under Spanish control. But Jackson's attack of Pensacola demonstrated that the feeble Spanish garrison was no match for the Americans if they were determined to take Florida.

Hadjo feared that his people faced impossible choices. Their future looked bleak. He resolved to do whatever it took to survive. Over the past few weeks, he had shared his concerns and ideas with the older men of their new village.

Now, for a moment, all was quiet around the fire, and Hadjo hoped the meeting was drawing to a close. He hadn't expected anything to be decided, and he felt himself begin to nod off.

The first of the old men to speak struggled again to his feet. "We have one among us who has skill as a hunter. One who fought beside the great Tecumseh. One who has savored victory against the whites but also suffered defeat. One who has no illusions about the challenges our people face. All who have wished to speak have had an opportunity this evening, but we have not heard from one who is wise beyond his years."

Hadjo had only been half listening, but the mention of Tecumseh had aroused his attention.

Once again all fell silent. Hadjo glanced around. In the flickering light, he could see the faces of the men seated around the dying fire. They were looking to him.

A sadness crept over Hadjo as he realized what he must do for his family and his people. Slowly, he grasped his war club and stood tall in front of the fire. At the sight of a legendary Red Stick war club, several young men cheered. Hadjo wished he had the words that had seemed to come so naturally to Tecumseh.

Hadjo paused, allowing his mind another chance to reconsider the alternatives, knowing the words he spoke next might very well determine the fate of those who now eagerly awaited his counsel.

CHAPTER FIFTY-SIX

FEBRUARY 1815, PLATTSBURGH, NEW YORK

Corporal Silas Shackleton sat in a wooden chair outside Captain Humphrey's office at the headquarters of Fort Brown. The captain had sent for him, and Silas wondered what the company commander wanted. Silas reviewed his actions and words over the past several days, wondering what offense he might have committed.

His term of enlistment was just a month away, and he had been looking forward to returning to New York City. He had no interest in farming, so he would sell the land he had been promised when he was recruited in Boston. Hopefully the money he had earned would be enough to get him by until he found new employment.

A private strode out of Humphrey's office. "The captain will see you now, corporal."

Silas rose and dusted off his uniform. With his shoulders back and his chest thrust forward, he slipped his shako hat under his arm and strode into the office.

The captain was nearly bald and had a dark-brown handlebar mustache that framed his grim expression. He was sitting behind a desk reviewing some papers. Silas stepped in front of the desk and stood at attention. The fort's parade ground was visible through a window behind the captain's desk.

"At ease, corporal."

Silas relaxed a little. If the captain planned to chew him out, he probably would have left him standing at attention.

"I see that you enlisted in Boston in the fall of 1812. Why did you sign up?"

Silas wondered what the captain was fishing for. "I was cold and hungry, sir, without prospects for employment."

"Your record shows you have a way of finding trouble."

Silas hesitated. He didn't know how to respond. What did the record say?

"You fought at Queenston Heights? How did you escape without capture?"

Silas wondered if the captain was going to charge him with desertion. "Once the battle was lost, sir, my sergeant and I floated a log across the Niagara River."

Humphrey frowned and shook his head. "Your sergeant had balls. Good sense, too. That whole operation was a shambles." The captain flipped to another piece of paper. "You served under General Scott during the capture of Fort George?"

"Yes, sir."

"And also at Chippewa—and Lundy's Lane?"

"Yes, sir."

"In your opinion, corporal, what made the difference at Chippewa compared to previous battles?"

Silas cleared his throat before answering. "Well, sir, General Scott kept us healthy and well fed, but mostly it was the training. We knew what we were supposed to do without thinking about it. General Scott marched us in front of the redcoats. We fought them face to face and whipped them, sir."

Humphrey reached for the last paper in his stack. "I understand that you volunteered to serve with Commodore Macdonough?"

"Yes, sir."

The captain glanced up from the papers, and frowned. "Corporal, you are aware that it is expressly against regulations for army personnel to serve under the command of naval officers?"

Damn it, thought Silas. He was going to get reprimanded for *that?*

The captain chuckled. "Well, as it turned out, it's a good thing General Macomb loaned the navy a few of our lads, isn't it?"

Silas relaxed a little. "Yes, sir."

"How do you like life in the army, corporal?"

"Like it?" Silas cleared his throat. "I guess it's all right, sir."

The captain laid the papers on his desktop, then leaned back in his chair. "What are your plans after your term of enlistment ends?"

"No definite plans, sir. I guess I'll go home to New York City."

Humphrey stood and gazed out the window. "Corporal, this war has demonstrated that our nation needs a professional army. We need good men to train and lead the next generation of recruits, and to help them prepare for whatever challenges our nation faces in the future. Our new army will be relatively small, I'm sure, but we want the best men we can find." The captain turned and looked Silas in the eyes. "If you reenlist for another five years, I'll promote you to sergeant. Would that interest you?"

Silas didn't know what to say. His mind raced. He thought back to his life as a youngster on the streets of New York City. The year of forced labor aboard the *Guerriere*. The miserable years as an infantryman in a poorly fed, poorly equipped, and poorly led army.

But over the past year, conditions had improved and the army had become his home, his way of life. Then he thought about the new recruits, and how he could help mold them into professionals.

Silas snapped to attention. "Yes, sir."

CHAPTER FIFTY-SEVEN

FEBRUARY 1815, WASHINGTON CITY

"Any news yet?"

Rachel Thurston studied the young man's face but didn't recognize him. She shook her head. "Sorry, we have heard nothing since the courier arrived yesterday."

Even though it was almost noon, Rachel's cheeks had numbed in the frosty air. She slipped her gloved hand through the crook of her father's arm and pulled close to him. She stared past leafless trees to the street sign at the corner. New York and 18th streets. A crowd had grown over the last hour, and more people continued to arrive.

Looming above them stood Octagon House, the three-story residence of the president. The Madisons had been living in the house since shortly after the British burned the president's mansion. Only a block away the charred walls of the executive residence stood in ruin, but that would soon change. On February 15 the senate had passed a resolution to appropriate funds for repairing and rebuilding the public buildings of Washington City.

Rachel tried to think of something more pleasant, but just that morning she had read that Robert Fulton had died. She remembered meeting the famous inventor and steamship operator at the Madisons' dinner party several years before. Inspired by Fulton's success in running steamboats on the Hudson and Mississippi Rivers, enterprising businessmen were launching steamboats as fast as they could build them. There was already renewed talk of building the canal Fulton had championed—from Albany to Lake Erie.

Her father nudged her. "A stagecoach just turned onto New York Avenue."

Rachel stood on tiptoes. The coach was still a block away. The day before, a courier on horseback reached Octagon House from New York City. Rumors quickly circulated that a sloop of war had arrived from Ghent, Belgium, with a peace document. Rachel's mind reeled with both relief and sadness. The war might finally be over, ending the spread of grief and suffering. But she was sure that a peace treaty would also seal the fate of Federalists.

News of General Jackson's victory at New Orleans had upstaged Federalist demands for changes in the constitution, making their calls for reform seem petty and irrelevant. When members of the convention presented their recommendation to the congress, they were laughed at. The Federalists quickly withdrew their resolutions.

Rachel realized that as a political faction the Federalists were doomed to extinction. History would be written by the victors, and the Federalists would probably be portrayed as fools.

Rachael fumed. The war had vindicated many of the Federalist policies, including the need for a robust military, a national bank, a strong central government, and higher taxes to support it all. But little of that would be remembered, and the Federalists would most likely fade into the dustbin of history. New England would gradually lose influence as the States expanded westward. Even the plantation aristocrats of the southern coastal states would be overrun by the damned Irish.

The war had left the new nation all but bankrupt, cost countless lives and immeasurable suffering, and had left the capital in ruins. But the Madisons and the Democratic-Republicans had won.

The stage coach pulled up in front of Octagon House. Out stepped a well-dressed gentlemen carrying a valise. The crowd cheered.

"It's Mr. Carroll!" shouted someone. "Henry Carroll—one of the peace commissioners."

Soldiers in dark blue had cordoned off the entrance to the Madisons' house, but Carroll paused at the top of the steps, turned, and smiled. Then with a wave he disappeared through the door.

The crowd went wild, screaming, "Huzzah!"

After a few minutes the door opened again. Out stepped Dolley Madison in a sky-blue dress, her hair piled high. "The President and his cabinet have adjourned upstairs. But please, all of you, come in to the warmth of our home while we all await the news."

Rachel and her father followed the crowd inside the house. Towering above most of her guests, Dolley moved about the room offering refreshments. The people in the room seemed crazy with joy.

"Peace! Peace!" someone shouted from the head of the stairs.

A butler served wine to all.

Paul Jennings played "The President's March" on the violin.

Shortly, Rachel was sure, history would be rewritten by the victors. Whatever the terms of the peace treaty, she suspected Madison would lose little time in putting the entire war in a favorable light. She imagined a front-page article in the *National Intelligencer* in which the president described the treaty as highly honorable to the States and the war a most brilliant success.

A wave of newfound patriotism and pride would probably sweep the nation. Newspapers were already promoting a poem inspired by the battle at Baltimore. Written by a local attorney, Francis Scott Key, and set to the tune of an old tavern song, "The Defense of Fort McHenry" was rapidly gaining popularity.

Rachel noticed a rise in volume of voices around her, and she caught bits and pieces of conversation.

". . . terms of the treaty. . ."

". . . *status quo ante bellum* . . ."

Rachel was stunned. The phrase meant that conditions would be returned to the status before the war started. If the rumor was accurate, then both sides had agreed to end all hostilities, with neither side agreeing to any concessions. The borders between British territory and U.S. soil would remain as they had been before the war.

Not that the war hadn't had other consequences. Britain's reputation as a power had been tarnished, Rachel was certain. Despite its many victories in North America and its defeat of Napoleon, Great Britain had been stung by early American victories at sea and had been thwarted in the latest battles on land.

The Americans had learned from their early mistakes in the war and had matured somewhat as a nation. No doubt they would continue to encroach into the Spanish territory of Florida, probably using the hostility of the Indians as an excuse. Meanwhile Spain, weakened by war, could do little about it.

With the death of Tecumseh and the defeat of the Red Sticks, the Indians had little hope of uniting against the land-grabbing Americans. The natives, Rachel realized, were clearly the greatest losers in the conflict.

On the northern border, the vast majority of heavy fighting had been conducted by British regulars. But Canadians, both English- and French-speaking whites, had put their differences aside against a common enemy and had even joined with native Americans in repulsing the American invaders. Who knew? maybe Great Britain would begin to treat the Canadas more like a nation than merely a collection of colonies.

The war had begun when two sides, with conflicting views and goals, had failed to resolve their differences peacefully. But over time the relationship between the States and Britain might involve a little more mutual respect. With so many things in common, at some point they might even be able to work together as allies against mutual threats.

Meanwhile, after a costly war, both America and Great Britain would each have to deal with staggering debts. No doubt both countries would use whatever time of peace lay ahead to energetically get about the business of making money.

Rachel figured that the nations would mend their wounds and prosper, at least for a while. But she couldn't help but think of the thousands of lives lost during the war, on both sides. With three or four times as many wounded, many would face a lifetime of suffering and pain. Her heart ached for those who had lost loved ones.

Rachel realized that, in comparison, she and her father had weathered the war in relatively good shape. But after the disappointing convention in Hartford, Rachel had plunged into despair. Her father had been humiliated and disgraced. His political influence had been destroyed. She lashed out at him for his failure.

Over the following weeks Rachel had felt like crawling into a cocoon and never coming out. She had slept until the afternoon and rarely left the house.

Then, over the last month she began to realize her father had never been the titan she had imagined. He had substantial intellect and skills, no question, but he could also fail. Something she hadn't imagined possible.

She had been amazed and confused to see that within weeks of the failure of the convention in Hartford, he renewed his interest in land speculation and shipping.

As she watched her father rebuild his life, she wondered if somehow she, too, could start again. If a man could fail and then recover, why couldn't a woman. Then the truth overwhelmed her. She hadn't actually failed, because she hadn't actually tried to accomplish anything. She had been using her gender as an excuse for not even trying.

For several days she mulled over this realization and began to consider her options for the future.

Over the last few weeks she had formulated a plan and had only recently decided to proceed. Her father no longer needed her to draft letters to editors throughout the States, but she found that she missed the challenge of formulating thought and crafting them into persuasive argument.

"Excuse me, miss."

Rachel turned to see a gray-haired black man in a white jacket.

"Would you care for some cider?" he asked.

She smiled and nodded then lifted a glass from his tray. As he moved away she studied him. Even after living in Washington City for several years, she marveled at the darkness of black skin. No doubt he had been born a slave and knew no other way of life. That didn't make it right.

The war had transformed the new nation in many ways and had probably propelled it forward to whatever future was destined. But the nation still allowed slavery. And she decided that she would do something about that.

She would dedicate her life to the abolition of slavery. She would write letters to editors throughout the States, and she would sign them with her own name. She would develop her speaking skills and present her arguments in front of any group, large or small. She would make her case in writing and orally until slavery was banned forever. The task would be daunting, but to fail was unthinkable.

She and her father had decided that they would not live in Washington City, and neither wished to return to Gloucester. He was inclined to move to Boston, but she had persuaded him that New York City would provide both of them exciting opportunities. They were packed and ready to leave.

Rachel glanced around the room and noticed a young man staring at her. She quickly looked away. After her experience with George Sherbourne, or whatever his name was, she wasn't about to trust another man anytime soon. But then again, if she was making a new start, maybe she should keep an open mind. Forget George. Forget omens and superstition, she would chart her own course. She glanced back at the man. He raised his glass and smiled.

CHAPTER FIFTY-EIGHT

FEBRUARY 1815, BATON ROUGE, LOUISIANA

Lemuel Wyckliffe leaned against the bulwark of the steamboat as it pulled away from the dock in a cloud of smoke. Ashore, a crowd of onlookers waved at the soldiers and militiamen on board. The paddle wheeler's whistle shrilled as the boat headed upriver for the last half of its journey to Natchez from New Orleans.

Docks and warehouses along the riverbank soon gave way to shacks and then overgrown forest. Lemuel gazed up the wide, winding river. Once the steamboat reached Natchez, its passengers would disembark, and its cargo of cotton, rice, and sugar would be unloaded. For the return trip downriver, tobacco, whiskey, lumber, and bricks would be loaded, and another crowd of passengers would board.

Before leaving New Orleans, Lemuel had taken his leave of General Jackson. The general thanked Lemuel for his service and asked about his plans for the future. After listening carefully to Lemuel, Jackson wished him well but also reminded him that many of the remaining Red Sticks had fled to Florida, and sooner or later they would be a problem.

Lemuel hadn't needed to ask Jackson what the solution would be. He had heard the general tell others that the natives who didn't adopt civilized ways, even those who had sided with the States against the Red Sticks and the British, would have to go. Jackson asked Lemuel to rejoin him in Tennessee, for he needed scouts to keep an eye on the renegades now hiding in Florida.

Lemuel noticed movement in the trees upriver along the shoreline. He spotted an Indian watching the steamboat from the cover of brush. Lemuel brought his rifle to his shoulder and eased the hammer to full cock. Putting a ball through the native's chest would be a challenging shot, given the motion of the boat. He kept the Indian in his sights as the boat pulled closer. If the native even pointed a weapon toward the steamboat, Lemuel would fire without hesitation.

As he waited to see what the Indian would do next, Lemuel thought back to the brutal murder of his mother and little sister. And that he had vowed revenge. At Tippecanoe he had killed his first Indian and taken his first scalp. After the death of his father, Lemuel had renewed his vow. And then again and again after the loss of Stubby and of so many other friends, he had avenged their death.

As the steamboat passed the spot on the river where the Indian sat hidden in the brush, Lemuel curled his finger around the trigger. The Indian showed no sign of hostility toward those on the boat, but Lemuel was tempted to shoot him anyway. The native had probably been up to no good in the past and was bound to cause mischief sometime again. Besides, a dead Indian never caused anyone trouble.

The boat continued upriver, and the native was lost to Lemuel's view. He slipped his finger off the trigger and eased the hammer back over the pan. As he set the rifle butt down on the deck, his hand brushed against the cluster of scalps tied to his belt. He had worn the old relics so long that he rarely noticed them anymore. The hides were dry and gnarled, and the black hair had lost its oily sheen.

He fingered the grisly patches and studied them, trying to remember the battles that had yielded each. In his mind he relived the battle at Horseshoe Bend, where he had helped slaughter the Red Sticks by the hundreds. He had lost track of the number he had killed.

Lemuel felt very tired. He suspected that he would have reason to kill again. But he no longer felt the need for revenge. He glanced at the scalps and thought of the Indian-hide bridle reins in his pack and the tomahawk hanging from his belt. He considered tossing them all into the river. They would bob in the muddy water until a swirl of current caught them. In an instant the river would claim them and whisk them downstream.

He tightened his grip on the rail as the paddle wheeler swerved to avoid a huge log. High above the river flew a large bird. An eagle. In the bright sunlight, Lemuel could plainly see the bird's white head. With its wings spread wide, the eagle completed a tight circle over the river, then glided toward the west.

Lemuel glanced to the western horizon. Much of the Louisiana Purchase had not yet been explored. Even the boundaries of the vast territory were in dispute. The States claimed that the territory north of the Rio Grande River was theirs as part of the Louisiana Purchase, but Spain argued that the territory they called Tejas was part of Mexico.

Lemuel's gaze returned to the river ahead. He would travel to Missouri and see if he could find Daniel Boone. Then maybe he would head farther west. There might be more work for an Indian fighter.

TO THE READER

The idea for this novel began while I was at a convention in New Orleans. I've always been a history buff, and I couldn't resist the opportunity to visit the site of the Battle of New Orleans. The self-guided tour was fascinating, but it also caused me to realize how little I knew about the War of 1812. I picked up several books at the visitor center, and began to read them that night.

Having recently completed a manuscript for a novel, I was looking for another story idea. As I learned more about the War of 1812, I began to toy with the idea of telling its story in the form of a novel. I had also recently read Tom Clancy's *Red Storm Rising* about an armed conflict with the Soviet Union, and it provided an example of how to structure an exciting novel with multiple viewpoints and vast geographic scope.

The deeper I dug into the subject, the more I realized that there are dozens of nonfiction books about the War of 1812, its battles, and the individuals involved. My goal became to write a novel that depicted the major events and real-life participants of the war from the intimate viewpoint of fictional characters. The result was a novel that I hope readers find both entertaining and informative.

Mike Klaassen

SPECIAL ACKNOWLEDGMENTS

In addition to the following bibliography, I acknowledge the following individuals and organizations who provided research assistance in this project.

Buffalo and Erie County Historical Society. Copies of material about the Battle of Queenston Heights.

Rick Conwell, Tippecanoe County Historical Association, Lafayette, Indiana.

Ron Dale, author, historian and former Superintendent of Niagara National Historic Sites of Canada.

Detroit Public Library, Burton Historical Collection. Copies of various documents and maps related to Fort Detroit and related action in 1812.

Fort Meigs: Ohio's War of 1812 Battlefield, Perrysburg, Ohio.

Keith A. Herkalo, War of 1812 Museum & Battle of Plattsburgh Association, Plattsburgh, New York.

Doug Kohler, Erie County Historical Society, Erie, Pennsylvania.

University of West Florida. Photocopies of material regarding Tecumseh's visit to the Muscogees in 1811.

BIBLIOGRAPHY

Allgor, Catherine. *A Perfect Union: Dolley Madison and the creation of the American nation.* New York: Henry Holt and Company, 2006.

Altoff, Gerard T. *Oliver Hazard Perry and the Battle of Lake Erie.* Put-in-Bay, Ohio: The Perry Group, 1999.

Babcock, Louis L. *The War of 1812 on the Niagara Frontier.* Buffalo, New York: Buffalo Historical Society, 1927.

Claiborne, John Francis Hamtramck. *Life and Times of General Samuel Dale.* Photocopy of Chapter 3. Courtesy of the Library of the University of West Florida.

Clift, G. Glenn. *Remember the Raisin!: Kentucky and Kentuckians in the Battles and Massacre at Frenchtown, Michigan Territory, in the War of 1812.* Baltimore: Clearfield Company, Inc., 2002.

Coles, Harry L. *The War of 1812.* Chicago: The University of Chicago Press, 1965.

Collins, Gilbert. *Guidebook to the Historic Sites of the War of 1812.* Toronto: Dundurn Press, 1998.

Cruikshank, Brigadier-General E. A. *The Battle of Queenston Heights.* An abridgement by permission of the Lundy's Lane Historical Society. Niagara Publishers, 1948.

Cruikshank, Lieutenant-Colonel Earnest, V.D. *The Battle of Fort George*. Third printing. Niagara-on-the-Lake, Ontario: Niagara Historical Society, 2009.

Elting, John R. *Amateurs, to Arms!: A military history of the War of 1812*. Chapel Hill, North Carolina: De Capo Press, 1995.

Everest, Allan S. *The War of 1812 in the Champlain Valley*. Syracuse, New York: Syracuse University Press, 1981.

Fischer, David Hackett. *Albion's Seed: Four British folkways in America*. New York: Oxford University Press, 1989.

Genealogy Trails History Group. "Baltimore Riot of 1812." Newspaper Accounts transcribed by Nancy Piper. http://genealogytrails.com/mary/balticity/riot_1812.html

George, Christopher T. *Terror on the Chesapeake: The War of 1812 on the Bay*. Shippensburg, Pennsylvania: White Mane Books, 2000.

Gerson, Noel B. *The Velvet Glove: A life of Dolly Madison*. Nashville, Tennessee: Thomas Nelson, Inc., 1975.

Graves, Donald E. *Field of Glory: The Battle of Crysler's Farm, 1813*. Toronto: Robin Brass Studio, 2000.

Graves, Donald E. *Where Right and Glory Lead!: The Battle of Lundy's Lane, 1814*. Toronto: Robin Brass Studio, 2000.

Haythornthwaite, Philip J. *Napoleonic Weapons and Warfare: Napoleonic Infantry*. London: Cassell & Co., 2001.

Heidler, David S. and Jeanne T. Heidler, editors. *Encyclopedia of the War of 1812*. Santa Barbara, California: ABC-CLIO, Inc., 1997.

Herkalo, Keith A. *The Battles at Plattsburgh: September 11, 1814.* Charleston, South Carolina: The History Press, 2012.

Hitsman, J. Mackay, updated by Donald E. Graves. *The Incredible War of 1812: A military history.* Toronto: Robin Brass Studio, 1999.

Katcher, Philip and Bryan Fosten. *Men-at-Arms Series: The American War, 1812-1814.* Oxford: Osprey Publishing, 1990.

Lake, Martin. *Volume 3, The Mississineway Expedition: December 17-18, 1812.* Marion, Indiana: Grant County Historical Society, 1997.

Latimer, Jon. *1812: War with America.* Cambridge, Massachusetts: The Belknap Press of Harvard University Press, 2007.

McCutcheon, Marc. *Everyday Life in the 1800s: A guide for writers, students & historians.* Cincinnati, Ohio: Writer's Digest Books, 1993.

Madsen, Axel. *John Jacob Astor: America's First Multimillionaire.* New York: John Wiley & Sons, Inc., 2001.

Mosier, Joseph C. "The Battle of Craney Island: The defense of Norfolk in the War of 1812." Norfolk, Virginia: Hampton Roads Naval Museum, 1997.

Muller, Charles G. *The Darkest Day: The Washington-Baltimore campaign during the War of 1812.* Philadelphia: University of Pennsylvania Press, 1963.

O'Brien, Sean Michael. *In Bitterness and In Tears: Andrew Jackson's Destruction of the Creeks and Seminoles.* Westport, Connecticut: Praeger, 2003.

Peskin, Allan. *Winfield Scott: And the profession of arms*. Kent, Ohio: The Kent State University Press, 2003.

Philip, Cynthia Owen. *Robert Fulton: A biography*. Author's Guild Backprint.com edition. Lincoln, Nebraska: iUniverse, 2002.

Pickles, Tim. *New Orleans 1815: Andrew Jackson crushes the British*. Oxford: Osprey Publishing, 1993.

Pitch, Anthony S. *The Burning of Washington: The British Invasion of 1814*. Annapolis, Maryland: Bluejacket Books, Naval Institute Press, 2000.

Reid, Stuart and Graham Turner. *Warrior Series: British Redcoat (2), 1793-1815*. Oxford: Osprey Publishing, 2000.

Remini, Robert V. *The Battle of New Orleans: Andrew Jackson and America's first military victory*. New York: Viking, 1999.

Rose, Alexander. *Washington's Spies: The story of America's first spy ring*. New York: Bantam Books, 2006.

Skaggs, David Curtis and Gerard T. Altoff. *A Signal Victory: The Lake Erie Campaign, 1812-1813*. Annapolis, Maryland: Bluejacket Books, Naval Institute Press, 1997.

Sugden, John. *Tecumseh's Last Stand*. Norman, Oklahoma: University of Oklahoma Press, 1985.

Tippecanoe County Historical Association, Research and Publications Committee. *The Battle of Tippecanoe: November 7, 1811*. 2nd Edition. LaFayette, Indiana: Tippecanoe County Historical Association, 1999.

Von Steuben, Baron Frederick William. *Baron von Steuben's Revolutionary War Drill Manual: A facsimile reprint of the 1794 edition.* New York: Dover Publications, Inc., 1985.

Webb, James. *Born Fighting: How the Scots-Irish shaped America.* Paperback edition. New York: Broadway Books, 2005.

Wills, Garry. *James Madison.* New York: Times Books, Henry Holt and Company, 2002.

Wise, Terence and Richard Hook. *Men-at-Arms Series: Artillery Equipments of the Napoleonic Wars.* London: Osprey Publishing, Ltd., 1979.

HAVE YOU CONSIDERED WRITING FICTION?

Consider *Scenes and Sequels: How to write page-turning fiction*, by Mike Klaassen.

Most books about the craft of writing fiction don't even define a scene, much less describe how to write one. Even fewer address sequels. Scenes are the exciting, turbocharged parts of fiction, driving the story forward. Sequels provide a breather, where the focal character can celebrate or lick his wounds and plan his next move. Together, scenes and sequels help create page-turning fiction.

The concepts of scenes and sequels were championed by Dwight V. Swain (1915-1992) and Jack M. Bickham (1930-1997). *Scenes and Sequels: How to Write Page-Turning Fiction*, builds on the work of Swain and Bickham to create the most comprehensive and concise explanation of scenes and sequels anywhere.

"Indispensable nuts-and-bolts advice for crafting successful fiction. Highly recommended."—Evan Marshall, co-creator of *The Marshall Plan® Novel Writing Software*

"I am a huge fan of Jack Bickham's classic craft book *Scene & Structure*, and consider it one of three essential books to a writer's library. When I learned of Mike Klaassen's new book, *Scenes & Sequels*, and its efforts to expand upon Bickham's work, I looked forward to reading it with great anticipation. Well, it doesn't disappoint! It's a great addition to Bickham's initial explanation of the two most important elements of story and delivers both an in-depth explanation of these elements and an important expansion of the principles it delivered. Highly recommended for serious writers."—Les Edgerton, Author of *Finding Your Voice* and *Hooked*.

ORDER YOUR COPY OF *SCENES AND SEQUELS* NOW FROM WHEREVER NEW BOOKS ARE SOLD.

ABOUT THE AUTHOR

Mike Klaassen is the author of two young-adult novels, *The Brute* and *Cracks*. He has also written two nonfiction books: *Fiction-Writing Modes: Eleven Essential Tools for Bringing Your Story to Life* and *Scenes and Sequels: How to Write Page-Turning Fiction*. He publishes *For Fiction Writers*, a free monthly ezine about the craft of writing fiction. For more, visit www.mikeklaassen.com